LEGION
OF BONES

T.A.FROST

Giulia Degarno watched the sun sink down towards the treeline. "We'll only have a few hours," she said. "I'd rather not do this in the dark."

Hugh of Kenton nodded. He had polished his breastplate that morning, and the afternoon sunlight made the steel glow. "You're right. If these local fellows don't show up soon, we'll head back to the inn."

Their three mercenary helpers stood a little way off, under a massive oak tree. Alberto and Vitale were chatting: they'd known each other for years. Alberto had the full beard and long hair of a freelance cavalryman, and the emblem of his old regiment was painted on the back of his armour. Vitale was dark-skinned and clean-shaven, a former marksman for the Averrian navy. He wore green and brown like a scout. He chuckled at something Alberto said, and Alberto spat into the undergrowth.

The third mercenary was seeing to their horses, tying the bridles to a low branch. Ludwig Kroner was seventeen, the bastard son of minor Teutic aristocracy. He was good-looking, a little chubby in the face, and skilled with a longsword.

"Did you say we can go back?" Ludwig asked. There was a nervous quality to him that Giulia didn't like. They had only recruited him a couple of weeks ago, and for all his training, she hadn't seen him fight for real. She had a nasty feeling that he might run at the sight of the undead.

"No," Giulia replied.

"Not yet, son," Hugh said, his voice a little softer. He was good with the mercenaries, Giulia thought – but then, being a man and a knight, he didn't have to win their respect. "Give it a little time."

1

"Not too long," Giulia said. She spoke quietly, so Ludwig wouldn't hear. "Is it true that the undead get stronger at night?"

The old knight shook his head. "I don't think so. They're much the same in the dark. It's just that we're worse."

"That's reassuring."

"Hey!" It was Vitale's voice. He pointed down the way they'd come. "Look there!"

Giulia shaded her eyes. Half a dozen men were approaching. The man at the front rode a big grey horse; the others walked. The leader, clearly a member of the local nobility, wore a steel cuirass and a flamboyant hat.

"That must be our man," Hugh said.

Alberto scowled. "About damned time."

From fifty yards away, the local militia looked like killers: grimy men armed with bows and knives. From twenty yards away, they seemed scrawny and tattered.

The rider dismounted and led his horse towards them. The other men hung back. He was tall, about thirty, with deep-set eyes. He'd be a local nobleman, of course: there were no guilds or councils to run things in the countryside. Giulia missed the certainty of streets and walls. This wasn't her terrain.

"I'm Ricardo Gordini," the nobleman said. "I take it you're the mercenaries?"

Giulia stepped forward from the others. She needed to take charge. "I'm Giulia Degarno. I'm pleased to meet you."

"They told me about you," he said.

"Let's hope they told you right." She put her hand out. It took him a moment to realise that she meant for him to shake it. She looked him in the eye as they shook. "This is Sir Hugh of Kenton, my comrade in arms."

"Sir Hugh," Gordini said, turning to the knight. "Are you the leader here?"

Hugh smoothed down his moustache. "We both are. Between us, we tend to make the right decisions."

"I see. And these are your men, then. Are you from the countryside, sir?"

"Yes, back in Albion. I was—" Hugh started.

"Thought so. Pleased to meet another countryman." He pointed at Giulia's horse. "That girth's too loose, by the way. Need to pull it in a couple of holes."

She looked at the horse. It had been fine so far. "Really?"

"Absolutely. Horse like that's long past its prime. Got to take it in hand."

Anger moved within her like a dragon stirring in its sleep. "Is that so?"

"You'd be best selling it for meat, to be honest. Cruel to let it walk around." He looked at Hugh. "Some folk get sentimental about horses. Too much time in the city."

Giulia looked straight at him. "I didn't ask for your advice."

His eyes widened; he stood up straight and his head tilted slightly, as if the experience of being answered was new and insulting. Hugh stepped between them. "The horse is fine," he said. "So's the saddle. Now, let's get going."

"I'm not your little peasant, so don't talk to me like one," Giulia said. "And if anyone touches my horse, they'll find out how 'sentimental' I am. Understand?"

Alberto and Vitale had been watching from a little way back – Alberto grinning, Vitale looking concerned –

3

but now, at the possibility of violence, they stepped closer. Even Ludwig had his hand near to his sword.

"I was just trying to give you some advice," Gordini said. "That's all."

"Well, don't," she replied. "Let's go."

"Your horse is fine," Hugh said as they walked up the hill. They were at the back of the group. An old peasant led the way, Gordini following.

"I know she is," Giulia replied. "He just needed to feel tough. God, there's some bloody arseholes walking around."

Gordini looked over his shoulder and called, "Have you fought revenants before, Sir Hugh?"

"We've fought all sorts of things," Hugh replied. "Two months ago, we took scales from a wyvern's nest."

Gordini slowed, so they would catch him up. "That can't have been easy. Well, hopefully this will be simple by comparison. Revenants are disgusting, but they're no good against skilled fighters. Or so I hear." He turned and nodded at the track. "My men are decent people, but they're afraid. Can't blame them, really. We thought having trained fighters here might, well, stiffen their sinews a bit."

Hugh said, "Good idea," and Gordini looked pleased. Giulia felt a little stab of resentment. People took notice when Hugh spoke. She wondered if she'd ever get used to using him as her mouthpiece, as though he translated her words into a language that other men would hear.

"Now then," Gordini said. "If you'd just follow me, Sir Hugh..."

They walked up the slope. The day was giving up: dusk was creeping in. *Should've done this in the morning,*

Giulia thought. She wondered about bedding down, destroying the revenants at first light. No – better meet them when she was alert and ready, not when some sentry woke her up.

"I hope the old man knows what he's doing," Alberto muttered as they followed Hugh up the slope. "Is he safe walking uphill at his age?"

Vitale gave a brief snort of amusement, Ludwig grinned awkwardly, and Giulia ignored them both. She turned her attention to Hugh.

"—quite like a man," the knight was saying. "Better than most men, in fact. Here, you mean?"

Gordini stopped, and his men drew to a halt around him. "This is the place."

Hugh put his hands on his hips. He was the tallest man present by several inches, and it made him look more like a scarecrow than ever. "Have you fellows observed our quarry?" he demanded.

"Observed?" The nearest villager sounded bitter. "We've watched 'em walk all the way up from Long Ditch to Guiseppe's field! On the march, they are. Tried to get the priest out but he's locked in his house, hiding. Bloody coward."

Gordini said, "That's enough of that talk. They shot at the morts earlier," he added. "They put one down and managed to pin a bell on one of the others with a crossbow. We'll hear them coming."

"Never saw a dead man walk about before," one of the militiamen said. He was about the same age as Hugh, but life had shrunk and buckled him. "When I was a boy, my old man told me about morts coming out of the ground. I didn't think it was true. Not until today. It's a blasphemy, that's what it is. An offence against God."

Giulia wanted to tell the man to be quiet. She could see the peasants talking themselves out of this. "Which way will they be coming from?" she asked.

The old man stared at her for a moment, as if he couldn't quite believe that she existed. Then he pointed into the trees. "Come from that way, I reckon."

"Let's fan out a bit," Giulia said. "We don't want to shoot each other by mistake."

They moved apart, into a rough semicircle facing the way that the old man had indicated. The peasants readied their bows; one carried an ancient crossbow. Only Hugh and Ludwig had no ranged weapons. Hugh drew his sword in a soft hiss of metal. The sound made Giulia tense.

It was starting to get cold. Gordini rubbed his gloved hands together and cracked his knuckles. A young militiaman pulled a wad of arrows from his belt and drove them into the ground head-first, so he could ready them quickly. It looked as if he was trying to plant them like saplings.

They waited. From between the trees came the soft tinkling of a bell.

There was sudden movement throughout the group, a ripple of fear. Ludwig readied his sword. Alberto hefted a short-barrelled musket, a cavalryman's weapon. Vitale drew the string of his crossbow back. His hands moved quickly, his eyes scanning the forest as he worked.

Gordini pulled a pistol from his belt. "Is everybody ready?" he demanded. The villagers ignored him. The bell tinkled again, then stopped.

Hugh stepped up beside Giulia as she loaded her crossbow. "See anything?"

She kept her eyes on the forest. "Nothing yet," she said, squinting. A shadow moved to the right and was gone, like a man passing between tree trunks. "Wait, there's someone. He's just gone out of sight – there, behind the hawthorn. See him?"

"I see him," Hugh said softly.

She watched the figure lurch into view, forty yards away: lanky and dishevelled, moving like a clockwork toy. She had expected something slow, but the revenant went as fast as a jogging man, head nodding in time with its rapid, stiff-limbed stride. Behind it came a woman in a torn blue dress. A crossbow bolt protruded from her shoulder, and from it hung a little bell on a string. She jangled as she came, like something from a fair.

"God almighty," Gordini muttered. One of the men made the Sign of the Sword across his chest.

"Look," Ludwig said. His Teutic accent gave his voice a jaunty lilt, even now. "There's another one, on the left!"

"Damn things're trying to outflank us," Hugh growled.

One of the villagers muttered something that Giulia couldn't make out. She kept her eyes on the forest, scanning between the trees.

"That's not possible," Gordini said. The certainty in his voice died among the trees. "The undead are too stupid to do that. They can't do that," he added.

Giulia watched the revenants, appalled and fascinated. They were walking impossibilities, moving without hearts, animated by magic. For a second she wondered what they thought, what they wanted, how she must seem to them, and then a cold, clear voice said in her mind: *They're in killing range.*

Loudly, she said, "I can see five. Anyone see more than that?"

"Six," Vitale replied. "One's hanging back."

Giulia peered at the morts as they struggled closer. Vitale was right: a sixth revenant lurched like a drunkard at the rear of the group.

Hugh called out, "Mark your target, everyone."

Bows were drawn, quick prayers muttered to the saints.

"Shoot!"

All around Giulia, people loosed arrows and bolts. One of the undead crashed into the mud and began to pull itself up. Giulia took aim at the nearest revenant's head.

She pulled the trigger but the mort stumbled and her bolt flew past. She hissed with annoyance and reloaded. On her left, Alberto raised his musket and took careful aim. He fired, and the gunshot was a quick, hard bang.

One of the morts was hit by his bullet and staggered backwards – and then an arrow struck it square in the brow, knocking the head back at a crazy angle. For a second it stood there, as if unsure how to respond, and then it collapsed, a puppet without strings. It lay on the earth looking like what it was – a corpse.

The other morts sped up. Hugh raised his sword and bent his long legs into a fighting stance. "Get ready!" he called.

Ludwig took up a duelling stance. Alberto drew his mace. Giulia worked the crank under her crossbow and slapped another bolt into the groove.

The revenant with the bell stumbled as an arrow hit her calf, and fell onto one knee. The bell tinkled crazily. One of the other morts staggered towards her and shoved her back onto her feet.

The act of helping repulsed Giulia far more than anything else she had seen this night. *But they don't know what's going on. Maybe they do. God, if they know that they've ended up like this—*

She pulled the bow in tight to her shoulder and fired. The bolt smacked into the woman's head, just above the eyebrow, and she dropped. The mort who had pushed her upright bared his teeth and rushed towards Giulia. Almost lazily, Alberto stepped in from the side, whipped his mace around and broke his skull.

The undead reached the villagers. One man cried "Oh, God!" and dropped his bow and fled. One of the morts stumbled into the midst of them, arms flailing, and knocked a bowman to the ground. An awful cry came from the left, an animal noise of horror and despair. Giulia saw Gordini trying to fend off a revenant with his hands. It had one hand on his neck already and was grabbing at his throat with the other, hissing as it tried to choke him.

"Hold it steady!" she shouted, thinking she could shoot the thing, but Gordini was too far gone to hear her. He lost his footing and crashed down. The revenant fell on top of him, scrabbling for his throat.

Giulia drew her knife and ran over. She ducked low and stabbed the revenant in the shoulder – that at least seemed to distract it. Then Hugh was standing over them all, and his sword swung down with the neat lethality of an executioner's axe. The revenant flopped forward, truly dead.

Gordini scrambled out of its clutches, up onto his feet again. His eyes were huge and white, like a damned man in a painting.

And that was it. Nobody was left to fight. Vitale said something under his breath: a prayer, perhaps. Giulia heard boots crunching on the dirt and looked around.

Hugh stood beside her, cleaning the blade of his sword on a rag.

A long second passed. The villagers began to pack their bows up. They said little and spoke too quietly for Giulia to hear, as though they were ashamed of what they'd done.

"Good work!" Gordini cried. "Well done, everybody! Now we can all go back and— yes, let's go back, shall we?"

The villagers walked away from him, and he followed them. Hugh stood still, hands on hips as he surveyed the corpses. "Someone ought to get these poor fellows underground," he said.

Gordini looked back at him. "A burial party will come out tomorrow. I'll sort you out a letter for the bounty: you can cash it when you're next in Astrago."

Giulia tapped Hugh on the arm. "Let's go."

They followed the locals through the dusk, back towards their horses. As Giulia passed Alberto, the mercenary spat into the bushes. "You know something?" he said. "I hate the living dead."

"I hate farmers, too," Alberto said, three hours later. They sat on a bench against the wall in the village inn, next to the spot on the floor where they would sleep. On the far side of the room, a dozen locals stood around Ricardo Gordini, listening to him describe the battle with the revenants. Two of the group were bowmen from the militia.

"I mean, just look at them." Alberto took a swig of beer. "It's always the same. They never stop telling you how smart they are, living off the damn land and all that, but as soon as a nobleman walks past they start bowing and scraping like heathen slaves. Makes me miss the Men of Repute. Say what you like about the Landsknecht chapters, but none of us would suck up to a man like that. You had to *earn* a man's respect in the chapter. We had dignity."

He had a point, Giulia thought. She liked the countryside but not many of the people in it: there was a casual brutality to rural life that unsettled her. First you beat your cows, then you beat your dog, then you beat your children and your wife. Giulia had slain half a dozen men, but there had been nothing casual in any of her killings.

"Haven't you got your whistle?" Vitale asked. "You could give us a tune, and we wouldn't have to listen to you complaining."

Alberto laughed. "It's in my saddlebags. Bad luck!"

Giulia tore a loaf of bread in two. "You know," she said, passing one half to Hugh, "I wouldn't mind living outside the city, provided my land was my own. I just wouldn't want to end up as some shitty tenant, paying all my money to some fool in a big house," she added, lowering her voice in case the locals could hear.

Hugh nodded. "A man should be close to the land. A true knight draws strength from the soil." He turned to her. "You did well back there, dealing with those dead fellows. A lot of men would have turned tail and run. Of course, you've always had a lot of backbone, but you've got real skill when it comes to fighting. It's one thing to be able to wave a blade about, quite another to wield it properly. True combat," he declared, "is an art."

"Right," Giulia said. Having seen true combat, she was not inclined to honour it with a fancy name. "We need a plan for tomorrow. Where's Ludwig?"

"Outside, talking to one of the villagers. He said the old men knew where the revenants had come from."

11

Alberto chuckled and twisted round to look at them. "He's probably gone chasing some girl. He may be young, but the lad moves fast." He turned back to Vitale. He said something Giulia didn't catch and Vitale laughed.

Hugh leaned back, cupping his drink in his big, bony hands. "It's a damned shame you're not a man, Giulia," he said. "I reckon that if you'd been born as a fellow, you'd be a knight by now."

"More likely I'd be a better criminal. And by better, I mean 'worse and more successful'."

"That's as may be. Fact is, you're bloody good at this."

She smiled. "Thanks, Hugh. I appreciate it."

He looked straight at her. He seemed thoughtful but alert, serious but not sad. "Giulia, if it wasn't for you, I'd still be drunk in some tavern, back in Pagalia."

That was probably true, but it felt awkward to hear. She smiled and said, "And now we're getting drunk in this tavern, in the middle of nowhere. I'm assuming that's an improvement."

The door opened and Ludwig entered. He closed the door and approached. Alberto rubbed his hands together and smirked.

Giulia said, "Did you have any luck?"

Ludwig pulled up a chair and sat down. "The locals say there's a manor house nearby. It's half-ruined, abandoned years ago. They won't go there. According to Maria, the girl I was just talking to, that's the source of all the morts they've seen recently."

"Maria, is it?" Alberto smirked. "Did she say anything else? What?" he added, looking at the others. "Just making sure the boy's not being taken for a ride. Some of these peasant girls are very untrustworthy."

"How far is it to this house?" Giulia said.

Vitale offered Ludwig a cup. The youth took a swig. "It's six miles north-east. Maria said her uncle once saw lights coming out of it. Apparently, years ago, a nobleman lived there, who made a pact with a devil to become rich. Then he tried to get out of the pact, and——"

"All that stuff," Alberto said.

Ludwig nodded. "All that stuff."

Hugh sipped his beer. "One hears a lot of stories like that."

"I know," the young man replied. He opened his hands apologetically. "It's not very reliable, I know, but it sounds worth a look."

Vitale said, "It's fairly out of the way. Good for a little quiet necromancy, I suppose."

Hugh looked at Giulia. "What do you think?"

"I think it's the best lead we've got," she replied. "Let's have a look tomorrow morning. We'll go in quietly, just the five of us. But don't tell the villagers we're going, in case they try to stop us. And Gordini doesn't need to know, just in case it's on his land. If it's nothing, we won't have wasted too much time. And if there is something there, well… then we can deal with Leth and get our bounty money."

"Then we're decided," Hugh said. "We'll get up early and ride over there. It's probably best to have as much light as possible for this kind of work."

Giulia woke up, sat up and leaned against the wall. The morning light framed the tavern door as if the outside world was on fire. She waited, trying to figure out whether she was hung over or just tired.

13

On the far side of the barn, Alberto was already at work, rolling up his blankets. He looked around, saw Giulia and gave her a small, friendly smile that made her wonder if he was quite as crass as she'd thought. Then she stood up, feeling as long-limbed and gawky as a colt, and woke Hugh.

They had bread and small beer for breakfast. It was Vitale's turn to ready the horses, and he returned to the inn smiling broadly. "It's a fine day out there," he announced. "Not too hot; good for riding."

They trooped outside, into the sunshine. It was strange, Giulia thought, that the same sky hung over herself and Constantin Leth. She wondered if God found it harder to see what people were doing if they were hidden from the sky, and whether that was why the undead avoided the daylight.

Constantin Leth, revenant and alchemist, was at least a thousand years old. He had once been a citizen of the Quaestan Empire, the great civilisation that had existed long before the Archangel Alexis had founded the holy Church. He had extended his life with black magic, hiding from the authorities and perfecting his techniques for raising the dead. Twenty years ago, he had traded occult knowledge with the Inquisition, in return for prisoners on whom to practice his arts. Those prisoners had included dwarrows and dryads. And now, the fey folk had put a huge bounty on Leth's head, and Giulia intended to collect it.

Hugh rode at the front, Giulia just behind him. Trees flanked the road, throwing shadow over the riders. Giulia looked between the trunks, thinking of the night before. She half-expected to see figures shambling about in there, to see faces staring out at her, full of the stupid fury of the undead.

Easy, she told herself. *Easy. There's nothing there.*

Behind her, Alberto was telling Ludwig about his career as a mercenary.

"Every chapter of the Landsknecht has its own colours, and its own name. Me, I rode with the best: the Men of Repute. That's their sign I've got painted on my armour. They're an honourable crew. But some of the others – the Death Cheaters or the Cold Heart Riders – they're just trash. Some of those fellows would just ride into a town, smash the place up, go chasing women around, all that. In the Men of Repute, we had rules."

"So why did you leave?" Ludwig asked.

"Because I broke the rules!" Alberto laughed and kicked his horse on. It trotted a few paces forward, hooves thumping softly against the ground. He bounced up beside Giulia, slowed to a walk and said, "How far off are we?"

"It shouldn't be far now." She glanced at the sun. It looked to be mid-afternoon. "At least, I hope not."

"Good. Last thing I want is to be walking through the front door in the pitch dark, with a bunch of angry stiffs waiting for me on the other side. Fighting's one thing – getting jumped is another."

"Don't worry," Hugh said. "If we've not got enough time, we'll make camp, then give it another look in the morning."

Giulia said, "Once we're inside, it'll be pretty dark no matter what." She felt warmth across her forehead. She put a hand there: travelling had left her slightly sunburned. She pulled her hood up. "I'll go in first and scout around. I don't mind the dark."

15

The road swung to the left, and on the right was a valley, where once a stream had run. A manor house lay at the bottom, the buildings spread out around it as if it had tumbled into the valley and broken into pieces. Hugh pulled on his reins and the others stopped around him.

"Well, there it is," Vitale said.

Giulia shielded her eyes with her hand. *There's nothing to worry about*, she told herself. *It's just like the jobs you used to do. Just another big house to rob.*

From the road, looking down, it seemed like a small hamlet: half-overgrown, the outbuildings sinking into a sea of vegetation. The main house, however, was oddly clear of plant life. The ground around it looked dead, as though the soil had been poisoned.

The house was big and empty, built as if to withstand gunfire. The windows were squares of blackness. Four huge columns flanked the entrance. There were only a couple of chimneys – not many for a house of that size – and no smoke rose from them.

"We'll leave the horses here," said Hugh. "If there's revenants around, we don't want them getting scared."

Giulia climbed down. The others dismounted around her. They armed themselves, pulling weapons from their saddlebags. Vitale took out his crossbow and peered at the workings. He licked his finger and rubbed it down the groove where the bolt would lie, cleaning out specks of dirt.

"Shit, that's a big house," Alberto said. He shielded his eyes with his hand. "It looks dead, though."

"Define 'dead'," Vitale replied.

Hugh looked at Giulia. "What do you think?"

She sized the house up as if it was an enemy. There were no horses or wagons in sight. None of the windows seemed to have shutters – that felt odd. A few tiles had come loose from the roof, but not enough to make the place uninhabitable. She could only see the front doors, but there would definitely be other ways in. There wasn't much in the way of handholds on the front, but someone skilled could probably climb up to the first floor without much trouble.

"All right," Giulia said. "First, if there's a lookout in there, there's no way we're getting across the grass without being seen. Unless we want to wait for nightfall—"

"No, we don't," Alberto said.

"That's what I thought. You see those little trees on the left? I could work my way around them and get to the house from the side. I'd see what's going on, and the rest of you could follow."

Vitale said, "I could cover you with my crossbow."

Ludwig raised his hand. "Er, what happens when we get there? I mean to say, if we all go in through the front, what's to stop Leth running out the back?"

"Go on," said Hugh.

"Well, I don't know. We could— when I went hunting with my father, we'd get the servants to beat the grass, to drive the animals out…"

"Flush him," Hugh said. "Like game."

"Exactly. I could go with Hugh and Alberto, and we could work our way towards the back. Then Giulia and Vitale could lie in wait, and shoot him if he comes out."

Alberto spat into the undergrowth. "That's not a bad idea. Assuming you two remember how to shoot straight."

Giulia looked at the house, at the black squares it had as windows. Each one looked like a hole, leading down into darkness. "I don't like it. What happens if Leth gets the jump on you?"

"You think he would?" Alberto said.

"I think he's a thousand years old and he's probably got some tricks up his sleeve."

Alberto shrugged. "We'll call for you."

Let's just hope it's shouting and not screaming. "Hugh? What do you think?"

The old knight rubbed his chin. He stared at the house. "Vitale, Giulia, go around the back. Stay just outside," he said. "Our voices will carry from inside. Alberto, have you got that whistle?"

"Right here."

"If we get into trouble, Alberto will give two blasts of the whistle. Then you come in and help us out. How does that sound?"

Giulia thought it over. "All right. And if Vitale and I get into trouble, we'll shout."

Vitale nodded. "Trust me," he said, "you'll hear us."

Giulia loaded her bow and set out towards the house. She picked her way through the undergrowth, crossbow lowered. The foliage was largely dead: stems and leaves crunched and broke under her boots. Vitale was close behind. For now, speed was more important than silence.

"The ground's dead," he said.

Giulia stepped behind a pale, twisted gorse bush the colour of ashes. "Maybe it's alchemy," she said, but she thought *Poison.*

They were twenty yards from the house. Giulia hurried on, pushing through the bracken and sidestepping the bits too large to flatten. She glanced at the windows: they were empty, but anything could have been hiding in there, watching from the dark. She

18

wondered if she would be able to feel Leth's eyes on her. Could revenants see like living people?

Vitale cursed softly; she heard cloth rip as he pulled himself free. "Just my cloak," he said.

To the left was a low wall, half-swallowed by vegetation. Giulia glanced at it, saw nothing trying to hide behind it, and kept going. She looked over her shoulder and saw the other three moving up behind them, Hugh leading the way.

The wall of the house was just ahead. God, it was big, she thought. It was like a fortress; it would have been a miserable place to live. She reached the wall and stepped into its shadow, covering the others as they approached. They seemed to be making hard work of it; Alberto had drawn his mace and was bashing through the dead gorse.

Vitale stopped beside her. He looked back at the other three and raised his eyebrows. "So much for the quiet approach."

A bird was singing, far away. Giulia looked back up the slope, and could just see their horses, standing in the shadow of a clump of trees. Her mouth was dry. She closed her eyes and listened, in case anything was moving within the house, but all she heard was the sound of the others approaching.

Hugh reached them first. "That was hard going."

Giulia kept her voice low. When everyone was close, she said, "All right. Vitale and I will sneak round to the back. You go in through the front. If anything comes our way, we'll shout. And hopefully shoot it, too."

Ludwig nodded. His round face was sweaty and pale. "You still got that whistle, Alberto?"

The mercenary reached down to his boot and pulled the whistle out as if it was a dagger. "Right here."

"If things get nasty, use it." She glanced from face to face, worried that she'd missed something. "I think that covers everything. Hugh?"

The old knight frowned. He stood still, as though listening to music that only he could hear, and said, "I can't think of anything else. We'll give you the count of a hundred before we go in. That way you'll be able to get in place."

"Good idea."

He reached out and put his hand on her shoulder. "Take care."

"You too, Hugh." She turned to Vitale. "Let's go."

They crept off. Together, they walked to the end of the house. Giulia glanced back: Ludwig was taking out a lantern, closing the shutters to reduce the glow. Then Giulia turned the corner and the three fighters were lost to view.

She and Vitale hurried down the side of the house. The only windows were high and dark. Twigs and leaves crunched softly under their boots. The air smelled stale, full of dying vegetation.

Giulia reached the end of the house and stopped. Slowly, carefully, she looked around the corner.

Once there had been a garden here: a rectangular space could still be made out, although its contents had long since died. At the rear were a few trees. She beckoned Vitale closer.

"Looks like they used to grow food here," he said.

"Not for a long while. See those trees? We can hide behind them."

"Sounds good."

She ran out. She rushed at the trees, trying not to think of the windows she'd be passing, or of how exposed she was. A low branch appeared before her and she hurdled it. The dead trees were only a few yards away. She could hear Vitale close behind, his panting breath and the pounding of his boots on the earth.

She reached the trees and ducked behind them. Her heart was still beating fast; she tried to calm herself as she looked over the rear of the house. The windows were pitch black. The back door was closed. It looked surprisingly new.

Quietly, Vitale said, "See anything?"

"Nothing."

"Me neither." He eased himself down onto the ground and placed the crossbow to the side, within easy reach. "You reckon they'll flush him out?"

"Maybe. If he's there. Or they'll kill him."

They waited. Giulia wondered how much time had passed. By now, Hugh, Ludwig and Alberto would be deep inside the house. She'd told Hugh about breaking into houses before, and she hoped he'd remember: sweep the floor you're on, make sure nobody can ambush you before you move on to the next. Hopefully the stairs and floor would be stone. Wood would rot, and the last thing they needed was someone breaking their leg when the stairs collapsed.

Don't worry, she thought. *Stay calm. They'll be fine.*

"I've been thinking," Vitale said. His voice was low and calm. "Say we kill Leth. What if he just turns to dust? How will we claim the bounty on that?"

"We'll collect the dust and take it to the fey folk as proof. They'll have some kind of magic. And the clothes would—"

"Did you hear that?"

She held her breath. A breeze stirred the trees at the top of the valley. She heard nothing. "No. What is it?"

21

Vitale picked up his crossbow. "Thought I heard a voice. Shouting."

In that moment, the whole valley seemed alive with tiny sounds. The leaves rustled on the trees; wood creaked softly. Vitale shifted position and a stick crunched under his boot.

Then Alberto's whistle blasted through it all, shrill and urgent.

"Shit! That's Alberto. Let's go!" Giulia pulled her crossbow up and stepped out of cover. Legs bent, she scurried towards the house. The whistle came again, a high piping squeal, like a bird in pain. Vitale cursed and ran past her.

"Careful!" Giulia called. She flicked the bow to cover the windows, saw nothing, and ran after him.

Vitale reached the door. He grabbed the handle. "Locked! Hold this." He shoved his crossbow at her, and Giulia grabbed it with her left hand. She stepped back, bow in each hand, and Vitale threw his shoulder against the door.

The whistle came again, long and high. It was moving, as if Alberto was running back and forth. Weirdly, it seemed to be coming from below the ground. A single shot boomed – that had to be his musket. Vitale slammed his shoulder into the door again, bounced back and did it a third time.

"Careful!" Giulia snapped. "It might be—" and the wood splintered and Vitale burst into the house. He stopped and stood in the wedge of light that had come through the doorway. There were chequerboard tiles under his boots, cracked and ancient. He stood there, looking left and right.

A scream of fury and a hand lashed out from the darkness. It clipped Vitale's head, sent him sprawling out of view. A man lurched into the doorway. The whistle blew again.

"Hey!" Giulia said.

The man turned. His skin was like wax, his eyes full of crazy rage. Giulia raised Vitale's crossbow one-handed and shot the revenant in the head. It stumbled backwards and collapsed. She dashed in and almost threw Vitale's bow at him. He grabbed it, hesitated, and drew his sword.

"This way!" Giulia called.

She ran deeper into the house. Shafts of light punched in through the window-holes, breaking up the shadow. She ran between the light and dark, towards the centre.

A figure loomed up ahead. Giulia stopped short, aimed her bow, and realised it was a statue of a girl, slightly bigger than life-size, screaming at the ceiling.

She heard Alberto yell "Hey! I'm over here!", and ran towards the sound. Giulia turned a corner. A door was almost closed, and daylight spilled around its edges. She grabbed the handle and threw it open.

She looked out into a square atrium, open to the sky. Dirt and rubble were heaped at the edges; the place was crumbling. The floor had partly collapsed, forming a kind of ramp down into the earth. Alberto stood in the centre, sword raised. Several figures lay at his feet, bloody and unmoving.

Where's Hugh? She ran forward and Alberto turned. Then she saw who lay beside him.

"Hugh!"

She ran to his side. The old knight stared up at her. His face was white, his neck a wet mess of blood. His hand was pressed to the vein. Blood pumped between his fingers, soaking his gloves.

"It was the boy," Alberto said. "The boy – Ludwig – he stabbed him. Dropped his sword and ran off. I couldn't stop him – the morts let him through. I swear to God."

She knelt beside her friend. His eyes recognised her: Hugh stared at Giulia as if he could heal himself through force of will alone. "Hugh, Hugh," she said. She looked up. "Bandage. We've got to make a bandage. I need some fucking cloth!"

Giulia drew her knife and half-cut, half-tore a chunk out of her cloak. She turned back to Hugh. His free hand came up and caught hold of hers. His fingers felt so strong, almost crushing her knuckles. His eyes were desperate, his lower jaw shook.

"I'm going to bandage your neck," she said.

He groaned and sagged back onto the broken tiles. The force went out of his grip, out of his face. She'd seen him unconscious before, gormless in sleep or drunkenness, but he had never looked like this before. He wasn't restful, just gone. Dead.

"Bandage," she said. "Come on, Hugh."

"Giulia." It was Vitale, standing over her. "Giulia!"

She looked up and felt rage. "Fucking help me, damn it."

"No," he replied. "Look!"

She looked up. The broken floor led down into the earth, into a hole, and things were crawling out of it. They were pale, spindly, almost naked, and they wore masks over their faces. She saw three – no, four – climbing over each other.

"Oh, fuck," Alberto said. "Oh, fuck, we've got to go."

More of them now, seven or eight, no more than a dozen yards away. They were spreading out, some of

24

them upright now, holding knives and spears. They reminded Giulia of spiders.

"We're not going," she said.

Vitale shouted, "To Hell with that! Alberto, you ready?"

The big mercenary took a step backwards, his mace held up ready to swing. "We're going."

Suddenly, Giulia realised what that meant. "We're not leaving him here! We've got to take him with us. The fey folk can— they can make him better."

Vitale turned, and his face was at once hard and kind. "Giulia, Hugh's dead. We have to go."

The revenants, or whatever they were, had started to creep closer.

Alberto barked "Fuck it, Vitale, just run! Leave her here!"

Vitale grabbed Giulia's shoulder and shook so hard that she nearly fell down. "Come on!" he bellowed. He turned and ran. Giulia ran after him. As if at a signal, the undead lunged forward.

Alberto swung his mace into the side of a revenant's head. It screamed and fell, thrashing. Vitale reached the door and turned to cover them, crossbow raised. He fired and Alberto and Giulia raced through the door.

Giulia looked back. At the edge of the hole, two of the skinny grey things had grabbed Hugh's feet and were trying to pull his boots off. No, she realised. They were pulling his body down the slope. A figure emerged from the hole, a tall bald man, graceful in a long white robe. He looked down at Hugh and nodded. His skin was like marble.

Leth.

Then the others were yelling at her again, Vitale was pulling her on, and she stumbled behind him: towards the sunlight, away from Hugh.

PART ONE

Chapter One

Alberto shielded his eyes against the sun and looked across the valley. The church stood on the highest point of the village of Mardino, and fields stretched around in all directions like a lake of corn. Families waded through the corn, bringing in the harvest. A young woman carried a basket almost as big as she was, a scarf over her head to protect her from the heat, and Alberto squinted to see whether she was good-looking. It was impossible to tell.

He turned towards the tree that marked the centre of the village and watched the two figures standing in its shade. From here, the smaller of the two looked like a doll made of burnt sticks, all thin limbs and dark clothing. The larger one wore a long robe, taut over his paunch as if he was pregnant. The fat man stepped back, his business concluded, and the dark figure began to walk towards the church.

"Is she done?" Vitale sat under the lich-gate, out of the sun.

"Looks like it," Alberto said. "Are you ready for this?"

Vitale climbed to his feet. "All set," he said, and he picked up the crossbow from the ground by his side. "Let's get it over with."

The city of Astrago loomed on the horizon as if it was about to fall off the edge of the world. Its towers formed a jagged silhouette against the blue sky, like the painted backdrop of a play.

27

The two mercenaries walked slowly down the hill. Alberto's musket was slung over his shoulder, his mace tied to his belt. He hooked his thumbs over his belt to make himself look casual.

"How'd it go?" he asked. "Did your man have anything good to say?"

Giulia nodded. "Nothing on Ludwig. But there's a man in Astrago looking for Leth. His name's Pietro Sepello, and he's some kind of priest who kills revenants. Or at least that's what that merchant's heard. You know how it is: traders swap stories along the road. Only thing is, five inns down the way and the story's completely changed. Hopefully we're close enough to Astrago for it to still be roughly accurate."

Alberto gave a derisory snort. "Merchants, eh?"

For a moment, everyone was quiet.

"What's wrong?" Giulia said.

"Giulia," Alberto replied, running a hand over his hair, "I've been meaning to say this for a while. To be honest, I've been waiting for some good news to come along. Some good news for you, I mean." He sighed, as if deflating. "Fact of it is, me and Vitale, well, we've been thinking about heading our separate ways."

She said, "You want to leave."

"We both do," Vitale said.

"That's about the sum of it." Alberto sighed. He was surprised to feel this sad. "It's not, you know, personal, but— we thought we'd hang on for a while, but, you know how it is…."

"It's not a matter of money," Vitale put in. "I know it's been hard for you to cover things recently, but it's not that. We're— well, things are a little slow for us, to be honest."

Alberto shrugged. He felt awkward, as if he was lying. "Men like us, we need action. I know we're doing good work and all, but it's been pretty quiet these last few months." He didn't say it, but it hardly needed saying: *since Hugh was killed.*

Giulia said, "We're near to finding Leth. I know we are. Listen: just a month more, maybe two, and we'll be onto the bastard. We can bring him in between us and collect our reward. Believe me, it won't be quiet then." She smiled at Alberto: a broad, flat smile that he didn't like. "I can feel it, honestly. We're nearly there."

Vitale's voice was quiet and calm. "Giulia, you said that last month."

"I mean it," she replied. "You'll have all the action you want. All the money, too."

"It's not for us," Vitale said.

Alberto nodded. "There's Landsknecht work going on up north in Vorland, you know. Good work, with regular pay – no offence, Giulia. Archduke Vanharren's hiring out pretty much any freelancer he can find, getting all the old chapters back together again. I reckon the Men of Repute would take me back. It'd be like the old days. I could put in a good word for you if you like – it's not often they get women riding with them, but it's happened before. You'd make a good scout—"

Giulia shook her head. "Thanks, but no."

There was a moment's pause, as if they had all forgotten why they were there.

"I'm really sorry about the old man," Alberto said. He clearly hadn't meant to say it: now that the words had been blurted out, they seemed to hang in the air between them, too big to be ignored. "Really."

"Thank you," Giulia said.

Vitale rubbed his stubble. "I am too," he said. "I liked him."

Giulia looked over her shoulder. Alberto wondered if she expected to see Hugh standing there.

"Look," she said, "I still owe you some wages. I've not got enough on me to cover it all, but if we all go to Astrago, I can get it from my savings in the bank. It's only a day's ride. Would you come with me?"

They looked at each other. "Of course," Alberto said. "We'll ride down there with you. Keep you company."

"Good," Giulia said. She glanced around, as if she had only just realised where she was. "Now, let's find something to eat. I could do with a good meal."

"Right!" Alberto slapped his palms together with too much jollity. "Good plan! Then you can tell everything that merchant said."

Giulia looked surprised. "You still want to know?"

Alberto felt slightly hurt. "Of course I do. Come on, I'm hungry."

*

The walls of Astrago were high and thick, designed to stop not just rocks and battering rams, but cannonballs. Earth had been piled up against the walls as well as stone, and now they were like the base of a mountain. Towers poked up above the walls like trees growing out of a crater, and gun emplacements squatted on the top of the fortifications.

Grass grew up some of the outer walls. As Giulia rode towards the gates, she saw children flinging themselves at the slope, laughing as they rolled back down. Women stood outside little shacks, trying to sell food to travellers. Giulia could smell roast meat.

They rode between two long embankments to the North Gate. The gates were open, and four bored guards stood chatting in the gap. They wore the livery of House DeFalci: yellow and blue stripes, with a unicorn courant in the centre of their chests.

As Giulia came near, they stepped into her way.

"Morning, lady," one said, laying a hand on the horse's bridle as he gave it a friendly pat. He took in Giulia's scars calmly, as if he planned to draw her face from memory later on. "Visiting friends, are we?"

"I'm here to finish up some business," she replied. She did have friends in Astrago, or at least acquaintances, but that could come later. "These two men are my guards on the road."

A second soldier strolled around the side of the horse. "And what sort of business is that, then?"

"Mort hunting. Bounty work for the militia."

"The militia? You?"

"Yes, me. I've got a letter to prove it, too." Giulia fished out Gordini's letter and passed it to the nearest man. She waited as he read it.

"You can come in," he declared, handing the paper back up. "But remember: keep those bows out of sight. Curfew's from midnight to five, all swords and knives are to be kept in view, no brewing, printing, killing or whoring without a licence – not that any of that affects you good people, I'm sure." The guard stepped back. "Go ahead."

Giulia nudged her horse along, into the city.

It had been over a year since she had seen this place. Astrago had become overgrown in her absence: not with plants, but with statues, buildings and fortifications. As she rode through the gates, she saw that the houses just behind the walls had been torn down, and mortars and trebuchet batteries erected in their place. Scaffolding covered the front of one massive tenement, as a team of masons used a spring-loaded pulley to lift the statue of a saint to the peak of the roof.

A giant clock-face rattled above her and, as she passed by, the hour hand thumped against the polished IX on the dial. A brass man standing on top of the clock stood up with a rattle of cogs and waved a flag.

They dismounted in the main street. The North Gate was not the most important way in – the most noble visitors rode in from the east, while the bulk of trade came across the sea, docking in the south of the city – but it was still impressive: so new as to still look unreal, as though Giulia was an insect crawling through an architect's model. In the centre of the road stood a statue of Mavlio's wife, Viola: dead in childbirth, now twice life size and dressed in robes that made her look like a cross between an orator and a goddess. There were fresh-cut flowers in the basket she carried. Her other arm reached across her body, ready to scatter them over her husband's city.

"Quite a town!" Vitale said. He peered down one of the wide streets. "Has it always been like this?"

"It's always been getting this way," Giulia replied. "Ever since Prince Mavlio overthrew Prince Diello and drove out House Sciata. But that was ten years ago, before I ever came here." She looked up the broad, busy street, past the crowds and carts rattling on the cobblestones, towards the nearest branch of the Bank of Promises.

The Bank of Promises had been opened by dwarrows, many years ago, and they had become successful – and scandalous – by holding money not just for God-fearing men, but for dwarrows, dryads, dissenters, New Churchers and even women. Giulia was slightly disappointed to find that the staff in the bank were human: she missed the dwarrows of Pagalia, and would have liked their company.

Giulia handed the teller the letter from Captain Gordini, and he read it slowly while she waited. "It says here there's five of you."

She nodded. "One of us was killed, and another ran away." She pointed at the letter. "There. Hugh de Kenton. And Ludwig Kroner." She didn't like saying their names together.

"I'll bring the coins out," the man replied. He seemed weary, as if he paid out bounty money every day of the week.

They sat on a bench at the edge of the courtyard while they waited for their pay. Alberto bought fresh bread from a street vendor and, as they ate it, they watched a group of swordsmen striding past in brand-new uniforms.

So this is it, Giulia thought. Soon the money would come, and that would be the end of their partnership. She realised that she didn't want Vitale and Alberto to go. Vitale was eccentric and Alberto was a crude, violent man – but without them she would only have herself for company. There would be no need to play the leader then, no obligation to put on a brave face. She held the bread out to Vitale and, as his dark hand tore off a chunk, a door opened in the side of the bank and the bank teller emerged with a cloth bag in his fist.

Giulia stood up. "Right then. Let's get paid."

Back in the street, Alberto surprised her. "End of the road," he announced, and he sighed and held out a big hand for her to shake. "It's been a pleasure, Giulia. Too bad about Sir Hugh, really it is."

She shook his hand, feeling strangely grateful. For a moment they both hesitated, and then they embraced. He patted her back.

"I've got to say, when I saw I'd be working for a woman, I thought *Here's trouble*, but it's been one of the best jobs I've ever done. I'm sorry it worked out this way, though. Me and Vitale'll head north, to Vorland," Alberto said, rubbing his beard. "I know people in the Landsknecht there, back in my old chapter. It'll be good to ride with the boys again."

"And I'll go for the infantry," Vitale added. "I've heard Vanharren wants good scouts. Besides, Alberto needs someone to show him which way north is."

Giulia smiled. "I hope it goes well." She hugged him. "It's been a pleasure working with you."

"You too, Giulia," Vitale said. "And if I see that whoreson Ludwig, I'll send his Teut arse straight to Hell for you!"

"Just tell me where he is," Giulia said, trying to sound tough and confident. For a moment they were all silent. A high-sided wagon rolled past, creaking and clattering on the cobbled street. "Well," she added, "good luck."

"Goodbye, Giulia," Vitale said. "Take care."

She watched them go as if she were watching her last boat home sailing out of port. Then she turned back to the city, and to the task in hand.

*

The ship lay eight miles off the coast of Astrago. There was only a light breeze and, with its anchor down, the vessel lay as still as a felled tree. As his own boat drew near, Francis Vale stood up and waved.

A soldier on the deck waved back. The marine wore a cuirass and helmet, a pistol at his side.

The ship was fairly small for a cargo vessel, built for speed. The sails were dirty-white, without heraldry. The name on the bows was faded and unreadable.

Built to go unseen.

The rowers pulled on the oars and Vale's boat came alongside the ship. Marines hurried to the side and tossed down a rope ladder. Above them, seagulls circled and screeched.

Vale scrambled up the ladder. The ropes smelled of rotten seaweed. One of the marines, a stern-faced young man, leaned in to help him up.

As he stepped on board Vale saw what had drawn the gulls. There was a feast laid out for them across the deck: a dozen corpses lay in the positions where they had fallen. They were dressed for working the ship, in tough, practical clothes. The marines had boarded so swiftly that few of the sailors had even drawn their weapons. The bodies did not smell, not yet.

The marine saluted him. "Welcome aboard, sir!"

Vale licked his lips and tasted salt. "Well, this makes a change. It's more fun than sitting around in the embassy back in Pagalia, at least."

"It's the Lord's work, sir."

"Quite so. You've been busy, I see. Is this all of them?"

"All but one, Sir Francis," said a voice. Vale turned and saw the sergeant of the marines. He was a massive man, with a glum face and eyes that had seen everything.

"Ah, Sergeant Merrick. You hit them hard, I see."

"Very much so, sir. We took a rowing boat over, all ten of us, told 'em we were inspectors from Astrago. The rest was easy. I thought they'd put up more of a fight, to

35

be honest. That fellow there" — he nodded towards a corpse at the bows — "had a sword on him, but we'd stuck the bugger before he drew it. Reckon he was their captain."

Vale frowned. "It's a shame you didn't take any of them alive."

"Half of them didn't speak Alexian, Sir Francis. They wouldn't have been any use to us."

"That's for me to decide. You said there was one left."

"Yes, Sir Francis. He's a foreigner, too. We thought he might be a wizard. Got him tied up below."

Until we're back in Albion, everyone is a foreigner.

"A wizard, eh?" Vale replied. "Well, that's something. Now, Sergeant, have you had the chance to search the hold?"

Sergeant Merrick grimaced. "Yes, Sir Francis, we did."

He turned and walked across the deck. Vale followed. A corpse lay beside the trapdoor that led into the hold. The man's skin was dark brown, and Vale wondered where he had been born. Vale looked at the empty, grimacing face, and reflected that in life he would have been a handsome man.

But he's not so fine now.

"You might want to cover your mouth, sir," the sergeant said. He pulled up the trapdoor. "And mind your head on the way down."

The alchemical stink that rose out made Vale want to back away. He stayed in place and reached into his sleeve. A scented handkerchief nestled beside his stiletto, and Vale held it over his nostrils and mouth to keep the tainted air away.

A wave slapped against the ship, and it tilted, throwing a square of light across the contents of the hold. Vale saw wooden crates and several locked trunks. They looked expensive, like the cases that mercenary captains took with them on campaign. Vale climbed down, the sergeant following.

Letters had been chalked on the lid of one of the crates: SVLFVRIUM. "Sulphur, eh?" said Vale. "Now, this is interesting."

"Devilry," the sergeant growled.

"Not devilry. Alchemy. There's a clear distinction."

Merrick looked unconvinced. Vale knew what he was thinking. On a boat like this, crewed by pirates, heathens and incense-sniffing Old Churchers, what else could you expect?

"I want the hold stripped," Vale said. "Take all the chemicals out and make an inventory. We can give any of the alchemical stuff that we don't need to Prince Mavlio as a gift."

Merrick nodded. "Yes, Sir Francis."

"There's two kegs of powder on my boat. Have the men bring them aboard and rig a three-minute fuse. I'll tell you when to light it."

"Yes, Sir Francis."

They climbed back onto the deck and the sergeant kicked the trapdoor shut. Vale pushed the handkerchief back into his sleeve. He took a deep breath of the sea air. "Now, then, Sergeant. Let's have a look at this pirate wizard of yours."

Merrick nodded grimly and stomped across the deck. He stopped at the captain's cabin, at the rear of the vessel. "He's in here." He opened the door, and Vale walked inside.

A man was tied to a chair in the centre of the room, his head hidden by a small sack. He wore a grey robe and black gloves. As they entered, the man raised his head and his breath quickened, puffing into his bag.

It's just fear. He'll be fine.

There was a table at the back of the cabin, full of books and instruments. Vale walked over to get a closer look. The prisoner flinched as he came close; Vale ignored him.

The table held a portable alchemy lab. Vale was no expert, but he recognised calcinators, refraction tubes, rows of bottles and small, razor-sharp knives. He reached behind a long, ornate condenser and took out two small books.

One was a text in some language of the East: columns of characters ran down the page like rows of tiny diagrams. There were pictures, though, that he understood full well. A soldier with a basket under his arm, tossing massive fangs onto the earth as if to sow a field with teeth. A few pages on, and he saw a second image: a decapitated body standing upright in a gown. A severed head hovered above it, smirking. *Yes*, Vale thought, *this is it, all right.*

Vale looked up from the book. "And now for our new friend." He picked up a chair from the edge of the room and set it down in the centre.

He sat down in the chair and looked at the man before him. Under the bag, the man was shivering. Vale snapped the book shut. The slap of closing paper made the captive wince.

"Let's see who we've got." Vale reached forward and pulled the bag away.

The man was indeed an Easterner. He was old, clean-shaven, with a deeply lined face. He blinked, glanced around, drew back in the chair and struggled to make himself still.

"Hello," Vale said. "And how are you today?"

The man stared at him. He said something that sounded like "Tinbudon". His voice was soft and hesitant. He shook his head. "Not speak much."

Vale crossed his legs. "Ah," he said, "I think you can understand me pretty well, if you put your mind to it. After all, how would you sell the goods in your hold if you couldn't argue a good price?"

"A little," said the man. His shoulders were tensed, as if to resist a blow.

The planks creaked by the door: Vale looked round and saw Sergeant Merrick standing there, looking both menacing and uncomfortable.

"So you do know a little Alexian! Excellent." Vale gave the prisoner an encouraging smile. "I'll make it easier for you. I'm going to mention a few names, and you'll tell me if you recognise any of them. And if that's still a bit difficult, perhaps this might help jog your memory."

He reached into his sleeve and drew the stiletto. The prisoner's eyes fixed themselves on the blade. He began to sweat; his breathing became heavier. Vale wondered if he was going to cry. "No," he said. "Please."

"So now," said Vale. "Let's start with the House of Orloque. Does that ring any bells? How about the Mutasharrin? The Lapis Philosophorum, then? No? Nothing at all?" Vale leaned forward. His fingers toyed with the knife. The captive's eyes were locked on the twinkling steel. "Let's try something a little easier, then. Constantin Leth."

*

Giulia walked through the district humming to herself, still left with the empty feeling of having seen friends depart.

She could smell meat cooking, and her stomach rumbled. A pair of bulky, broad-shouldered dwarrows marched past, glowering at the road ahead. She was surprised to see that they were militiamen: the emblem of the Citizen Guard was stitched onto their coats. Other cities tolerated the fey folk, but only Prince Mavlio had tried to recruit them.

The statues, the recruitment programme, even the purge of the criminal classes that had driven her out a year ago, had all been carefully thought out. The prince was binding his city together, turning Astrago into a single unit under his command.

She turned left, feeling the strange sense of nostalgia that came from returning to familiar ground, as if she was tracking a younger version of herself. To the right, she saw the tenement block where she'd once lived, up in a room on the top floor. She remembered crawling across the tiles on the night that she'd fled Astrago, climbing in through the roof to grab her things and run. She turned towards a narrow alleyway, and three small children burst out and dashed away like startled birds. Giulia shrugged and headed down between the whitewashed walls. She emerged into a wider street. On the far side, two hefty young men loitered outside an inn.

The Gauntlet.

One man stepped forward as she approached. He stared at her face for a moment, then drew back. Giulia nodded to him and opened the door.

The Gauntlet hadn't changed. It was long, dark and smoky inside, rumbling with low voices. If the drinkers there had changed, they'd been replaced by very similar people: different actors playing the same roles. A girl filled battered tankards from a row of barrels at the back of the room. She glanced at Giulia, clearly decided that she was of no importance, and got back to work.

"Hello," Giulia said. She fished out a coin. "I'll have a cup of wine. A big one. Is Irmgard in?"

The girl held out a mug. "Who's asking?"

"Yulia!"

Giulia turned. A stocky, middle-aged woman emerged from the back room. She had blonde hair and a pink face sheened with sweat. They embraced briefly.

"Welcome back, Yulia," Irmgard said. Her accent was as thick as ever. "Come back home to Astrago, eh?"

"I'm not sure I'd call it 'home', but yes. How's business?"

"Not too bad. Got to be careful, these days. Prince Mavlio doesn't like crime unless he's the one doing it. How about you? I thought you were going to make your fortune?"

"I'm still working on it. Have you got a room going?"

"Of course, if you can pay for it. You always were a little… slow with the coins, you know?"

"Not anymore. I'm better off now."

Irmgard snorted. "You can't be that rich if you're staying here." She leaned past Giulia and yelled down the length of the hall. "Tomas! Get that man out of here! These fucking drunkards," she muttered. "Some of these people…"

Giulia passed some coins over. "Food as well. Whatever you've got."

"It's good to see you," Irmgard said, and she sounded as if she meant it. "Last time you were here, I was worried you were in trouble."

41

"I was in trouble. I still am, but it's not the same trouble. I suppose that's a good thing."

"So long as it stays outside. Anything you need, Yulia, any gear, you ask me, right?"

"I will."

Giulia had got used to eating alone a long time ago, when she had been plotting her revenge on the men who had carved her face. She sat by the wall, in a small bubble of quiet in the hubbub of the inn, turning her options over.

There were things to do, leads to follow. The merchant at Mardino had given her a name to look into: Pietro Sepello. Apparently, he was some sort of churchman tracking the undead, and was staying in rooms behind the Chapel of Saint Cordelia in the centre of town. With a little luck, he would be able to help her in finding Leth.

If he's got any sense, he'll be glad to have my help. Although there's no telling with churchmen. She poured out another cup of wine. She felt sharp, cold and a little distant from everything, as if she was directing her body from afar.

Then there were the fey. A week after Hugh's death she had sent an update to Sethis and Arashina, her contacts among the fey folk and their unofficial ambassadors among the city-states. Sethis had sent a letter expressing his sadness at her news and stating that he would understand if Giulia wanted to give up the search for Leth. Giulia had got drunk and written back, stating her intention to hunt Leth down, set him alight and shit in his ashes. The thought of that letter made her wince, and she took another sip of cheap red wine. She'd have to contact the dryads again soon. They'd be wondering how she was faring. She'd need to reassure them that she was still working on the mission, even if she was going to do it alone.

Three men were getting steadily drunk at the far side of the room. Two of them suddenly launched into a song, and the third started to bang out a beat on the tabletop. A few people looked up – one long-haired drinker looked at the singers as if he meant to cut their throats – but nobody objected.

Giulia finished her cup. The room was a little too warm, the air too stale. The singers launched into something faster and more raucous, and a couple of other patrons joined in. Giulia felt uneasy: there was a certain kind of male revelry that could quickly turn from rowdy fun to violence. She got up, wanting to be out of sight. She trudged upstairs as if the soles of her boots were lined with lead.

Giulia sat in her room, feeling the thump of the beat below come ringing up through the floor. There had to be a way to get away from this, to leave this nasty room and her weariness behind, a home to run to.

I was your squire, she realised. She'd never put it like that before.

She owned almost nothing of Hugh: the knight had always travelled light, and with the loss of his body, he'd left almost no trace of his existence. She still had a book that she'd bought him, which he'd left in his saddlebag when they'd gone hunting for Leth. It was *The Lamentable Death of Alba the King* , a story from Hugh's homeland of Albion. Now she picked it up and flicked through the pages, but it just made her feel tired and sad.

Welcome back, Giulia. You thought you could get away, thought you could make another life, but here you are again, taking another revenge.

Well, so what if I am? It's what I do best.

43

Friends came and were stolen away, but the need for revenge and the fury born of being cheated were reliable company. She had been foolish to think that she'd escaped from this. The trail had just led back here, to the same tavern and the same sense of outrage that would not fade away.

It's been eighty-one days since Leth murdered Hugh. I was his squire.

The Chapel of Saint Cordelia stood between new tenement blocks like an old parish priest between two strong lads. It was small, rough, made of battered stone and chipped, slate. Giulia had visited it a few times in the old days. She had tended to worship at the grand basilica, at the shrine that Saint Senobina, patron of thieves, shared with other minor saints, but occasionally she had come here to ask Cordelia for a blessing. Once Giulia had turned herself into a killer, it had seemed only reasonable to ask Our Lady of Righteous Battle for help.

The door was heavy and iron-banded, but it opened easily. Giulia slipped inside.

The nave was made of massive stone blocks. The windows were high and small. It smelled of stone, dust and burning candles. Modern churches were like palaces for God, but old ones felt like strongholds. It suited a warrior-saint.

There was a rood screen by the altar, topped with a wooden figure of Alexis the Archangel, his wings spread almost as wide as the nave itself.

A figure loomed out of the dark by her side. Giulia turned and saw a tall, bony man in a robe long enough to brush the floor. His long face was made for misery, but he smiled at her.

"Holy father," she said.

44

"Daughter. Can I help you at all?" He examined her face. "Do I know you from somewhere?"

"I used to come here to pray. But that was a while ago," Giulia said. "I'm looking for someone. A churchman."

"Well, of course, I am—"

"He's called Father Sepello. A merchant on the road gave me his name."

"Ah," said the priest. He seemed disappointed that she didn't want to talk to him: perhaps he was just diligent, or perhaps he had been looking forward to hearing the story behind her scars. "There is a gentleman of that name staying here. He isn't a priest, though. I can see if he's available."

"I'd like to talk to him. There's a sinner we need to discuss."

"You'd best wait here," the priest said, and he walked away down the shadowed side of the nave, opened a small door and disappeared inside.

Giulia walked slowly down between the pews, slightly ill at ease. It was cool and quiet, and her boots softly scuffed the stones.

There was a picture of Saint Cordelia fighting the living dead painted on the wall to her right. It looked ancient. The figures were childish, their robes and armour barely shaded, their bodies lacking perspective as though they had been crushed flat.

Saint Cordelia stood in the centre, on top of a little hill. There was no mistaking her: the armour, the pudding-bowl haircut, the face at once pure and stern. A horde of undead reached for her with grey, clawed hands. Light was bursting from the saint, skewering the nearest revenants, making them throw up their arms and wither like dead plants.

"Quite a picture, isn't it?"

Giulia turned around. The man behind her was tall and healthy, wide across the shoulders. He was young, she realised, probably in his mid-twenties. His face was round and pleasant, and it stopped him looking intimidating. He smiled. "There's a painting of her ascension to Heaven on the other side of the nave."

"I'm looking for Pietro Sepello," she replied.

For half a second he appraised her, making some decision she couldn't read. "That's me."

"Pleased to meet you. My name's Giulia Degarno. A merchant in the next town down gave me your name," Giulia said. "He said you might be able to help."

"Oh yes?" Sepello nodded gently.

"He said you were an expert in killing morts. I wondered if I could talk to you about it."

"Feel free." She knew that he'd be wondering what she was up to, whether this was some kind of a trick. "If there's anything you need to know, I'd be happy to answer your questions. I should warn you, though, that some of the details aren't too pleasant. Revenant hunting's not the prettiest of jobs—"

"It's about one revenant in particular," Giulia said. "His name is Constantin Leth."

He hesitated. "Oh really?"

"Really." She waited.

Sepello glanced around, as if the statues were eavesdropping. "Perhaps you'd better come and sit down."

Giulia followed his gaze to the rear of the chapel, where it was shadowy and private. She thought about Ludwig, all smiles and nervous friendship, and said, "Let's go outside. I'd prefer to be in the sunshine."

"Fair enough. Lead on."

46

They stepped into the sunlight. Down the road, a man was strumming on a battered lute. A monkey on a chain hopped and scampered around his boots. People tossed coppers at his feet and the monkey bared its teeth, as if to laugh.

"Where would you like to go?" Sepello asked.

"The old riverside?" She remembered the gentle banks, where she had used to sit in the old days: at first lamenting the ruin of her face, then plotting revenge for it.

"Whatever you like."

They began to walk. Sepello coughed and said, "So, erm, how do you know of Constantin Leth?"

Giulia wondered whether to tell him about the plot she'd uncovered to bring dirty money into the city of Averrio, which had included Leth at its periphery, or the group of fey she'd met, who wanted to pay Leth back for the crimes he had committed with the Inquisition, or the reward that the elder folk had offered Giulia and Hugh to hunt Leth down. But the real answer was simple.

"He killed my friend."

"I'm sorry to hear it. Was this— did it happen recently?"

"Almost three months ago. My friend was a knight, a freelancer. He was trying to track Leth down. Leth paid a man to betray him. The bastard... well, he hit Hugh – my friend – from behind. If it'd been a fair fight he'd never have won, but he lied, you see, and caught him off guard..." She stopped before she could start rambling. Her voice wanted to become bitter. No, best keep this professional. "I want Leth brought to justice."

"So do I," Sepello said. He looked at the ground as he spoke. "So does my order. I'm sorry about your friend," he added. "Were you, er, close?"

"Yes, we were close. Just friends, but close." Outside his forge, a smith was dipping hot iron cogs into a trough. They hissed angrily as they met the water. "We worked together, as freelancers. I used to be a thief-taker. That was how we met. Sometimes people want a woman to confide in. Noble ladies especially."

"I can imagine," Sepello said.

"Down here."

They turned in to a narrow alley. Giulia said, "The priest said you weren't a churchman. Are you some kind of bounty hunter?"

"I'm in the Order of Saint Cordelia," Sepello replied. "I destroy the living dead: it's my job."

"That sounds dangerous."

"It is, but it's a good cause. And, sometimes, it pays well." Sepello smiled, then stopped smiling. "I've been tracking Leth for a while now. I'm close to catching him, but if you know anything, do tell me. If any information you give me leads me to him, I'll make sure some of the reward money comes your way."

Giulia shook her head. "Thanks, but I don't want any payment. I just want to kill the bastard, that's all."

The alley ended and they emerged into the bright light of the early afternoon. Suddenly they were at the water's edge. The land stopped as if cut away with a huge spade, and before them ran a straight, wide canal.

Giulia peered at it. "This isn't the riverside. Where are we?" She felt nervous, as if Sepello had led to the wrong place for some improper purpose: she moved her hand towards the sleeve where she kept her stiletto.

"This *is* the riverside." Sepello sighed. "They made a few changes."

"What happened? I remember there were trees, and a slope. People used to bathe in it…"

"The prince had it tidied up," Sepello said. "They use it for barges now; some of the water gets diverted into the poor quarter, too. They have these things like great screws to make it rise – augers, that's the word – taller than a man—"

"God. I've been away for too long."

"Maybe. But it's much better than it was. I remember coming into Astrago when I was just a boy, while Prince Diello was still on the throne, and it was like some little market town down south. It's incredible what Mavlio's done with the city."

She looked down at the canal, remembering the games at the water's edge, the women with baskets of washing, the children shrieking with glee. "I suppose so."

"Progress, eh?"

"Let's go somewhere else," Giulia said. "How about the Festival Plaza? Is that still there?"

"Good idea."

They turned away from the waterside. "So, have you found out where Leth's hiding yet?"

He shook his head. "Not yet. Not by a long way. He's crafty, you see. One of the smartest of all the undead. He's no mere mort, that's for sure."

"What's he like?"

"Very cunning, and very old. Some say he was alive during the Quaestan Empire, a thousand years ago. But revenants have to kill to keep going. Because of that, sooner or later they draw attention, so they have to work out ways to survive. Most of them go feral: they live like beasts. A lot are just crazy, completely deluded. But some are wily, too. And a few can even pass as people."

"And that's what Leth is?"

"Absolutely. Except – well, he's different. Look," Sepello said, staring down the road, "most revenants aren't that hard to track down. They're vain, arrogant, never as clever as they think. A lot of them hardly bother hiding themselves, once you start looking. I mean, they *are* dangerous, very dangerous once you're close, but if you know what to expect, you can get the upper hand.

"Leth's not like that. He doesn't show himself, he works through other people, he kills anyone he thinks could be a threat – he's more than just a monster. He thinks like a scholar." Sepello frowned. It seemed that he was not used to explaining his trade. "Your average undead is like a wolf or a big cat. Leth's more like a general in the army."

"He's their leader, then?"

"In a way. The undead don't often work together – they're too arrogant, and too likely to turn on one other. Leth tends to use living people to do his dirty work. He has a knack of offering people what they want. It's cleaner for him that way."

"That's what happened to me. He paid a man to turn on my friend."

The streets were widening as they walked. A row of small trees stretched down the centre of the avenue, dividing the road into two lanes. The shops and tenement blocks were giving way to the big houses of wealthy merchants and functionaries of the prince. The men who did well in Astrago were those who organised others, who directed people instead of hacking them on the battlefield. These days, the city-states needed bureaucrats, not knights. And there was Hugh again, flaring in her mind like a twinge from a wound she had thought was nearly healed.

She said, "How do you kill someone like Leth?"

"Well," Sepello replied, "a revenant that old would be very tough. Much tougher than you or I. They barely feel pain, and the older ones often have skin like leather. But they have weaknesses. Generally speaking, you cut off their head or sever the spine. That tends to do the job."

"I'll bet it does."

"Running them through the chest works pretty well, too," Sepello added. "Likewise blowing them up. Gunpowder has been an absolute blessing for the Order."

The road opened into a grand square. A wall ran along the left side of the square, with a pair of huge fortified gates in its centre. The gates were open for now, and Giulia could see the swarming mass of homes beyond. Prince Mavlio had built four walls through the centre of Astrago, quartering it. That was allegedly for defence: Giulia suspected that it was to keep his subjects in check.

On the far side of the square stood the Quincunx Palace, the home of House DeFalci. The four domes at its corners were blue with verdigris, and the great central dome shone gold in the afternoon sun. One of the outer towers was studded with weathervanes and lightning conductors. As Giulia looked, a figure moved across one of the upper windows, a spyglass in its hands.

Giulia said, "Do you ever work with the fey folk?"

"The fey?" Sepello looked surprised. "Saints, no. They can't stand the Order of Saint Cordelia." He lowered his voice a little: not out of secrecy, she thought, but embarrassment. "Back in the war, the Inquisition tried to get us on their side. They wanted to enlarge the Order, make it part of the Inquis Impugnans." He paused a moment, and Giulia realised what he was about to say. "They wanted to make it not just about hunting the undead, but the dryads and dwarrows as well. Some people went along with that. Some didn't. Of course, this is long before my time, but to the fey folk, it's like yesterday."

"I've got friends among the fey," Giulia said. She wondered whether to tell him that they were funding her – or at least that they had been – and decided against it. "They want Leth dead as much as any of us."

"Oh yes? Do they help you, then?"

"I'm on good terms with several – dwarrows as well as dryads. I thought you and I could pool our knowledge. You could use your links with the Church, and I could go back to the fey for information. Between us we ought to find Leth easily. Then, once we've got him cornered—"

"Wait." Sepello stopped walking. "How do you mean, between us?"

A voice called out from the far side of the square: a man was pushing a cart loaded with apples, shouting his prices.

"We could work together," Giulia replied. "Pool our resources."

Sepello shook his head. "I'm sorry, but no. It doesn't work like that. When you said about help, I thought you just meant information. Actually *destroying* him… no. I'd do that alone." He glanced round, as if for witnesses. "I'm sorry. I've given you the wrong idea."

"I know what I'm doing," said Giulia. "I've hunted morts before – I've hunted people too. I've seen all kinds of things—"

"I can't," Sepello replied. "I'm sure you've done a lot, but I can't work with you. It's just not possible. Sorry."

"Not with a woman? I'd have thought that if Saint Cordelia—"

"Not with *anyone*. It's part of the contract. I'm sorry, but I have to work alone if I'm to collect on this. It's part of the deal."

"The Church says you can't have any help?"

"It's not the Church. My terms of appointment require me to work alone."

He's holding back, she thought. *He's not working for the Church at all. Someone else is giving him orders. Who?*

"I'm sorry about your friend, I really am." Sepello went on. "If you knew the things Leth's done— Well, I'm sorry. But rest assured that I'll find him, and he will be destroyed. You've my word on that."

"Thanks," Giulia said. *This is a waste of time.*

"I wish I could help more, but my hands are tied."

"All right. Fair enough." She swallowed. "I understand."

"If there's anything else I can do…" he said.

"There isn't." Giulia extended her hand. "But thanks for hearing me out, anyway."

Sepello looked down at her hand, a little surprised. He shook it. "Goodbye, Giulia. I'll make sure your friend rests easy."

Fury rushed up in her like bile. *How dare you? Who are you to tell me that? Hugh rests easy when I nail the bastard that murdered him! Me, and no-one else!*

And then she was calm again.

Sepello said, "Can I give you a piece of advice?"

"Of course," she replied.

He leaned forward and said, "Listen, Giulia, I realise you want to pay Leth back, but you should keep away from this. The undead are poison: morts, revenants, all of them. It doesn't matter how many men and women you've crossed swords with – they're something else. Keep away, and if they come looking for you, run."

"Thanks. I'll bear that in mind."

"I don't mean to be rude, but you should leave this to the experts," Sepello said. "Really, you should."

"I will. Goodbye, Sepello."

"Goodbye." He paused again, as if preparing to say something more, and turned away. She watched him walk across the square, back towards the safety of the chapel. Twenty yards away, he looked back, saw she was still there, and kept on going. He turned the corner and was gone.

*

The barn had been empty for many years. In the loft there was an open window, and on the window sat the small cruel skull of a hawk. It had been tied carefully to a wooden jig, and a string dangled from its beak. The string hung down the side of the barn and disappeared into the earth below.

A speck appeared in the sky, and at once the hawk's jaw started to flap open and closed like the tail of a beached fish, jiggling the string. At the end of the string, fifteen feet beneath the ground, a tiny bell began to sound.

There was a workbench under the bell. The man at the workbench put down his tools, stoppered the jars around him and wiped his thin hands on his apron. He lifted the jangling bell and laid it on a high shelf to slacken the string. Then he climbed the stairs.

The stone stairs led up to a cellar. Narrow wooden steps rose from the cellar to a trapdoor. Three of the wooden steps had been weakened, so that they would collapse under an intruder's weight. Leth knew them by heart, and stepped over the trap as he ascended. He had done the cutting himself.

Leth unbolted the trapdoor and climbed up into the shadows.

The barn was little more than a shell. The breeze ruffled the long grass around Leth's boots. He climbed up to the loft, across boards that he had replaced while the rest of the floor had been left to fall apart, and reached the windowsill.

The hawk's skull had stopped jiggling. A pigeon waited beside it. Leth reached out and gently lifted it down. It was a plump, hefty specimen, and he cradled it like an infant in his left arm while his right hand slipped the message from its leg.

Friend –
We stand ready in the city. Once you make your move, then we shall make ours.

Leth looked out the window. His long fingers transferred the message to his mouth. He chewed it slowly and carefully until the paper was nothing more than a pellet. There was no need to answer it: his allies would strike when he needed them to.

The pigeon stirred in Leth's arms. He had almost forgotten about it. He looked down, lifted the bird in his hands and bit off its head. He chewed thoughtfully, watching the sun pick out the wheat in the fields beyond. It was nearly harvest time. The headless pigeon shuddered against his palms.

It was strange how some animals still moved after death, as if fighting the inevitable. *Nobody wants to accept their end.* Still holding the bird, still chewing, he walked downstairs.

*

As Giulia walked into Smithswell, the houses became heavier-built and more austere, reinforced with stone instead of timber as if a weight had settled on them.

Unlike most of the cities on the peninsula, there was no clear point in Astrago where the pagan district began. The houses of fey folk and dissenters were grouped together, but the boundary faded into the surrounding neighbourhood. Purists and dwarrows lived near good Old Church folk, and if they did not actually like one another, they were at least content to let each other go quietly to Hell.

A door opened on the opposite side of the road and two dwarrows strode out, wearing rucksacks bulging with food and kit. In the old days, Giulia had often seen little groups of the fey making their way out of the city via the western gate: gossips said they were heading into the woods to perform black magic. She knew better now: they were going to pass into Faery, the otherworld where men could not freely go. The fey folk had no temple inside Astrago from which they could enter Faery. The Inquisition had demolished it during the war, to keep the fey inside the city walls. Strange, she thought as she passed the rows of blocky houses, how the inquisitors had gone to such effort to trap and kill the fey folk instead of just driving them all away.

Up ahead was a communal workshop owned by four dwarrow engineers. Giulia ducked out of the sun and into the sweaty dark of the workshop. Several dwarrows laboured silently at a long bench against the wall. Their broad backs were a wall to keep her out. A table stood on the far side of the room, and it was covered by about a dozen large, half-dismantled clocks. Tiny cogs lay on the tabletop like scattered coins.

"Hello?"

One of the workers turned, grunted, and climbed down from his stool. He was an inch shorter than Giulia and looked strong enough to tear her in two. He pushed a strand of pale hair out of his eyes.

"What do you want?"

"I was told you could help me. I need to pass a message on to someone. A dryad. His name is Sethis."

"I see. Wait here."

The clockworker turned and lumbered into the back of the workshop. A wide door swung open and Giulia glimpsed a long table and solid chairs, a meeting-room. Then a figure stood up and walked out, shutting the door behind him.

The dwarrow who emerged had weary eyes and skin the colour of pale slate. He looked at Giulia with thoughtful suspicion. "Good day." His accent was heavy. "Can I assist you?"

"Yes, you can. My name is Giulia Degarno. I'm known to Grodrin of the Forge, master-smith of Pagalia, and Arashina, a dryad noblewoman from Averrio. I need to pass a message to the dryad Sethis, who works in the Scola san Cornelio in Averrio. I can get you letters to confirm who I am if you'd like, but to be honest, I'm a little short of time."

The foreman's gaze did not change. "If you know them, why not tell them yourself?"

"I could do, but I thought you would be able to do it quicker." *And they probably think I'm dead by now. Having my existence confirmed by the dwarrows of Astrago would probably help.*

"What shall I tell this Sethis?"

"Tell him that I'm well, and I want to meet. Is the Silver Garden still here?"

"Yes, of course. What was your name again?"

"Giulia Degarno. I'll be there at midday for the next three days. Tell him to come and meet me there."

*

Pietro Sepello rolled onto his side, less than half-awake. He had been dreaming about something – pushing a cart, he thought – but if the dream had had any meaning, it had vanished as soon as he remembered it. He thought about Clara Boucard, three hundred miles north of here. A pleasing image drifted through his head: returning in triumph to the Chapter House of the Order of Saint Cordelia, as the destroyer of Constantin Leth. They'd make him a knight senior for that.

Sepello imagined Clara's parents nodding and smiling, then of Clara leading him from the room, smiling over her shoulder as she took him into the cool dark of her house, towards her bed—

Something creaked at the back of the room.

He was awake in a second, sitting upright with his pistol in his hand. He stared into the shadows, trying to locate the source of the noise. Nothing moved. Sepello looked at the window. The shutters were closed.

Nothing there. He was safe, and alone. Sepello eased down slowly, as if his muscles were sighing with relief, and leaned over and put the gun back out of sight.

He lay there on the bed, trying to think of nothing. He thought about the woman with the scars on her face, who'd said Leth had murdered her friend. Had she been genuine? It was entirely possible, but he had to be careful. She could easily be one of Leth's hirelings, or just some lunatic.

Destroying revenants was a loner's game. It was risky enough involving another hunter, even one you trusted, but to join forces with an outsider, one you could neither trust nor command…

Sepello closed his eyes, rolled onto his side and hoped that Giulia, whoever she was, would be a long way away by now.

∗

In the shadows at the far end of the room, Giulia waited for Sepello to fall asleep. She made herself count to fifty, then a hundred, then a hundred more, until Sepello's breathing became deeper and more mechanical, and his sheet rose and fell as if a clockwork bellows was pumping away under the cloth. Even then she did not step out of the dark.

On the floor by her boots was a little stack of notes and journals, removed from the revenant-hunter's bags. One was a sketchbook, crammed with odd little diagrams and what seemed to be recipes, the sort of things a village witch might know. Another couple were ledger-books, the names all written in code.

She opened the fourth of Sepello's little books. A wad of pages had been ripped out at the front, leaving ragged stubs in the binding. At the top of the sheet now facing her was the word "Astrago".

Her eyes flicked over the big, looping handwriting and her mouth drew back into a smile.

Giulia returned to the Gauntlet an hour later. Irmgard's son nodded to her as she came in, and watched her go upstairs.

She took off her boots and cloak, unfastened her knives and got into bed. She had expected the raid on Sepello's lodgings to make her feel successful, almost triumphant. But as soon as Giulia lay down to sleep the Melancholia was with her again.

It wasn't just that Hugh was dead. That was awful, but his death was an excuse for the Melancholia to come flooding in, and to let her undammed mind return to its natural state: a mixture of fury and despair. His murder was another indication – an especially cruel one – of the way the world worked, and the fact that as soon as you cared about anything, anything at all, God would notice and snatch it all away.

Grief, like nausea, exhausted her. She drew her legs up and folded her arms, and in that shape she eventually fell asleep.

Chapter 2

Giulia reached the Silver Garden half an hour before noon. Sethis was waiting for her.

The garden was little more than a courtyard between the dwarrow workshops, and there was only one tree big enough to provide any shade. Sethis sat on a bench beneath it. At the far end of the garden, the dwarrows had erected one of their smooth, organic sculptures. It looked like a stocky man under a sheet, raising one fist.

Sethis saw Giulia and stood up. He was a little taller than her, slim and wiry. He wore a white shirt, dark britches and spectacles. His huge brown eyes were quick and friendly.

Giulia stepped in and embraced him. He smelled, as usual, of freshly cut grass.

"It's good to see you, Giulia. You had me worried. Come and sit down."

She lowered herself onto the bench beside him. The sun soaked the garden in light, as if to deny the Melancholia of the last few days had ever happened. It seemed ridiculous in the daytime, that you could sit in bed feeling as if you were going mad with fury, fighting the urge to scream.

She leaned back. The Silver Garden was an odd little spot of calm, a sanctuary within a busy district of a bustling city.

"So, how are you?"

Giulia shrugged. "Not bad. And you?"

"Fine, thank you. I'm very sorry about Hugh," Sethis said. "He was a good man. He deserved better than that."

"Yes, he did. Thank you, Sethis."

"Look, if you need some time away from all this, a break from it, I'm sure it'll be fine. We can have someone else—"

"No. I'm still in. Hugh was a good friend. I can't let this go, Sethis, not now." She swallowed down the hard lump forming in her throat. "If you're willing to let me carry on with this, I'll find Leth for you." *And then kill him.*

Sethis said, "Good. We still want you. Arashina asked me to send her best wishes, by the way."

Giulia had found it hard to warm to Arashina, who was Sethis' senior colleague in all of this, and the original source of the operation to hunt down Leth. *She's on my side*, she reminded herself. *The right side.* "Tell her thanks. And send her my regards."

"I will. I got your letter a couple of months ago, and I, ah, wondered if you wanted to carry on…"

"Yes, sorry about that." She opened her hands. "I was in a bad way when I wrote that, to be honest. I shouldn't have sent it. I'm sorry if I worried you."

The dryad nodded. "I did worry, to be honest. There were some aspects of it that made me think you ought to have a break from all of this."

"The bit about having a shit in Leth's ashes, you mean?"

Sethis chuckled, and Giulia grinned awkwardly. He was much more human than the other dryads Giulia had met. He still had the features – the pointed chin, neat little mouth and huge eyes, almond-shaped and nearly twice the size of a human's – but he lacked the stern, immobile quality common to a lot of their faces. It was as though he had learned to lower his guard. He was not conventionally attractive, but when he laughed it was impossible not to warm to him.

The dryad pushed his spectacles back up his nose. "Yes, that did trouble me a little. But I understand why you felt that way." He stood up and brushed his long hands together. "Now, do you know what I think we should do?"

"No."

"We should find some food. I'm absolutely starving!"

They found a bakery and joined a group of people waiting outside the door. The smell of fresh bread made Giulia's stomach turn with anticipation, but she felt uncomfortable being here: she noticed heads turning to look at Sethis, saw people smirk and whisper into their friends' ears. If the dryad was aware of it, he did not show it. Giulia found her hands moving together, where her right hand could pull the stiletto from her left sleeve.

"So, have you still got the hired men?" Sethis asked.

"No." The chatter around them hid their voices. She tried to sound confident, as if she'd made the decision to get rid of Vitale and Alberto. "I didn't need them, and to be honest, they were more Hugh's people than mine. Besides, there was better work for them elsewhere. I move quicker without them."

"I'm sure you do."

A man in front of them looked back over his shoulder. His hair was dark, and there were pockmarks on his cheek. He stared slowly and carefully at Sethis, then at Giulia. He turned away.

The baker glanced at Giulia and managed not to look surprised. "Two," she said, pointing to the small loaves. She passed a couple of coins over. "Let's go," she called back to Sethis.

As she slipped through the queue the man with the pockmarks calmly said, "Pixie-loving whore."

Outside, Giulia exhaled and leaned against the wall. "God, it's hot. Listen, Sethis, why don't you find us somewhere good to sit, eh? We could go to the south gates and sit in the market square. I'll catch you up."

"Are you all right?"

"I'm fine. I just want to rest a little. I'll be there in a moment."

"Right," he said, and he walked away.

She waited. Maybe there was nothing to worry about.

The dark-haired man wandered out the door. He had that satisfied look she'd seen on a wide range of male bastards, of having put things right with a firm hand.

In one move she stepped in close, pulled the stiletto from her sleeve and pressed the blade against his cheek as if playing a trump card. The man froze. The tip of the knife lay just under his eye, at the bulge of the lower eyelid. He couldn't quite look at it, try as he might.

Giulia kept close, as though they were talking. She watched him try not to breathe.

"Watch your mouth," she said, and she drew back, slipping the knife away out of sight. She took another long step away from him, skirt swishing out behind her, turned and strode away. She slipped into an alleyway and ran. At the end of the alley, Giulia stopped and turned. The pockmarked man was nowhere to be seen.

What the hell did you do that for? That was stupid, making a show like that. There's never any need to make threats. Either stab him or don't, and not in the fucking street. What were you thinking?

Bloody fool.

Sethis was waiting further up the road. He watched her, his eyes hard and angry. "What did you do to that man, if you don't mind me asking?" he asked as she came near.

"Nothing. I told him to watch himself." She saw his expression and said, "God damn it, Sethis, I'm not taking that. Not from anyone."

Sethis peered down the road, then started walking. "I didn't hear him properly. What did he say?"

"Nothing much."

"Really."

"He said I was a whore. Your whore, to be exact."

Sethis looked around them, as though he expected an attack. "You've got to be careful," he said. "Working for us, especially. Mavlio might not mind having fey folk here, but there's plenty of others who do."

"Yes, and I'm not inclined to take their shit."

"It's about more than just you. Come on."

They walked on, Sethis looking wary and annoyed, Giulia quiet and angry beside him. The marketplace was one of the finest public spaces in Astrago: the architect and natural philosopher Cosimo Lannato had designed it, and it had been opened with much fanfare two years ago. They sat under a row of trees on the south side of the square. A bored watchman looked down at them as he walked by on patrol, then wandered on.

Sethis reached into his bag and took out a small flask and a pair of cups. He poured out wine for them both, and accepted a chunk of bread from Giulia.

"So," he said, "tell me about this news of yours."

Giulia leaned forward. "Right. Up to about two weeks ago we were hunting for Leth – me and the hired men, that is – following up all sorts of rumours, getting nowhere. Then we happened to be in this village called Mardino, and I got talking to a merchant who I thought would be able to help . He said there was a priest at Saint

Cordelia's church – here, in Astrago – looking for information on Leth. So I got the others paid off and went there yesterday afternoon." She took a sip of wine. "The man's called Sepello. Turns out he's not a priest at all, but he's from the Order of Saint Cordelia. You know them?"

The dryad nodded. "I've heard of them. Witch hunters. Some of them used to work for the Inquisition."

"Sepello said he wasn't a member then, and I believe him. He's too young. As far as I could tell, he's like a bounty hunter, except that his bounties are on the undead. I asked him about Leth, and he gave me a bit of information on revenants on the whole, but not much I didn't already know. Then I asked about working together. I thought we could join forces: he'd have the information from the Church, and I'd have your people backing me up."

"Hold on." Sethis took his glasses off and blew onto the lenses. "I doubt Arashina would allow that. I'm not sure I could either. Working with a man whose organisation used to be linked to the Inquis Impugnans… that would be a problem for us."

"It doesn't really matter. Sepello didn't want any help at all. Perhaps he thought I'd want half of the bounty money. In fact, he wouldn't even say who was helping him to go after Leth."

Sethis slipped his spectacles back on. "Your Church, I suppose."

"I'm not so sure. I got the feeling that there was more to it than just that. Anyhow, trying to talk to him was a dead loss, so I said goodbye and headed home. Then I went through his books later on."

The dryad looked shocked. "You robbed him?"

"No, no. Just burglary. Robbery involves violence. Not my sort of thing. Actually," she added, "I didn't really burgle him anyhow. I burgled this priest he was staying with."

"You burgled a *priest?*"

"So? You're a pagan. I'd have thought you'd be glad."

Sethis gave her a hard stare. She stared back. Slowly, the corner of Sethis' mouth twitched up into a smile. He shook his head sadly. "By the Lord and Lady of the forest, Giulia, what am I supposed to do with you?"

She grinned. "You tell me."

He ran a hand through his thick hair and sighed and said, "All right then, what did you find?"

"Sepello had some books with him, handwritten things. A lot of it was in code. I didn't find out who Sepello's working for. But what I did find was this: Sepello is waiting for a ship called the *Comaru* coming in from Dalagar. It's something to do with Leth. Maybe he's on it, or it's carrying something he needs. I don't know. But I'm going to find out when it's due, and when it arrives… I'll be there to see what's on board."

"*Comaru*," Sethis repeated. "I wonder what that means? Actually, it's strange that it should dock here at all. Dalagar's a province of Averrio. It sounds like it's unloading in the wrong city-state."

"Leth was linked to the smuggling ring back in Averrio. It's not safe for him there anymore. Maybe that's why his ship is coming here."

For a few seconds Sethis said nothing. He bit off a piece of bread and chewed it carefully, then finished his wine. "Well," he said, "I suppose you ought to look at the docks. But please be careful. Just have a look around and tell me what you find: don't put yourself in danger."

"I won't." Giulia finished her wine. "I'll let you know about this ship, then." She stood up, and Sethis followed. Up ahead, the patrolling guard was walking back towards them. He looked like boredom personified.

"Take care of yourself," Sethis said.

Giulia had always thought of him as being about her own age. He reminded her of a young scholar, or an artist not quite noted enough to have his own patron yet. It suddenly occurred to her that he might be much older. After all, the fey folk lived longer and aged differently. "You too."

"If there's anything you need, let me know."

Why doesn't he go? Giulia wondered. The guard wandered past and, as Sethis stepped towards her, she realised why: *He doesn't want the guard to see us embrace.* People said things about the dryads, that they liked to steal children and corrupt young maids. Giulia had never seen any evidence, but she didn't think of herself as a young maid, either.

The guard walked on. Sethis embraced Giulia and kissed her cheek. Then he stepped back.

He strolled down the slope and back into the streets, polishing his glasses on his sleeve as he walked. Right now, he was about the only person she trusted.

*

"Ship from Dalagar, you say? The *Comaru*?" The harbourmaster shook his head. Giulia sat in his office, at the top of three narrow flights of wooden steps. It was full of mismatched furniture. The harbourmaster stood at the window, his beard and belly jutting out before him, looking down at the men working below. A clockwork crane rattled as it swung a pallet of sacks onto the land. It made Giulia think of a siege engine.

"Yes," Giulia said, "the *Comaru*." She had put on an accent, somewhere between her own and Hugh's, and hopefully sufficiently exotic to make herself seem worth listening to. She glanced at the guild crest on the far wall, then to the pile of record-books under it. They would probably be boring reading, she thought. The only interesting thing about the dock records would be what the stevedores decided to leave out.

"No ship of that name here," said the man. "But there's a group of ships due to come out of Dalagar soon. They travel from Dalagar in a group, so it's harder for pirates to attack them. Every month or so, we get a bunch of five or six turning up at once – carracks, for the most part. Your ship might be one of the group."

"Could pirates have captured all of them?"

"There's always a chance." The harbourmaster shrugged. "But it's very unlikely."

Giulia ran a hand through her hair. She'd met people like him before: affable, business-like, and of no help at all. The harbourmaster leaned out the window to wave to someone, and she thought, *He knows as much as I do. What next?*

"Has the *Comaru* ever unloaded any cargo here before?" she asked.

"Maybe." He glanced at the window, as if the answer was on a sign outside. "But I don't remember it."

"Could I look at the records, perhaps?"

"No. That's private."

A second passed.

"Of course," Giulia replied. "Thank you for your help. Could you show me the way out, please?"

He led her down the narrow stairs and out into the sunshine. Men worked around them, loading and unloading, piling sacks and boxes on the great curve of the harbour. The cranes rattled and creaked as they moved. Wagons struggled up from the waterside, pulled by oxen bred for size. The harbourmaster squinted at the sky and hooked his thumbs into his belt. Giulia had a feeling that standing there was his idea of hard work.

There was one angle of approach left. "Thank you for your help," she said. Before he could reply, she added, "Just one thing: did you work here when Boar Carbini was running the dock?"

Stiffly, he said, "I've never heard of him."

"Really? Everyone's heard of him on the waterside, criminal or not." She turned to him, as if they had only just met. "Look, I'll be honest with you. I'm looking to bring some cargo in without the guards seeing what I've got – nothing nasty, just stuff I'd like to bring in quietly. You know somewhere I could unload spice easily?"

"I ought to bloody slap you," he replied. The affability was gone. He just looked fat and hard. "I knew it was a bad idea to let a woman up here, asking questions. Round here, we don't like smugglers, and we don't like people who don't pay their way. If you come round here talking like that, you'll end up wishing you hadn't. Understand?"

"Yes I do," she said. She tried to sound chastened.

"My men work hard on these docks," he said. "And when someone insults our good name, we don't take it kindly. You follow me?"

"I'll be going, then," Giulia said. "Thanks again."

"You do that, and don't come back. We don't need women down here, poking around. There are worse men than me on this dock, and they won't be as kind as I am. Remember that."

She nodded, turned and started walking back up the hill. She could feel his eyes on her: her hands wanted to clench into fists. A thin, tanned man watched her go past, looked at her face and then her body, and shook his head. She kept on walking, the prospect of violence winding up in her like a spring. Nobody grabbed her, nobody tried to drag her out of sight.

At the edge of the dock, she glanced back. The harbourmaster was talking to a younger man. They leaned in close to each other, like conspirators.

*

Tarrus saw the dust move long before he heard the sound of boots. Motes stirred on the tiled floor of his bedroom, and the little mosaic fish suddenly seemed to lie beneath a grey, rippling stream. Tarrus looked down, saw dust on his fingers, and wondered how long he had been lying here. He stood up in a soft avalanche.

A deep groan came from down below, like something wrenched out of the earth, and then the sound of a fist beating slowly on his front door. A myrmex. He gathered his robes around him and walked downstairs.

In the atrium, a statue stood facing the doors: life size, showing Tarrus himself raising a hand in greeting, benevolent but stern. Age had roughened the stone, sent cracks through it like poisoned veins, chipped and blurred the features. Sometimes Tarrus wondered whether visitors would tell him apart if he stood motionless beside the statue. But visitors were rare these days.

Another thump on his front door. Tarrus slipped a shortsword into the folds of his robe and reached out to the bolts.

It was as he had expected. A myrmex stood just outside, hulking under its armour and massive helmet.

Tarrus hesitated. He opened his mouth, licked his lips and remembered how to speak.

"Looking for me?"

The brute growled.

"Senate meeting, is it?"

The figure did not respond. Behind the perforated faceplate, Tarrus glimpsed flesh as grey as his own. The myrmex groaned and turned as clumsily as a wagon. It stomped back down the steps.

Tarrus locked his house and followed. There was nothing much to steal in his home – nothing that the noxi and their kind might want – but it was habit. He still liked the place, and he knew the sort of damage that the raiding parties liked to inflict: the furniture broken, slogans scrawled on the walls, heads knocked off statues and busts shattered on the floor.

The myrmex lumbered down the path, past the skeletons of trees and the spindly legs of a long-smashed marble faun, and they stepped onto the road. Tarrus knew the way, and he walked in front, the myrmex looming behind him like a metal ape.

Sometimes, he could almost believe that Oppidium was its old self. The cavern roof could be the night sky, the twinkling impurities in the rocks above him could be stars, the little fires that burned in the centre of the town could be the work of living men.

A long, gabbling howl rose out of the rubble behind them. It could have been a cry of despair or a gleeful laugh. The myrmex stopped, looked over its shoulder as best as its helmet would allow, and growled. Tarrus touched it on the arm. "Come on. It's nothing." The guardian grunted, shrugged in a clatter of armour, and started to walk again.

The great chamber of the Council stood behind rows of stone columns as if it had been trapped in a gigantic cage. Chance, or perhaps magic, had saved the building from the earthquake and the civil war that had followed it. Save for a few chips and cracks, the masonry was entirely intact. The myrmex stopped at the bottom of the steps. Tarrus walked up the stairs, between the columns, and he was alone.

Tarrus passed murals of gods he had forgotten about, irrelevant scenes of war and triumph, and entered the Chamber of Debate. The rows of stone seats were empty. Once, this chamber had housed two hundred delegates; now two people waited for him.

Stulcus stood near the door, all seven feet of him. He had been a massive man in life; now he was a grey-skinned hulk, a caricature of the sculptors' ideal physique. Beside him was Crespis, the half-skeletal priestess who had advised them before the earthquake. Her face had that patched-up tautness common to the older undead – at least, to those created by Constantius Leccius Varso.

"Where is he?" Tarrus demanded.

Crespis looked as if she might fall apart if she moved too quickly. "You took your time. Where've you been?"

"He's been busy dusting off his honour," said Stulcus. "Haven't you?"

A figure appeared in the doorway at the far end of the chamber. Robes brushed the ground as Leth entered the room.

He was tall, dignified, and inhuman. His cheekbones and forehead were completely smooth, like a plaster mask. He was so pale that it was hard to tell where his clothing ended and his skin began.

The sight of him made something inside Tarrus crumple and die. Crespis and Stulcus were the same as he was – less, in fact – but Leth was much greater than any of them. He had perfected his techniques on himself.

"I have good news," Leth announced. "Our friends in Astrago are ready. We're all set."

Stulcus nodded, apparently satisfied.

Crespis seemed to relax. "Good news indeed."

"Stulcus, get your fighters ready. Crespis, I want auguries for the next two months. Come with me, Tarrus. I'd like to speak to you alone."

Tarrus felt both worried and strangely gratified that Leth would want to talk to him on his own. He wondered if he could defeat Leth in a fight. Almost certainly not. Would his sword even cut the alchemist's flesh?

They left the main hall and passed through the rear doors, into the town. The Great Chamber stood on a slight rise, and Tarrus could see almost the whole of Oppidium. At the edges, the broken homes were just jagged chunks of shadow, but the centre glowed with fire. He wondered if it was night-time in the world above, and what it would be like to see daylight again.

"The forges are busy, then," Tarrus said.

"We're almost done," Leth replied. "It's good to see Oppidium coming to life again. Do you remember how it was after we changed? All the fighting, the squabbling for whatever animus we could drain out of one another."

You did that, Tarrus thought. *Your alchemy turned us into that.*

"It was men like you who brought the place back together," Leth said. "It took force of will."

A plume of flame shot into the air in the centre of the city, as if a dragon had blown fire into the sky. It triggered something in Tarrus, made him angry and rebellious. "Something had to be done. Something had to be salvaged of the city, after you wrecked it with your sorcery."

"That's as may be," Leth said. "What matters is what happens *now*. Tell me, Tarrus: are you going to take advantage of the opportunities that our situation presents? To use undeath as best as it can be used?"

"What do you mean?"

"I'll show you."

Leth turned away, his robe brushing the grey dust, and walked back into the hall. Tarrus followed him into a side room. It had that empty look of most rooms in the city: anything not made of stone had been either looted or allowed to decay. There was a table in the centre, and a map had been spread across it, held down at the edges with lumps of rock.

Looking at the map made Tarrus feel like his old self. He stood over it, recognising the coastline, the arrangement of the rivers and towns. It made him feel strong, as if he was one of the gods gazing at the world below.

"They call it Astrago, these days," Leth said. "The City-State of Astrago and its territories."

"I recognise the land."

"Even locked away in that villa of yours, you can't have missed the work I've been doing. Gathering our strength, our numbers. The centre of Oppidium is quite a hive of activity these days – perhaps not in quite the way that our founders envisaged, but still..."

Tarrus remembered the lair that Leth had made inside the grand bath-house, how centuries ago the noxi had pulled him out of hiding and dragged him there, screaming and fighting. His last day of true life, before Leth had administered his medicine.

"How long has it been since you went overground?"

Tarrus said, "A long time, Leth. At least a hundred years. It was… a lot had changed since our day." He did not want to admit it, but the world above had been even more dangerous than the one below.

"But you know a little of their ways. And you speak their language."

Tarrus shrugged. "So do you."

"We've spent too long cowering," Leth said. "We Quaestans used to be a conquering people, a race of rulers. We brought civilisation to the barbarians, back in the day: we defeated them, educated them, enslaved them. We should be doing that now, not skulking underground like worms."

"Why me? Why do you want me for this?"

"Because you had backbone, Tarrus. You opposed me in the forum, back in the old days. You called me out in the market-square. You were the last to accept the gift of undeath. You were a soldier with the Legion, after all. You fought the dryads and savages in the Teutberg Forest."

"That was a thousand years ago."

"It doesn't matter. The martial virtues don't die in a man unless he lets them. The noxi are mad; the myrmex and the legionaries are little more than automata. But you kept your mind. You and I have the strength of will to go on forever. The same minds, the same will that brought civilisation to the provinces all those years ago, can do it again. I have all the manpower I need, Tarrus. But I need an expert commander."

Tarrus paused. Leth was right, and the fact that he was a monster didn't make it any less so. A man ought to be strong and clever, and ought to fight for the betterment of the Republic and the Empire. And if Leth had a plan to drag Oppidium out of this gods-forsaken hole, to give it a chance of becoming great again, it had to be worth hearing.

"For the glory of the Republic," Leth explained.

Tarrus looked down at the map. He recognised the location of some of the towns, but not their names. The upper-earth people, the living people, had given them new names in honour of their one weak god and its feeble, doe-eyed saints.

"Supposing we do attack them," Tarrus said. "Where are we going to strike?"

Leth smiled. "Everywhere."

*

Giulia stood in her room, readying herself. Sepello would need a warrant of entry and permission from the city guard before he could search the docks. He could be waiting a week for that. Giulia needed nothing but her tools.

Her room was on the first floor, directly above the main fireplace. It was comfortable enough but, more importantly, she could climb into and out of the window. It was best not to walk through a busy inn wielding a loaded crossbow, after all.

Voices and music filtered up from below. Irmgard had hired a singer for the night, and he was performing gentle, skilful songs rather than the shouty ballads the less reputable inns preferred. All the more reason to get out. Love songs made her gloomy, even the ones with happy endings. Their tenderness was painful, like probing a wound. She slipped her lockpicks into the leather bracer on her right forearm.

Time to get moving. You want Leth dead, you go and do the work.

She opened the window and felt the warm night air, and smelled the smoke from thousands of houses. Giulia put her hands together and lowered her head. It seemed right somehow to pray into the night.

Saint Senobina, patron of thieves, watch over me. Keep me safe and hide me from my enemies. You looked after me when I took revenge for my own face — well, this is for someone else, a proper noble cause, like in books. Help me find justice for my friend.

She opened her eyes, then closed them again.

Saint Cordelia, fighter of the undead, help me find this murdering bastard. Protect me as if I was in your Order. Keep me safe from revenants. Amen.

Giulia slung her bag across her back. She draped her cloak over her crossbow and tucked the bundle under her arm. Then she locked her door and headed downstairs.

Nobody seemed to notice her entering the ground floor of the tavern, and she was certain that nobody cared. Giulia picked her way through the shadows and smoke, the singing and loud conversation. She reached the door and slipped out into the quiet, fresh night air. She strode off in the direction of the port.

She passed a bakery, still open to serve the little group of people who lingered around the door, then a tavern at the far end of the road. Lights glowed red inside, and smoke hung in the air. A serving-girl stepped outside, took a few deep breaths and turned back to the crowd indoors.

As Giulia rounded the corner, a drunk staggered out of nowhere and she had to sidestep to avoid bumping into him. He stumbled away, muttering apologies. Further on, three lads were lowering a sign down from a cooper's shop — whether to repair it or steal it, she couldn't tell.

The docks were near now. She had never spent much time there, back in the day. A person with her skills could make more money in the centre of town.

No need for killing. Just break in and find out what's going on – unless Leth's there.

Up ahead, a pair of gates separated the docks from the rest of the city. Two bored guards stood at one side, talking quietly. Giulia braced herself.

As she approached, one of them looked up at her, nodded, and got back to the conversation. Giulia walked straight through.

Well, that's a first. Now then, to business.

First of all, she needed to visit the harbourmaster's office. He had claimed ignorance when she'd mentioned Boar Carbini, which was suspicious in itself. Whether you loved the man or hated him, if you worked on the docks of Astrago, you'd have remembered his name.

She remembered the way he'd faltered when she asked about the *Comaru*. It sounded as if it had been here before and, if any of the cargo had been unloaded legitimately, there would be records. Giulia looked across the docks, squinting against the dark.

The harbourmaster's office was a three-storey tower of worn red brick. It loomed over the dock as if to challenge ships as they came in.

Giulia slipped through the administrative buildings without difficulty, towards the rotten smell of the sea.

Boots crunched on cobbles to the right. She stepped into the dark and drew herself up against the wall. A golden stripe of light swung across the ground. Giulia moved back very slowly, one foot at a time as if the ground might give way, until the door to one of the clerking buildings was at her side. She pressed herself behind one of the pillars that flanked the door. She held her breath. The lantern-beam swung across the pillars and beyond. The guard wandered on, sighing and idly swinging his stick.

Giulia exhaled. Her heart had risen in her chest, beating high and fast. She counted to a hundred as the watchman's boots faded away, then slipped out of hiding and continued.

Above the double doors to the harbourmaster's offices, dolphins and mermaids gambolled on a marble frieze. A wild, bearded man stood on a chariot pulled by sea monsters, brandishing a trident. He looked like a drunken prophet. A lamp burned in the left-hand window above one of the mermaids' heads. Giulia could hear water lapping at the dock.

Never go in through the front door. She walked down the side of the building, keeping in shadow. There was a rear entrance, smaller and darker, and she crouched down and slipped the lockpicks from her bracer.

It took ten minutes before the tumblers clicked open. Giulia paused, listening. From inland came a loose cheer, followed by laughs and shouts. They sounded happy and far away. She opened the door.

It led straight onto a narrow flight of stairs, lit by thin moonlight. She climbed them two at a time, keeping close to the wall where they were less likely to creak.

The stairs stopped at a small landing. Light seeped out of the room to her right, and with it, faint snoring. Giulia crept across the landing, crouched down and peeked around the door. An elderly man sat at a battered, empty desk, his legs crossed before him. His head hung back as if about to drop off, and as she watched he let out a long, satisfied snore.

Giulia smiled, feeling a sort of affection for a watchman so incompetent, and climbed to the harbourmaster's office. She slipped inside and closed the door behind her.

The room had looked so normal when she had been sitting here this morning: the moonlight made it mysterious. There was just about enough light to work by. Giulia checked the desk. It contained an old, unloaded pistol, a knife with a bone handle, a pay-book and a few copper coins, which she decided not to take. No need to get the old fellow downstairs into trouble, especially when he'd been decent enough to sleep through her arrival.

A massive cabinet stood against the wall. That looked promising. People had a tendency to keep their dirty secrets close.

The lock was primitive but large, the tumblers so heavy that she wondered if the effort of moving them would twist her picks out of shape. She crouched down and got to work.

It wasn't easy, and soon the muscles in her legs ached. After ten more minutes, the lock clicked open. Giulia looked inside and smiled. Piles of thin books lay on a shelf.

She lifted them out, stirring up a small cloud of dust. She checked the dates on each book. Each volume covered a season. She started with spring.

Giulia leaned against the wall beside the window, flicking through the pages in the moonlight, occasionally pausing to listen to the street below. No-one approached the building, and nobody moved downstairs.

She ran her finger down the page, past the names of the ships: *Marie-Annique*, *Fortuna*, *Sant'Luciana del Prasca*, *Trade Wind*, *The Pride of Callarne*. And there, at the bottom: *Comaru*.

It docked two and a half months ago, with a cargo of spice. Just as you would, coming from Dalagar. She looked back through the book. The *Comaru* had unloaded five cargoes over the last year, at eight-week intervals. It ought to have delivered another cargo a week ago.

I wonder what happened to it?

She ran her finger across the page. In the past, import duties had been paid, the *Comaru* had berthed on the Western Wharf, and the goods had been unloaded into the warehouse of Giovanni Felasco. Giulia looked up from the book. The warehouses lay in rows on the slope leading up from the waterfront, like a set of gigantic kennels. There were at least twenty of them.

The books didn't say which warehouse belonged to Felasco. She grimaced. This could be a long night. Giulia replaced the books, locked the cabinet and headed downstairs.

On the landing, an idea struck her. Keeping low, walking slowly and carefully, she crept back to the room where the watchman continued to snore. Maybe he would have a map of the docks. She stood in the doorway, looking around the room. There was nothing. Giulia mouthed "Shit", and sneaked back down the stairs. She locked the rear door behind her and frowned into the night. Sometimes thievery was just hard work.

Without a lantern to check the signs, she had to get close to each warehouse to see the name painted above the doors. By the ninth warehouse her legs ached, and the warm summer air was beginning to feel oppressively close. Worse than that, the dockside inns were closing, and soon the sailors would be wandering home to their ships.

The fifteenth building was Felasco's.

The warehouse doors would have shamed a castle, and the padlock holding them closed was as big as a fist. Giulia grimaced. Then the light caught on the wood, and she saw that there was a smaller door set into it.

The small door had its own lock. It was recessed into the wood, much smaller than the padlock. She got to work.

Five minutes in, voices rose up to the left. Giulia stood, slid her pick out of the mechanism and pulled her hood up. A voice came out of the dark, coarse and proud and male.

"I told him so, I said it's the best fucking ship there is, mate, the best he'll ever fucking see! You or anyone else, too!"

Giulia walked away from the doors.

A woman's voice now, hard-edged with drink. "Let's stop here, eh? Just for a minute."

"No, we're going to the boats. I'll show you the boats – beautiful, they are. Come on."

"But—"

"I said we're going to the boats."

Giulia slipped into the alley beside the warehouse and waited for them to pass. They strode by, surprisingly quick for drunks, and Giulia saw that the woman was younger than she'd thought, perhaps no more than sixteen. She wondered if the man was paying for her company.

As soon as they had gone, she returned to the lock. With a little effort, the tumblers turned and the bolt drew back.

Giulia stepped to one side and pulled her crossbow into her hands. She worked the ratchet and laid a bolt into the groove.

She pushed the door with her boot and it swung open silently. The air smelled of dust and rats and, very faintly, spice. Giulia stepped inside, leaving the door ajar to let the moonlight in.

She spotted a lantern hanging from a metal ring. She took her little roll of thieves' tinder out of her satchel, broke a piece off and spat across the tip. As the stuff flared into life, she pushed it into the lantern and waited for the wick to catch.

She closed the door and lifted the lantern down.

The walls were brick. Vaults supported the ceiling as though she was in a vast cellar. Boxes, chests and full sacks stood against the walls. The centre of the room was clear. Against the back wall, a set of wooden stairs rose to the floor above.

Leth won't be here, surely, but there might be something to help me. What am I looking for – gold, potions, ingredients for alchemy? Maybe bits of dead bodies. The thought made her hands tighten on the bow. She began to climb the stairs.

The upstairs was empty and dark. A table and chair stood on the far side of the room. A couple of barrels lay in the corner opposite the stairs.

Nothing strange.

The lantern-light showed a mess of bootprints in the dust around the stairs. Someone besides Giulia had been here recently. That was something: at least the trail wasn't quite cold. She carried the lamp downstairs, wondering where to begin.

Giulia laid the crossbow on one of the boxes and began to examine the largest heap of goods. The smell of spice hit her. Tangy and strange, it made her both hungry and eager to sneeze. The Anglians loved all sorts of spice: Hugh had liked stew spiced to the point where it stung Giulia's mouth.

This was hopeless. She'd never find anything here, not in all these boxes, with only a shitty lamp to help her. Besides, what if the *Comaru* had been legitimate? What if all the illicit goods had already been smuggled off-site?

Sepello thinks the ship belongs to Leth. He said so in his notes.

Giulia straightened up and scowled into the dark. Perhaps she'd missed something upstairs. She crossed the room, suddenly angry. At the bottom of the staircase, she paused.

There were things under the stairs, lumps of something. She reached in and picked one out: it was half a brick. *Half a fucking useless brick.* She tossed it back.

A row of bricks stuck a couple of inches out of the ground. Bits of brick protruded from the ground like broken teeth. She stared at the bricks, unsure why they had caught her attention.

There used to be a wall in front of the stairs.

Something stirred in her mind. She thought about the big houses she'd entered, and then wondered what the other warehouses looked like inside. *You wall the stairs off. You have stairs going up, and under them—*

Giulia touched the floor under the staircase, and felt wood covered by a thin layer of dirt.

Stairs going down.

The breath tightened in her chest. She put the lantern down and scrabbled at the floor. Yes – there! There it was, a square of planks. Her hands traced its outline, and they found a tiny loop of rope. She readied her crossbow. Giulia positioned herself close to the wall, out of the way of anything that might shoot up from below. She licked her lips, bent down and tugged on the rope with her left hand. Smoothly, in a shower of dirt, the trapdoor opened before her.

Nothing burst out. Giulia waited, listening. Nothing moved. She raised the lantern in her left hand, holding it as far from her body as she could, and aimed the bow down the stairs in her right. As she descended, light spread across the room below.

It was a cellar made of ancient, crumbling brick. A table stood in the centre of the empty vault, and on it was an unlit candlestick and a fancy wooden box like the coffin of a wealthy child. Giulia could hear herself breathe.

She crouched down and put the lantern on the ground. She crept down the length of the cellar, bow raised in front of her.

She reached the corner of the room and saw that there was a gap in the wall. A passage stretched away. The passage smelled of raw earth.

Giulia approached the table. Carefully, she picked up the candlestick and lit it off the lantern.

The box might be trapped. She walked around the back of the table and lifted the lid of the box from behind. She counted to twenty, and then she walked to the front.

The inside was padded with wool. Nestled among the wool were half a dozen things like bone spear-tips, each a foot long and slightly curved. *Horns?* She lifted one out. The object was smooth in her hand, flattened and subtly grooved as if eroded by water. It curled back on itself, like the blade of a scimitar, and the curved side was razor sharp.

God almighty, it's something's tooth.

Giulia put it back into the box and closed the lid. A hidden cellar and a box full of colossal teeth. What in God's name did it mean?

She looked at the passage in the opposite wall. If there was an answer, it was down there.

Saint Senobina, watch over me.

She readied the crossbow, took a deep breath and stepped into the passage.

The walls were rough earth, shored up in places with wooden planks. The corridor sloped downwards and twisted out of sight. The air was stale and wet, like the air of a marsh.

Giulia descended. The damp air surrounded her like a cloud. The ground crunched softly under her boots. She followed the corridor round and down, as if corkscrewing into the ground. Light seeped down the passage. She had gone about thirty yards before she heard a voice.

She froze.

The voice snapped out of the dark: angry and educated, urgent and clipped. "Utter rubbish," it barked. "Lies! I found them that way! Not my fault if they're too bloody ignorant to know…" It dropped into muttering, too low to make out properly.

Footsteps followed it. They thumped the earth, drawing closer, and Giulia raised the bow to eye-level, her hands and stomach tensing. The man seemed to turn away, and stomped off to the side. "Question my judgement, would you? It's a matter of humeric alignment, you imbecile."

I could nail him, whoever he is. And yet—

It wasn't Leth. It couldn't be. Leth wouldn't sound so petty, or so close to rage. But it sounded too educated for a criminal. Perhaps it was a merchant smuggler, or some corrupt nobleman in the revenant's pay. She listened to the bootsteps fade, and followed them deeper underground.

Giulia emerged in the entrance to a low cellar, smaller than the one before. Workbenches lined the walls, and on them sat masses of candles melted together into heaps of wax. At the far end of the room was a fireplace, half-hidden by a pillar, and from the pillar there stretched the shadow of a man looking at his hands.

Giulia took a step into the room. She kept her eyes on the shadow, but she could see things on the workbenches: mortars, pestles, rows of jars. Glass condensers, flasks, paper packets and little heaps of luminescent dust. She'd bought enough tinctures against Melancholia to know what this was. She was in an alchemist's laboratory.

"Back to work now. I'm *achieving* things here. I'm my own master now. I'm my own master now."

A wicker box with a cage door sat on the next bench down. It contained a live cat. A neat pile of dead rats lay on the far end of the bench, stretched out and piled up like logs.

As she crept closer, she saw a door set into the wall. It had metal bars at eye-height, like the bars of a cell. She saw darkness behind it.

Giulia sidestepped and saw the back of the alchemist. He wore a long maroon robe. She lined up the crossbow bolt with the back of his bald head. He bent down to tend to the fire, and Giulia tilted the crossbow down, keeping the tip of the bolt lined up with his skull.

She made her voice loud and hard. "Stand up slowly and turn around. Keep your hands out."

As smooth as clockwork, the alchemist stood up and turned to face her. He wore a cloth mask across his mouth and nose. The firelight made his face look waxy, unnaturally smooth. He took a step towards her.

"Keep back," she said.

He raised his left hand. "It's all right. Everything's fine. Don't shoot. I'm an apothecary."

Giulia's voice sounded far more confident than she felt. "Don't move."

The alchemist's raised palm began to shake. "Easy, now. Easy." His mask puffed in and out as he spoke. "Easy there, girl."

"Don't come any closer," Giulia said, but he was already taking another step.

"It's all right," the alchemist said. "I know what I'm doing. I know, I *know*." He took another step towards her, his palm still raised. Giulia took a step back, covering him with the bow. "It's all right. You see my hand, yes? They say my hands shake, but I know much better than that. I know!"

He's mad. "Shut up. Stay where you are."

He paused, and when he spoke his voice was much softer than before, as if he was comforting a child. "But look at your poor face. Look at what they've done to it. All those scars. All lopsided. You should talk to your apothecary, have him expelled from the guild. They'll expel a man for anything, you know."

"I didn't come here for you," Giulia said. "I'm looking for Constantin Leth."

The raised palm became a wagging finger. "I could help you, you know." The mask pulsed in and out of his face like a gill. "Your face is all uneven. It's unbalanced."

"Shut up about my face. Where's Leth?"

He took another step forward, the finger wiggling in reproach.

"Let's even it up!"

His right hand slashed out and she darted aside, heard the knife in his fist cut the air where her cheek had been. "You see my hands shaking now, you bitch?" he snarled behind his mask, and suddenly she caught the dead, meaty stink of him.

Giulia glanced at the door, and the apothecary sprang. She sidestepped and he leaped past her as if hurled from a catapult, landed on the edge of the bench behind her on all fours.

He crouched froglike in his dirty surgeon's robe. In the candlelight his high forehead looked like marble. He hissed behind his mask and the sound filled the room.

"Let's tidy up that face of yours!"

He's not a man. And then, as he opened his mouth behind the mask and growled, she thought, *Your kind murdered Hugh.*

He pounced. Giulia dropped low, the bow kicked in her hands and the madman slammed into her, knocked her stumbling towards the wall. *Don't fall, don't fall,* she thought and she twisted aside and scrambled to her feet, drawing her long knife ready to fight.

Her opponent lay flat upon the floor. The bolt had caught him just below the cheekbone and punched up through his skull. It was a brain-wound, a guaranteed kill. But she reloaded the crossbow as fast as she could.

The alchemist did not move. Giulia prodded the body with her boot, and felt the same nasty mixture of weight and give that there would be from any corpse.

She backed away, not turning from the body until she was at the passage. Then she hurried off, back the way she'd come.

*

Sepello stood up from the body and wiped his knife on a scrap of cloth. He stepped back to join Giulia and the captain of the Citizen Guard on the far side of the room.

"Is he dead?" the captain asked. He was an earnest young man, probably a part-timer from a prosperous family. He looked queasy. "Really, properly dead?"

Sepello nodded. "Yes. He's not going anywhere. You can take him out. But be careful: there'll be things in the blood, poisons, that you don't want to touch. Make sure your men are wearing gloves – thick ones, like pikemen use."

"Right," the captain replied. "I'll make sure they do that."

"And burn the body."

"Yes, sir." The guardsman paced away, past the benches and towards the warehouse exit.

Giulia wanted to get out too. She crossed the room and looked down at the corpse, small-looking in its dark red robe. "That's not Leth," she said. "If you're wondering."

Sepello sniffed. "I know. One of his people. A revenant, but not Leth."

"You were right about them being crazy," Giulia said. "This fellow was spouting all kinds of rubbish before he went for me. Something about people thinking he was a bad doctor. It must have been when he was alive."

"It happens," Sepello replied. "They brood over things. Even the smarter ones have their obsessions. It's often how we catch them out." He looked straight at her. "What you did was very dangerous."

"I thought you'd thank me."

"Oh, I'm grateful. Pretty impressed, too. But hunting the undead is a good way to get killed. It's not for amateurs."

There was a ladder by the fireplace, in the shadows. It led up into a small, run-down townhouse. The house looked disused, but it had the advantage of being inside the city. An ideal way for a smuggler to get past the gates.

Giulia leaned against the wall and folded her arms. "Have you ever heard of someone called Giovanni Felasco?"

"Never," Sepello said. "I'll check with the authorities tomorrow morning, but he sounds like a front man for Leth. It's probably a false name. You know, it must have taken a hell of a lot of work, digging that tunnel between here and the warehouse."

Giulia said, "Maybe it was there to begin with. It looks like a smuggler's hideout to me. It was probably left behind when Prince Mavlio cleared out Diello Sciata's people."

"It can't have been easy to set all of this up, especially all the alchemical gear." Sepello looked around slowly. "How did you figure out where to find it?"

"That's a trade secret," Giulia replied. "Although probably much the same way you would have done." She stood up and walked to the table. She reached out and lifted one of the teeth from the box. It was as heavy as a dagger, as cold as stone. "What are these things, anyway?"

"I'm not sure. But I think they're dragons' teeth."

She turned to him. "You're joking. There's no such thing as dragons."

"Not here, no. At least, not that I know of. But in the East they have them. At least, that's what I've heard. They say the emperor of Sinia is a dragon. He lives in a secret city that no man is allowed to enter."

It sounded like nonsense, but Giulia still shuddered. "And these are… their teeth?"

"The teeth of a small one. I've never seen them before, but I've heard stories. The Sineans damn near worship the things. It's forbidden to take them out of the country."

"Why would you want them?"

Sepello looked extremely serious, as if he was breaking the news of a death. "Like I say, I've never seen anything like this before. But there are legends that dragons' teeth act as an – what's the word – an accelerant in necromancy. It makes the spells stronger. The Quaestans used to say that if you sowed a field with dragons' teeth, it would bring up a crop of dead men."

"Is that true?"

He opened his hands and shrugged. "I've never come across it before. But that's the only thing I can think of."

"And Leth wants these things."

"He's probably got a load of them already, brought in from Dalagar."

Giulia hefted the tooth in her hand. "I want in, Sepello."

"How do you mean?"

"I want to work with you, to find Leth."

He shook his head. "I don't think that's a good idea."

"You owe me. I found this place."

"I would have done anyway."

She pointed to the body on the floor. "You'd have needed warrants and things. By then this arsehole would've been long gone." She suspected this wasn't true, but it was worth a try. The revenant that she had killed would probably not have been sane enough to make a clean escape. "Listen, one way or another I'm going after Leth. I owe him. You and I are both good at what we do – more than that, we're experts. I'll help you find Leth and nail him, once and for all. And for free. You don't even have to pay me anything."

Sepello smiled. It was an open, slightly foolish smile, as though he knew his bluff had been called. It made him look much younger. "You make a good case, I'll give you that."

"You don't even have to tell your order about me, if you don't want to."

"I'd give you credit. That would only be fair." He hesitated a moment, then said, "All right, Giulia, you're in. From now on, you're working for the Order of Saint Cordelia. But I'm in charge here. You defer to me, understand?"

"Yes." Giulia put her hand out, and Sepello shook it.

"All that remains now," he said, "is for me to introduce you to the prince."

She felt surprised, and slightly alarmed. Everything felt a notch bigger, a degree more intense. She felt as if she suddenly had more power, and yet less control over the situation. "The prince? Prince Mavlio?"

"Naturally. I thought you'd realised that."

"Shit. You mean to say you're working for Prince Mavlio?"

"Of course. This is his city. He doesn't want Leth anywhere near it."

"So I'd have to… talk to him?"

"You'd need to be introduced, yes. He's keeping a close eye on things. We'll go to see him the day after tomorrow," Sepello said. "It's when the prince receives his visitors."

"Fine," Giulia said. *God almighty, the fucking prince.* "I'll see you then."

"You will." Sepello yawned. His face was slightly too bland to be handsome. "I'll get one of the palace people to come and fetch you. Five in the afternoon's the usual time. And Giulia?"

"Yes?"

"You will have to dress like a woman. And smartly."

"I think I can handle that," she replied.

He looked slightly worried, as if he suspected that she'd turn up naked.

"Trust me," she said. "I know how to deal with people."

"I'm sure you do," he replied, but he didn't sound very reassured.

Chapter 3

"So then," said the lady to the right, "who do *you* know?"

She had blonde hair and slim hands with long, clean nails. When she spoke, she got too close; when she smiled, as she was smiling now, she bared her teeth.

"Well," Giulia said, "I don't really know anyone here. I mean, not very well. I don't live in Astrago, not permanently."

Sepello stood at her side, hands clasped behind his back. He smiled and said, "She's with me."

The queue shuffled forward slightly, and Giulia passed by another two feet of the bucolic mural on her left, as if she was walking very slowly through a country scene. On the wall, two well-proportioned young men gazed at a crumbling temple on the horizon, whilst a statue loomed over them, inexplicably missing its head. Giulia rather wished she was in the picture, instead of here.

She looked back to the smiling woman and said, "I'm deputised to the Order of Saint Cordelia." She gestured towards Sepello, who was deep in conversation with the skinny merchant behind him. "My colleague here is one of their members."

From somewhere further down the corridor, three boy singers began to chirp over a twanging lute.

"Oh really?" The woman stopped smiling for a moment, then started again. "Is that a contemplative order?"

"Well, not exactly—"

"The Order is sworn to the protection of mankind against devilry," Sepello said grandly, turning towards them. "In the manner of Saint Cordelia herself, we work to counter the undead."

The woman nodded carefully.

"And you?" Giulia asked. "What brings you here?"

The queue advanced two feet more.

"Well," the woman said, "I'm escorting Philia here." She took a step back and the young woman by her side, obviously her daughter, met Giulia's eye for the first time. "Our family lives nearby, and" – she lowered her voice – "the princess is well known to be lacking in company of her own age."

And maybe the prince wants company, too, Giulia thought. She said, "So you and your sister—"

"Daughter, please!"

"Really? I would never have known."

The woman laughed. Giulia caught a glimpse of Sepello. He looked deeply unimpressed. It was crude flattery, but Giulia needed allies in a place like this. She had no rank to rely on in society, and her face put her at a disadvantage from the start.

She had considered buying an alchemical potion to create the illusion that she had no scars. But if Mavlio was half as slippery as she'd heard, he would be able to see through any magical trickery.

A servant appeared at her side. "Name and station?"

"Giulia Degarno. I'm—"

"I meant the gentleman, madam."

Giulia decided that the rural idyll in the mural looked much more appealing than the prince's soiree, provided she wouldn't have to wear this God-damned dress once she got there. As she reached the front of the queue, she braced herself to be announced to the gathering.

However, the herald simply ushered them through, and they moved on unannounced. Surprised and vaguely disappointed, Giulia walked into the entrance hall.

Most grand mansions had an open courtyard in the centre. The Quincunx Palace, however, had a covered hall in the Anglian style. The high walls curved up into timbers the size of wyvern ribs, studded with carvings and bosses. Singers stood on a mezzanine decorated with Mavlio's coat of arms. At the rear of the hall, a massive staircase rose towards the private rooms. Guards in palace livery stood at each doorway, and at the bottom and top of the stairs.

A servant with a tray stepped in to Giulia's left like a Watchman making a quiet arrest. "Wine, madam?"

"Thanks," she said, accepting a glass. The servant did not even glance at her scars: he seemed thoroughly uninterested in her. The musicians began a song that she recognised, performed at half its usual speed and with a fraction of the usual enthusiasm. The servant drew back like receding mist.

"Keep walking," Sepello said from behind. "Go in."

"What does it look like I'm doing?" Giulia hissed and, putting on her most innocent expression, she walked into the room.

People stood and talked in small groups. An elderly woman peered at Giulia, then shuffled off, frowning. A greedy-looking little girl peeked from behind a woman's skirts. She looked like a scaled-down adult.

Giulia wanted to adjust her collar, which had seemed much less ostentatious in the hire shop, and check her ludicrously flimsy shoes. She could already tell the places where her feet would be sore in a few hours' time.

She strolled in, sipping her wine, thinking *Bollocks to it all.* She'd picked the word up from Hugh: for a moment she could almost see him, striding through the guests, drinking from a tankard as he walked.

If only Hugh was here. If only Sethis was here, or even Arashina. She'd put the word out through the dwarrow clockworkers again, but neither dryad had appeared. So much for a friendly face.

The singers stopped, and trumpets sounded from the mezzanine. Giulia turned to look. A suit of armour stood at the top of the grand staircase, held up by a frame. A drum hung around its neck. Slowly and jerkily, the suit raised its arms, and she saw drumsticks in its fists. Gleaming, the metal hands flashed up and down and the suit beat out a rapid tattoo. It dropped the drumsticks and awkwardly, as if it was a great effort to do so, lifted off its helmet.

There was nothing underneath. People gasped and laughed, and a little ripple of applause ran through the hall. Giulia glimpsed gears and wires in the armour, and thought: *Natural philosophy. It must run on clockwork.*

The suit held out its left arm as if welcoming a performer to the stage.

Prince Mavlio DeFalci stood on the far side of the staircase, one hand resting on the banister. He wore a loose dark robe over a red tunic. His clothes were plain but well-cut and expensive-looking. His face was clean-shaven and his short dark hair could have been painted straight onto his skull. The prince smiled, and Giulia noticed how taut his skin seemed to be, as if it had been stretched too tight over the bones.

Mavlio bowed to his guests and two people stepped onto the staircase behind him. The first, a slim man with a full beard that didn't suit him, was Cosimo Lannato, the famous scholar and engineer. No doubt the drum-playing automaton had been his work. The second was a girl in her late teens. She was smallish, pretty but not striking, with large eyes and a small mouth. Her hair was dark red. She had to be Mavlio's daughter, Carmina.

The three of them descended. Giulia had seen Lannato before, had probably glimpsed him while she had been cutting purse-strings at the unveiling of one of the prince's civic projects. Carmina was new to her. It was surprising, she thought, that a ruler so committed to securing his position should have no male heir to continue his line.

Mavlio reached the bottom of the stairs and advanced through the hall, greeting and shaking hands, bowing to the women as they curtseyed to him. He looked affable and interested in his guests. Perhaps he was just a good actor.

Sepello stood a little way to Giulia's left, peering into the crowd. She finished her wine and followed his gaze. She was surprised to realise that he was looking closely at Princess Carmina. Surely he didn't think he'd be in with a chance with her. *Good luck with that*, she thought, stepping to his side. *Royalty marries royalty.*

"There he is," Sepello said.

"So, what happens now?" Giulia asked.

He glanced at her. "We wait. He knows I'm here."

"Is there any food?"

"I don't think so. Maybe they'll bring some in."

Giulia folded her arms. Her sleeves felt enormous compared to her usual clothes. Apparently that was very popular in Bergania. *So is religious warfare. Doesn't mean I want any of it. Come on, get round to us*, she thought, watching the prince do his rounds.

Mavlio was deep in conversation now. She clearly had a little while to wait. A priest in a purple robe began to speak to Sepello. They leaned in close to each other, as if sharing secrets.

Cosimo Lannato stood a little way back, accepting a glass of wine from a servant. He seemed to be alone.

What the hell. Giulia took a deep breath and approached.

"Master Lannato," she said, standing in front of him and curtseying as best she could.

"Hello," Lannato replied. He looked slightly surprised, but nothing more. His eyes were very shiny behind his excessive beard, like two gems in a magpie's nest. "I don't believe we've met."

"My name is Giulia Degarno, sir," Giulia said. "I'm a colleague of Master Sepello there, from the Order of Saint Cordelia. I'm sorry to bother you, but might I ask if you made that suit of armour?"

"Oh." The servant by Lannato's side stepped back, out of the conversation. "Well, yes. I didn't make the actual armour, of course, but the mechanism inside is mine, indeed. It's very simple, really," Lannato added.

The musicians resumed their singing. "I'm very interested in such things," Giulia said. "I'm a friend of Marcellus van Auer, of Pagalia."

"Oh really?" Lannato seemed more awake. "The natural philosopher?"

"Yes, sir," she said. "I know him quite well. He's a very interesting man."

"Ah," Lannato said, "he certainly is. I've heard a lot about his machines. He's very keen on efficiency, I've heard. The last I heard he was trying to build a boiler that would need no enchantment at all."

Giulia nodded. "I saw it in Pagalia last year. He's still working on it."

"Intriguing. I ought to take the flying machines over to Pagalia sometime. You know, there aren't many women with an interest in this kind of thing. Do you know Amelia Brunelli of Astrago, by any chance? She a painter – a very good one, too."

"I'm afraid not. I do know the Scola san Marcello, though. I had some dealing with Battista Iacono the cartographer a few months ago. Is Madam Brunelli a member of the Scola?"

"Indeed she is," Lannato said, impressed. "Well, I never. Small world, isn't it? Ah, Master Sepello. Enjoying the evening?"

The revenant-hunter bowed. "I certainly am, sir. That display of yours with the armour was remarkable. I wondered if the prince would be able to speak with us soon. We have important information, and I'd like him to meet Madam Degarno here."

Lannato glanced at the clock above the stairs. "He should be free on the hour. I expect that he'll want to talk to you in private, in the solar."

Another blast of trumpets, and they looked around. A man in a dark coat stood on the staircase, by Mavlio's side: he had a neat, close-trimmed beard and white cuffs. There was something slightly exotic about the fellow: perhaps the shape of his beard, or the cut of his clothes.

Mavlio clapped his hands smartly, and the room settled down.

"Good evening, ladies and gentlemen," the prince announced. His voice was quick and clear. "Welcome to the Quincunx Palace. It is of course a pleasure to see you all here, and I'm delighted that you could attend. Today, we are honoured by a special visitor: here this afternoon is someone from outside the principality, here on important business."

Giulia glanced at Sepello: his face gave nothing away.

"The gentleman in question stands beside me. Formerly of the ambassadorial party to Pagalia, and representative here of Queen Gloria herself, I am honoured to present Sir Francis Vale of the court of Albion."

The man in the dark coat smiled and made a small, stiff bow. "You're too kind, Prince," Vale said, "although I'd ask you all not to judge me too harshly for coming here from Pagalia." There was a little laughter: Pagalia was traditionally Astrago's rival. "As a matter of fact, Queen Gloria wishes to strengthen links with *all* of the city-states, not just your fellows across the bay. I am here to express that wish in person and, in the spirit of friendship between nations, to present you, Prince Mavlio, with this gift as a token of our goodwill."

Mavlio raised his eyebrows at "gift", pantomiming surprise. There were smiles in the audience. Two servants stepped forward, bearing a gilded picture frame. The painting itself was covered by a cloth.

"Several years ago, Prince Mavlio was kind enough to permit Master Lannato, the greatest scholar of this age, to visit our queen. From his instructions, Anglia's first clockwork fortress has now been constructed, which we have named *Iconoclast*. Just as our privateers safeguard the seas, we trust that the land-ship *Iconoclast* will protect our country. In thanks, Queen Gloria sends this painting as a token of her appreciation, and a recognition of the bond between our nations."

Giulia felt eyes on her. She glanced around the room, looking to see who was watching her. Princess Carmina looked away too fast. Giulia glanced away too, turning her attention to the musicians on the mezzanine. Best not to stare at a princess, especially not in her home.

Vale pulled the sheet away from the frame, and the painting was revealed. A pale, wise-looking queen sat in a high-backed chair. Her hair was bright red, her face plaster-white. She wore a strange mixture of court dress and polished armour, as though warfare had become a fashion where she ruled. The woman's expression was cool and knowing.

Mavlio leaned in and peered at the signature in the corner of the painting. "Hans Harbrecht, eh?" he said. "That's very kind. I shall hang it somewhere suitably prominent. My guest: Sir Francis Vale!" he exclaimed, and another burst of clapping broke out. A man cheered. Giulia clapped along, careful not to spill her wine.

The prince nodded at the mezzanine. At once the band launched into "My Lady of the Spring", and in the sudden noise Mavlio slipped behind one of the drapes, through a little door and out of sight.

Nicely done, Giulia thought. *The prince has got this place sewn up tighter than a magic lock. I wonder how many of the guests are also on the payroll? God help the man who tries to walk out with the silverware.*

When she looked back, she saw that Lannato had wandered off. He now stood with a couple of young men a few yards away, earnestly explaining something with both hands. Sepello touched Giulia's arm and, when she looked at him, he pointed to the clock. "Come on," he said. "We'd better head to the solar. Do you need to use the facilities first?"

"No," she said. "This is as good as I get." She finished her wine off and took a fresh glass from one of the servants. The servant frowned slightly and walked away. Giulia took a swig of wine and followed Sepello, feeling that this fancy business maybe wasn't beyond her after all.

*

As Mavlio stepped out of the hall, one of his guards approached. "My prince, Rinalto Sciata is here. He wishes to speak with you urgently."

Quickly and quietly Mavlio said, "What, now? I've got people to talk to. People I actually like."

"I'm afraid so, my prince. Sciata says he has news about his father. Apparently it's a matter of life and death."

Hopefully, just a matter of death. "Where is he?"

"He's waiting in the small hall. There are two uniformed guards there, and a crossbowman hidden in the usual place."

"Good. I can give him a minute or two."

Diello's nephew. The only one of his wretched clan that I'd allow into my city. Unless his holiness the Pontifex shows up, of course. Or the queen of Bergania.

Sometimes, Mavlio wondered if it had been a good idea to cross House Sciata. Even the Vanharren family didn't have power like the Sciatas: their distant relations included several royals and the head of the Old Church. But he'd owed it to the city to shove that tyrant Diello off the throne – and owed it to himself.

A young man waited in the entrance hall, casual and relaxed. Two liveried guards stood just behind him, halberds at the ready. As Mavlio approached, Rinalto Sciata bowed and opened his hands in greeting, showing the prince that they were empty. Mavlio hoped that his men had checked Sciata's sleeves.

"Good evening, Prince Mavlio. May God grant you good health." Rinalto Sciata was no older than eighteen, with the black hair and dark eyes of his family. His jaw was hard and his eyes were close together: it was only charm that stopped him looking like a thug. Charm was something, Mavlio recalled, that Rinalto's family generally lacked.

"Welcome to my home, Rinalto. Now, I'm rather busy at the moment, so we'll have to be quick, I'm afraid."

"Of course, my prince. It's an honour to visit the palace. I am here at my father's request."

"Ah yes. And how is Ricardo?" *Dead yet?*

"Well enough, my prince, but mindful of his age. He grows old, and fears he will not see the inside of his home city before he dies."

He won't if I can help it. Ricardo Sciata had been one of Prince Diello's chief advisors, and a vicious persecutor of potential rivals to the Sciata line – including House DeFalci. "That is unfortunate," Mavlio replied. "But I would rather think a country estate would be more, ah, restive to an old man than the bustle of the city. All those vineyards, plenty of good fresh air…"

The youth shifted position. Mavlio glanced at the guards and prepared to make the hand signal for them to step in.

"My prince, my father thinks increasingly on matters of the spirit. Recently, he has been in correspondence with the Pontifex Justus."

"Oh really? I didn't know he was so pious."

Rinalto smiled. "They are close, my prince." He lowered his voice. "Were my father's banishment to be lifted, you would have a loyal ally in Sanctus City."

"Interesting." *I very much doubt it. As if Justus would ever forgive me for deposing his rotten cousin. As soon as I let any of your criminal relatives back within the city walls, they'll try to stage a coup and get the Pontifex to denounce me as a heretic. I'd cut my own balls off before letting your family of vipers within striking range.*

106

"May I say, my prince, that Princess Carmina looks most beautiful this evening."

That was a step too far. Mavlio kept smiling. "Thank you for coming to speak to me, Rinalto. I shall give your father's offer all the consideration it deserves. Now, if you would excuse me? I really need to speak to my other guests."

"Of course, my prince." Rinalto bowed again and took a step backwards.

As he walked away, Mavlio could feel Rinalto Sciata's eyes boring into his back, like a knife between his shoulder-blades.

I was too kind to the Sciatas. I ought to have wiped them out.

*

Giulia and Sepello were ushered into a large room with a high ceiling. The walls were light green, and a set of springs and belts set in the roof enabled mirrors to turn in the rafters, amplifying the sunlight from outside. The servants offered Giulia a high-backed chair. She sat down, tried and failed to get comfortable, and held her wine instead of drinking it. She needed to be alert for this.

Sepello took an equally hard-looking chair beside Giulia, as though they were a king and queen. Lannato sat down at one end of a two-person chaise. The natural philosopher crossed his legs and smiled vacantly.

A side door opened and the prince entered the room, followed by Carmina. Everyone in the room stood up in recognition of royalty, Lannato slightly slower than the others. Giulia glimpsed three guards outside, and the door swung shut.

It was strange to be so close to the prince: it set Giulia on edge. She feared him, but a small, treacherous part of her mind wanted to win his favour. *Just be careful.*

"Sit down, everyone, please," Mavlio said. "Sorry I'm a little late. I had to deal with a small matter."

Carmina quietly took a place on the end of Lannato's seat, as if she were an afterthought. *He's probably training her in affairs of state*, Giulia thought. *So he can have some influence over whichever nobleman gets to marry her.*

Mavlio stood beside the empty fireplace. His eyes flicked across the room – and stopped on Giulia. "You must be Madam Degarno, the newest edition to the party. Are you enjoying yourself tonight?"

It was a strange sort of fear: a kind of heightened nervousness, almost stage-fright. She was not surprised to be wary of him, but there was a feeling of not wanting to disappoint.

"Very much, my prince."

"Not what you're used to?"

"Not at all, Prince Mavlio. Your palace is beautiful," she added, needing to say something more.

She expected him to nod and get on with ignoring her. Instead he said, "Thank you. I'm very fortunate to live in such a magnificent home. I have Lannato's skill and Carmina's good taste to thank for that. If it was left to me, the whole place would look like a shed." He grinned, which made it look as if invisible hooks were tugging the skin at the edges of his jaw. Giulia smiled politely. "Now then: Master Sepello's told me a little about your background. You're some sort of freelancer working for the Order of Saint Cordelia, I take it?"

"Yes, my prince."

"And before that? Bodyguard to a lady?"

"Yes, I've done work like that."

It didn't seem to surprise him that a woman might be a fighter. "Have you been employed by anyone I'd know?"

"I did some work recently for Marcellus van Auer, the scholar."

"Ah, Lannato's colleague across the bay. Or should I say 'rival'? Sepello here tells me that you've some experience in tracking the undead. I gather you'll be assisting him while he's here."

"Yes, my prince."

"Good. Well, I suppose a warning is in order. The rules here are fairly simple. None of what we discuss now goes any further, at all. You can speak freely here, but that's it. If you need to discuss the orders that Sepello here gives you, you'll do it with him and nobody else. Understand?"

Orders. It was hardly surprising to hear it put like that, but the idea of taking orders still irritated her. "As you wish, my prince."

"Indeed I do. I think it's fair to say that the penalties for doing otherwise are rather stern. Fair, but definitely stern." Mavlio rocked on his heels. "Now then, let's get down to business. What do you understand our purpose here to be, madam?"

Giulia tried to think of a catch, something that might be intended to trip her up. "To find and destroy Constantin Leth."

"Good," Mavlio replied. "The first priority is indeed killing Leth. Find him and wipe him out as soon as you do. No matter what he says or does, whatever special circumstances he may try to plead, execute him immediately and bring me proof."

On the far side of the room, Carmina nodded earnestly.

"The other objective is to find any information on alchemy that Leth may have. It's well known that he's an apothecary of great skill. Whatever he's got – books, papers, ingredients and the like – bring them to either Lannato or myself. Understood?"

"Kill Leth, bring you the papers, tell nobody," Giulia replied.

"Very good! You'll find that people loyal to their city and prince do well here."

And those who cause trouble end up taking a short trip off a high gallows.

Mavlio sipped his wine. "I understand you helped Sepello kill one of Leth's underlings at the docks."

Helped? "You could say that, my prince."

"That's excellent. Let's hope it was only the first of your successes. Now, Cosimo, you were able to look at the alchemical equipment that Leth's little minion was keeping down there. Perhaps you could tell us about that."

"Certainly." Lannato leaned forward in his seat. "The equipment down there was fairly standard: pestles and mortars, condensers, that sort of thing. All of good quality but not much you wouldn't see outside a good apothecary's shop in town. There were also a number of syringes." He glanced at Giulia. "A syringe is a tool for drawing blood, a recent invention. It has a very thin needle with a tube down the centre, that's pushed into the skin. Blood can then be drawn out of the veins, through the needle. You could also use it for inserting something straight into the bloodstream: a dissolved tincture, say. That way it takes effect faster than just drinking it."

Giulia nodded. "I see."

"Leth's man had a number of rats down there. It seems he was trying to inject them with something he'd been mixing up. From what we found, I think he was dosing them with a potion made from ground-up dragons' teeth. Hence the box you found." Lannato reached to the floor, picked up his glass and took a sip. "In Quaestan legend, dragons' teeth act as a powerful reanimating agent. That, mixed with a suitable base, would be enough to duplicate the effects of the humours enough to simulate actual life."

Giulia raised a hand and Lannato stopped. "I'm sorry to interrupt," she said. "What's a reanimating agent, please?"

"It brings things back to life," Carmina said. She had a level, pleasant voice. "Sort of. Makes them undead."

"Thanks," Giulia replied. Then, realising her mistake: "Thank you, Princess."

Carmina looked her in the eye. "It's a pleasure," she said, and she smiled and glanced away.

"So," Mavlio put in, "it looks like Leth had a laboratory of his own set up in the docks, allowing him to work within the city walls, where he's had this assistant of his bringing rats to life. And no doubt he was planning to move from rats to people soon enough. What's the phrase?" Mavlio asked the ceiling, and it was clear as soon as he spoke that he was about to answer himself. "'From necromancy comes only the liveliest awfulness'."

"'False and empty are the Devil's works'," Sepello replied. Despite his profession, it sounded strange to hear him quoting the Holy Codex.

"Quite so. Sepello, tell us about the house above the cellar."

"As you wish," Sepello said. "There were two ways into the laboratory – one from the warehouse at the docks, and one from a house directly above the laboratory. The house was empty. It was rented out by a merchant named Gustavo Giari to two brothers called Luca and Pietro Travina."

The prince said, "I'll have my people speak to them all. Privately, of course."

"That won't be easy," Sepello replied. "The local captain of the guard told me both brothers have been dead and buried for about ten years."

"Ah. Hardly likely conspirators – unless they've been dug up again. So, what about this Gustavo Giari, then? I know the name." He paused. "They were a family – quite a large one. Criminals, all of them, friends of House Sciata. I executed several of them just after I came to power. I exiled the rest. They settled down the coast, in Brancanza."

Executed was the wrong word, Giulia thought. *Massacred would be more appropriate.* After he'd overthrown Prince Diello Sciata, Mavlio had secured his position by killing anyone who could oppose him, and driving the rest into hiding. Diello had ruled with the help of the big criminal families, and Mavlio had murdered or banished them all within a year, leaving only a few distant relations. Giulia felt no sympathy for them. Perhaps it was hypocrisy, or perhaps just good sense, but a life of crime had taught her to despise almost every criminal except herself.

Sepello said, "How far away is Brancanza?"

"You think the Giari family arranged this business from there?" Mavlio frowned. "It's possible, certainly. I could imagine Leth using people like that to do his dirty-work. Brancanza is about three days' ride south-west from here, past Paraldo. "

"I've never been there."

112

"You didn't miss much," Carmina said quietly.

Giulia wondered if Carmina was melancholic, or perhaps phlegmatic. She seemed withdrawn, slightly shy and quietly unhappy: all signs of a defect in the humours. *Strange.*

"It's a fishing port," Mavlio replied. "Not the finest town in the state, but very industrious."

Nicely put, Prince. Giulia sipped her wine. *Even the smugglers give it a miss. You don't stop there in case they steal the horse from under you.*

"Perhaps we should take a look," Sepello said.

"It's not too far," Lannato said. "Maybe we could arrange to have one of the flying machines carry you there—"

"No," said the prince. "Ride there. Go quietly. Find out if anything is going on there and come straight back. Then we can decide how best to deal with Leth. If we need the flying machines, we'll use them then." He turned to Giulia. "We have two: Lannato built them both, but we loaned one to the Pagalians for a while. It's back with us now. *Zephyrous* and *Resplendence*. Marvels of the modern age."

"I'm sure they are, Prince Mavlio."

Giulia had an image of the flying machine dropping from the sky onto Leth's hideout, packed with soldiers and weaponry. Leth would die, but it wasn't what she wanted. No: if he was killed without her being there – if he was killed by anyone else, in fact – she would be cheated. He needed a crossbow bolt in the skull, or a knife to the neck. Giulia's crossbow, Giulia's knife.

He belongs to me.

Ten minutes later, they were in the main hall again, back in the hum of music and conversation. Giulia stood at the back of the room, suddenly weary. Mavlio had returned to his guests, chatting and nodding, giving and receiving compliments. She wondered if the prince felt genuine affection for them, or whether he just knew that they would be of use.

Her shoes were starting to hurt, so she found a large chair by the side of the room. She was already tired, bored of the rumble of voices and the band tootling stupidly above. A shriek of wince-making laughter rose out of the centre of the room, and Giulia thought, *Have I had too much wine, or not enough?*

A black-haired woman, probably a courtesan, tottered by in platform-soled chopines. She paused and looked down at Giulia as if unsure what she was. The woman was incredibly well-groomed, to an almost inhuman level. How long did it take to make yourself look like that?

"Makes your feet sore, doesn't it?" Giulia said. The courtesan snorted and turned away.

Suddenly, Giulia was sick of the whole thing: of smiling, of being quiet and appreciative, of men who stood in the shadow of the prince and women straining their faces with the effort of looking sweet.

God, how can you get so rich and have so little fun? If I had money like these idiots I'd buy a tavern and a library and sit drinking by the fire, like I used to do—

"Giulia? Is everything all right?"

Sepello stood beside her chair. There was a thin stripe of sweat at his hairline.

"My shoes are a bit tight," she replied. "But otherwise I'm fine. Are we finished here?"

He looked around the room. "Yes, I think so. Unless you were planning to stay longer. I gather there's dancing later on—"

"Then I'm definitely leaving. The sooner we get back to normal the better."

"Normal?"

"My kind of normal."

Sepello smiled. "Well then, let's go. I was thinking of getting ready tomorrow and heading out the day after. It sounds like we've got a few days' journey ahead of us."

That sounded good. She'd have enough time to buy supplies, check her horse and send a message to Sethis. If the fey folk wanted to meet her, they'd have the chance to arrange it. "Fine with me. Do you reckon we can slip out of here?"

"It shouldn't be a problem." Sepello nodded at a group of men on the far side of the hall. "Looks as if Francis Vale's on centre stage tonight."

He was right. Vale stood in the centre of a group of wealthy merchants, talking earnestly. He looked nothing like Hugh had done, but his mannerisms were surprisingly similar: that seriousness, the lack of gesticulation as he spoke. Vale seemed to make some important point, and everyone around him nodded.

Cosimo Lannato was also doing the rounds, smiling and chatting. Carmina was by his side. Giulia wondered if they were romantically involved. Probably not, she thought: Lannato was like her chaperone, like a doctor accompanying a sickly friend. *My God, imagine having Mavlio as a father-in-law*, she thought. *Or a father*. She stood up and followed Sepello towards the door.

*

"So, you're working for Prince Mavlio now?" Arashina the dryad fanned herself with her floppy, wide-brimmed hat. Her dark hair hung around her face like curling smoke. "Interesting."

It had been the usual strange, informal business. Giulia had given a message to the dwarrows at their workshop, requesting an urgent meeting. They had been waiting with a response the next morning and now, in the afternoon, she had gone to find Sethis and Arashina in a copse near the main road out of Astrago. Giulia had walked half a mile, turned left at a huge black stump, and found Arashina sitting on a fallen oak with her shoes and sword on the trunk beside her, as casual as a farmer about to eat his lunch.

"Giulia works *with* this man Sepello. She still works *for* us." Sethis stood a little way away, arms folded. He looked friendly but a little cautious. Giulia was not sure whether he was Arashina's servant, interpreter or rival – she was pretty sure he wasn't her lover, though – but there was a certain wariness between them. "That's right, isn't it, Giulia?"

"Yes, that's right." The sunlight dappled Giulia's forearms, where she had rolled up the sleeves of her dress. A sunbeam poked through the leaves and into her eyes. She squinted. "We head out tomorrow."

Arashina swung her legs up onto the trunk. Her dress was outrageously short, allowing Giulia to see not just her feet and ankles but a fair amount of the dryad's calves. She hoped that was not for her benefit. Rumour had it that the dryads would sleep with anything. Arashina stretched. "Do you think you'll find him there?"

"Leth? Probably not. But hopefully I'll learn something useful. That's the aim: slowly get closer, and then when he's not expecting it – hit the bastard."

"Be careful," Sethis said. "If you think it'll be too dangerous, let me know. Really."

"Thanks," Giulia replied. She had seen Sethis in action: he was no master-swordsman, but he was tough and brave.

Far away, it seemed, a cart rattled along the road. Giulia wondered if its driver would overhear them. Probably not: things worked differently in the forests. Deep in the woods, the real world ebbed into Faery, the otherworld that humans could not enter unless invited by the fey.

"I don't know the family we're going after," Giulia explained, "but if they're anything like what they say about Brancanza, they'll be tough people. From what I've heard it's the kind of place where they send half an army to collect the taxes."

Arashina closed her huge eyes and tilted her head back to catch the sun. Watching her bathe in the sun was like watching a lizard on a rock.

"Giulia, be careful of Mavlio," Sethis said. "I've heard he's pretty good at being charming, but—"

"Don't worry about that," Giulia replied. "I don't trust him at all. He's out for himself and his family. I wouldn't turn my back on any of them, just in case they stabbed it out of principle. Sepello's probably all right, though – not that I'd give him the opportunity."

"The prince's family narrowly escaped being killed by the Inquisition in the war," Arashina said. "He knows of Leth's crimes. One would expect him to be eager to see Leth destroyed – but, as they say, it is the doom of men that they forget." She smiled, without humour, and looked Giulia in the eyes. "A creature like Leth knows how to play on the greed and vanity of human beings. I think you are smart enough not to listen to him, Giulia, but others of your race are less intelligent. Find Leth and come back to Sethis and I, and then we'll root him out together." She tilted her head back. "Good luck."

It took Giulia a moment to realise that the conversation was over. Sethis said, "Be careful out there, Giulia."

Arashina stretched out on her fallen tree and closed her eyes.

"I'll lead you back to the road," Sethis said. "Come on."

Giulia followed him to the roadside. She felt a curious levity, as though something fun was about to happen. Sethis had a good figure, and for a moment she was filled with the urge to slap him across the arse, if only to see the look on his face.

They stood beside the road, where the trees had been cut back a little way. The road ran off into the distance, well-made and straight.

"This used to be an old Quaestan highway," Sethis observed. "They built hundreds of them." He pushed his glasses back on his nose. "They say you could ride straight from Sanctus City to Lexopolis and never have to leave the road."

"Were you alive then?"

"With the Quaestans?" He laughed. "Lord, no. That was a thousand years ago."

Giulia looked down the empty road. "What about Arashina?"

"Now that I don't know. I wouldn't be surprised."

On the other side of the road a pair of rabbits scoured the grass, half-hopping, half-creeping around the road's edge. "If you don't mind me saying, she doesn't seem to like you very much."

Sethis nodded. "Don't worry, she's very much on our side." He frowned, which made him look scholarly. "But you're right. She thinks I'm rather too much like you people. I think she rather respects *you*, actually."

"I wouldn't have guessed it. Well," Giulia said, "I'd best head off. I'll be in touch again in a few days. Don't worry if it takes a bit longer: I might have found something good."

"Fine. Do you need me to come back to the city with you?"

She shook her head. "Thanks, but if I can't walk half a mile without dying, you've hired the wrong woman."

He smiled. "Take care. Remember: it's better that Leth gets away than you get hurt. Seriously."

"Thank you," Giulia said. "But he won't be getting away."

*

Giulia spent the rest of the day preparing for the trip. She sat in her room, sharpening her knives. She returned the dress that she'd worn at the palace to the hire shop and stopped at a cartographer's office on the way back, where she paid an apprentice three silver saviours to sketch the route to Brancanza on a piece of paper.

There would be inns along the roadside, but it was still worth getting provisions, just in case. She purchased two wineskins of weak beer, some dried fruit, half a dozen nasty-looking strips of cured beef and some dry bread that looked as if it might be edible in an emergency. Then she bought thirty crossbow bolts, standard size, with long armour-piercing tips.

Back in her room, she checked her crossbow and put a little oil in the mechanism. Two quick pulls on the ratcheted lever under the body of the weapon would cock the string. She could have a bolt ready to fire in six seconds. Giulia stashed the bow under her bed and went to sleep.

She rose with the dawn and dressed in her dark shirt and britches. She carried her things down to the stable. The stable-boy brought her saddle out and she loaded up.

Sepello was waiting at the West Gate under a statue of the Imperator Sanguissimus. He rode a big, dark mare that looked as if it had warhorse blood. The panniers were heavy with kit. For the first time since they'd met, he looked really capable.

"Morning," he called as Giulia drew near. "You're looking well-equipped."

"You too," she said.

Sepello said, "It shouldn't be too bad a ride, so long as the weather holds up. Once we leave the city we just need to stay on the road until Paraldo, then head south to Brancanza. The road should be good until then." He settled back in the saddle. "All set?"

Giulia looked at her horse's ears and tried to remember if she'd forgotten anything. "Yes," she said at last. "I'm ready. Let's go."

Chapter 4

They set out west from the city, on the same Quaestan road that Giulia had walked down to meet Arashina the day before. The sun was steady and strong, and Giulia pulled her hood up to shade her face. They rode at a fast trot, slowing every hour or two to rest the horses, and reached their inn with a few hours to spare.

The inn was a grand establishment by country standards and, to Giulia's surprise, Sepello insisted that he pay for her room as well as his own. She hung back as Sepello bantered with the fat landlord, aware that it was not quite right for a woman to travel without her husband, even if Sepello was claiming to be her hired guide.

Up in her room, she suddenly felt dog-tired. She yawned as she pulled off her boots. A sort of tranquil depression fell over her, like grey snow, and she slept.

On the second day, an hour or two into the afternoon, Giulia heard a drum and whistle as they rode past the edge of a big village. A procession of people danced out in front of them, laughing and drinking, and Giulia and Sepello stopped in the road as the revellers surrounded them like merry bandits from one of Hugh's stories of old Albion.

They sat under a tree and watched the wedding party. Tomorrow the villagers would be working their land again, backs bent and tools scraping at the soil, but for now they would drink to anything. Giulia and Sepello were offered a jug of thin peasant ale, tried to pay for it and were refused, and were formally welcomed by the local priest, whose hand wobbled as he blessed them both. Then both Sepello and Giulia were hauled up to dance.

It took half an hour to escape the dancing. Giulia returned to the shade and sat down with her back to the tree. Another bout of singing started, and the locals cheered on the newlyweds.

"Are you married?" Giulia asked.

"Me?" Sepello said. "No." He took a drink of ale from the jug and handed it over to Giulia. "But I'm courting a lady. She's called Clara Louise De Valcourt Boucard," he declared, as if the sound of her name was a magic spell.

"Are you sure that's just one lady? She's got enough names for half a dozen."

Sepello looked at her, puzzled. Giulia raised her eyebrows, and he laughed. "She's Berganian nobility. They all have names like that."

"What's she like?"

"Very pretty." Sepello saw that Giulia was waiting, and added, "She's quite tall, a bit taller than you, and blonde. She's clever, and very gentle. She's got a good sense of humour."

Giulia sipped at the ale. "You should have got her to come to Astrago. You could have introduced her to the prince."

"She lives about three hundred miles away. Besides, it's not quite like that. We're not betrothed – not yet."

Giulia sipped again, wondering what it was like to love someone who lived so far away. "Three hundred miles," she said. "That's a long way to go."

"She's worth the journey." Sepello clambered to his feet. "Come on. Let's head off before they make us dance again. The groom's mother keeps giving me the eye."

They reached Paraldo in the late afternoon. It stood on the top of a low, wide hill, with Brancanza twenty miles south-west. It was almost aggressively respectable, humming with honest labour. Carpenters worked in the streets, sawing away under awnings with their sleeves rolled up. A blacksmith pounded out horseshoes on his anvil, and the *p'ping, p'ping* of his hammer made a beat for the rest of the town to work to.

That night, they stayed in a big, busy inn. As they sat eating soup at a long communal table, a peddler with a round, angry face told them repeatedly that Brancanza was the worst place on the Peninsula. The innkeeper's son, who seemed a little simple, came round with a pot to dish out second helpings. "You got to give me a penny," he kept saying. "That soup costs a penny."

"Brancanza is a shithole," the peddler grunted, ripping the crust off his bread as if tearing an enemy in two. "Half the families down there are bandits and the other half are smugglers. I was lucky to get out without my head broken, I'm telling you. You don't want to be there unless you're cleaning the place up, and if you want to do that, I'd suggest you take a company of soldiers, sir. It's no place for a woman, that's for sure."

"Sounds charming," Giulia said.

"Well, it isn't," the peddler replied. He looked down the table and called, "Hey, could you bring me some more soup?"

"You want more, you got to give me a penny," said the innkeeper's son. He seemed to notice Giulia for the first time. "Hey, you're a lady! What're you doing here?"

"Enjoying the soup," Giulia replied. "Come on," she said to Sepello. "Let's go outside and sample the country air."

123

They strolled down the long street. Giulia felt an odd tenseness in her limbs, as though the tendons were slightly overstretched. Sepello was watching her. "If you don't mind me asking," he inquired, "how did you get into this line of work?"

"Revenant hunting? I told you when we met. Leth murdered my friend."

"I meant this in general. Mercenary work. You've been doing it for a while, haven't you?"

Giulia shrugged. For half a second, she wasn't sure either. It felt as if she'd always been travelling, always looking for revenge of some kind. "Accident and bad luck, basically. I was a thief-taker for a while. You make quite good money, if you're clever about it. I got a lot of jobs from ladies – you know, stuff that has to be done quietly. Getting letters back, that sort of thing."

"I can imagine," Sepello replied.

"And before that, well—" *It doesn't matter now*, she thought. "Well, I had some trouble of my own." She touched her scars. "Some bad people crossed me. I suppose I wasn't all that good a person back then, either."

"Poacher turned gamekeeper, eh?"

"Something like that. How about you?"

"It was always a possibility that I'd join the Order of Saint Cordelia," he replied. "One of the Knights Senior knew my father. To begin with, I liked the company, the sense of purpose – and the bounty money I could claim from the Church. Then I realised it was the right thing to do. I'm protecting people, and I'm good at it. And if you're good at something and it's the right thing to do, that's what you ought to be doing with your life, isn't it?"

They rode south and made good progress. That night, they camped outdoors a few miles north of Brancanza. The weather was warm enough not to need a tent, and the midges hadn't come this far inland. Fifty yards from the road, there was a little copse with a dip in the centre. Someone had made a campfire there, and Giulia fetched wood while Sepello tended to the horses. She used a scrap of thieves' tinder and a wad of moss to get the fire going and, by the time he returned, she was feeling pleased with herself and feeding sticks into the flames.

"Good work," Sepello said, dumping his pack beside the fire. He pulled out a bottle. "I have precisely no fresh meat, but on the plus side I do have a full bottle of wine. Here."

Giulia took the bottle from him and swigged. Sepello poured water into a pot and added herbs, beans and some of Giulia's dried meat. "I can't promise this'll taste good," he said.

"Put some wine in," Giulia replied. "It never fails."

After eating, they sat on opposite sides of the fire, hardly needing its warmth. Giulia sat reading while Sepello cleaned his pistol. It was really two guns fused together, she saw: one pistol barrel above the other, the triggers both linked. It looked complicated and lethal.

"What's the book?" Sepello asked. He sounded surprised: she realised that he hadn't expected her to be able to read.

"*The Sorrowful Death of Alba the King*," Giulia replied, quoting the front page. "It's good."

"Can I see?"

"All right," she replied, "but be careful. It's not mine."

Sepello took it very gently and opened the first page. "'This is a book for noble people to read in, and learn from acts pious, base, brave and cowardly' – well, noble people is us, all right. Causes don't come much more just than ours. Where'd you get the book?"

"It belonged to my friend," she said. "The one Leth killed. It was his favourite book." *And probably the only one he'd ever read.*

"Good choice," Sepello said. He passed the book back. "What was he like, your friend?"

Giulia put the book back in her pack. She felt suddenly sick of knights and ladies and their gentle predicaments. The world had changed.

"He was older than me, quite a lot older. People sometimes thought I was his daughter. He was tall, and thin, but really tough – the best fighter I've ever known. He used to say that keeping to the knightly code kept him strong. It didn't help him in the end, though."

"I'm sorry."

"That's all right. I'm not the first person who's lost friends because of Leth. Hopefully, I'll be the last." She stared at the flames. "Where did the undead come from? To begin with, I mean."

"It depends who you ask. Some say it was a curse from God. You know the story of Thantome, the dancing-girl in the Holy Codex?"

"Yes." The fire was small, but it was hypnotic; the flames seemed themselves to dance. "She performed for the sultan of Jallar, and he told her she could have anything she wanted. So she said, 'I want the head of the prophet Jehan'."

"'And so they struck his head from his body and she kissed his lips, and so did she taste of the prophet's holy blood'. They say God cursed her so that no food could

126

nourish her, so she struck a deal with the Devil: she would prey on the living, and thus do the Devil's work. And so she became the first revenant."

"Is that true?"

"I don't know. Some people think that revenancy is an alchemical disease, a sort of plague. Others reckon the fey folk invented it, or that it's a punishment for the wickedness of the world."

"What do you think?"

Sepello hesitated, as if he'd never considered the issue before. "I don't know how it came about, exactly. But it's evil, no doubt about that."

Suddenly, the campfire seemed smaller, the woods vast and dark around them. Giulia said, "Let's not mess about tomorrow. Let's get there early, go in, find what we need and get out. The quicker we can get this done, the better."

Sepello said nothing for a little while and stared into the trees. Then he nodded. "You're right. There's no point wasting time. We'll leave at dawn."

*

It was mid-morning. Sepello sat on his horse at the side of the road, watching for trouble. He held the bridle of Giulia's horse in his left hand and kept his right hand close to his gun.

They were about a mile from Brancanza. The road wound down towards the bay, screened by trees. Sepello could see why the town was so popular with smugglers: it was almost impossible to see from the road.

A sparrow chirruped above the road and fluttered from one side to the other. Sepello watched it, wondering what kept it in the air. God's will, perhaps. But then wyverns could fly, dragons too, and they were fey creatures, creations of the pagan gods. Even Prince Mavlio had a flying machine, and Sepello very much doubted that God was involved in that.

Come on, Giulia, he thought, peering into the trees. She had been gone about a quarter of an hour, climbing up the hill at the side of the road to scout out the town below. She'd gone at it like a soldier, scrambling up the slope with real enthusiasm. *She really wants Leth dead*, Sepello thought, and then, *She'd better not mess this up.*

But he suspected that she wouldn't. Whatever she was – strange as she might be – she was a professional. Perhaps Saint Cordelia herself had been like that. He thought of the few fighting women he'd known, tough warriors from his own order, and shrugged.

Giulia's horse threw its head back and tossed its mane. Sepello looked over his shoulder. The road was still empty. His impatience was rising. How long could it take to climb a hill? For a moment he wondered if Giulia had been attacked, or whether she had walked into the town to sort the business out on her own. No; she was too good a hunter to break cover that easily.

He heard a rattle of loose dirt to his left and the sound of a body slipping through trees. Giulia appeared at the edge of the forest, shadowed by branches. She beckoned to him and ran back up the slope. Sepello dropped down from his horse, tied the bridles to a branch and jogged between the trees after her.

He found Giulia crouching at the top of the rise, her crossbow on the ground beside her. Brancanza sprawled out before them across the bay. The stubby, whitewashed houses reminded Sepello of yellowing teeth. The streets were empty. There were no boats in the harbour.

Sepello dropped down and crept up beside Giulia. Together they looked across the rooftops.

"Trouble," Giulia said.

Sepello shielded his eyes with his hand. "What's happening?"

"Nothing. That's the problem."

It took him a moment to see what she meant. The air above the town was clear. He looked at her and scowled.

"No smoke," he said.

*

Giulia walked quietly into the town. She kept to the side of the street and held her crossbow ready to fire. Sepello walked beside her, his massive pistol raised.

The buildings on either side were high and the colour of bone. A few birds passed overhead, not circling.

"It's empty," Sepello said.

Giulia nodded. "If they're hiding, they're doing it well."

They walked on down the main street, further into the town. Sepello glanced into an alleyway and stepped quickly across the opening. He halted by a door, and gestured for Giulia to come closer.

She stopped beside him. Sepello pointed. A basket lay in the doorway on its side, wedging it slightly ajar. Apples had spilled out into the road.

"That's not good," she said. "Let's look inside."

Sepello pushed the door open with his boot. Giulia checked the road behind them, saw nothing, and followed Sepello indoors.

The room was cool and square, the ceiling low and the plaster rough. Someone had ransacked the place: curved shards of pot were scattered across the floor. A man's shoe lay below the window.

Sepello bent over in the corner. "Ah, *fuck*," he said bitterly, as if realising that he had been cheated. Giulia saw what he was looking at: a reddish-brown mark low down on the wall, almost the colour of rust.

"Whoever did this is gone," she said. "So's whoever they did it to. Come on. Let's look in another."

They entered the next three houses, and then a carpenter's shop on the other side of the road. All of the doors were open. Two of the houses showed signs of a struggle: to judge from the tools scattered across the floor of the shop, the carpenter had put up a fierce fight. But he'd been taken away, all the same.

Sepello ran his hand over the workbench, sending a snowdrift of wood shavings onto the ground. "Let's try the church," he replied. "They might have taken refuge in there."

They're dead. "All right," Giulia replied. "Let's look in the church."

They returned to the street. The sun cast angular shadows into the road, and the air felt oppressively hot. Giulia shaded her eyes and scanned the horizon: she saw a steeple with a sword on end at its peak. Sepello crossed the road so that he was under the eaves at the other side, and they walked towards the church as if to take it by surprise.

Giulia remembered scraps of war stories: villagers herded out into the fields to be killed, whole towns left empty after the Inquisition had done its work. She passed an open window, saw household objects strewn across the floor, and heard Hugh's voice in her mind: "The buggers used to leave traps behind them, to surprise our men…"

Sepello stopped at the end of the street. Giulia ran across the road to join him. "There's the church," he said, nodding to the right.

It'd be the best place in town to hold out, Giulia thought. *Against the living, anyway.* "Hey," she said. "Can revenants enter a church? It's consecrated ground."

"It seems to vary," he replied.

Great. "Let's go, then."

The church stood a little way back, surrounded by a yellowing lawn. They ran across the grass and reached the whitewashed side of the nave. "The doors are open," Sepello said. "That's not a good sign."

They walked in, their weapons ready. The church was empty, and its emptiness made it seem vast. Someone had painted a mural along the left wall: villagers in bright colours brought bread and fish to offer to an angel. For a crazy moment Giulia wondered if the locals had somehow been sucked into the mural. She glanced around and saw silver candlesticks and a gold sword above the rood screen.

"It's not been looted," she said. "Doesn't even look like there was a fight."

Sepello lowered himself onto a seat beside the wall. He sighed and ran his left hand over his face. "I half-thought they'd be in here," he said, "hiding behind the pews. Or piled up dead."

"Me too." Giulia looked back: the summer sun made the doorway glow like a portal into Heaven. Her skin crawled, as if someone was watching her. "Have you ever seen anything like this before?"

"Not like this," Sepello replied. "Not people just disappearing, without any reason." He stood up and made himself sound less weary. "Perhaps it was smugglers. Maybe they took everyone away as slaves or something. Maybe they all went to sea."

"So they all went," Giulia said. "Everyone in the town. But they didn't all want to go – some of them fought back. But they didn't lock themselves in the church, didn't make any organised defence. Maybe they didn't get the chance."

"And whoever took them away didn't bother robbing the church."

"Revenants don't know what money is, do they?"

Sepello shook his head. "Not morts. The smarter ones would."

"And they took the bodies with them." Giulia felt cold; sick. It was like looking at the paraphernalia of a black Mass: the pieces made no sense on their own, but together it stank of evil. She shuddered. "This is Leth's work, isn't it?"

Sepello swallowed. "I don't know. It's hard to tell without more. But yes, I think it is."

"We should look at the harbour, make sure there's no-one there."

"All right. Then we'll go back."

They walked back down the aisle. At the doors, they stopped and checked their weapons. Sepello crouched down and looked out of the church. He beckoned to Giulia and they headed out.

As she returned to the sunshine, Giulia thought, *What if everybody's just disappeared? What if Sepello and I are the only people left in the world?* She felt a strange fear, not of any one thing but of the world itself. It seemed to press in around her like gas. She felt sweat on her back, on her neck.

A single row of houses separated them from the waterfront. Giulia and Sepello slipped down a little alley, and the bay opened before them. Baskets lay heaped on one side; a few had rolled into the road. Fish guts had been dumped on sticky, reeking tables, a feast for flies. Boats lay in the harbour, most of them only big enough for a pair of fishermen. A couple of hulls rested on trestles for repair. It looked like any small fishing town, except that its citizens were gone.

Several big knives lay around the tables. Behind a boat, broken wood showed where something heavy – perhaps a man – had been hurled through a table. Giulia looked down. The bare earth was scuffed as though some frenzied dance had broken out on the waterfront.

"There was a fight here," she said.

Sepello nodded. "Maybe they threw the bodies in the water."

She stood up and looked at the gentle water of the bay. As she walked towards the waterside, she had a sudden fear that there would be corpses there. Giulia imagined the dead lying and waving lazily with the tide, as if to beckon her in. She thought of the time her face had been cut, when she had been thrown into the canal in Pagalia to drown… but there was nothing in the water.

A pair of gulls circled the harbour, screeching. Sepello wandered down to Giulia's side. He shook his head. "Well," he said heavily, "I don't know what to say."

She looked at the silent houses. "Someone took them all away," she said. "Leth couldn't do this on his own, could he?"

"No. He'd be tough – all revenants are – but he's not an army. You'd need a lot of men to empty out a whole town like this."

"I thought the locals would have more boats," Giulia said. "Maybe they escaped in them." She took a deep breath and looked at the sky. "We ought to go back.

We're not achieving anything here." *And there's no way I'll be staying around after dark.*

Sepello pushed his gun back into his coat. "Maybe we should come back tomorrow."

"In case the locals return?" She shook her head. "I hate to say it, but I don't think they're coming back. I reckon we should put some distance between us and here. Go back, tell the prince, see what he wants to do."

"There's a guard station in Paraldo. We ought to let them know."

They turned away from the waterfront. As they walked up the slope, towards the edge of town, Giulia said, "How many people do you think would live in a place like this?"

"Probably a couple of thousand."

"God almighty. Two thousand people, gone just like that."

Sepello climbed up the ridge that they'd used to spy on the town. Giulia led the horses off the road and waited for him to return. It occurred to her that they had been talking about the citizens of Brancanza as though they were already dead.

They found a different place to sleep, eight miles up the road. They saw nobody on the way.

Sepello sat on the far side of the dying fire. The shadows made his brows look heavy and his cheeks puffy, as though the flames had made him sick.

He held out a bottle to her. "Here, have some wine."

"Thanks." Giulia took it from him and drank. She had made dinner while he checked the horses, and the wine did a lot to take the taste away. "Sorry about the stew."

He shrugged. "It was fine. When you're travelling, you don't expect a banquet."

"I suppose not." Giulia looked around, into the summer night. "You know, I used to want to live in the countryside." She took another swig. The wine tasted like copper coins. "I still do, in a way, but there's too many arseholes out here. There's plenty in the cities, too, but they don't get away with so much."

She took another swig. The wine was warm and sour. She passed him the bottle, knowing that, if she didn't, she would soon be tempted to drink the lot. "You'd need a lot of men to make two thousand people go missing, right? Even if you were up against a bunch of fishermen."

"Absolutely. You'd need two or three hundred soldiers, at least. You'd have to hit it fast and hard, like the Inquisition used to do. And Brancanza has a tough reputation. It wouldn't be easy."

She nodded. "So he's not working alone, then."

"Evidently not."

"You think he's hired mercenaries? Or maybe there's some mad nobleman he's got working for him."

Sepello prodded the embers of the fire with a twig. "It's possible. The undead have allies. Beyond Polsk, there are whole tribes of bandits who swear loyalty to them. Maybe Leth's made some alliance with the Landsknecht. But if he has, it's new to me."

"What about the weaker undead? Could he command them?"

"Oh, definitely. But morts would be too stupid to pull off something like this. They'd wander in like a herd of cows, kill whatever they found, and wander off again. They wouldn't know how to hide the bodies."

It stinks of magic, Giulia thought. She looked into the fire, and for the first time in a long while, the shadows no longer seemed like her friend.

*

Paraldo was so busy that Giulia wondered if Brancanza's missing inhabitants had migrated there. Boats filled the harbour, and women on the water's edge helped haul in baskets of fish. Little carts wound their way through the alleys towards the rear of the town, and teams of chandlers sawed and hammered outside their boatsheds. Smoke curled up from chimneys across the sheltered bay: it was bizarre to think that, twenty miles further up the coast, Brancanza lay silent as a grave.

They walked through the babble of voices and the stink of fish, past coils of rope and stacks of barrels. They stopped to ask if anything unusual had been heard about Brancanza recently. Giulia let Sepello do the talking. A cooper told them that he knew nothing about Brancanza except to keep away. An old woman explained that it wasn't her sort of place, not her sort of people. "They bring all kinds of things ashore down there," she said, waving a bloody knife as if to illustrate her point, and then she got back to gutting fish.

Sepello got talking to a girl selling freshly cooked sea bass from a tray. Giulia waited in the shade on the far side of the road and watched him joke with her. The girl reminded her of herself many years ago, coy and pleased to have the attention of a gentleman. It must be strange, Giulia thought, to be young and pretty, where the big adventures in your life would be getting married and having children.

After a while, Sepello left the girl and walked back to Giulia. The smile faded from his face as he approached.

"They've nothing on Brancanza. A trader went down there last week and came back three days ago. Everything was fine, apparently. I didn't say anything about what we saw."

"Let's try the guard-house, then."

The guard station stood in the centre of town, a squat little fort with three whitewashed storeys. A young lieutenant met them at the door and led them upstairs to his boss.

The guard captain finished reading Sepello's letter of patronage and handed it back to him. "Interesting. So, how can I help you both?"

Sepello said, "We've just come back from Brancanza. We were sent there by Prince Mavlio, to look into smuggling. The town's empty."

The captain frowned. "Empty? What do you mean, exactly, by 'empty'?"

"There's no-one in it," Giulia said. "Nobody. Absolutely everyone's gone. There's signs of a fight, but no bodies."

"What kind of a fight?"

Giulia shrugged. "We saw blood, tables overturned, things broken, but no organised defences. It looks like whatever happened took the people by surprise. It's hard to say more than that."

"Are there still boats in the harbour?"

"Quite a few. Some of them might have gone, I can't tell for certain."

The captain looked at Sepello. "Is this true?"

"Just like she said. I'll swear it on the Holy Codex, if you want."

The captain glanced away. He had thin lips and a rather pointed chin, which only just stopped him from being handsome. He reminded Giulia of a harder, less intelligent Sethis. "The whole town was completely empty?"

"Totally deserted," Sepello said. "We didn't see a soul."

"Bloody hell," the captain replied. He stood up and looked out the window, as if checking that his own townsfolk hadn't also disappeared. "That can't be true. They must have gone somewhere... unless it's magic, somehow..."

He doesn't want to mess with sorcery, Giulia realised, *and I don't blame him.*

"All right," the captain said. "I'll take some men and have a look. But you're coming with me, both of you. I'll warn you now: if you're lying, you'll be straight up before the magistrate. So if this is just some kind of trick, I'd suggest you stop right now."

"I'm not lying," Giulia said. The captain glanced at Sepello. "He's not lying either," she added.

"Then we'll set off tomorrow morning, good and early. You're staying here tonight, under my protection. You can bring your own bedding in. I'll make sure your horses are cared for." The captain took a deep breath. "I'll need your weapons, please."

Giulia stared at him. "What?"

"Like I said, you're under our protection." He gestured to someone behind them. Giulia looked around, and saw two guardsmen in the doorway. The captain beckoned. "Lucio, Guiseppe, would you show these good people to the storeroom, please?"

Sepello sighed and leaned back against the stone wall. The candlelight caught on the folds of his coat. "I can't believe it," he said. "I've got a letter of patronage from

138

the prince and they still lock us up. What did he want, angels to come down and sing our praises?"

Giulia shrugged. "I see his point. He probably thinks we're trying to pull some kind of trick on him. Maybe he reckons we're banditti, or even bounty hunters. Half of that lot are just as bad as the people they bring in. At least they didn't put us in the cellar."

Sepello lay back on his bedroll. "So you're happy with them just locking us up?"

"I didn't say that." Giulia drew her leg up and slid her lockpicks out of the top of her right boot. "I got these out when they took our weapons. Not that I suggest we use them yet."

Sepello laughed quietly. "Nice work! Have you ever thought about joining the Order? We could use someone like you. I could get you an interview with one of our leaders if you'd like."

"Thanks, but I doubt I'd fit in."

"In this line of work, nobody fits in." He sighed. "God, I hope we're close to getting Leth. I'm tired of chasing the bastard. Polsk, Thanemark – I've been all the way down to Jallar to find him, for God's sake."

Giulia watched his outline. She had nothing to say. She had seen none of those places, and probably never would.

"I've hunted this son of a whore halfway around the world," Sepello said, "and I'm getting sick of it. *He's* got all the time he wants: I haven't. I want to make the kill, take what's owed to me and go. Trouble is, he's so damned clever. Leth's not like the other revenants – he's got ambition, you see? Most of them just want to kill and sleep, or else flounce around like drunken noblemen. Leth's smarter than that, the bastard."

"We'll get him," Giulia said. "Don't worry about that."

"I wasn't worrying," Sepello said, and he rolled over onto his side. "I know we will: I just would like it sooner than later. Goodnight, Giulia."

"Goodnight."

"Thanks for helping me."

"You too." She leaned over and blew the candle out. "See you tomorrow."

*

Mavlio woke. He lay in bed, suddenly conscious, eyes fixed on the ceiling. He stayed still, trying to remember something.

Sometimes he had nightmares. They were impossible to remember, dissolving into smoke the moment his brain tried to take hold of them. Mavlio sighed and shifted onto his side. An insect fluttered at the window, its wings a soft patter against the glass.

A cry came from outside the room. In one motion Mavlio stood up and slipped his feet into his shoes. He stood beside the bed in a loose shirt and britches, legs bent, waiting.

"Urrh!"

It was muffled, but definitely there. He put his hand by the bed and slid a knife from under the mattress. He pulled the scabbard off the blade and walked to the door.

Mavlio dropped down and checked the spyhole by the bottom of the door. Nobody moved in the corridor outside. He opened the door with his left hand, the right held back ready to stab.

The corridor was empty, lit by a single ornate lamp. As he left his room he heard the sound again, louder and more urgent. It was not exactly a cry, or a grunt, but something in between – the sort of noise that no-one made naturally, that had to be torn out of someone.

He hurried down to Carmina's room. The door was locked with a mechanism of Lannato's design disguised as a doorknob. Mavlio reached out and turned the doorknob a half-turn, then back a quarter.

The cry again, loud and keening.

Mavlio spun the knob a full turn, pushed it in and heard the mechanism fall into place. The door swung open silently.

A wedge of moonlight cut across the room. At its apex, Carmina sat at her writing-desk, her head cocked back at a weird angle. Red hair dangled towards the floor like wilted fronds.

Mavlio took a step into the room. Carmina shook her head. She drew back in her chair, her voice rising. "Get away! Get away from me!"

She raised a hand as if to fend something off, and for a second Mavlio wondered if there really was something there, some invisible monster hovering in front of her. Then he reached out and took hold of her shoulder.

Carmina staggered to her feet, tripped and fell onto the rug. She kicked out, knocking the chair over, and lay there blinking.

"Father?"

Mavlio slipped the knife away. He crouched down and made himself smile. "It's all right. You were having a nightmare. It's over now. You're in your room. Look."

Carmina looked around slowly, as if she didn't know how she had got here. "A dream," she said. "I had a horrible dream."

Mavlio glanced at the window. He didn't know what he was checking for: there was nothing there. There couldn't be. "You should go to bed."

"No." There was an intensity in her face that he didn't like, a kind of desperation. "You don't understand. I dreamed you found me a husband."

"Well, that's good, isn't it?"

"We came to visit you, and he killed you, and I helped him. And then – then we cut off your head."

Mavlio fought down a shiver. He forced himself to smile. "Come on, it was just a dream. This is what happens when you fall asleep sitting down: you have bad dreams. Come on." Mavlio held his arms open, like wings. She stepped into his embrace. "Goodnight, Carmina."

"Goodnight, Father. I'm sorry I got you up."

"Anything for my girl." He crossed to the window, looked out for a moment and closed the curtains. Nothing. "Get ready for bed now. Goodnight – and sleep well this time, all right?"

She smiled as he closed the door. The prince turned the lock so that Carmina would be unable to leave if she was sleepwalking. He walked back to his room, closed the door and slid the bolts. Mavlio slipped off his shoes, returned the knife to its hiding place and climbed back into bed.

Seventeen, he thought, *seventeen and still having nightmares. Any normal girl would have grown out of it.*

He leaned back and drew the covers around him.

And then we cut off your head.

Chapter 5

Giulia was locked in a house with a madwoman who ran from room to room. There were mirrors in each room, and whenever the woman saw a mirror, she shrieked and fled. She ran around like an animal thrashing in a trap, with Giulia following and unable to intervene.

"Giulia!" Something gripped her arm. Her shoulder shook. "Wake up!"

Sepello was leaning over her. Light flooded the room through high, narrow windows. *The storeroom,* she remembered. *They locked us in here.*

"Get up," Sepello said. "Get the door open."

Suddenly, she was fully awake. "What?" she said, scrambling upright. She shook her head. "What's going on?"

"I don't know. Something's happening outside. I heard people going past, shouting. There's fighting out there. Come on, we've got to go."

"Is it Leth?"

"I don't know. Maybe. Just get the door open, would you?"

Giulia slid the picks out of her boot. Her heart was tight in her chest. She bent down and got to work.

A minute in, a woman screamed. A gun banged just outside the building. Giulia whipped around, thinking that someone was trying to shoot in through the small windows, and heard shoes pounding the earth as somebody ran away. Sepello said, "Hurry up. We've got to get out."

"What do you think I'm doing?" she replied.

"Are you nearly done?" Sepello demanded. *God,* she thought, *he's really scared.*

She felt the tumblers shudder and drop away. The lock clicked. "There."

Sepello pushed the door open and they crept into the corridor. "We need to get our gear," he said.

The early morning light ran down the stairs like poured honey. The door to the main office was open. The room was empty. Giulia heard muffled shouts from outside.

"Sounds like it's coming from the waterfront," she said.

"Our stuff'll be in there," Sepello said, pointing at the far wall. "You take the big chest; I'll do the cupboard."

An iron-banded chest squatted in the corner of the room. Giulia crouched down and drew her picks. There was a high cupboard beside it, also locked. As she started work, Sepello ran up and smashed his heel into the cupboard as if kicking down a door.

She flinched, surprised by his violence. She turned her attention back to the lock.

Giulia felt the tumblers shudder and turn. Sepello bashed at the cupboard door, got a hold and wrenched it. Shouts came from the harbour, and among them, shrieks.

Sepello tore the door open. He reached in and rummaged around. "Nothing. Fuck!"

Giulia closed her eyes and tried to shut out the mayhem from outside. The lock clicked open. She lifted the lid of the chest and took her crossbow out. "It's all here," she said.

Sepello retrieved his pistol and his hunting knife. Giulia loaded up her knives and slipped the picks back into her sleeve. She worked the lever under her bow and the ratchet hauled back the string.

Howls rang up from the street.

"It's Leth," Sepello said. "It's got to be."

Giulia had an image of the revenant as she took out a crossbow bolt. *This is for you*, she thought, setting the bolt down snug in its groove.

She walked to the door with the crossbow raised. "Ready?"

Sepello nodded.

"Right then. Let's go."

She opened the door and stepped out into the morning.

The street was broad enough for a cart, flanked by whitewashed houses the colour of teeth. Three bodies lay in the road: two women and a man, all unarmed, and all bloody from waist to neck. From the look of it, they had been stabbed.

Side by side, Giulia and Sepello headed towards the bay.

A man ran into the street, a scabbard flapping at his side. He had no sword. Sepello raised his pistol.

"Wait!" the man cried. "Don't shoot!"

It took Giulia a moment to realise that he was the captain from the night before, the one who was not quite handsome, the one who had reminded her of Sethis. His face was grotesque with horror, like something carved onto a cathedral roof.

"What's going on?" she demanded. "Who's fighting?"

"It's the Judgement," the man replied. "This is it: the counting-out." He glanced left, then right, and rushed off to the right. "God have mercy on you!" he shouted, and he ran out of view.

Voices yelled and screamed on the waterfront. Fear twisted in Giulia's guts, fluttered in her chest.

Sepello caught Giulia's eye. "Come on."

145

Together they jogged deeper into the town, into the sound of chaos. Shouting, sobbing, howls of pain that suddenly rose and stopped. It sounded as though Paraldo was shaking itself apart.

There was an alley to the right. Sepello looked at Giulia for a long moment, as if worried he might forget her face. "Down here," he said, pointing into the alleyway.

They walked into the alley. Giulia saw blue water in the gap at the end, then an upturned handcart on a cobbled street. A woman lay under the little cart, trying to pull herself free. She heaved herself onto her side, then onto her back. Behind her, a high-sided boat slipped towards the shore.

The woman threw up her hands, and Death stepped into view.

It was a white stick-man, a human skeleton that somehow stood upright. It bent over the woman, quick and jerky as a marionette, and drove a short-bladed sword into her chest. Her hands shot out imploringly, shuddered, fell. A cry came out of Giulia's mouth. She hardly knew who was making it.

The skeleton looked up. It straightened like a mechanism, turned and strode towards them.

It can't be, Giulia thought, *that can't happen.*

The skeleton broke into a lumbering jog, sword in hand. The bone feet sounded like hollow sticks.

Can't be, can't be. Surely not.

Sepello lifted his pistol in both hands and took careful aim. Giulia pulled up the crossbow and fired. Her bolt hit the skeleton's shoulder-blade. It stumbled, righted itself and ran at them.

The pistol boomed. Sepello's bullet struck the skeleton in the chest and it burst. Bones showered the alleyway. The jawbone shattered, the skull rolled away.

"Reload," Sepello said, pulling out the ramrod for his gun, but Giulia was doing that already.

"What was that?" Her fingers worked without her, drawing back the string and snapping a fresh bolt into place. "What was that?" Thoughts ran through her mind, a jumble of ideas: the end of the world, the fact that she had seen a walking skeleton kill a woman, the question of whether Leth had created it – *Saint Senobina, watch over me.*

Sepello was muttering something as he reloaded. He tugged a paper cartridge from his belt and rammed it home. He looked up. "I'm ready."

Together, they crept to the end of the alleyway.

The scene was crazy, totally impossible. Giulia's head swam; she thought that her brain might break. Skeletons swarmed the waterfront. The sheer number of revenants made it hard to tell them apart. Several long boats had slid up to the dock, and dozens more bone-men were climbing out. Corpses lay in a jumble across the harbour, scattered like thrown dice. The citizens' clothes were different colours – a few were naked or in nightshirts, hauled out of their beds.

All Giulia could think was *Don't look this way. For God's sake, don't look over here.*

The undead were ransacking the houses around the waterside. A few had skin, like old parchment. One wore a cuirass, another had a mail shirt, but the great majority were naked bone. She could see the water through their ribs.

Oh God.

Two emerged from a building, carrying a fishing net between them: a man thrashed in the net, entangled. He was shouting things, but terror turned his words to gibberish. A woman in a red dress and fur cape ran out of a house shrieking. One of the skeletons chased her, knocked her down and climbed on top, and its arm jerked up and down as it stabbed her to death.

Strange how they could move, a little piece of Giulia's mind thought. Why didn't they fall apart?

She ducked back into the alley, her mind spinning. Sepello was leaning against the wall, pistol lowered. His skin was the colour of wax. There was a wild glint in his eyes, as if there were screams trapped behind his face. He said, "We have to go."

The little voice in the back of Giulia's head was telling her that she hadn't really seen anything. It was a dream, a silly thought. She could stay here and look at the wall, close her ears and everything would be fine. Just wait here…

She nodded. Noises still came from the waterfront, but they were sounds of movement, not of killing. *They're searching the place.*

Sepello and Giulia retreated down the alley, back the way they had come. *Careful,* she told herself. *We're going to get out of here. Got to keep sharp.*

At the far end of the alleyway, a shadow flickered across the ground.

Giulia pressed herself against the wall. She saw the holes in the skeleton's shadow before the skinny body followed it: the impossible gaps between the ribs. It strode past the alley, skull facing forward, and was gone.

Sepello peered around the corner, looked back and shook his head. "They're in the road."

Giulia felt her chest constrict, felt panic start to push up from below. *We're cut off! What do we do now?*

She pointed to a doorway. "Through here. Maybe we can go through the houses."

A crash came from the waterside, like a cart being overturned. Giulia darted across the alley, to the door. "Keep a look out."

Sepello stood guard as she bent down. There was no lock on the little door. She turned the handle. It did not move.

Giulia stood up and squinted at the frame. "Shit!" she hissed. "It's bolted from inside."

Sepello closed his eyes as if in pain, then opened them.

"Can you break it open?" Giulia asked.

"They'll hear," he whispered back.

She looked at the alley walls. There were no window-frames to support her. If she stood on his shoulders she could get onto the roof – assuming that the roof would take her weight.

From the sound of it, the undead had started tearing the waterfront apart. Giulia remembered Hugh's stories of the war, of Inquisition men ripping up floorboards in their frenzy to find dissenters.

"Fuck it," Sepello said, and he brought his leg up and stamped into the door. His bootheel smashed into the wood just above the handle and he staggered backwards. The door shuddered. Giulia checked the alley – nothing, yet. Sepello kicked again. The door crashed open and he stumbled into the house, jabbing his pistol into the dark. Giulia took a deep breath and followed him.

It was small and dim inside. The room smelled of smoke and old blankets. "The bolt won't hold now," Sepello said. "Let's get the table—"

"Shush!" Giulia's hand flicked up and Sepello froze. It was only a very faint thing, a half-conscious suspicion, but as soon as he fell silent, she knew that it was true. "Someone's coming."

The first skeleton stepped over the threshold. A second followed. They saw Sepello sprawled across a chair at the far side of the room and strode forward to kill him.

Giulia leaned out from behind the door and shot the nearest skeleton in the head.

The bolt punched straight through its skull and it fell apart. Giulia kicked the door shut and Sepello was on his feet, big knife drawn, rushing forward. The second revenant was trapped inside. It lunged at Giulia, shortsword turned to slide between her ribs.

She dodged to the left. Sepello charged it from the flank. He jabbed its side with his knife and the thing flailed. He hooked his hand under the jawbone. "The neck! Get the neck!"

Giulia drew her stiletto and drove it under the revenant's chin, where the windpipe should have been. She felt resistance, as if she was pushing the blade into a ripe fruit, and then the bones dropped around her as though she had untied a bundle of sticks. Giulia and Sepello stood there, surrounded by a scattered mess of bones.

"Well," Sepello said, "we can fight them up close."

"And we can take them by surprise."

They carried a table across the room. It would hold the door closed, but it wouldn't take long for a determined attacker to shove it aside.

"We need to get to the horses," Sepello said. "Then we'll ride back to Astrago. This place is done for."

Giulia thought of the people dying on the waterfront, the woman in the red dress. Sepello was right, of course. There was no hope of saving anyone. "Out the back window, then."

On the far side of the little room was a shuttered window. Giulia put her eye to the crack between the shutters and felt a warm stripe of light on her face. She saw a corpse lying in a dusty street. Nothing moved. A long way away, a man was bellowing with rage. Perhaps it was the young captain of the guard, rallying his men. Or perhaps the captain had fled the town, just as they were about to do.

"Is it safe?" Sepello asked.

"I think so." She paused, listening, then opened the shutter a crack. She pushed it open smoothly and quietly, looked out and climbed onto the sill.

Giulia dropped into the road and Sepello passed her crossbow out. He sprang down after her, landing with a soft thump. "The main road's that way."

"Keep to the alleys. It's safer."

She led the way, ducking low. She scurried into a narrow gap between walls. It smelled of sewage. Something about the end of the passage was familiar, she realised. She'd been here before, somehow, not last night, but—

They looked at the front of the inn where they had stayed three nights ago. It hadn't been burned, or wrecked, but somehow it was dead, unfit for human use. From inside the inn came a slow, mournful cry, a heartbroken noise.

Fear closed around Giulia like a fist, chilling her, trying to hold her to the spot. She shielded her eyes with her hand.

A young man squatted in the dark of the doorway, over something that lay stretched out across the floor. The young man was the innkeeper's son, the simple lad who had demanded a penny for a second helping of stew.

As Giulia stood up, she heard the creak of cartwheels. She paused, uncertain, and Sepello grabbed her shoulder. "Careful."

They pulled back into the shadows, and watched.

A high-sided cart rolled into the square. A skeleton sat at the front, a blanket draped over its shoulders. There was a bag over the horse's head. The flanks had caved in, showing ribs like the bars of a cage. *It's so thin*, Giulia thought, and then she realised: *It's dead*.

From the inn came another cry of sorrow. The cart rolled on. It stopped before the inn.

Sepello crept to the edge of the alley. His face looked like tallow. The cart shook as something moved within it, out of view. A skeleton climbed down. Then another.

From inside the inn came another moan.

The skeletons had shortswords. One carried a shield as big as a door, the edges curved to protect its body. They turned towards the inn.

They're going to kill him, she realised.

"Follow me," Giulia said. She broke cover and ran into the sunlight. She dashed across the road and dropped down behind the cart. Sepello stopped next to her. He raised his hand and motioned, jabbing at Giulia and then himself: they would flank the undead, hitting them from either side of the cart.

She nodded. Sepello reached out and grabbed her arm, looked her in the eye. Then he let go and slapped her shoulder, hard, and he was up and moving and now Giulia was too. She rounded the edge of the cart, ready to fire, and suddenly there were bare feet to her right, the

152

dead pink feet of people heaped in the cart, and in that half-second she faltered and one of the skeletons turned and spotted her.

She fired. Her bolt hit its massive shield. Sepello grabbed the other skeleton from the side, pulled its head back and drove his knife through its neck. The blade punched between the vertebrae and it collapsed.

The other revenant braced itself and raised its shield. Giulia dropped her crossbow and drew her fighting-knife.

The skeleton raised its shortsword and pounded on the shield – three quick, hard blows. A moment's pause and the thin arm beat down again, three more.

"It's a signal!" Sepello cried, and he ran in. The undead whipped around and struck. Sepello staggered aside, cursing. Giulia looked at him, back to the skeleton, and a shape rushed out of the inn.

It was the innkeeper's son. He wailed with grief and fear and the skeleton spun on its heel and ran him through. He stared at Giulia over the undead's shoulder. There was nothing in his face except horror. He fell back onto the road, and the skeleton raised its arm to stab again.

Thunder blasted the air and the skeleton burst apart like a heap of leaves in a storm. Sepello stood five yards away. He lowered his gun. "It was calling the others," he said. "We've got to go."

The lad was not quite dead. Blood came out of his mouth with each breath. He looked at Giulia, understanding nothing except that the world had gone terribly wrong.

"He's done for," Sepello said.

Giulia felt embarrassed that he had spoken like that in front of the boy. She bent down beside him and tried to think of what to do.

She took his hand. "You'll be all right," she said. "It's all right." The lad made a choking sound. For a moment he looked straight at her. Then he died.

She got up from the body and turned and picked up her crossbow. She looked at the cart – *They'll put him in there, with all the others!* – and said, "Let's get the horses."

Sepello paused, looking down at the huge shield and the shortsword among the bones. He seemed to be trying to remember something. A memory stirred in Giulia's mind, very faintly. Then it was gone, and she turned back to him.

There was blood on his sleeve, rust-coloured against the brown leather. "You're hurt."

"It's not bad," he said quickly. "Come on."

They ran up the road towards the guardhouse. The midday heat pressed on her like a weight.

The guardhouse was still deserted. The door hung open. "Round the back," Sepello said.

As they ran around the side, Giulia heard noises. She stopped and loaded her bow. Beside her, Sepello readied his gun. His left sleeve was torn and bloody.

The stable door was open. In the dim light of the stable, a horse turned as someone tried to climb onto it. Giulia flexed her fingers, readied the bow – and Sepello strode straight in, gun held out before him like an accusing finger. "Hey! Get off my horse!"

A soldier looked around, his boot in the stirrup, and the angry response he'd been about to make dropped off his face. He climbed down and stepped back. Five nervous horses watched him.

Sepello grabbed the reins off him and led his horse outside. "Steal someone else's," he said. His face softened slightly, and he added, "You might as well. No-one's going to want them now."

"He's right," Giulia said. "They're all dead." She stepped past. "That one's mine."

Sepello took a couple of minutes getting his horse ready. The soldier stood to one side, his hands shaking. Giulia mounted up and looked down. The soldier smiled thinly at her. *He thinks we'd shoot him. Maybe Sepello would.*

Sepello gathered the reins. "Wait for me," the soldier said. "Please."

Giulia looked at the stable gates. She imagined the undead gathering outside, mustering their numbers to attack. "Be quick," she replied.

Sepello stared at her: not accusing, just hard. The left sleeve of his coat was ripped and sticky with blood. He held his injured arm across his body, the fingers gripping the pommel of his saddle. By now, she reckoned, it would really be starting to hurt.

Giulia realised that the town was almost silent now. She could hear a heavy dragging sound to the west, as though someone was hauling a chest down the street. Perhaps they were looting the town for money. Or maybe they were loading the cart.

Bring out your dead. Like the plague.

It took the soldier four long minutes to join them. He untied the horses and left the stable door open. He rode out, and the two remaining horses wandered out after him.

They rode into the road. The hooves sounded deafening. Giulia glanced back into the town.

A single skeleton stood in front of a row of houses, completely motionless. It looked as if someone had drawn it onto the wall. Even without eyes, it was watching her. She shuddered. Sepello kicked his horse and cantered away, and Giulia followed.

They lost the soldier three miles up the road. Sepello slowed his big horse from a steady canter to a slow trot and said, "I need to sort this out." He meant his arm.

The soldier pretended not to hear. Giulia dismounted and Sepello climbed down beside her. Sepello watched the young man ride off. "I give it two hours before he lames that horse," he said.

Giulia looked over her shoulder.

"You think we're being followed?" Sepello asked.

"I can't see anyone. But let's keep moving, anyway."

They rode for two hours, keeping up a good pace. At last, Sepello slowed his horse. "Got to stop," he said. "I've got to see to my arm."

They led their horses off the road into the woodland. Deer had worn a thin track through the bushes. After fifty yards, the trees opened up into a little glade. Giulia took one last glance over her shoulder. "This ought to do," she said.

They stopped under a laurel tree and tied the horses up, surrounded by the smell of bark. Giulia watched the way they had come while Sepello began to remove his coat. She helped him slide it off, heard him hiss with pain as it dropped onto the ground. He reached over and tried to roll up his sleeve, but the blood had glued it to his arm.

"Damn it," he said, and he drew his knife and began to hack at his sleeve.

"Here," Giulia said. Her knives were sharper than his. She cut away the cloth just below his shoulder, poured a little water onto the blood to loosen it and gently slid the sleeve away. Sepello grimaced.

The cut was long but clean. The blade had sliced across his arm just below the shoulder, and as Sepello flexed his fingers fresh red blood welled out of the slit. "Shit," he said miserably.

"You need stitches," Giulia said. "Let's get it washed. I'll make you a sling."

Sepello looked down at his arm and grimaced. "There's a box in my saddlebag. It's got salves in it."

She paced across the clearing and rummaged in the bag. She looked over the horse's back, checking the woods. It was hard to see past the foliage. She wondered if the skeletons were clever enough to creep up on them.

The box was small and smelled faintly of perfume and spice, the sort of thing a nobleman might take on a long journey. Giulia carried it back and flipped the catch. Inside, there were half a dozen neat little bottles, each carefully stoppered, with a tiny label pasted to the side. "It's called Torment's Ease," Sepello muttered.

Giulia opened the bottle and passed it over. "Do you need me to—"

"I'll do it."

Very carefully, Sepello lifted the bottle and trickled the contents onto the wound. He moved his arm slightly, opening the cut a little. Suddenly, his face tightened, and he leaned to one side and kicked the tree beside him as if to knock it over. "Fuck, that hurts!" he gasped. "Ah, shit!" Slowly, Sepello's face relaxed, and he drew himself upright.

"That should do it." The pain had made him short of breath. "There might've been something on that sword. Poison, maybe. A lot of dirt. The salve should clean the wound. It won't hurt as much now, either." He looked at his arm. "I guess we know what happened to the people from Brancanza, then."

"Yes."

"I've never seen anything like that. Never. I mean, I've seen groups of the undead – but that many? There must have been fifty of those things on the dock. There's a bottle of Healing Hand in there: it's not got a label. Could you get it out, please?"

Giulia turned back to the medicine box.

"I can't believe it," Sepello said. "I really can't."

"I know." They were standing in a glade, in the middle of summer, with birds singing in the leaves above them. How could the dead walk in a place like this? It was impossible, surely, but then the sight of Leth standing over Hugh's body had been impossible too.

She unplugged the bottle and passed it to Sepello. "Here."

He raised the bottle and tipped it until a trickle ran onto the gash in his arm. It clearly hurt to do so, but not as much as applying the Torment's Ease had done. Sepello's face uncreased, and he set the bottle down. "That should seal it for now. It'll need more work when we get back."

"I'm sure you'll be fine," Giulia replied, uncertain how true that was. "You'll just have to lay off the duelling for a week or two." She stoppered the bottle and put it back in the case.

Giulia leaned against the tree and sighed. "I think we ought to go back to the city."

"You're right," Sepello replied. "There's no way that I'm going back into Paraldo, not without more people. You'd need half an army to clear that place out."

Giulia said, "The same thing's happened to Brancanza, hasn't it?"

"I reckon so. The undead must have just rowed in on boats, blocked the harbour off and moved up through the town. Then, last night, they did the same to Paraldo."

She didn't want to say it, but it had to be said. "That cart we saw, outside the inn. It was full of bodies. They were collecting them, weren't they?"

"I think so."

"Are they going to… turn them into more skeletons? Could Leth do that?"

Sepello shook his head. "I don't know. They don't usually do that. I— I don't know what Leth's powers are, how much he can do before he runs out of magic. They say he's the greatest necromancer in history."

Giulia said, "He's got a load of dragons' teeth."

Sepello closed his eyes, as if in pain. "He can't do that. I'm sure he can't. I mean, if Leth could raise the whole of Brancanza to do his bidding, that'd be two thousand walking skeletons."

"Four thousand now," Giulia replied, and as Sepello stared at her she added, "Paraldo *and* Brancanza."

Sepello looked down at the grass. "I suppose so."

He flexed his arm cautiously, as if he was not quite sure what its purpose was. He picked up the shirtsleeve. "Can you help me cut this up? We can boil it up for a bandage."

"Certainly. Then I'll find some wood and we'll start a fire – if you think it's safe, that is."

Sepello stared off into the trees. "It'll be safe. I don't think they'll come this way."

"Do revenants need light to see?"

"Most of the time. But they don't need as much as us."

"Maybe we should go on watch. Take turns."

Sepello said, "You should get some rest. I don't think I'll be sleeping much tonight."

"Me neither."

Giulia woke just after dawn. She sat up, her shoulders aching from the ground, and shivered in the morning air. Sepello was a silent lump of shadow.

Somewhere behind her, birds were tweeting, as if in argument. The forest was waking up, the night creatures creeping away while the deer and birds came alive, like two shifts of the Watch switching over. The world seemed safe here, reliable.

As Giulia pulled her blanket around her shoulders, she wondered if any of the day before had really happened. It felt like a bad dream, a nightmare inspired by a hellfire sermon. But it was real, sure as anything. She remembered the scene at the end of the alley, framed by walls and shadow: a skeleton stabbing a woman as she tried to crawl away.

The undead were out there, and they were close. Only the good things seemed a long way off: Sethis' kind voice, and safety behind the city walls.

Giulia clambered to her feet and ran her hands through her hair. It was time to get moving.

Chapter 6

On the scaffolding around the new library, three workmen were about to have their lunch. They lowered a basket down on a rope, and a couple of women loaded it up with bread and ale. One of the workmen said something and pointed up to the brass weathervane, showing a dragon holding up an hourglass, and even through the thick window Giulia thought she could hear them laugh.

She sat in a side room, waiting to speak to the prince and his closest colleagues. There had been no time to return to her lodgings: Giulia and Sepello had gone straight to the Quincunx Palace to give their report. Prince Mavlio's doctors had quickly stitched and bandaged Sepello's wound and, as soon as the bandages were tied, he had been taken to the prince. Explaining what had happened seemed to be a man's job, but it hadn't excused Giulia from being required to sit here for the past hour and a half.

The door opened and a servant looked in. "May I fetch you a glass of wine, madam?"

"Please."

He returned a few minutes later. Giulia was disappointed to find that he hadn't brought the bottle. "Do you know if they'll call me soon?"

The servant shook his head. "I'm afraid not, madam. If you require anything else…" The man retreated from view.

She stood at the window, sipping her wine. Astrago still looked unreal, with its busyness, its high towers and its neat, straight roads.

The door handle rattled and turned. Giulia started, managed to spill a little wine on the tiled floor, and stood up, wondering what to do with her glass.

The figure in the doorway was a head shorter than she had expected.

"Princess Carmina." Giulia curtseyed.

"Oh, don't worry about that," said Carmina DeFalci. "Really."

She looked more alert than Giulia remembered. Carmina had bright, quick eyes, and a friendly, crooked smile. "You're supposed to be going to the New Hall. It struck me that you probably don't know where that is."

"I don't, I'm afraid."

"Come with me, I'll show you. Come along," Carmina added, like a man telling his dog to follow. "You can bring your wine."

They walked together down the corridor. A single guard followed them: a tubby man who looked unusually ineffectual for one of Mavlio's men. Giulia wondered what you said to a princess. Did someone like Carmina watch plays, or drink, or ever leave the palace at all? Perhaps she read books. Giulia walked a pace behind Carmina. The princess' skirts hissed softly on the floor.

"Left here," Carmina said.

"Thank you, Princess."

"You don't have to call me that, not while there's no other people around."

"Oh. Well, thank you anyway. It's a big building. It must be hard not to get lost."

"You get used to it," Carmina replied.

God, Giulia thought, what must it be like to live in a palace: always guarded, always supervised? The world was a strange place: either you were dirt-poor and no-one cared what you did because it would never matter, or you were rich and lived behind locked doors and bodyguards, forever grubbing up to your superiors. There had to be some alternative, some way of neither starving nor having to grovel, but she was damned if she knew what it might be.

"Do you know, we have eight chapels here," Carmina said. "And you know what else is interesting? They say the foundations of the palace date back to Quaestan times. Of course, Father's had a lot changed. Cosimo rebuilt the palace almost from scratch after Prince Diello was overthrown and House Sciata was driven out. This way!"

They headed down a broad wooden staircase. It reeked of polish. At the bottom a small, fat woman was clearing away her cleaning tools.

The corridor was wide and well-lit. "We can cut through here," Carmina announced, as though they were embarking on an adventure. She opened a door and motioned Giulia into a library.

All four walls were covered in books. They stretched eight feet to the ceiling. Rows of shelves had been erected in the centre of the room. It smelled of dust and old smoke. The carpet was soft and thick.

"You know," Carmina said, "we have over a thousand books in the palace. It's one of the biggest collections of books on the peninsula. Only the great libraries have more."

"I didn't know there *were* a thousand books," Giulia said, and Carmina laughed. Giulia smiled.

"I spend a lot of time here," Carmina said. "Do you know how to read?"

"Yes, I do. I like reading."

"You could read here, I suppose, if you're careful with the books. I like this picture," Carmina added, pointing to one of the few sections of wall not covered by bookcases. The painting showed a woman in a white robe reading from a tablet to a group of other women. The background was full of broken columns. "It's called *The Poetess*," Carmina explained.

"Lovely," Giulia said.

"Isn't it?" Carmina replied, and they went through to the next room.

It was an octagonal hall, the walls painted white. A table stood in the centre of the room. Books were piled on the table, and a set of jointed metal arms was clamped to its edge. Each arm ended in a large lens. It made Giulia think of the tools that the dwarrow clockworkers used. That reminded her that she needed to speak to Sethis, to let him know what had happened at Brancanza.

"Here we are!" Carmina announced, motioning towards a chair. "The New Hall. Do sit down."

A large painting hung over the fireplace. It showed a procession of some kind, perhaps a pagan celebration. A robed man stood on the back of a chariot, gesturing towards a huge white building in the background. Bullocks and wagons followed the chariot. Behind that were bearded, savage-looking men, chained together and guarded by soldiers.

Wait. I know that symbol. "Princess?"

Carmina had been messing about with candles at the edge of the room. "Yes?"

"That picture up there. What's it of, please?"

"That?" Carmina seemed surprised. "Um, a triumph, I suppose. Quaestan, I think."

"May I?" Giulia asked and, when Carmina shrugged, she walked over and peered at the engraved title fixed to the picture frame.

164

The triumph of Scorpio Moroccus. The title meant nothing to her, but he looked like an ancient of some kind – a king, perhaps. That was unimportant, though. What mattered were the men at the edge of the picture, guarding and prodding the captives. They wore metal armour made of overlapping plates, and carried short swords and huge shields like curved doors.

Just like that skeleton had, outside the inn.

"How old is this, please?"

Carmina took a deep breath. "Well, it was painted when I was about ten, so I suppose—"

"I mean the people in the picture."

"They're Quaestans. So it must be…" Carmina frowned. "Well, about a thousand years ago, maybe?"

The doors opened at the far end of the room. Sepello entered, followed by Prince Mavlio, Cosimo Lannato and a slim man with a neat, pointed beard.

Sir Francis Vale, the man from Albion.

Giulia turned and curtseyed. Sepello's arm was in a sling.

"It's good to see you again, Madam Degarno," Mavlio said. "Please feel free to speak your mind, without fear of repercussion. We're all on the same side, after all."

"Thank you, Prince Mavlio," she said.

The men pulled chairs back and took places around the table. Carmina sat down a little way back, and Giulia followed her example.

"Master Sepello has been telling us about what happened," Mavlio said. "That two towns have been wiped out by the risen dead. Am I correct in thinking that's right?"

"Yes." She glanced around the room. "That is, there may have been a few survivors. But not many."

"I gather that you encountered some new kind of undead. From what I understand, morts tend to stumble around like people in a dream. But these were walking skeletons, and they were quick and organised."

"That's right," Giulia replied. "These were something else. They moved fast, as fast as living men."

"A lot of people would doubt your story," Mavlio said. "They'd say you were mad, or that you had made it all up in order to trick me into giving you money. I have a lot of enemies, you know. They'd like to make a fool of me by having me run after some cock-and-bull story about skeletons marching around." He swallowed, as if it was hard to continue. "But I think you're right. I think the undead either killed or kidnapped everyone in Brancanza. The question now is how we respond. First, we need to know where these things are coming from."

"It's Leth," Giulia replied. "He's an alchemist: he must be making them."

"I agree. Now, Master Sepello is wounded." Mavlio smiled his thin smile. "He may say otherwise, but he's in no state to be out in the countryside. I wouldn't send a man against a monster like Leth unless he was in the best of health, and he is not. So, until Leth is found and destroyed, Sepello will be acting as an advisor. If there's any fighting to be done, my guards will do it."

Giulia glanced at Sepello. He looked grim. "Thank you, Prince Mavlio."

"As for you, Madam Degarno, while you were out the room, we've been discussing your work over the last few days. Master Sepello has presented me with a glowing report. He assures me that few men could have conducted themselves as well as you did."

"Thank you, Prince Mavlio." *And…*

"Until Sepello is ready to take over again, you will be his chief man – or perhaps I should say woman – in the field. You will, of course, have no direct command over any of my troops, or anyone else for that matter. You'll follow Sepello's instructions to the letter. Should you require further assistance, you will inform him before seeking to involve anyone else. But should there be any, ah, difficulties, I will make sure that you receive the same help that Sepello would do."

Mavlio looked around slowly, as if trying to find something hidden in their faces. He gestured to Francis Vale. "Sir Francis shares our interest in defeating Constantin Leth and has been doing some investigations of his own. Now is the time to pool our findings. Sir Francis, would you be so kind?"

"Gladly, Prince Mavlio." Vale shifted in his chair and leaned forward, as if to whisper.

Giulia settled back in her seat and took a sip of wine. *Now, this might be interesting. Tell us what you know, Ambassador.*

Vale was a courtier, which Giulia took to mean "spy". His duties, he explained, included visiting other countries and – on an informal basis – deciding whether they were suitable for alliance before reporting back to Queen Gloria. He also dealt with more... sensitive issues, things that had to be done quietly. He looked around the table, as if everyone knew just what he meant.

Some months ago, a group of criminals had been planning to steal a magical treasure from the city of Clados, which was the capital of Plennyd. From the way Vale spoke, Giulia couldn't work out whether Plennyd was part of Anglia or a separate country. Whatever it was, it contained many magical treasures. One of them was a cauldron said to be able to raise the dead.

Vale had intercepted the plotters' correspondence. He had captured the conspirators and questioned them. The plotters had – after some encouragement – informed him that they worked for Leth.

"Their leader told me that Leth was collecting items that would help him to raise large numbers of undead at once," Vale explained. "He told me that Leth was coming home. He was paying criminals to bring alchemical supplies to Astrago. Unfortunately, Leth's man never told me any more than that. His heart gave out under the – ah – pressure of the conversation. I thought I should pass on a warning to you."

As Vale spoke, Giulia wondered what he might be holding back. Why had he come to Astrago in person, when a messenger would have sufficed? And if all he had meant to do was to warn Mavlio about Leth, why was he still here?

"Thank you," Mavlio said. "Sepello: what do you make of that?"

Sepello frowned. "I hate to say this, but I believe that Leth is trying to make an army of the dead. First, there were the dragons' teeth that we found in the alchemical workshop in the docks. It's well known that they act as an accelerant to spells of necromancy. This cauldron you mention, Sir Francis, would serve much the same purpose."

"Indeed," Vale said grimly.

"We – Giulia, really – was able to stop one shipment of dragons' teeth from reaching Leth. But the records in the docks said that the *Comaru* has come to Astrago several times before. Who knows how many shipments got through before we prevented it?

"And that's not all," Sepello added. "In Paraldo, Giulia and I saw the skeletons collecting the dead citizens in carts. There's only one conclusion to be drawn. Leth is trying to raise large numbers of revenants. It is possible that, by now, Leth will have turned the citizens of Brancanza and Paraldo. That gives him a potential force of four thousand revenants."

Vale pinched the bridge of his nose and closed his eyes. He looked up and took a slow, deep breath. "I see."

Lannato leaned over and whispered to Carmina: she opened one of the books at a map of the Peninsula.

"Four thousand isn't much of an army, as I understand it, but it's a substantial raiding force." Sepello said. "I doubt that Leth could take your own army on, especially since he won't be able to get hold of cavalry and gunpowder. However, that many revenants could easily raid other towns, in order to get more soldiers." Sepello drew his hand across the map. "Maybe Leth wants to launch more raids along the coast, to swell his numbers – that would be my first plan, if I was him. But, as you can see, there aren't that many other towns to choose from between Paraldo and here. Everywhere else is inland. If he's still using boats to attack, he can either go west down the coast, in which case he's looking at fifty miles or more before he finds another town worth the taking, or he can go east."

"Which brings him here," Mavlio said.

"I'm no general, but neither option seems very good," Sepello added. "Heading west brings Leth almost nothing, and going east takes him straight to Astrago. And this must be one of the best-defended cities on the Peninsula."

"*The* best," Lannato put in. "If you don't mind me saying so."

Mavlio looked at his daughter. "What do you think, Carmina?"

She peered at the map. "So neither east nor west is good for Leth. What would happen if he sent his men – his revenants, I mean – inland?"

"Well," Sepello replied, "I don't think it would help him much. Say he advances through the countryside. You can't move four thousand living men without people noticing, let alone the sort of monstrosities that he's using. Whichever way he goes, there'd be a bow wave of people fleeing the area, and we'd hear about it. Leth would lose the advantage of surprise, and no doubt you'd send an army to meet him. As I say, four thousand fighters isn't that much, even if they are undead."

"Four thousand," the prince repeated. He shook his head sadly. "God almighty." He looked up. "You said you killed one of these skeletons, Sepello?"

"We killed several," Sepello replied, "although 'destroyed' is a better word for it. They died as easily as men, pretty much. When they took enough damage, they fell apart."

"So they could be beaten by a conventional force." Mavlio stared at the map. "Correct me if I'm wrong, but it seems Leth is in an awkward position here. His force is currently too small to be a serious threat to any determined army, and too large to go undetected. So, his options are limited. Either he hides the revenants that he's already got, acquires new minions from somewhere, or attacks us immediately. And if he attacks immediately, he'll lose. Am I right?"

"I think so," Sepello said. He folded his arms and said, "But Leth is very crafty. He won't throw his fighters away. If he thinks that he needs to wait, he will – and the undead can wait forever."

"The longer he waits, the more men I can mobilise," Mavlio replied. "As it stands, time is against him. Unless he goes to ground very quickly, he's exposed. And if he does go to ground, he'll have to find somewhere to stash his forces." He looked around the table. "I suggest we go after him now. Strike while the iron's hot."

"It would take a while," Sepello said. "You'd have to find him first, track his movements. And if he's using boats to move his revenants, that could be difficult."

The prince smiled. "Easily done. Cosimo?"

Lannato pushed his chair back, the legs squeaking on the marble. "We've got two flying machines available. I can have them both ready to fly in a day's time. We can use them to travel along the coastline. We'll be able to see Leth's soldiers from the air."

Flying machines? Giulia felt a tremor of fear. *Shit, I hope you're not expecting me to go on something like that.* Flying through the air was unnatural: something for wyverns and birds. *But then, if it's what it takes to find Leth...*

"Good," Mavlio added. "That's what we'll do. Each flying machine will take a group of palace soldiers. If we catch Leth on his own, or with just a few of these revenants, we'll go straight in and put an end to him. If he's with a bigger group, then we'll head back to the city and send out the troops. Does anyone have any objections?"

Giulia raised her hand.

Sepello said, "It sounds good to me. In terms of the way we hunt the undead, it makes a lot of sense. Of course, I'm no military expert. I'm used to dealing with smaller groups of revenants. I don't think there's been this many undead in one pack for... I don't know. Maybe not since the days of Saint Cordelia."

Lannato said, "I'd suggest sweeping out, covering the coastline and then working inland. Each flying machine will watch out for the other. You'd need to stay fairly close, so you could signal if you saw anything."

"Good thinking," Mavlio replied.

Giulia said, "Prince Mavlio?"

"May I add something?" Vale asked. "I have fifty marines at my disposal: a personal guard who accompanied me from the embassy in Pagalia. These men are experts in boarding actions and ship-to-ship work – basically, in close-quarter fighting. I'd like to put them forward for the scouting work you describe."

Mavlio paused. Giulia watched the prince's tight, smiling face, realising what was going on behind it. He was weighing up the options, working through the possible results in his mind like a gambler about to throw down a card. She remembered something she'd heard from Nicolo One-Hand, her first tutor in thievery: *The best gamblers hardly ever trust to luck.*

"Why not?" Mavlio said. "That sounds like an excellent idea."

"Splendid. Thank you." Vale's face was not built for smiling. *Probably a Purist*, she thought. Hugh had always said that there were a lot of extreme New Churchers in Albion.

Carmina nudged her father. "I think Giulia wants to say something."

"Ah," Mavlio said. He turned to look at Giulia. "Did you want to speak?"

"Yes. Some of the" – it sounded absurd, in this warm, cultured room – "the walking skeletons we saw had big shields, like Quaestans. They had short swords as well, like the soldiers in that picture above the fireplace."

"Oh yes?"

Vale looked vaguely disgusted. "What are you implying?"

She looked at Sepello. "Leth's old, isn't he? Hundreds of years old?"

He nodded. "Yes."

"Old enough to have lived back then?"

"Very likely."

Giulia looked at Vale. "Sir Francis just said that when he, er, questioned those robbers in Plennyd, they said that Leth was coming home. The Peninsula is home to him, isn't it?"

Nobody replied. Prince Mavlio shifted in his chair. When he spoke, his voice was flat, calm, serious. "Yes," he said.

"If Leth's trying to keep out of sight for now, he'll need a hiding place. Somewhere he can stay out of sight, gather his forces, make his plans. Right?"

"Right," Sepello said. "A lair."

"Are there any old Quaestan buildings near here?"

The prince glanced at his daughter. "Carmina, could you turn the map around?"

She rotated the map and pushed it over. Carmina pointed. "There are some ruins nearby, Father. Maybe we should look at them."

Sepello nodded slowly, approvingly.

"Ruins, Prince Mavlio?" Vale sounded doubtful. "How would four thousand undead hide in a ruin?"

Giulia said, "Not all of them. Just Leth."

"Well," Mavlio said, "there are three large sets of ruins in the principality. Leaving aside a couple of Questan buildings in Astrago itself, there are Portia and Virtulania near the northern border, and Oppidium about fifty miles west." He rubbed his smooth chin thoughtfully. "Virtulania isn't ten miles from here. It's a ruin, very picturesque but useless to anyone. Painters take their students there to learn how to draw in the classical style. You've been there recently, haven't you, Cosimo?"

Lannato nodded. "It's pleasant enough, but there's nothing much there. Portia and Oppidium are much more substantial. They were big towns, almost cities."

Giulia said, "What happened to them?"

"They collapsed," the philosopher replied. "The ground swallowed them up. Personally, I'd put my money on an earthquake, but nobody knows why. I've heard people blame it on the dwarrows or on huge worms, digging up under the foundations. Some say they went the same way as Sorron in the Holy Codex, destroyed by God as a punishment for vice. Nobody knows for sure."

Giulia knew the story: she'd heard her fair share of angry sermons. God had blasted the city of Sorron off the face of the earth when he discovered its citizens dabbling in buggery. God didn't like buggery.

Mavlio looked at Sepello and raised his eyebrows. "Well?"

"It's worth checking," Sepello said. "In this line of work, everything is."

The prince looked at Carmina. "What do you think?"

"I agree," Carmina said. "I think we should look at the ruins. That's how you hunt an animal, isn't it? You block off all the places it can hide, force it into the open."

Mavlio grinned. "Well said. I agree with my daughter! My marines will go to Portia. Vale, your men will go to Oppidium. I'll make sure your steersman has a good map. You're on Vale's flyer," Mavlio added, looking at

Giulia. "And Sepello – you'll be with my men. Not fighting this time, though. Just giving advice."

"As you wish, Prince Mavlio," Sepello replied.

Carmina smiled. Her smile was unlike her father's: it made her look less devious, more like a friend. The right man would have found her very attractive.

Mavlio slapped his hand down on the table. "Right then, we have a plan. Leth has stuck his head above the parapet: now we have a chance to cut it off. We'll leave the day after tomorrow, at first light." His chair scraped on the tiles as he stood up. The others rose up around him; Giulia got to her feet. "Our work against Leth will remain completely secret, as before. Madam Degarno, I'll need you to stay here tonight. Master Sepello, would you come with us for a moment, please?"

Giulia curtseyed and waited for the others to leave the room. Vale was the last to depart. "Goodbye, madam," he said, and his eyes were hard and keen, as though he was trying to look straight through her. He turned and left.

The door closed and Giulia was on her own. She sat down. The room seemed very empty, the walls cold and dead. She thought about the white walls of Pasaldo, the impossible sight of a skeleton walking up an alleyway, as implacable as clockwork.

She glanced at the door, wondering if some spy – or Mavlio himself – was at the keyhole, watching for disloyalty.

The big clock at the far end of the room said that it was half past five. She had time to slip into the city, to buy new bolts and thieves' tinder, and to pray at the chapel where she'd first met Sepello. She needed to seek the help of Saint Cordelia as well as Saint Senobina. And while she was in town, she would give the dwarrows an

175

urgent message for Sethis, telling him to meet her tomorrow.

Plans within plans, she thought, and she wondered what the others really had in mind.

*

Giulia leaned back in her chair and watched the evening begin outside. There was a small table under the window, which held a tall glass and a bottle of what she suspected was fairly decent wine.

Her room wasn't much by palace standards, but it still felt large and exceptionally clean. There was even a clock mounted on the far wall, whose ticking was going to keep her awake if she didn't go to sleep half-drunk. *Better get on with it*, then. She poured out another glass.

Giulia had slipped out and left a message with the dwarrows at the clockworking shop. Tomorrow night, she'd meet with Sethis and update him. God only knew what he'd make of it all. She was drawing closer to Leth, but that meant involving others: Sepello, Mavlio, and now Vale. More dangers, more ways for it all to go wrong.

She stood up and paced the room. Now that the prince's soldiers were involved, Leth could be dead by the end of next week. She sipped her wine.

She doubted that it would be that simple. At times like this, with hours to kill and not enough drink to send her to sleep, she knew that there would always be another hurdle to jump, another obstacle to clear before she would be free to live normally again.

Stop it. Soon you'll have Leth. And as she finished off the glass she wondered, *And what then? Who'll be next on the list of enemies to polish off? This is a waste*, she thought. *Everything I've done has been a waste.*

176

She put the glass down. The Melancholia was rising: she needed to distract herself. She had Hugh's copy of *The Sorrowful Death of Alba the King* in her bags, but that would just make her think of him. Giulia remembered the library downstairs, the one Carmina had led her through. Mavlio wouldn't mind if she borrowed a couple of books. For one thing, she was his guest. And, for another, he wouldn't have the chance to mind, because he wouldn't know.

Giulia left her room. The corridor was dim, lit by a single lamp. She walked towards the stairs, her boots quiet on the carpet. The smell of roast pork seeped up from the kitchens, as though a banquet was being held in silence down below.

The stairs barely creaked as she descended. Halfway down, she heard footsteps beneath her, and froze.

She drew back into the shadow of the banisters, and a young guard crossed the hall and opened a side door. He disappeared from view.

Giulia crept down after him. She paused for a moment at the bottom of the stairs, listening, wondering what would happen if she was caught.

The corridor had a high ceiling and ornamental columns down the sides. In a niche, a fat stone child was wrestling with an eagle: no doubt the sculpture portrayed some ancient legend or other.

A couple of lanterns lit the corridor, throwing deep shadow into the recesses. Did princes impose curfews in their own homes? It would not have surprised her, especially here.

She kept on going, ducked past a statue and reached the library door. As she touched the handle, she heard voices.

"Yes, I remember it myself. 'All Bergania is divided into three parts' – not the sort of thing I'd expected, personally." *Lannato*. His voice was less flippant-sounding than the prince's, more thoughtful, kinder. "Still, it makes a change from all that poetry." Lannato grunted with exertion. "Here we are. It's a good copy, this: Gossberg press, I believe."

Giulia ducked down and put her ear to the keyhole.

Carmina's voice did not carry well. "Thank you."

"Goodness knows what you're looking to find in it. It's hardly good reading for ladies. Still, if you want to see plotters coming, I suppose there's worse people to study than Yullicus." Giulia frowned, trying to think where she'd heard that name before. "Just remember," Lannato said, "Yullicus trusted the wrong man, and we know what happened to *him*." He put on a deep orator's voice. "'You too, Stultus?'" he cried, and Carmina laughed as he faked a cough. Giulia recognised the quote: she'd seen a play about it a few years ago. Yullicus had been an ancient warlord, stabbed by his own jealous minions.

Lannato sighed. "You always have to know who to trust," he said, and there was no laughter in his voice any more. "Always know who to trust, and always be discreet. That's what's kept me safe all these years. And if you find you've trusted the wrong man – then it's time to start taking your father's advice."

Giulia looked over her shoulder, at the darkened corridor. *Nobody there except the statues.* She thought of the house where Hugh had died, the marble girl screaming at nothing.

Carmina's voice: "Will it always be like this?"

"Maybe not forever. Now, come along. I'll take the book—"

Giulia heard his boots on the library floor. The realisation dropped in her like a rock: he was close, much closer than she'd thought. In ten steps he'd reach the door, maybe five –

She turned and ran back down the corridor. Giulia bounded from rug to rug across the hall so that her boots wouldn't make any noise. She reached the stairs and dropped into the dark. Carmina and Lannato stood outside the library, almost silhouetted. Giulia ducked down and crept back up the stairs.

Slipping away the next morning proved harder than she'd expected. The palace seemed to be clogged with a sudden influx of guards, their striped uniforms giving them the look of acrobats waiting to be sent on stage. Giulia watched them from her window, then cautiously made her way downstairs.

She ate with Sepello in a servants' hall. They sat at the same long table as a group of craftsmen. The craftsmen leaned in and talked quietly, as if they were plotting something. Sepello's arm was still bandaged and in a sling.

Giulia tore off a lump of bread. She bit into it, chewed it. "This is good."

"They bake it here. The palace has got its own ovens."

"Very handy. Especially for getting rid of the evidence."

Sepello looked shocked for a moment, and then chuckled. "Well, today they're getting ready. Vale's bringing up his marines, Lannato's getting the flying machines sorted out... and you and I get to sit around and wait."

He reached across the table, and Giulia broke off a piece of bread for him. "Lucky us. How's your arm?"

"It doesn't hurt much, but it's a fair way from being healed. I'm being careful. I've got mixtures upstairs to help speed up the healing. It'll be fine, given time, but for now I might as well not have the damn thing. Pass the small beer, would you?"

Giulia poured out two cups. "Sepello, what do you think of it here?"

"In the palace?" He sipped his beer. "I think keep quiet and busy, and you'll be fine. Let's talk about this upstairs. I've got something for you in my room."

Sepello's chamber was bigger than hers and considerably more lavish. She sat in the ante-room while he opened a travelling-chest on a table beside his bed. He moved the chest so she couldn't see the lock; she wondered if he was doing it on purpose.

"Here we are," he said, slamming the lid down. He produced a tiny bottle and a brown leather strap, and put them on a table next to a statue of a hawk.

"Here. Drink some of this." He handed the bottle over.

"What is it?"

"We call it Bitter-blood in the Order. If you die, it'll stop anyone raising you from the dead. The revenants do that for spite sometimes. I guess it amuses them to see their worst enemies marching in their ranks."

Giulia opened the bottle and took a cautious sniff.

"It's safe," Sepello added. "Leave some for me."

"How long does it last for?"

"One sip is good for a few days."

She took a cautious sip and passed it back. It was bitter and sour at once, and clung to the roof of her mouth with the consistency of cream. "Shit, that's nasty."

Sepello finished the little bottle. "I always forget how bloody awful it tastes. And this is for you to wear," he added, passing her the strap.

It was a mastiff's collar, wider than usual. Giulia accepted the thing warily. It smelled of grease, like old riding gear. "It goes around the neck," he explained.

"I realise that. I just wondered why you wanted me to wear a dog collar, that's all."

"The undead tend to go for the big veins, the way wolves do. It'll stop any of them biting through. I wear one under my shirt when I'm in the field."

Giulia rolled it up and put it in her bag. "Well, if I didn't look like an old hound before, now I really will."

Sepello paused.

"You did a good job back in Brancanza," he said. "Really. There's not many people I know outside the Order who could have pulled that off."

"Thank you," she replied, trying to swallow away the rest of the unpleasant taste. She lowered her voice. "Listen, what do you think of all this?"

He rubbed his hand over his chin. He needed to shave. "Mavlio you can trust so long as you're on his side. Cross him, and you'd be in a lot of trouble."

She nodded, and waited.

"Lannato's a good man, from what I've heard, but he doesn't deal in politics. And as for Vale – he's new to me. I can't say I trust him, but I hardly know the fellow. Still, they all want Leth, so they can't be all bad…"

"That's what I thought." She wanted to say more – and checked herself. What was the point of telling Sepello to watch his back? You didn't go killing revenants without knowing who to trust. And maybe *he* couldn't be trusted, either. Fine, she'd fought beside him, but what did that really mean? All that stuff about not knowing a man until you'd fought at his side was tavern-talk, brothers-of-the-sword shit that mercenaries said to sound tough.

"I'll see you later," Giulia said. "I need to get ready for tomorrow." She looked around the room. The palace was starting to feel like a prison. "Right now, I could do with a change of scenery."

Sepello smiled. "To be honest, it's the change of scenery I'm not looking forward to."

Giulia left him in his room. She had business to conduct outside the palace.

She reckoned that Mavlio's guards would be reluctant to let her go into the city, at least without a chaperone. She waited until just before lunch-time, when the corridors were full of servants and the prince's family would be getting ready to eat. She slipped into the warren of service corridors and left the palace via a door behind the kitchens. It went so smoothly that she wondered if someone was following discreetly to see where she went.

She was relieved to be back in the town. It felt good to be a nobody again.

Giulia needed to get blessed: against a monster like Leth, the protection of the saints could be vital. The old priest let her into the chapel where Sepello had been staying. She knelt before the image of Saint Cordelia, and prayed to her and to Saint Senobina, patron of thieves. Between them, the two women surely understood Giulia's predicament.

Giulia checked that she wasn't being followed, then headed into the pagan district. The dwarrows at the clockwork shop had been expecting her, and they told her the address of a house in a street nearby. She thanked them and headed out, quick and discreet.

The house was in a district she always remembered as being full of poor artisans and religious dissenters: the sort of place where the most popular crime was heresy, closely followed by theft. Two women in black dresses and white headscarves talked by the side of the road: New Churchers, Giulia reckoned, and probably Purists. They made her feel uncomfortable: religious cranks seemed more alien than the fey folk. At least the dryads wanted to enjoy life: to Purists, sin and happiness were the same thing.

Giulia found the right building and climbed a set of narrow stairs to a third-floor apartment. She knocked four times on a narrow door and waited on a landing that smelled of dust.

Sethis opened the apartment door. He wore a white shirt and loose trousers. His spectacles were pushed up onto his forehead: an oddly human thing to do. "I'm afraid I'm not at my smartest," he said, ushering her inside.

She walked in and closed the door behind her. It looked like a lot of hired apartments: neither dingy nor luxurious, clean-swept and impersonal. "How is everything?" she asked.

"Oh, the same as ever. Arashina's a bit difficult, but she's very keen. I've got some wine," Sethis said. "It's not great stuff, but it'll do."

"You shouldn't tell me that until I've drunk it. I wouldn't recognise the good stuff anyway."

Giulia walked to the window and looked out at the street. Across the way, four young men lounged against a wall, playing dice. One of them glanced up and she pulled back, out of sight. "You know those lads throwing dice outside?"

"Giulia, I've only been here a few days. They're probably just wasting time. Apprentices , I suppose."

"Be careful, Sethis. There's always some fucking arsehole trying to stir up trouble for you people." Her voice sounded coarse and angry. She regretted cursing in front of him. "Just be careful, that's all."

"That makes a change. It's usually me who says that to you."

She glanced around and made herself smile at him. *They could be working for Leth*, she thought, and she felt anger start to form inside her. *If they are, then—* A little surprised by the rage she felt about nothing at all , she pulled a chair over and sat down. *Don't be absurd.*

Sethis passed her a cup and took a seat on the other side of the little table. "So," he said, "tell me what's happened."

Giulia told him about the visit to Brancanza, and then about the skeletons. It felt like recounting some wild, awful dream. She described Sepello's injury and their return to the palace, the conference with Mavlio, and Vale volunteering the use of his men. She did not tell him about the conversation that she'd overheard between Lannato and Carmina. It felt too vague to be of use.

Sethis listened carefully, his head tilted to one side in that thoughtful, birdlike way of his. When she stopped, he remained silent. After nearly a minute, he looked up and said, "And that's it, then?"

"Yes," Giulia replied. "That's it." She sat back. "You think the revenants will march on the city?"

"I don't know," he replied. "Your guess is as good as mine. They'll need more soldiers if they do. That means he'll need to raid more towns."

More soldiers. She thought of the people outside, going about their lives. *They don't know. Nobody knows.* She wanted to warn them – felt that it was her duty, somehow – but knew at once that it would be a waste of time. Nobody would believe her, and even if they did, what would people do apart from panic? And what would Mavlio do to her in response?

Voices filtered in from the road. Someone was selling oranges. A hammer bashed nails into wood. Giulia thought about the wedding that she and Sepello had seen on the way to Brancanza. What were those peasants doing now? Hopefully, they were still going about their lives – and not fleeing from the living dead.

"I'll report this back to Arashina," Sethis said. "It's the first time I've ever heard of such a thing happening. Maybe she'll know more about it, but I've never heard of undead like this."

Giulia said, "Let me know if she comes up with anything."

Sethis sipped his wine cautiously. "Giulia, what do Mavlio and Vale want from Leth?"

"To kill him, I suppose."

"Do you know why?"

She hadn't really thought about it. "I guess Mavlio sees it as his duty to destroy anything that threatens his people. As for Vale, well, he's some kind of New Churcher, probably a Purist. He probably sees it as a sacred task."

"I see." Sethis poured himself another cup, then offered the bottle to her.

"Thanks."

"People – humans – always wonder what they can get out of a creature like Leth," the dryad explained. "They forget that Leth is always asking the same question. Arashina thinks that only one of the fey could really understand that."

"Do you agree with her?"

"I think there are exceptions."

She reached across the table before she could think about it and squeezed his hand. "I'm one of them."

His long fingers closed around her hand and squeezed back, with a hard, constant strength. "I know."

She took her hand away. "No matter what, I'm going after Leth. I don't care who tries to stop me." Giulia felt anger and desperation rising within her. *Easy, girl.* She sipped her wine, made herself calm again. "Do you know anything about this Oppidium place, then?"

"A little. It was a town about a thousand years ago. I don't think it was much different to any other Quaestan town: well-supplied, prosperous... I think they did mining there. It would've been primitive compared to the sort of thing the dwarrows do but, if I remember rightly, they used to dig up tin."

"But it got destroyed, right?"

"Yes." Sethis took his glasses off, blew across the lenses and rubbed them on his sleeve. "What happened to it depends on who you ask. Some people say the slaves in the mine rebelled and collapsed it. I've heard others say your god blew the town to pieces to punish the citizens for, er, unnatural practices. In reality, it was probably subsidence."

"What's that?"

"Movement of the ground. I suspect they over-mined the place and the town collapsed into the tunnels under it."

"Do you think it'll be safe to go there?"

"Nothing involving Leth is safe," Sethis replied. "But you'll at least have a lot of soldiers with you. It seems rather a long shot to me," he added. "But perhaps there is a link to Leth there. Or maybe he just likes dressing his minions up as Quaestan soldiers. It's hard to say."

"So what would Oppidium be like now? Just a load of ruins?"

"Yes. Just a big heap of stone, if that. There might be a few columns still standing, but it's likely that it'll be either overgrown or the locals will have taken most of the stone for themselves. But that doesn't mean you shouldn't be careful."

"I will, don't worry about that. If there's anything there, I'll let you know." She stood up and said, "I've got the rest of the day to kill. There's probably a play on this evening, if you're interested."

Sethis shook his head. "I'm sorry. I've got a lot of work to do. For one thing, I need to find Arashina, and that's never straightforward." He stretched. "Besides, if I went to the theatre, people would probably think I was trying to burn it down."

"It's not that bad."

"Maybe not quite that bad, not these days. But I'd better not. Perhaps we can go when we're done with all this?"

"All right," she said, "we will. I'll hold you to that."

"Good luck tomorrow," he added, getting up. "Take care."

They embraced. Even in the city, he smelled of cut grass. "I wish I could help you more," Sethis said, stepping back. "I'll talk to Arashina about getting some good fighters together. Goodness knows there's enough of us who'd like to see Leth put down." For a moment his face was stern, almost vicious. It was the same hard face she'd seen at the House of Glass, back in Averrio. It was easy to see Sethis as weak – he might not be the most skilful fighter she'd met – but his determination could be frightening.

Outside, the little group of gambling youths had dispersed. Giulia still felt as if she was being watched. A thin young man walked down the road carrying a wad of pamphlets in his fist. As Giulia passed, he thrust a sheet of paper at her.

She took it and walked on, keen to leave the area. If there was anyone looking for her, she needed to lead them away from Sethis.

Going to watch a play with a dryad – ridiculous. It sounds like the sort of thing Breakshafte would put into one of his comedies. But it still sounded good.

Right now, there were more important things to consider. She wanted more crossbow bolts, a good whetstone for her knives and a fresh supply of thieves' tinder, so she'd need to visit the shops along Illuminary Way, and then stop off at old Kronda's black-market alchemy shop, assuming it was still there.

She turned right, ducked into a doorway and checked the road behind her, just in case.

Giulia pretended to study the pamphlet and looked along the street. Nobody stopped walking, nobody signalled to a friend to keep out of view. Either she was in the clear, or the prince's men had improved their tradecraft since the last time she'd been here.

The tract was so badly printed that it was almost illegible. The picture on the front showed a four-headed beast, coiling out of Hell on clockwork wings. The smaller heads seemed to represent a dwarrow, a natural philosopher, and a Purist in a broad-brimmed hat, but the main one was crowned, and could only be Mavlio. Giulia wondered who would be stupid enough to print such seditious stuff – a religious maniac, presumably. She folded the tract up and dropped it in the doorway. Best not to be caught with a thing like that.

She strode off down the street. There was a lot to do.

Chapter 7

Giulia got up before dawn and heard Mass in a small chapel with half a dozen staff members. Then she hurried back upstairs and armed herself. The big brass clock on the wall said it was a quarter to eight.

She slid her stiletto into the bracer on her left arm and looked out of the window, across the square. On the far side, two men were unloading rolls of cloth from a wagon. A woman was hanging clothes from her window. Two houses down, a door flew open and a young man stumbled out, as though his wife had thrown him into the road. Giulia smiled briefly. Normal life, the sort of life she didn't have. Ten to eight.

In an hour's time, I'll be flying through the air. God in Heaven, that's bad enough without the living dead at the other end.

She felt as if she'd drunk weak poison: a mixture of worry, fear and nervousness that seemed to run though her muscles. She took a few deep breaths, picked up her crossbow and headed downstairs.

Sepello stood in the east vestibule, talking to one of Mavlio's guards. The prince's man wore a breastplate with a high collar, and both knives and cartridges hung from his belt. He looked like an expert, more like an old street-fighter than someone plucked from a pristine row of soldiers. Giulia hoped that all her new colleagues would be that tough.

"Good morning, Giulia!" Sepello's arm was in a more rugged sling today, and he had rearranged his knife and pistol to compensate for the injury. "Good luck today. Your machine's in the courtyard at the back: it's called the *Resplendence*. I'm on the other one, the *Zephyrous*. We'll be heading out soon. I'm told the *Resplendence* is the smaller of the two fliers, but it's faster. You won't have such a long journey."

Well, that's something. "Good luck. And take care of yourself."

"You too," Sepello said. "May Saint Cordelia keep you strong."

"Thanks," Giulia said. "And may Saint Senobina keep you hidden."

She strode away. The two men started talking again.

Giulia turned the corner and saw a door open ahead. Sunshine glowed in the doorway, and she squinted as she emerged into the yard behind the palace.

The *Resplendence* was about forty feet from end to end. Jointed frames stuck out of the sides like huge fins, made of wooden poles connected with leather. Instead of a sail, a broad wooden spiral wound its way around the mast, like an apple peeling stretched out taut.

I thought it would be bigger than that.

Men swarmed over it. Sailors were strapping down loose cargo, tucking the ends of ropes out of the way. An engineer – not Lannato himself, but one of his men – was checking the wings with a brass instrument like a big sextant. A trapdoor hung open in the side of the flying machine, and a leather belt ran out onto a small windlass mounted on a tripod. Two men were furiously cranking the handles of the windlass, winding something up within the hull.

She approached. The craft looked no better at close range.

A stocky man was peering into the workings at the rear of the craft. He stood up, pulled a scarf down from his mouth and walked over to meet her. "You the woman?"

"Yes, I'm the woman."

"Carlo Torca. I steer the ship through the air. You know it's bad luck to have a woman on board?"

"I thought that was boats."

"This ship too. They say you're coming no matter what." Torca sniffed. "So you go to the hold and you sit tight, yes? No messing about."

"Aye-aye, captain. I'll be as quiet as a church mouse, unless I have to kill someone." Knowing that she irritated him made Giulia feel somewhat better. "Actually, I'm pretty quiet when I do that, too."

He scowled. "Just keep out of the way until we land."

"That's fine by me." Giulia walked up the gangplank and looked around. Being on board felt unnatural, even while the thing was still on the ground. She stepped aside to let one of the soldiers past. He wore a heavy brown coat under his cuirass, like an Anglian cavalryman.

On the far side of the ship, Vale leaned against the rails, checking the supplies against a piece of paper. He wore a long, black coat. He looked up and gave her a brief nod.

"Good morning, Sir Francis," she said, walking over to join him.

"Madam. You look… equipped. I assume you're joining us today?"

"Definitely." She looked over her shoulder. "Need any help with anything?"

"Not until we reach the ground. I'll tell you when you're needed." He seemed to soften slightly. "Sepello says that you're a good scout."

She nodded. "I used to work as a thief-taker. Then I worked freelance with a knight, Sir Hugh of Kenton. I've tracked people before."

"Hugh of Kenton. I know the name. He used to work at the embassy in Pagalia. A drunkard, if I remember rightly."

"You don't. He was a good man. Constantin Leth murdered him. That's why I'm here: to bring Leth to justice."

Vale looked surprised. "I'm sorry to hear that. Clearly I was mistaken. I hope today we'll avenge your friend. But you'll be taking orders from me, understand? Neither I nor my marines will look kindly on it if you do otherwise."

"Don't worry, you can trust me."

Vale seemed pleased. "I'm glad to hear it." He patted the railing. "Remarkable contraption, this."

"Let me know when we get there," Giulia said, and she climbed down the ladder into the hold.

Inside it was dim, poky, and smelled of tar and sap. There was enough room for a dozen men to sit. Giulia walked down the length of the hold. The low ceiling made her feel trapped. She took the seat at the end. Above, Vale shouted something, and people began to climb aboard. Boots thumped the deck above her. A big man clambered down into the hold, then another.

Vale's marines wore tough, customised gear, like soldiers who had looted a battlefield. More came in, climbing down the ladder until the hold was full. The soldiers put their muskets and swords on the floor, between their legs. They chatted, greeted one another, picked up conversations they'd left off outside. Their accents were not quite the same as Hugh's had been; their voices were more raucous, more aggressive. *They'd better not make a racket when we land.*

Vale entered the hold and the men quietened. He wore a breastplate over his coat. "We're ready to go!" he shouted at the sky, and he yanked the trapdoor shut. The sunlight was suddenly gone. Only a single lantern lit the hold.

A coffin made for twelve.

Behind her, in the mechanisms, something creaked. The flying machine shuddered. There was a fast, descending rattle like a chain being released, and the mast-rotor ripped into life. Noise ran through the hold like a drumroll, like growing thunder. The walls shuddered as if in fear. Giulia leaned forward, rested her hands on her knees and closed her eyes.

Oh shit. No getting out now. Blessed Senobina, watch over me.

The walls rumbled and the flying machine lurched upward, as though yanked on a string. The rotor was poundingly loud, a steady *thrum, thrum* that was as much a feeling in her guts as a sound.

Oh, fuck.

The *Resplendence* rose, one steady beat after another, climbing in increments like the handholds on a ladder. Her stomach churned. With a sick sense of horror, Giulia realised that they were in the air. She clenched her fists, leaned back and exhaled.

Oh God, here we go.

*

The *Zephyrous* was big enough to have one cabin. In the absence of the prince, it was given to Sepello. He sat at a tiny desk in the cramped little room and opened the bandages on his arm. Sepello poured a little more of the Healing Hand onto the skin, grimacing as the potion ran over his stitches. He fastened the bandage and reattached his sling. It didn't hurt too much: the wound was progressing well enough, and in a week it would be entirely healed.

As he put the little bottle back in his bag, somebody knocked on the door. He glanced up. "Who's there?"

"Just a humble servant, with a message from the prince."

Sepello opened the door and found himself looking at Mavlio DeFalci. The prince was wearing a hooded cloak. He grinned. "Mind if I join you?"

"Of course, Prince Mavlio." Numbly, Sepello stepped back and Mavlio squeezed into the cabin.

"Apologies for the surprise. A prince has to go quietly sometimes. Right now, my carriage is rolling round the city, with my best impersonator inside. He'll be giving out alms soon. It's amazing how much more work you can do when there's two of you." The hull creaked softly. Mavlio looked around the cabin and smiled. "I love this machine," he said. "Absolutely love it. To think of it: right now, you and I are flying through the air itself. Can you imagine that?"

"It is quite an experience," Sepello said. He was glad not to be on deck.

"It's more than that. You could take every man in this city, me included, and I'd wager that Cosimo Lannato is smarter than the whole lot put together. God made that man for greatness. He can damn near work miracles." The prince gestured around the room. "Twenty years ago, they would have queued up to burn a man like that at the stake. But I gave him the chance to work wonders, and this is the result."

Mavlio's battle-happy, Sepello thought. He'd seen it in plenty of men before: the speeding up that came from danger, as if the possibility of death gave them a fresh burst of life.

"That's why I want Leth destroyed," Mavlio said. "His type want to see mankind grovelling again, dead or enslaved, just like we did under the Inquisition. God's an artist, Sepello. He wants us to do great things. He doesn't want his greatest creation crawling face-down in the dirt. You want to praise God? Do great things."

"I'll remember that, Prince Mavlio."

"Now then," the prince added, and he shrugged a bag off his shoulder and onto the bed. "I've got a couple of new pistols here. Show me if I'm loading them right. I've never liked gunpowder too much – so damn noisy."

*

"So, we're in the tavern at the back of the playhouse and John's talking to this girl – long golden hair, fancy dress, all of that. But what John didn't realise was that she was really one of the actors who'd just come off the stage, a lad dressed up as a woman! Well, he fucking found out later on!"

Four men burst out laughing. The rocking of their bodies made Giulia nervous, as if it might shake the *Resplendence* out of the sky. A man opposite called out "Don't knock it till you try it, brother!"

Giulia moved her hand close to her knife. Men made her nervous when they got like this, lewd and jocular. She wondered what she'd do if Vale's marines turned on her. No matter what, she wouldn't last against them in a fight. Would she stab a couple of them, and get cut apart for it? Or let them have their fun, and try to hunt them down later on? *Bunch of fucking arseholes*, she thought, angry that they had even put the question into her head.

"Hey." Someone tapped her knee; she whipped around. It was the soldier opposite. He had a wide peasant face and a neat beard like a black seam along his jaw. He sounded like Hugh impersonating a yokel. "Easy, lady, easy. Are you all right?"

She had to call over the mechanism. "Yes, I'm fine."

"You don't look too happy." He seemed keen to talk: no doubt he had never seen anything like her and wanted to discover what this strange woman was like. "They say you're some kind of scout. That you're magic or something."

"I'm not magic," Giulia replied. "I'm with the Order of Saint Cordelia."

"Is this what you do, hunt undead?"

"Sometimes. Most of the time, I'm a thief-taker."

"You ever kill anyone?"

A roar of laughter came from the bows. Giulia glanced down and saw Vale lean in to speak with the sergeant. "All right, that's enough," the sergeant called.

"Back home in Anglia, the fey folk do a lot of our scouting. Me," the soldier opposite said, "I'm a navy man. Used to fight with the privateers. I'm Will," he said, pointing to himself.

"Giulia."

"Pleased to meet you. That's a fine crossbow," he added. "When I was a boy, my old dad—"

The flying machine rocked. Giulia's innards lurched. Someone cursed. The trapdoor opened and air rushed in. A face appeared at the hole, and Vale stood up to speak to it. The door slammed shut again and Vale cupped his hands around his mouth. "The place is in sight!" he shouted. "Bow your heads!"

Will shuffled back in his seat. The men closed their eyes and lowered their heads.

The sergeant stood up, bracing his arms against the hull. "Almighty God!" he roared down the hold. "Almighty God, make us pure in faith, and guide our hands! Give us your soldiers the strength to fight and crush your enemies. For above all nations, the Lord has chosen Albion and its soldiers to be his own! Amen!"

So much for humility before God. Giulia wondered if she counted as a heretic to them. Even if she didn't, she was probably a moral weakling in their eyes: well-meaning, perhaps, but soft.

"Everyone up!" the sergeant shouted. "Get ready!"

Men scooped up muskets and crossbows and stood, ready to climb onto the deck. The ship began to descend.

Giulia clambered up the ladder, into brilliant sunlight and open sky. The light, the cold wind, the sound of the rotors, were like a blow to the head.

Oh my God. The sky yawned above her, as though she was about to float off the ground and into it. The spinning mast was a white blur. She could not tell whether the sickness in her gut came from her fear or the sense of falling.

Captain Torca stood at the ship's wheel, shouting orders to the sailors around him. They were loosening ropes, which appeared to be slowing the descent. Giulia swallowed hard.

"Places!" Vale's sergeant yelled. His marines were ready – used to boarding actions, they clutched the railings to steady themselves. They had slung their guns and swords across their backs. One huge man had a small cannonet strapped to his chest.

The ship descended; Giulia fought down a rush of nausea. The wings thumped like great soft drums. She crouched down and grabbed hold of the railing, breathed in and braced herself. *What if we land wrong? What if the hull breaks?*

The *Resplendence* hit the ground. It lurched forward as if a battering ram had struck the stern, shuddered violently and was abruptly still. The thump of the wings was gone. Giulia let go of the railing and stood up. Around her, the marines readied their guns. The spinning rotor started to slow, and the thrumming racket began to fade. Then the sergeant yelled, "Everybody up! Get going, you lazy bastards!"

The men were slower on their feet than Giulia, bulky with weapons and armour. She paused, unsure what would happen next. She saw hills around them, rough scrub and scraggy plants in the morning sun, and then someone dropped his hand onto her shoulder.

It was Vale. "You come with me, scout," he said.

"Right behind you," Giulia replied. She scowled, swung her bow into her hands and loaded a bolt as she followed Vale across the deck.

The soldiers dropped a gangplank and jogged down. They fanned out at the bottom of the ramp, hefting their weapons like a street-gang looking for trouble. Giulia was the last to descend. Her legs were a little shaky.

Now the flight was finished, she took a good look at the surroundings. Low, broken walls ran along the ground. None was more than a few bricks high. Patches of long grass grew up alongside them. Giulia looked down and thought, *This is it, then? This is the great town of Oppidium?*

"We're at the top of the valley," Vale said, pointing. "The flying machine will stay here. If the crew see anything, they'll shout. Watch the ground for rubble," he added. "There may be potholes, too. Let's go." He turned to Giulia. "You, keep back for now. Tell me if you see anything."

The soldiers walked away from the flying machine, their guns readied as if expecting an ambush. Giulia followed. She looked around, too nervous to trust anyone except herself. The only movement in the valley was grass stirring in the breeze.

They picked their way down the slope, between outcrops of gorse and trees blown out of shape. The men's gear tinkled softly, as if they were travelling merchants. Their boots were very quiet. The heat of the sun lay like a weight on Giulia's shoulders. On the far hills, a hawk rode the thermals, wheeled and flew away.

The ruins of Oppidium stretched before them, criss-crossed by broken walls. At the bottom of the valley the ruins became more substantial: first she saw square plinths sticking out of the foliage, then the shells of smashed urns and the corners of ancient homes, and then, at the bottom, two rows of broken pillars eight feet high, like the remains of a great stone cage.

The sergeant turned around slowly, as if to memorise the view. "So this was their town, eh?"

"Until it was struck down." Vale glanced about. Crickets rattled in the grass. "I bet it was quite a sight."

"Doesn't look like much now."

"Hold up," one of the marines called. It was Will, the friendly man from the flying machine. "There's footprints here. Looks like they're recent."

The soldiers stopped. Vale walked over to see. Giulia followed him. She felt tense, as if someone was watching her. She looked back: the flying machine still sat at the peak of the valley like a ship riding a wave. The sun made the backs of her hands itch.

Vale crouched down and peered at the dry earth. "Boots and bare feet," he said. "The ground's too hard to see much more than that."

Giulia looked at the footprints. They were faint, but the bare prints were deeper than she would have expected, the toes and heel like six holes drilled into the dirt.

Bare feet, or bare bones?

Vale turned to Giulia. "Have you seen something?"

"No more than you."

"Keep going," the sergeant called.

They walked on, deeper into the quiet valley. The soldiers moved as Giulia would have done: covering each other, spreading out, advancing round the low ruins so as to leave no hiding places unchecked.

Now nothing moved, not even the breeze. *This place is dead*, she thought. *Properly dead. Maybe God really did destroy it.*

Movement on the right. Giulia turned, and a lizard skittered off an exposed stone and disappeared into the undergrowth.

"Sir?" The marine with the cannonet stood at a stone window, like a portrait in a frame. There was nothing behind the window, just scrub. "I've found something."

Giulia's insides wound themselves tighter.

They advanced. Giulia checked the way behind. The flying machine was still there. A tiny figure moved across the deck. She wondered how long it would take to run back to it.

"Here, sir," the soldier said, pointing.

A small wooden jig had been wedged into the corner of the window-frame. Someone had fixed an owl's skull into the jig, the head left loose so it could be moved up and down.

"What is that?" the marine asked. "Some kind of pagan thing?"

"Don't touch it," Vale said. He reached the rear side of the window-frame and bent down, frowning.

"It doesn't look fey," Giulia said. It was too crude for the dryads or dwarrows. It looked more like some kind of yokel charm. She thought *Black magic* and pushed the idea aside.

Vale raised his hand as though there was water cupped in it. A thin string lay across his palm. "It's tied to this—"

For a terrifying moment, she thought he was going to yank on the string. "Careful!" Giulia hissed. "It might be trapped!"

Vale looked at her wearily. "I realise that," he replied. Still crouching, he turned and scraped away at the ground with his hands. "The string goes into the masonry. This looks recent." He drew a knife. "Let's see."

"I'll do it," Giulia said.

"I'm fine, thank you." Vale scratched at the soil. "Yes, it's—" He looked up. "It goes underground."

Giulia said, "Just be careful." She glanced around again. The sergeant was looking closely at her, as though this was all her fault. "Lannato said there were mines in Oppidium."

Vale got up, brushed his hands together. "Listen, everyone! I want you to search the ruins. Look for any doors, trapdoors, cellars, anything like that. There may be something below ground." He glanced at Giulia. "If you see anything, say."

"You heard!" the sergeant barked. "Everyone in groups of three. Nobody go out of sight of the rest of us."

Vale looked at her. "Come with me," he said. He started off towards the two rows of big pillars.

Giulia followed. The stillness of the place felt unreal, as though she had wandered into the background of a painting. *If I was hiding down here*, she thought, *I'd make a lair away from all the ruins. Dig a tunnel so it came out at the top of the valley, maybe. Somewhere nobody would think of.* She looked through a stone front door, into the atrium of a house that was no longer there.

She leaned against a wall, glad to be in shadow, and watched the far side of the valley. At first, she wasn't sure what she was looking for. Then she realised: stick-thin figures made of bone, as quick and unreal as puppets. She felt queasy.

"Scout! Come over here: I've found something!"

We should play a trumpet and put a flag up, Giulia thought, *just so Leth knows that we've arrived.* She hurried out and saw a soldier standing over Vale. The ambassador crouched in the shadow of a ruined wall.

"It's clever," Vale said as she approached. The grin on his face looked completely out of place, as though he had drawn it on.

The marines spread out around him in a loose half-circle. "It seems like nothing, but look," Vale said, and he reached into the thick grass that had grown in the shadow of the wall. His fingers caught a loop of rope and tugged it upwards. A square of grass came loose, and in one quick movement Vale lifted out a wooden tray three feet across. The tray was several inches deep, thick enough to allow the grass to grow. Vale hauled the tray aside. Beneath it was a trapdoor.

Giulia's mouth was very dry. She licked her lips. The trapdoor seemed like the centre of the entire world.

Vale stepped away. "Sergeant Merrick! Get it open."

"Everybody stand back," the sergeant ordered. "Henry, you're with me. Get to one side and be ready for whatever's in there."

Henry carried the cannonet. He pulled it up and pointed the massive barrel at the trapdoor.

The sergeant crouched down and took hold of the handle. "On three," he said. "One, two, three." He stood up and threw the trapdoor open.

Nothing moved. They stared at the black square, waiting. A gentle breeze stirred the grass.

Giulia took a step forward, leaned over and peered into the hole. She saw a floor twenty feet below. Grey tiles lay scattered across the ground, most of them chipped and broken. The only light was that coming in through the trapdoor.

Someone said, "What is that, a cellar?"

"I don't know," Giulia replied.

Vale pointed at the ruins and clicked his fingers. One of the men looped the end of a rope around a pillar and tied it fast. Vale turned to look at Giulia. "Right then, Saint Cordelia," he said. "It's your turn."

"Right." She took her lantern and lit it with a piece of thieves' tinder. Then she closed the little metal doors and hooked it onto her belt. She unloaded her crossbow and slung it over her back.

A soldier tossed the coiled rope into the hole. The end of the coil struck the tiles with a soft thud.

Giulia looked at Vale, then at the sergeant. "Wait for me," she said. "If anything happens, pull me up. If you have to go, you take me back with you. Understand?"

"Of course," Vale replied.

She tugged on the rope. It was tied fast. "Do I have your word on that?"

"Yes."

Giulia sat down on the edge of the trapdoor, her legs dangling over the hole. She felt their eyes on her. She took a deep breath, then another, as if she was about to plunge into the sea.

Here we go.

Giulia took hold of the rope and climbed down. The shadows fell over her like water: the warmth of the sun was suddenly gone. She descended as fast as she could, hand over hand, hardly taking in the room around her. Somehow, she knew that it was huge and empty. She let go, and dropped the last six feet. Giulia landed neatly and froze, listening.

She unhitched the lantern from her belt. Carefully, she opened it a little.

The room spread itself out in the lantern-light. It was like a stone barn, loaf-shaped, three times her height. Life-sized statues stood against the walls: blank-eyed women holding vases. There were arches built into the walls, dozens of them, shaped like fireplaces but stacked four-high.

Bloody hell.

The air was cool and still. At the far end of the hall, a corridor stretched away, curving out of view.

Giulia looked up at the trapdoor: a head appeared in the square of light. "What do you see?" Vale asked.

Giulia raised the lantern higher. There were pictures all over the ceiling. People in robes and tunics laboured in a field, sowing crops, then reaping them; then eating a feast; and, finally, bowing before a king in a grey winter scene. The king scowled, surrounded by dead, leafless trees.

"Shit," she muttered, half in disbelief. "God almighty!"

It must be some kind of storeroom. But why all the decoration? This place is incredible.

"What do you *see*?" Vale demanded.

"This place is enormous," Giulia called back. "There're holes in the walls. There's a picture on the ceiling of the seasons – you can't see it from here, but it's huge. I think it's a storeroom."

Vale said, "It's a tomb."

"I don't think so. There aren't any gravestones."

"Are there urns?"

"Are there what?" Giulia didn't like shouting up at him like this. If it mattered so much, he could come down and see for himself. She glanced around, checking the shadows. Anyone could be hiding in this place. Someone had wanted to conceal it, after all.

"Urns, woman. Burial urns. Big pots."

Who cares? "I don't see anything," she called up. "I'm going to look for a way out of here. Stay there."

He said nothing.

"Vale?"

The ambassador held up a hand. "Shush. I can't hear." He glanced at someone to his left, out of sight. "What did you say?"

Vale pulled back from the hole. "Hey!" Giulia called. "Vale!"

A gunshot cracked out above her. A voice yelled something. Vale appeared at the hole again. "Stay there. Don't move. Just stay there."

Another gunshot. "What's going on?" she cried.

Vale was gone. All she could see was a square of sky, a blue hole in the ancient picture.

"Vale? Vale! Sir Francis!"

One of the men yelled "Over there!"

Fear closed its hand around her heart. Giulia put the lantern down and backed away from the light. She pulled her crossbow into her hands. A rattle of gunfire came from above, followed by a shriek.

"Back up the hill!" the sergeant roared. "Back to the ship! Everybody get—" Something knocked the breath out of him. Then he was bellowing like an animal, like a stricken bull. A sharp bang and a stream of loose earth slid down from above, pattering on the stone floor. Metal scraped on stone. A man screamed.

Two pale bare arms slammed the trapdoor shut.

Suddenly she was on her own. Muffled shouts came from above. Giulia heard a loud, choking cough, and that was it. The sounds were gone. She stood there, the lantern before her, alone in the tomb.

In the stillness, Giulia heard her own breath. She was panting with shock. Fear crawled over her skin like insects. As the quiet settled into her, so did the understanding.

They're all dead. I'm trapped down here. Oh, fuck!

Terror rose in her gut. She saw the skeletons back at Brancanza, saw them marching out of the dark for her, and the memory made her stagger back against the wall and stuff her hand in her mouth so she wouldn't cry out. She took a deep breath and stepped towards the lantern.

The trapdoor jerked open again. Slowly, almost mockingly, forty feet of rope slithered over the edge and dropped onto the ground in front of her. The door slammed shut again. She heard scratching above, then a soft, steady thumping sound. It took her a moment to realise what was happening. Someone was stamping the tray back into place, so that nobody would know she had ever been here .

The stamping stopped. The chamber was silent. Something worse than fear began to form within Giulia: the mounting horror that would lead to despair. The Melancholia was rising now, a black tide that would freeze her solid. *Get out*, she thought. *I've got to get out of here.*

She picked up the lantern. Giulia gathered the rope up and quickly wound it round her arm. She tied up the ends and threw it over her shoulder. Then she raised the crossbow and looked for an exit.

There was an archway on the far side of the chamber. It led into a long passage. She felt the weight of the stone around her, as though it had seeped into the air. Giulia paused, listening. When she heard nothing, she advanced.

A doorway opened on the right. Letters had been carved into the lintel: FESTINVS. Giulia put the lantern down and leaned around the edge. She saw a white face, a bare arm – and realised that it was a statue of a girl standing against the opposite wall. The girl held a scroll in both hands. An angel, maybe. Had the Quaestans believed in angels?

The corridor became straight and wide. It ran like an avenue through a hall of doorways, each with a word carved into the lintel: ALLATRIS, CORDVS. Each doorway led into a stone room, empty except for urns left in niches in the wall.

Saint Senobina, Saint Cordelia, watch over me. Help me find the way out of here.

Giulia shook her head. There was nothing for her here – nothing of use to anyone alive. Maybe there'd be a way out further on. She kept walking. The corridor stretched on and on, further than her lamp's light could reach, a thoroughfare in the city of the dead.

*

The ruins of Portia were oddly still. No wind stirred the long grass around the fallen columns. The stumps of buildings jutted out of the earth in a broken row, like old teeth in a jawbone. Sepello holstered his gun and climbed up onto a low wall. It was surprisingly hard to balance with one arm in a sling. He walked along the wall until he reached its high point and looked across what was left of the town.

Portia had been utterly smashed, as though giants had rolled boulders over it. Mavlio's guards walked through what had been the streets, slow and cautious, finding nothing. They had that hard-eyed, wary look of professionals, too intent on their work to be interested in the town itself.

"Sepello!"

He glanced around, almost lost his footing and rocked on the wall, twisting his body to stay upright. Mavlio stood below, hands behind his back. The prince looked intrigued, like a patron admiring the work of a promising artist.

"Find anything up there, Sepello?"

"Nothing, Prince Mavlio."

"No traces? Do the undead leave spoor, anything like that?"

"I'm afraid not, Prince Mavlio." Sepello started to climb down.

Mavlio rubbed his chin. "There's nothing here, is there?"

"I don't think so."

The prince turned and watched his men. He cupped his hands around his mouth and called, "Anyone seen anything yet?"

"No, sir!" Mavlio's sergeant-at-arms shouted.

"Right, then. We're going back to the flying machine!" Mavlio whirled his hand in the air, then pointed to the *Zephyrous*. "Check everything once more, and then we'll head down to the coast. Everyone have another look!"

"You heard the prince!" the sergeant called. "Get on with it!"

Sepello jumped down. The prince waited for him at the bottom of the wall. "Disappointed?" Mavlio asked.

"Not really. I didn't know what we'd find here. Although Leth's much too smart to be standing outdoors, waiting for us to get him."

"True. Now then: one last look, and we'll be on our way."

*

CALLITVS, AMENTIS, BVCCO. Giulia walked past more doorways, more stone maidens holding pots and scrolls. She looked into the nearest doorway: another tomb. She'd seen half a dozen of them now, all utterly empty.

There must be an end to this. There'll be stairs leading out, surely. Come on, God, show me the way out.

The corridor ended in a carved frieze. A hooded rower sat in a boat, on a sea of chiselled curls that represented waves. Worried-looking people stood at the stern, wrapped in shrouds.

What if there isn't a way out? What if that trapdoor was it? God, no, that can't be.

The Melancholia was rising now. First there would be terror, then panic, then real, absolute despair. She felt the beginnings of hunger.

I need to sit down, work out a plan. I just need to think, that's all.

She looked into another doorway. This tomb looked identical to the last six or seven.

They're all the same. It just goes on and on.

Giulia wandered into the tomb. She wondered if the flying machine had escaped.

210

No. Leth will have killed them all. Besides, even if they had got away, she doubted that Vale would risk his men to help her. Maybe Sepello would intervene. Or perhaps Carmina. They all seemed a million miles away. Giulia stopped and looked around. *Mind if I rest here awhile? Just paying my respects, that's all.*

How long before I start calling for help? Would anyone hear me? And if they did, what would come?

She sat down and put her back against the wall. It would be a hard choice, between calling for the undead and just staying here. Maybe, if she yelled, she could kill whatever came looking for her, and escape the way it had come. Assuming anyone heard her. And then there was the small matter of food.

Giulia looked down at the lantern. *Oh fuck, how much more light have I got? I just need a rest*, she thought, *I just need to get my thoughts in order*, and suddenly the Melancholia came flooding in, as if it had broken through her defences.

I'll never get out of here. Never. God help me, I'm stuck down here. She pulled her cloak around her and her hood down low, clenched her fists and wept with fury. *I'm sorry, Hugh. I tried.*

It might have taken five minutes, or perhaps half an hour. You lost time with the Melancholia. After a long while, she heard her breathing slow down. There was an ache in her chest, below the ribs. Swallowing was uncomfortable, as though she was gulping a pebble down.

Her eyes were damp and gluey. She wiped them off, feeling hardened and ashamed.

Get up, she told herself. *You're wasting time. There has to be another way out. Where? God only knows, and this isn't exactly God's home turf.*

Giulia clambered to her feet.

If they ambushed Vale, they must have another way to get to the surface.

Giulia picked up the lantern and walked back down the corridor. She stopped at the frieze of the boatman rowing his charges to the land of the dead. She peered at the sculpted faces. The Quaestans had been able to build marvels. Perhaps there was a hidden button to make the wall swing back: concealed in an eye, maybe, or the top of a staff…

There was nothing. She exhaled slowly, determined to stay calm. *You're the expert here. Look again.*

As she looked over the faces, she heard the trickle of water.

She had to close her eyes and stand still to make it out properly. She put her hand on the frieze. The stone was soft with ancient dust.

Slowly, she crouched down. As she drew closer to the ground, the sound grew louder: still faint, barely a trickle, but definitely there.

Under the ground. There's water under the ground.

Giulia moved back a few feet and stopped, listening. The sound was still there. There was some kind of channel under the floor. She drew her fighting knife, pushed it into the mixture of soil and tiles, and began to cut an opening into the ground. The ancient mortar gave easily. She levered the tiles up and put them to the side. Soon her knife touched stone – not natural rock, but slabs. She hooked her fingers around a slab, heaved it up and pulled it out of the way.

There was a hole underneath. Giulia glimpsed a second floor, about two feet lower down. She lowered the lantern into the hole and heard frantic squeaking, the scurrying of rats. She smelled stagnant water. Giulia pulled her hood up and put her head into the hole.

It was as if the entire corridor had been built on stone stilts, or as if someone had made a cellar two feet deep below it all. It had to be some kind of drainage system, to allow water to run down from the tombs and be carried away.

I could get under there, she thought, and the idea filled her with energy. The apathy of despair was gone. She felt fierce and clever.

Giulia placed her crossbow in the hole, next to the lantern. She knelt beside the opening and slid her head and upper body into the gap. Her arse and legs felt very vulnerable. Dank mud began to seep through her cloak and shirt. She crawled forward, squeezing more of her body into the hole. Clumsily, she pushed the crossbow and lantern before her.

It was dirty, stinking, awkward work. Her body was pressed flat against the ground: her chest and stomach were cold with grime. Giulia felt grit between her fingers, under her nails.

Six feet more, and she'd be underneath the frieze – underneath the wall. She shoved the lantern and crossbow forward, and crawled on.

Her face was streaked with dirt. Surely she'd gone far enough now. Much longer in this fucking hole and she'd start to go crazy. She rolled over with a grunt of effort. There was hardly enough room to turn her body.

Giulia lay on her back, the tiles a few inches above her nose. Pulling her hands up, she shoved at the stone slab above her head.

The damned thing would barely move. From the looks of it, the filth was sucking it into place. Cursing, Giulia tugged the stiletto out of her left sleeve and began to jab at the edge of the slab. The blade was made for bursting chainmail and human necks: it had no trouble punching into crumbled mortar and packed earth. She wiggled the knife back and forth, chewing her lower lip as she worked.

Dirt trickled onto her face. The cold spread across her back as the muck soaked into her clothes. She pulled the knife down the edge of the slab, cursing the tight space, the long-dead bastards who'd built this mausoleum, and suddenly with a wet slurp the slab came free. With a grunt of effort, she shoved the slab up and pushed it aside.

Giulia looked up. She couldn't see the roof. There was a very faint glow in the air above her face. She slid out of the hole in one movement, pulling the crossbow out behind her, stood up and turned around.

"Holy God!" she whispered, and her free hand traced the Sign of the Sword across her body.

She stood at the edge of a gigantic cave. Its size was beyond her – perhaps a mile across, maybe three. The roof had to be a hundred feet high. The rock twinkled with impurities. Hundreds of buildings stood in the middle of the cavern. Most had been wrecked: stone columns lay like felled trees, empty plinths jutted up like stumps. Huge statues towered over the ruins, left at strange angles by subsidence like the figureheads of shipwrecked galleons.

But not all of it was dead. Through the entire city there crept a soft, blue-grey phosphorescence, a light without heat. In the centre of the cavern, massive buildings rose up above the ruined homes – battered, but intact. She recognised an arena like the one in Pagalia. Beside it stood a huge square block fronted by a row of columns that might have been a temple of some kind.

The scattered ruins on the surface had been nothing. *This* was Oppidium: hidden and sprawling down below.

I'll never find Leth in there. No, she realised. *That's wrong. He'll never see me coming.*

Giulia readied her crossbow and entered the city of the dead. She walked between the empty buildings as she had done in Brancanza. She kept to the shadows, well aware this was Leth's territory. She checked rooftops, ducked under windows and paused in doorways to check the way ahead. Giulia weaved from street to street so as not to take a straight course, and twice she doubled back on herself, to catch anyone who might be following. She spotted nobody.

The only faces she saw were on the statues of heroes and gods. One or two she half-recognised, from old legends and the gardens of the rich. Almost all were damaged: faces were leprous with cracks and dents; outstretched limbs had fallen like dead branches; and robes were riddled with holes as if they had been blasted with grapeshot. Some had been vandalised. A horse and rider were untouched except for the careful removal of their heads. Further down, clay had been smeared over the face of one orator to make a crude mask. Someone had drawn two eyes and an idiotic grin into the clay. Whatever his new face meant, it unsettled her.

Giulia turned a corner and the street opened into a marketplace. Stone pillars supported the tattered remains of stripy awnings. The tables were empty.

Wooden scaffolding had been erected between the pillars, and nooses dangled from the beams. There was no mistaking the ropes. She had seen those in plenty of places, knotted thick and tight, ten feet off the ground. They had been hanging people here – many of them.

It looks as if the town went to war with itself. Was that Leth's doing?

She remembered something Sethis had said: Constantin Leth was poison. Everything he touched turned into evil.

He would be in the centre, in the big building she'd seen earlier, living like the prince of this rotten little city. No doubt he would also be guarded. She needed a better view of the place, so she could work out the best way to get at him.

A large house stood across the street. It reminded her of the tenement buildings in Astrago. Giulia slipped inside. She saw empty rooms, scraps of pot and bits of metal that had rusted into nothing. Tiny pieces of coloured tile crackled beneath her boots. It smelled of ancient dirt.

The stairs had collapsed, but the holes in the stone for the timbers remained. She strapped her crossbow across her back and began to climb, using the holes as handholds. Giulia reached the first floor and looked up. Two more to go. She caught her breath and started to ascend.

Quickly and quietly, Giulia clambered to the next floor. Her arms ached; weariness had seeped into the backs of her legs. She crawled onto the landing and pulled her bow into her hands, ready to fire.

Very carefully, testing the floor before each step, Giulia crept towards the window. She was halfway across the room when flames roared in the street outside. She dropped down, saw fire billowing from the roof of an apartment block several streets away. The fire rolled back and disappeared. The city was grey-blue again.

What in God's name is happening here?

Giulia stopped beside the window and peeked around the frame. The big building with the pillars was several streets away, a little to the right. It had to be a palace, or the Quaestan version of a cathedral. That looked promising.

Something drew her eyes back to the plaza. It had changed somehow. Giulia looked over the ruins and nooses, then down to the shelves and counters. Then she looked past them, at the row of smaller statues at the far side of the square.

Three life-sized figures. They hadn't been there before.

Oh shit.

The fire roared. She ducked back and the glow of flames filled the room. The rumble died away, the light faded, and she looked around the window-frame. The statues had gone.

She had only seen them for a moment: she remembered long, thin limbs, skinny bodies and smooth white faces. They were not skeletons, but they had to be her enemies. Giulia turned from the window and crept back towards the stairwell.

Something rattled on the windowsill. She whipped around, and one of them was crawling through the window like a grey-pink spider, all pale arms and knives. A mask covered the head, a hideous grinning mask.

She fired. The crossbow kicked against her shoulder and the bolt slammed into the mask just above the right eye. The mask cracked. Blood ran out of the hole, around the shaft, and the thing fell into the room, flopped onto one side and lay still.

Giulia's hands worked the ratchet. She heard the string click back and dropped a fresh bolt into the groove. The creature did not move.

There was no time to waste. Giulia crept to the stairwell and began to climb down. She dropped the last six feet, landing in a crouch. She scurried across the ground floor, reached the doorway and paused to check the street. Nothing moved outside: Giulia stared at the defaced statues, half-expecting them to come to life.

She stepped out, keeping her back against the wall. Giulia followed the wall down towards the marketplace. The market square looked clear, but it was always dangerous to cross open ground. Giulia kept to the wall, working her way around. The air smelled of chemicals and burning, an unnatural smell of alchemy.

The palace couldn't be far away. She would need to pass the arena, and then find a way inside. Giulia turned into an alleyway, tried to get her bearings.

Something moved on the rooftops. She turned and raised the bow, and a net sailed out, a grid dropping over her from the sky. Giulia yelped and threw herself aside. She rolled on her right shoulder and the crossbow went off in her hands. The net hit the ground behind her. Giulia drew her fighting knife as she stood up, and one of the creatures dropped into the road.

It wore a mask too, the face a caricature of despair. A voice muttered behind the sad face. The creature took a step towards Giulia. Spindly hands flexed at the end of gangling arms.

She held the knife up. "Keep back!"

The undead thing stepped forward, still muttering, and opened its arms as if playing to the gallery. The eyes tried hard to lock her own. Its voice sounded like a crazy priest's – *Quaestan*, she realised. *It's talking Quaestan.*

218

She glanced aside and the voice rose, gabbling. Hands waved furiously around the face, trying to keep her watching, keep her occupied—

Giulia spun around, slashed and her blade met flesh. A second monster stumbled away, its bare shoulder gashed. Behind it, others came: creeping down the street, crawling over the walls like lizards.

She knew what they were doing: in a moment they'd have her surrounded. They'd be on the roofs, ready with their nets.

Sad-face was creeping up from the left – she turned and snarled at him. The undead with the gashed shoulder stepped forward, his pack behind him, and hissed at her.

His mask had sculpted curls and stopped just below the nose. His mouth was a mass of scars and sharp, broken teeth, as though he'd eaten something angry and alive. "*Reste, puella*," he crooned, picking up a trident. "*Reste.*"

A giggle from the left and Sad-face lunged. Giulia jumped aside, sliced at his groping hand, missed and heard the pack come to life behind her. Sad-face darted into the way and she twisted, jumped at the wall and drove off it with both legs. Her shoulder knocked his arm aside and suddenly she was free, landing, rolling, coming up again and sprinting away.

Behind her, the revenants whooped and howled. Her boots pounded the tiles; her heart tried to bash itself free from her chest. Bare feet slapped the ground and she weaved. Not long before they caught her now. She needed somewhere to hide, where the shadows would help her fight. She veered right, and the curved side of the arena rose up in front of her.

There was an opening in the side of the arena, a ramp leading down. She tore down the ramp. The shadows swallowed her. Giulia forced herself to stop, to hold her breath and brace herself. She slung her crossbow onto her back and readied her blade.

Sad-face bounded after her into the dark. She heard him lope into the chamber, smelled the awful dead reek of him, and saw the smooth ghostly face swing left, then right, away from her.

She leaped on him, drove her long knife into his ribs, tore it free, yanked his head back and rammed the blade into the side of his neck. She ripped the knife forward and out, slicing the windpipe, blood flicking from his slit throat like seeds scattered by a farmer's hand. Sad-face thrashed in her arms and she felt heat on her face, tasted blood in her mouth, and then he fell.

He dropped across the entrance. Outside, the others cried out. Giulia backed into the dark, bumped into something, spun around, caught her breath and slipped further into the shadows. The undead stood on the threshold, snarling and jabbering, gathering their strength.

Her heart rattled against her chest. Giulia glanced around, trying to find a way out of here.

The room was full of wooden frames like enormous easels, each mounted on a tripod. She weaved between them, feeling that they were somehow familiar. There had to be another door. Yes – at the far end, there was a crack of grey light. A corridor must lead out of here.

Something rattled overhead. The undead were scaling the arena walls. Giulia picked her way towards the light.

She realised what the frames were. Each was an outsized crossbow, big enough to fire spears.

As Giulia reached the corridor, she heard a noise behind her. She turned and saw the first of the hunters creep down the slope. Another followed it, crawling halfway up the wall. Giulia hurried to the corridor.

The passage turned left into another ramp. She jogged up the slope, onto sand. Suddenly the walls were gone, and she was in a vast open space.

I'm in the arena.

A metal hand grabbed her shoulder. Giulia spun around, saw a huge steel bowl of a helmet, and the hand tossed her onto the ground. She landed on her bow and pain jolted up her spine. She looked up at the armoured man towering over her.

He wore robes over a patchwork of leather and plate. The helmet completely hid the head; it was punched with dozens of tiny eyeholes. Armour stretched over the chest and arms. There were mechanisms on the forearms: some sort of crossbow and a set of leather tubes that curled up the arm like vines.

Giulia lay on the arena floor. The hunters were crawling over the stands now, carrying spikes and nets, hissing and muttering behind their masks. She scrabbled back from the armoured revenant, her legs moving too slowly to let her get away. Giulia cursed and scrambled half-upright, and saw the first of the hunters drop down onto the arena floor.

The big undead raised its arm, as if to greet them – and the crossbow on its wrist released a bolt. One of the hunters screamed, clutching at its chest. More of them dashed forward.

The armoured revenant drew a shortsword and stabbed the nearest hunter in the chest. A second leaped onto its back, clawing at its breastplate. The brute dropped its sword, bellowing under its helmet, grabbed the spidery limbs and tossed the undead onto the dirt, then stamped on its head. Giulia heard bone crack and stumbled away. She saw people in the stands, half a dozen grey figures watching the fight. One was applauding – and she recognised his face. It was the same face that had looked down when Hugh had fallen, three months ago.

Leth.

The sight of him was oil on flame. Her legs took off under her, her hands came up before her as if to strangle him, and she tore across the arena towards the stands. Behind her came a long, gabbling scream. Giulia raced across the sand. Leth didn't seem to have realised who she was.

She glanced over her shoulder: the undead were still fighting one another. The hunters had backed away, and the armoured fighter bellowed at the stands like an enraged bear.

The way was clear. Up ahead stood the arena wall, ten feet high. *I can do this*, Giulia thought, legs picking up speed under her. *I can do this, I can get you, you piece of shit, I will get you, right now—*

Giulia leaped. Her hands caught the edge of the stand, her boots scrabbled on the stone. She heaved herself into the stand and stood up grinning. Leth was straight ahead of her, five yards away.

A man stepped in from the side, a big solemn slab of a man, some kind of bodyguard. She lashed out to stab him, but he was quick. His hand snapped closed around her wrist. She reached to her belt with her free hand, to draw another knife – and he shoved her in the chest.

Giulia fell over the edge and slammed down onto the sand. The armoured revenant stepped in, looming over her. It put its boot on her arm, pinning her in place.

Leth and his robed lieutenants gazed down at her from the stand. Leth's face was drawn and stern, utterly serious.

Giulia lay on her back, staring up at the armour-plated giant and the pale faces of Leth and his comrades. She could hardly breathe. "I'll kill you!" she screamed at the stand, "I'll fucking kill you, I swear it!" The armoured monster pushed her back down.

Constantin Leth stood up and walked to the edge of the stand. His face was calm and grim, deeply lined. His flesh was grey: even the lips had no colour. His pupils were black.

"Giulia Degarno." Leth's voice was hard and deep.

"Fuck you!" It sounded impotent as soon as she said it, just empty sound. "Come down here! I'll fucking murder you!"

"I know who you are. You killed Ramon Azul and destroyed the Hidden Hand's operation in Averrio. You also killed Publius Severra, whose men scarred your face. I salute you.

"I have a proposal, Giulia Degarno. I want you to kill two men for me. I will pay you to do it – not in gold, but in a better currency. You probably think that the best reward I could offer you would be my own death, but I can make a better offer than that. Show your face."

For a moment, Giulia thought he was talking to her. Then the armoured soldier lifted its hands and unfastened the buckles that held its helmet in place. The gauntlets lifted the massive helm. Giulia thought of the faces of the undead, the endless possibilities for withering and rot.

But there was no decay, just the pallor of the newly-dead. She saw a pointed chin, a drooping moustache, a long face and tired eyes with scruffy white hair on top of it.

No, she thought. *It can't be.*

Her head swam as if from a blow. "Hugh?"

It was him, without a doubt. But his eyes didn't know her. Leth was saying something. She hardly heard.

"Like most diseases, undeath can be treated if it is detected early enough. It just takes a skilled physician, and enough of a body to be brought back – are you listening to me? Listen to me, Giulia! *Ecce!* Look at me!"

Her head turned to look at him.

"Listen! *I can bring him back*," Leth said. "That will be your reward."

She stared at him.

"I want you to kill two men: Mavlio DeFalci and Cosimo Lannato. You can get close to them. Bring me proof and Hugh of Kenton will be restored. You have my word." Leth's bodyguard leaned in and whispered to him, then stepped back. Leth nodded. "Now, go back to Astrago. The noxi will guide you out. When you return, tell your superiors that you were attacked by ghouls and hid in order to survive. Once Mavlio and Lannato are satisfied with your story and you have their trust, kill them both. Bring me their heads and our deal will be complete." His eyes were almost furious, their stare was so intent. "Do you understand?"

Her mouth moved, but she did not say anything.

"I asked you a question. Do you understand?"

Her voice seemed to come from someone else. "How long have I got?"

"Two weeks. By then your friend will be beyond repair. Remember: two heads. You'll know where to find me." He looked away from her. "Put your helmet back on."

The gloved hands lifted the helmet and lowered it into place, and Hugh's face disappeared.

PART TWO

Chapter 8

Giulia shifted the crossbow on her back and thought, *I'll go mad. My mind will break, I know it will.*

Perhaps it had been a mistake, some kind of waking dream brought on by too much hope. But if that was true, when had the dream begun? Leth had been real: his minions too. One of them had splashed its blood across her face when she'd cut its throat.

Three more revenants surrounded her now, the mask-faced things that Leth had called the noxi. She walked up the road, with her guides crawling along the rooftops on either side, like a disgraced ambassador being escorted to the city gates.

Lannato and the prince. Kill them and I get Hugh back. Oh God, is that possible? What if Leth's lying? Of course he's lying. He's a monster, for God's sake. Why would he tell the truth?

Fire blossomed in the depths of Oppidium, and she shuddered. She thought about the rows of bolt-throwers she had seen, then about the forges. She stopped, not sure what she was hoping to see. Leth's dead body? Hugh running to greet her, alive and well?

No, she realised, she couldn't kill Leth now, not the way that Arashina and Sepello wanted. If he had ever needed special protection from her knife, he'd got it now: while there was a chance the undead bastard could heal Hugh, she wouldn't be able to give him the death he so richly deserved.

A voice called down from the rooftops. "*Venite, puella! Festinate!*"

She turned and kept walking. Her body was aching and shivery, as if she had caught a cold. Exhaustion, probably. She needed to eat.

At the corner of the street lay a pile of bones. Most did not look human, but they had been heaped here carefully. A message had been written on the wall of the house above them, in mud or dung: *Non etiam Servii, sed Deii.* Whatever that meant. As she passed, Giulia wondered whether Leth had started the fighting in this place or had just happened to be on the winning side.

"Festinate, puella! Leccius imperat!"

She walked on. Her legs felt old and weak, like overstretched bowstrings. Somehow, she had to take control of all this. But how?

"Wait," she said. "I need to rest."

One of the noxi dropped down in front of her. It wore a set of overlapping metal plates on its left shoulder, stretching down its arm. The revenants made Giulia think of the sea: their nets and tridents, and their pale, gangly bodies, like creatures from the ocean bed.

She flopped against a wall, suddenly light-headed. "I just need a minute, all right?"

It crept closer, on all fours, and pushed its masked face out at her. *"Tempus fugit, assassinatrix."* The thing gestured up the road, towards the edge of the cavern. *"Venite!"*

She knew they were talking the old language, the stuff priests used at Mass, but she was too weary to try to work out what it meant exactly. She could guess the gist of it.

A second cracked voice called down from the rooftop. This one seemed to be female.

"Just give me a little while," Giulia said. "I'm not feeling good."

Hot saliva rushed into her mouth. She turned aside and spat it out. Giulia stood against the wall, knees bent and one hand braced against the wall like a drunkard having a piss, waiting to throw up. Nothing came.

After a little while she swallowed and stepped away. Her guides drew back. The male stood up and, with exaggerated grace, he beckoned her further up the avenue.

By the side of the road stood a broad, imposing building. Perhaps it had once been a block of apartments or the home of a wealthy merchant family. The noxi motioned her inside and she followed, her hands ready to draw her knives.

The house was a ruined shell. The ceiling had given way, leaving the upper floors hollow and useless. The ground sloped downwards, as it had done in the arena. Giulia walked down a ramp of flattened earth into a tunnel. Beckoning, the male revenant led her towards the end.

His mask looked as pale as the moon. His throat was like a plucked chicken's neck. "*Venite*," he said, gesturing to the tunnel.

She looked back, towards the centre of Oppidium. "I'll see you soon," Giulia replied. The revenant seemed to understand: at any rate, he chuckled behind his mask.

*

Tarrus waited in the Chamber of Debate. Around him were endless benches, the seats where the great men of Oppidium had once gathered to argue. They were empty now: most of the senators were dust, and those who still moved were automatons in Leth's army. Tarrus curled his hands into fists, relishing the stiffness of his new leather gauntlets.

"Feels good, doesn't it?" Crespis sat in the Throne of the Seeress at the far end of the chamber. Her thin hands gripped the armrests as if to rip them loose. Her face was painted in the old style, but she wore a breastplate over her robes in the manner of Sapienta, the goddess of knowledge. The city was going to war, and everyone in it was a warrior now. "To wear the old uniform again, I mean."

Despite himself, Tarrus smiled. "Yes, it does. Good to have a purpose again."

A thousand years, he thought. *While I was wandering the surface, or hiding in the ruins of my house, Leth was making this happen. Gathering supplies, digging tunnels, raiding tombs – turning us into an army.* It was impossible not to be awed by the sheer determination of it all, the sheer scale of Leth's ambition. Undeath had brought fear and horror to Tarrus, but it had made Leth great.

The door opened. The massive form of Captain Stulcus entered, carrying a cloth-wrapped bundle under his arm. He had always been big-boned: undeath had dried him out, turned his flesh to leather. "The general is here," Stulcus announced.

Tarrus stood to attention. Crespis got to her feet.

Constantin Leth walked in. He flicked his hand up in the old greeting, spoke the old army words. "My honour is my loyalty!"

"My honour is my loyalty!" Tarrus barked back. It was instinctive; he hardly knew that he was speaking.

Leth nodded to him. "Stand easy. Now, the living woman has left the city. The noxi led her out."

Crespis said, "Do you think she'll be able to do it?"

Leth hesitated. "My understanding is that she is very skilled, but... no. Perhaps she'll kill one of them, Lannato or DeFalci, but not both. It's enough that she causes trouble among the enemy. Besides, I have no intention of letting her live once we are done. One way or another, she'll die."

Tarrus frowned. "A soldier honours his promises, Leth."

"Not to heathens and barbarians. She'll be reunited with her old friend soon enough, just not quite how she would like. Now, friends, I have a gift for you. Bring it over, Stulcus."

The massive captain unrolled the bundle. Tarrus saw wooden rods tied around an executioner's axe. He felt a rush of excitement, of eager familiarity, like a hungry man looking at food.

Leth's voice was hard and clear. "Fifteen hundred years ago, a heretic cult preached against the gods, teaching mankind weakness instead of strength. In the old days, we threw those cultists to the lions. Now, their heresy has spread over the lands we once owned, and the world is full of weakness. The living have turned themselves from wolves into sheep.

"I give you the symbols of empire: the rods that beat and the axe that kills. You three are my generals in this: go into the barbarian country, conquer the land above and make them as we are."

Stulcus said, "We shall!"

"Good. The enemy is crafty: Lannato and DeFalci are skilled. They have gunpowder, but when it runs dry, they will fall. Their soldiers will be too terrified to fight. Cavalry will not stand against our legionaries. Cannons are slow and clumsy compared to our siege machines."

Crespis said, "What of the flying machine we captured?"

"It will be dismantled. I don't have the time to figure out its workings. But I have two other cards to play. For one thing, the machine itself will help to power a... device that I have been working on. A union of necromancy and siegeworking, you might say. And for another, it wasn't just the machine we took, but the man who rode in it, and he shall be very useful to us. Their loss is our gain."

Tarrus wondered what Leth's "device" might be. It was best not to think of it. For one thing, Tarrus probably wouldn't understand it: he was a soldier, not a scholar. For another, the intricacies of magic disgusted him. Trying to see the future in spilled blood was unfitting of a military man. Let priests deal in bones and spells: a real man's currency was steel.

"Good," Crespis said. She rubbed her hands together. "So, when do we start this campaign?"

Leth smiled. "Right now."

*

Standing at the railing beside the prince, Sepello wondered what exactly was keeping the flying machine aloft. The mechanism, he knew, was made of magically-enhanced clockwork of Lannato's design, built around a specially lightened hull. *Amazing*, he thought, *how these city-states can exist in near-chaos most of the time, and yet produce such wonders.*

They had been out for the whole day, scouring the coast. Dusk was drawing in, and the sun was rapidly sinking in the sky. Lanterns hung on the bows and stern, and the *Zephyrous* glowed like a firefly.

Mavlio checked their progress against a map. "We're about here, moving south-westerly towards the sea. Then we'll follow the coast up east, like this." His finger ran across the vellum. "On a day like this, we should have a viewing range of about ten miles either side. Taking into account the lighting conditions, that probably comes down to about five. Still a fair range."

"Do you ever use this thing in war?" Sepello asked. He had to raise his voice over the whistle of the wind and the steady thump of rotors and wings.

Mavlio smiled. "I've never had to. But I've used it to see what people are doing. I could just fly above everyone and look down to see what they're up to. Maybe that's how God feels." He smiled, but only briefly. "I once heard that Gloria of Anglia didn't presume to look into her subjects' hearts. I feel much like that myself – so long as they're loyal to me, they can think what they like."

"Very wise," Sepello replied, not believing a word of it.

"Sir!" A lad ran down the length of the ship from the lookout station in the bows. "There's a big fire on the ground ahead, south-southwest."

Mavlio twisted around to look at Captain Comi, a hulking man with a thick beard and long hair like a Landsknecht mercenary. "Bring us round on that course," he said.

"As you wish, my prince," the captain said. He cupped his hands around his mouth and bellowed, "South-southwest! Take us round, good and slow!" He turned to Mavlio. "You'll want to look over the port railing, my prince. If you need a spyglass, one of the lads can fetch—"

"Beacons!" a voice yelled. "Fires below – four, five of them!"

Sepello felt the urge to draw his pistol.

"You there!" Mavlio called to a crewman. "Fetch the spyglass for my man here!"

Sepello reached the side of the ship, took hold of the rail and gripped it hard. He could see the beacons through the gathering dusk, little red dots like approaching fireflies. The sailor unclamped a long brass telescope from the rail and handed it to Sepello.

"Why do people light beacons round here?" Sepello asked. "Is it an emergency?"

The prince pulled out his own spyglass and studied the land below. "They're not beacons," he said, and there was something like wonder in his voice. He lowered the spyglass. "Get us lower!" he shouted. "I want a better view!"

Sepello bent down to the railing and put his eye to the big telescope. For a moment, he saw nothing but darkness: then he swung the telescope up, over the boundary of a field, up past a farmhouse, and saw the glow of fire. It was on a wagon: two big torches were mounted above the driver's perch. The driver himself was hidden, covered in a white cloak like a sheet. Sepello saw his cargo and his stomach lurched. Fear made him flinch – for a moment he thought he would fall over the railing. The back of the wagon was crammed with skeletons.

They were packed in like propped timber, upright and motionless except for the shaking of the cart.

A skeleton paced beside the wagon – no, Sepello realised, not just one but a row of them. Huge shields were slung across their backs. They walked quickly, with long, hard strides. A horse's head appeared in the bottom of the lens, then its body and the yoke connecting it to a second wagon. Sepello swung the telescope down, his horror growing. He lowered the telescope and squinted. He counted seven red fires crawling across the countryside. As the flying machine drew closer, he made out more wagons: dozens of them, in several rows. Horses hauled boxes, barrels, big wooden machines that looked like portable gallows. No, not gallows. They were catapults.

And between each wagon strode the dead. An army of skeletons, pacing across the land, looking to kill and recruit.

Sepello turned to look at Mavlio. "God have mercy, there's thousands of them! That's not four thousand. Where've they all come from?"

"You tell me," Mavlio replied. He sounded numb.

"I don't know... Plague-pits, maybe; cemeteries, battlefields, I don't know. Mavlio, it's an army down there! Leth's got a fucking army!"

The prince did not respond. Sepello waited, and the wind made his collar flap against his face. Cries were breaking out across the ship. Appalled voices hollered from the lookout points: the captain was shouting their panic down. "Stay calm, God damn it! Keep to your places!"

Mavlio turned. "Captain Comi!"

The big man strode over. "Yes, my prince?"

"Captain, are there any large towns between here and the city, going north-east?"

"No, my prince."

Mavlio nodded. "Take us back to the city as fast as you can. Right now. Fast as you can, Captain."

*

The air tasted cleaner now, as if breathing it in washed Giulia's lungs free of Oppidium. *Kill the prince*, she thought, and she stumbled in the dark. *Fine. Anything else you'd like? Oh yes, kill Lannato too. First, murder the most devious man alive, and then kill the cleverest man, too.*

234

Her feet were dragging. Giulia paused, and her head seemed to take a second longer than her body to stop moving. She pinched the bridge of her nose. *Hell of a hangover*, she thought and, although it wasn't funny, she smiled.

You need a rest. Sleep for a week, then go after Mavlio.

The smell of earth was almost gone, replaced by cool air, pine sap and long grass. *Thank God. I can rest soon.*

Light filtered into the tunnel. It was red, but gentle and warming, not like Leth's forges. Again she wondered what he was making in there. Armour for his guards, like Hugh had been wearing? *I'll get you out of there, I swear it.* Her toe snagged on a root and she stumbled, sending her head and stomach swinging like two pendulums. *I'll rescue you, Hugh, like you rescued me back in Pagalia.*

Bushes clogged the end of the tunnel. The dusk seeped through the leaves, as though they were about to catch alight. Giulia stumbled into the evening and sat down on the earth.

I shouldn't feel this bad.

She hauled herself upright. To the right, she could make out white pillars rising above the scrub. They were the ruins she had seen this morning. She squinted across the valley. She saw no trace of the flying machine.

As she walked away, it occurred to her that the undead must have used this tunnel to ambush Vale and his men. That made her feel even more unwell. Giulia trudged on. It would be pitch black soon. She would need to find shelter. Summer nights had never felt this cold before.

Then there was the minor problem of getting back to the city at all. She wondered how much distance the flying machine had covered. It hadn't looked very far on the map. *Three inches. It could be sixty miles.*

She needed to find a road, and from there somewhere to rest. Giulia had a few coins, and the name of Saint Cordelia would hopefully go some way to explaining why she was dressed like a stage murderer and covered in muck and blood.

She walked on, past the lip of the valley where the flying machine had sat, into a loose forest of widely-spaced pines. She found that she was shivering.

Climb a tree. That's what I should do. Climb a tree and get a decent view, work out where I can get some shelter. Either that or it's back to the ruins to hide.

No – not back to the ruins. Not with those things crawling around. Shit, it's nearly dark.

Giulia stepped back, trying to work out which of the pines to climb. Her legs rocked under her, as if she was staggering drunk.

Something caught her foot. She stumbled, dropped hard onto her back and gasped as the crossbow jabbed her in the spine. Giulia twisted around to ease the discomfort. She wondered whether she'd broken the bow: it made her angry, thinking of her tools being damaged.

The trees loomed up ahead, challenging her. *I'll just rest here*, she thought. *Just get my breath back.*

Giulia woke up in the dark. Something pushed her leg and she felt it move. It prodded her leg again.

She was up in one motion, rising and drawing her knife, knees bent in a fighting stance. "Keep back!" she barked, and a bolt of pain shot through her head like a nail hammered into her skull. "Back!"

A light spread and grew among the trees. A puzzled face peered back at her: pale, but living. Two huge, almond-shaped eyes stared out above a little frowning mouth. The hair was drawn back, the clothing dark enough to seep into the night. He was holding a long stick.

A dryad, thank God. One of Sethis' people.

"Undead?" the dryad asked.

Giulia could hear herself breathe. It sounded like air being pumped out from a bellows. She nodded. "Down in the valley. By the ruins." She stopped, wondering whether she ought to continue. If they found Leth's hiding-place, they might find Hugh. And then they'd kill him. "I think."

The dryad looked her over. "Undead?"

He didn't speak much Alexian. Giulia nodded. "Yes," she said, "undead."

For a while the dryad was silent. He stared at her face, searching for something, until she turned away so that the shadows hid her scars.

At last, the dryad shrugged. He reached to his side and drew a sword. It came out with a sound like sighing. "Undead," he said, rather sadly, and he swung it up over his head.

"Wait!" Giulia yelled. "Not me, you stupid bastard! Over there! *There!*" She pointed into the dark. "That's where the undead are." The dryad lowered the sword. She put her head into her hands. Her saliva was hot in her mouth.

She took her hands away from her face. The dryad looked straight into her eyes. "Yes," he said. "You, undead."

*

The flying machine touched down in the courtyard, and fear spread from the sailors to the men awaiting them. The crew were frightened and desperate to talk about

237

what they had seen. The slackness of the landing-crew angered them, and the bewildered groundsmen caught the ropes and pulled the ship in as fast as they could.

Sepello licked his lips. The flight back had been fast and grim. He felt that he ought to be more ready, that he should know exactly what to do.

Mavlio was full of nervous energy. "Captain Comi? Your crew must stay in the palace. Nobody leaves. We can't allow the news to spread. If any of the men gets into the city, I'll hold you responsible. Understand? That rotten whoreson's coming for my city," he snapped at Sepello as the boarding plank went down. "He's going to try to storm the walls, isn't he?"

"I think so," Sepello replied. He felt like an apothecary giving bad news to a patient's family. "Where's the other ship?"

"The *Resplendence* must still be out. I've known it for years," Mavlio replied, not quite talking to him. "Knew someone would try to take it from me. Of course, I thought it would be House Sciata who would try, after I kicked Diello off the throne, not Leth… If that walking corpse thinks he's having my city – I'll kill him, Sepello – properly, for good. You!" he shouted, pointing at two guards on the far side of the quadrangle. "Run and wake Lannato! Tell him I want him in private council in five minutes, up in the map room. Get my daughter as well. And as soon as the other ship comes in, send everyone on board to me!"

Ten yards from the palace doors, Mavlio stopped. He turned to Sepello. "You and I are going to win this, my friend. We are going to work together, Master Sepello. Between us, we'll finish this bastard once and for all, understand?"

"Absolutely, Prince Mavlio."

238

"Good fellow. Now, have you got everything you need? Nothing left on the flying machine?"

"I think so."

"Excellent. Let's go inside."

They passed through the doors into the palace. They took a side passage, hurried up a narrow staircase and past a couple of maids carrying piles of washing. Mavlio pulled a curtain aside and they climbed more stairs, even smaller and narrower. The prince slipped a key from his belt and opened another door, and they entered another, wider room.

"Not exactly a secret passage," the prince said, "but it does have its uses."

The room was roughly circular, lit by candelabra and mirrors in the ceiling. In the centre stood a large round table, covered by a sheet. Objects of differing heights lay under the sheet. Sepello wondered if it was set for a meal. A map of the principality had been pinned to the wall. A wine-rack stood against the side, next to a silver tray and half a dozen glasses.

Mavlio leaned over the table and carefully lifted the sheet away. Sepello saw wooden walls and tiny buildings. As the prince drew the sheet back, he realised that he was looking at a model of Astrago.

"It's to scale," said the prince. "Lannato made it last winter – just for fun, I think."

As he folded the sheet, Carmina and Lannato entered the room. Carmina wore a gown over a nightdress, and seemed to have just woken up. Sepello couldn't help thinking that she looked pretty good like that. There was something about some women, when they stopped being prim. Lannato was dressed in old clothes like a workman. His hands were stained with ink, and fine sawdust dusted the front of his tunic. He pulled out a chair and sat down, nodding to each man in turn. Carmina took a seat. She looked keen and very worried.

"We got back about ten minutes ago," Mavlio said. His eyes glistened. "Listen: we're in trouble, a lot of trouble. Leth doesn't just have a few thousand revenants: he's got a whole army of undead, and it's coming this way."

Lannato said, "I see." He seemed weirdly calm. "How many revenants are we talking about?"

"Thousands. It was dusk when we caught sight of them. It was hard to tell. Would you agree with that, Sepello?"

"It was hard to be sure," Sepello replied. He wanted to say something encouraging. But there was only the truth, and they had to know. "But I would say ten thousand, at the very least. And they're not just morts. These were skeletal, like the ones that Giulia and I saw at Brancanza, and they were equipped with swords and armour. These are *soldiers*."

Carmina said, "So they won't rot, then?"

"No. There's no flesh on them to rot." Sepello's mouth was dry. "I reckon they'll just keep going until they're destroyed."

The princess frowned. "Where did they all come from?"

"We don't know for sure. Probably the populations of Brancanza and Paraldo, but Leth must have had a load of them before that. Country graveyards, maybe. Plague pits, anything like that."

Carmina shook her head. "That's not what I mean. Where have they been hiding all this time? Surely someone must have seen them – I don't know – coming together to march out. I know you can kill all the

240

witnesses, but not when there's *ten thousand* of you. And where did they get their armour, and their weapons?"

God only knows. Sepello opened his hands. "I don't know, Princess. We searched all day and saw no trace of a camp. Then we saw them marching, and we flew straight back."

Her voice was getting quicker, higher. "It doesn't make sense. Are you certain that's what you saw?"

Mavlio said, "We're sure."

"Then maybe they've been hiding underground. Or in a ship, out to sea. Brancanza and Paraldo are both on the coast—"

The prince said, "Carmina, wait. First things first. We have to deal with what we know. We have to defend the city."

Carmina scowled. *She's clever*, Sepello thought.

Mavlio pointed to the map of the principality on the wall beside him. "They were heading north-northeast, roughly parallel with the coast. I reckon they've marched straight out of Paraldo. There's no significant town between that point and the city of Astrago itself. Unless they change direction, which I very much doubt they will, they are coming right here."

Lannato said, "Were they carrying torches?"

"Yes."

"So they need light to see."

Sepello nodded. "My colleagues in the Order think that the undead have some kind of vision – even when they don't have eyes. They can be taken by surprise if they're looking in the wrong direction. When I was in Brancanza, Giulia Degarno stabbed one in the back." He swallowed. "Undead don't need to sleep. They'll be able to march twice as fast as an army of living men."

Lannato exhaled. "I see. What were they armed with, exactly?"

Sepello said, "I'd say they were armed like Quaestans. They carried spears and big shields. Some seemed to be wearing armour. Most had helmets."

Lannato looked thoughtful. "Did they have guns at all? Any cannons?"

"No. I think they had siege engines, though. The soldiers were flanking a row of wagons. I think there were bolt throwers in the wagons. I'm pretty sure they had at least one catapult, too."

"So no cannons," Lannato said. "That's something, at least." He leaned his head on his hand and slowly rubbed his eyes. "Master Sepello, are you completely sure about this? That they're coming here?"

"That's certainly how it looks."

"Then I'll do what I can," Lannato replied. "How do you want to meet them, my prince? We could send out troops—"

Mavlio shook his head. "We don't have enough men for a pitched battle. We've got almost no cavalry in the area, and I've no idea if horses would even stand against the undead unless they were treated alchemically. To raise a full army would take time, either to train our people or to bring in mercenaries. But the city guard are very good, likewise the other regiments stationed here. The question is: if this horde of skeletons gets to the walls, will our defences hold?"

Lannato was silent. Arms folded, he looked down at the model city. *Come on*, Sepello thought, *just tell the truth.* "It's well known that the Quaestans were masters of siegecraft. If Leth wants to storm the city, he's kitted out his army exactly the right way to do it." A small smile appeared at the edge of the scholar's mouth. "On the plus side, he's chosen exactly the wrong city to attack. Let me show you."

Lannato stood up, looming over the model buildings like a god. Mavlio caught Sepello's eye and smiled, as if to say *Wait and see*. Sepello didn't smile back.

The philosopher pointed. "Almost the entire outer wall has been reinforced with earth and sloping brickwork. Not only are the ramparts thicker than usual, but the shape means most cannonballs will simply bounce off or embed themselves in the earth. The same would happen with rocks thrown from a catapult – not that I intend to let Leth use any. The city towers are rounded for the same reason."

Sepello said, "What if he tries to break the gates down?"

"Well, Astrago has four gates. The South Gate grants access to the docks and is probably the weakest. That's why I had the cannon batteries enhanced round there, to sink enemy shipping." Lannato's hands were quick as a harpist's over the model, his delicate fingers picking out the towers. "Here, here and here are rotating cannon batteries, each built on an ox-wound clockwork engine. Each gun could sink a warship. We can keep up about six shots per minute, I hope. Should infantry come near, we've got fanned-barrelled organ guns mounted closer to the walls. That ought to thin them out."

"It sounds good," Sepello replied. It did indeed, but he could not help wondering how much of this was for show. Real weapons were robust and trustworthy. All this talk of clockwork and spinning forts sounded like trickery to impress guests.

"The city has four main internal walls, which divide it into quarters," Lannato added, tracing a cross-shape over the model. "Should one quarter fall, we can fall back and continue to defend from the others. Obviously, the palace is roughly central, but it's only accessible from the north-west quarter."

Mavlio said, "Cosimo, when these things arrive, you and your engineers will have full command of the defences. If you need to fall back or abandon any of the walls, you'll need my permission first – otherwise, run it how you see fit. So long as you put these bastards back in the grave, do as you will."

The philosopher stood up and bowed. "Thank you, my prince."

"Now: Sepello. How is Leth making all these skeletons? His magic surely must have limits. Won't he wear himself out?"

"I don't know," Sepello admitted. Suddenly, he felt completely lost. *All this time I've been chasing Leth. I've finally found him and I've no idea what to do.* "Normally, even a powerful necromancer wouldn't be able to raise more than fifty or so revenants, and they'd be very weak morts. But given what we found at the docks, Leth may have been bringing in large amounts of alchemical materials, including dragons' teeth. We know that Leth is a very skilled alchemist. Maybe he's found a new way of creating servants."

Mavlio said, "So he's got a method for raising them *en masse*. All he needs is a supply of bones."

Carmina had been quiet for so long that Sepello was almost surprised to hear her voice. "The Quaestans kept the bones of their dead. They had big mausoleums. Maybe he's digging the bones up…" Her voice tailed off, unsure.

"Maybe," Sepello replied. He thought of a skeleton on its knees, scrabbling in the dirt. Then a hundred of them, scratching tirelessly at the earth. He shivered. "The bones would be old, and brittle, but if Leth can bring them back to life, he can probably make them strong enough as well." He looked at them all, from face to face. "Look, I've got to be honest with you. This is new to me – new to my whole order, I expect. I've never heard of so many in one place, not since Saint Cordelia fought against the Grey Ague. This – this ability to just create more and more of these things – isn't like anything I've ever come across. Leth may have whole legions of them by now."

"Understood," Mavlio said grimly. "I'll send messengers to all the big towns in the principality, telling them to get their men mobilised." He looked up. "Our defences are strong, Master Sepello. It would take a mighty army to break into Astrago. My feeling is that we can hold them outside the city walls and severely deplete their numbers, by which time the rest of the principality's soldiers will be able to hit the undead from the rear. Assuming our weapons are up to the job."

Sepello said: "Well, they may not rest like men, but they can be stopped like men. Do enough damage to them and they fall apart. They don't feel pain, but they're not much tougher than you or I, so bows, guns, swords, maces – all will work fine. Could you drop rocks out of the flying machine, onto them?"

Lannato opened his hands. "It could be tried. It would be very risky and inaccurate, though, especially if Leth has bolt-throwers. To be honest, I'd rather not take the risk."

"What about magic?" Carmina asked. "If they're held together by a spell, wouldn't another spell just make them fall apart?"

"Possibly," Sepello said. "I have a tincture upstairs I use to prevent them bringing me back to life, should I die. It might harm them. The trouble is I've got about a bottleful, and I don't know how it's made."

Lannato raised a hand. "I'll look into it. The palace apothecaries might be able to help too. And the fey folk. We should talk to them."

Mavlio said, "I will." He had been gazing at the model of the city, glowering over the streets and walls as if expecting to see tiny people fighting on the battlements. "No doubt the countryside is filling up with all kinds of rumours. Those don't worry me too much – yet – but I won't have panic breaking out. If people panic, they'll come here to take shelter, and the last thing we need is the city filling up with useless mouths. We are going to meet these bastards head-on, and we are going to win."

He looked left and right, as if checking that they were paying attention. Lannato sat up in his chair. Carmina pushed her hair away from her face with two quick strokes. "Tomorrow morning," Mavlio said, "we will put out the story that we've heard that a large group of mercenaries is roaming the countryside. They paint themselves white and wear masks to intimidate people. We think they may try to raid the outskirts of the city, so all troops will be stood to until they hear otherwise. That means firing drill, stockpiling food and all the rest of it. It's not much of a story, but it's the best I can think of. The last thing I want people thinking is that the day of judgement is at hand.

"Which brings me onto the clergy. I want them totally on our side – Old Church, New Church, fey folk and anyone else. They will be telling their people to defend Astrago and their prince with their lives, or they won't be telling them anything at all. The price of living in this city is loyalty."

"That's right," Carmina said.

"In the meantime, I will put together letters to go to Princess Leonora of Pagalia, General Attelani of Averrio, and the Pontifex. The ones to Leonora and Attelani will propose a three-way alliance. The one for the Pontifex will call for a crusade against the undead, and so on." He glanced at the map. "We will only send those out when absolutely necessary. God knows there are enough people on the Peninsula looking for an opportunity to grab my land. Does that meet with your approval?"

"It sounds good to me," Lannato said.

Sepello said, "Prince Mavlio, if I might be so bold – whatever help you can get, you should ask for it."

"Understood," said the prince, and Sepello realised that Mavlio would do no such thing. "I think we're done here. I'll meet with the heads of the army at once. Sepello, I want you to help Lannato as much as you can. Carmina, I'll need your assistance here. Questions, anyone?"

"I have a question, Father," Carmina said. "Where's the other flying machine?"

*

There was a clean simplicity to the undead. Leth liked their unity, their determination, their lack of the grubby complexity of human lives. Oppidium was better without its living inhabitants, too. Its streets were pleasantly empty. Most of the time, the town was perfectly still. But when it moved, it moved with purpose.

It had a purpose now. He watched from the high window of the grand temple, as the legions marched out to war. Leth watched them leave the alchemical factories with deep satisfaction. The skeletons formed up in a mass of armour and shields, each with a shortsword on its belt and two javelins slung across its back, identical in undeath.

Another block of revenants marched off. They'd take the tunnels out of the city, and their bones would see the sunlight for the first time in a thousand years. They'd head north-east, homing in on Astrago like a dog on a scent.

A grey-pink figure moved at the edge of his vision. Leth turned, and saw one of the noxi squatting on the stone beside him.

Leth said, "You have the man?"

"Yes, my lord."

"Lead me to him." The noxi strode off, and he followed.

They took the stairs to ground level. In the grand hall, where the priests had once prayed and chanted, rows of skeletons were sorting bones. They worked smoothly and tirelessly. The living could keep their clockwork, Leth thought. It was nothing compared to the precision of the undead.

He walked between the tables. At the end of the room, bones were piled up like firewood, according to size and type. A skeleton loaded them into sacks for transport to the reanimating chamber.

The noxi led him out of the temple, into the cavern. The ground was scattered with broken tiles. Leth remembered when they had been torn up for use as ammunition. The last priests had climbed onto the temple roof, hurling tiles and cursing the gods as Leth's creatures had scrambled up the walls to recruit them.

The bath-house loomed up: pale, battered, magnificent. A masked revenant crouched on the steps, smearing plaster dust over its shoulders. It stood up as he approached, and dipped its head in submission.

Inside the bath-house, murals stretched across the walls. They were faded and chipped, but Leth remembered when they had shone out, promising all kinds of strength and beauty to the visitors. And, for a while, he'd made those promises come true. He walked past the cloakrooms, past the old steam rooms, and into the main hall.

Light rippled on chipped plaster. Alchemical fumes clogged the air. At the rear, four skeletons sorted the bundles of bones, made approximately human shapes on wooden stretchers and lowered them into the glowing water. They did not notice their master, did not respond to him.

The surface broke at the far end of the pool. A glistening cranium appeared, then a skull, and then the skeleton's shoulder-bones rose from the water. The revenant walked out of the pool, and stood still to allow the alchemical liquid to run off its bones. A second skull rose behind it, then a third.

Leth walked to the rear of the hall and ducked into an archway. Stairs led down. Beneath the bath-house were the beauty rooms, where Leth had administered his special treatments. His men had brought prisoners here, back in the old days.

At the bottom of the stairs he turned left, into a low-ceilinged chamber. Athletes leaped and wrestled on the walls. The mural was chipped: their faces had been carefully scratched away.

A living man stood in the centre of a little group of the noxi. Pasty hands held him in place: his armour was gone and his black jacket was open, as if he was about to be frisked by thieves.

Leth approached. The man fought the urge to try to back away. He succeeded.

"*Ecce homo*," Leth said, and one of the noxi laughed.

The man cleared his throat. "*Ego sum legatus*," he said carefully. "*Gloria, regina Anglorum—*"

"I speak your language," Leth replied. "You will answer my questions truthfully. Who are you?"

"My name is Sir Francis Vale," said the man. "I am the ambassador of Queen Gloria, who is the ruler of Anglia and pre-eminent in the alliance of the kingdoms of holy Albion. I speak on her behalf to the city-states of the Astalian Peninsula. I am a man of considerable influence—"

"So, you are an ambassador," Leth said. "A man who knows the ways of the living. Tell me something, ambassador: what use can you be to me?"

Chapter 9

It was a fine day, one of those windless, cloudless days that felt as if the world had frozen in the sunshine. As Sepello looked over the parapet at the land beyond, it seemed as if the whole world had stopped.

Metal clanked behind him, a dull, heavy sound. He looked around and saw a couple of workmen unloading iron balls from a handcart for the mortars mounted behind the curtain wall. They piled the balls beside the mortars in stacks of ten, then pushed their cart away to fetch another load.

Sepello walked along the wall, aware that he was out of his field of expertise. Engagements against the undead were usually fought at close quarters, between sides of a dozen at most: even now, it was still hard to imagine facing a whole army of revenants.

How the hell is Leth doing this?

He passed a couple of men cleaning a six-barrelled organ gun, one of Lannato's tools for clearing boarding parties off the walls. "Some sort of war-priest, I've heard," one of the men said as Sepello passed.

A cannon boomed on the far side of the city. Sepello whirled around, his arm twisting uncomfortably in its sling. Was this it? Had the fighting started? The testing flag flew above the battlements to show that it was a practice shot, but he hesitated, his heart tight in his chest, waiting for the sign that the attack had come.

Nothing. Sepello looked back and saw that none of the men had paid the cannon any heed. He sighed and leaned back against the battlements.

A dark-haired girl waved up at him from the street. "Good day, noble sir! Are you new in Astrago? Do you need a companion to show you the sights?"

Her dress was fancy and very low cut, but it looked as if it had been repaired several times. She had to be one of the prostitutes from the brothel near the northern gate. Mavlio permitted prostitution in his city and, Sepello suspected, probably took a cut of the earnings. After all, if men were in the brothel, they were happy, and happy men made for good citizens. No whore had ever incited a rebellion against a prince: plenty of preachers had.

"Sorry, sister," Sepello called back. "I've got duties, and my arm—" But by then he was of no use to her and she had disappeared inside.

He looked over the wall, at the great flat expanse of half-tamed countryside beyond the city, and wondered what Clara Boucard was doing now. Helping run her father's farm, perhaps, or at one of her viol lessons. He felt very lonely and, as if to spite him, his arm began to ache.

Two days passed. The *Resplendence* did not return. Sepello felt fear in his chest like a parasite, like ivy clinging to a tree.

He walked the streets of Astrago, watching the city wind itself tight in preparation for violence. He tried to look calm and strong, but he ached to stand at the battlements and watch the horizon, waiting for the inevitable.

Slowly, bits of truth were being fed to the populace. The citizens knew that enemies were coming – a large band of mercenaries, Mavlio had said. Now that they were used to the idea of closing the gates and helping out in a fight, they were being told that the men would be accompanied by revenants. Church attendance and public drunkenness rose together.

Giulia Degarno was very likely dead. Sepello hoped that she'd survived, that she'd had the sense to flee, but it was almost certainly not the case. He'd liked her, in a slightly brotherly way. At least Giulia wouldn't end up as a revenant: the potion she'd taken would make sure of that. Sepello felt sad, and then furious, as if he'd inherited Giulia's thirst for revenge.

Princess Carmina toured the city – carefully guarded, of course – and gave out bread and fruit to the poor. She was sweet and cheerful, and the paupers seemed to love her. Sepello wondered how they'd feel after a few weeks of siege, when the bread wasn't so forthcoming.

God willing, it'll never come to that.

The next morning, Sepello got permission to ride out the West Gate. He claimed that he needed to scout out the area, but in truth he just wanted to feel what it was like to be outside the city. *One last time.* One of Mavlio's men, a sleek, bald fellow called Gordo Lidi, accompanied him: ostensibly as a guard, but probably to drag him back to Astrago in case he tried to flee. But Sepello wouldn't be running. He'd stick it out, and help destroy Constantin Leth. And then he'd return to his order, and to Clara, as a hero. Somehow.

Sepello stood at the window of his room and watched the setting sun. It hovered over the city towers like a predator, awaiting the signal to sink into the streets and scorch the roofs. He sipped his wine and imagined the soldiers changing watch on the parapets. Fear lay in his gut like a sleeping animal.

Just like everyone else.

Soon the great and good of Astrago would be here, as summoned by the prince. Sepello was to provide expert advice. He wondered what to say apart from "Fight to the death". You couldn't ever really prepare people for the undead. All you could do was to make them as determined as possible, and hope to God that they didn't panic when the moment came.

The first refugees had started to arrive in the late afternoon, a stream of frightened people with a few overladen animals in tow. None of them had seen Leth's army, but they'd heard rumours and fled, leaving their farms and cattle behind. The prince had been furious that rumours had got out, but it felt inevitable to Sepello. The refugees were granted sanctuary in the city and given work preparing for the attack.

It can't be long now. And the waiting will seem like a pleasure once the revenants arrive. At least I won't feel so useless then.

Somebody knocked at the door. Sepello said, "Come!"

A guard opened the door. "Master Sepello. The others are all here. I'm to bring you to the hall."

Sepello finished his wine in two hard swallows. He checked that the sling on his left arm was comfortable. "Let's go, then."

Fourteen people were packed into the solar, either sitting on chairs or leaning against the wall. Sepello remembered the last time he'd been here, when he'd brought Giulia to Mavlio's party. He felt a rush of sorrow and fought it down. He had to concentrate.

The men were mostly commanders of the city guard, but there were others: the head of a mounted infantry unit stationed three miles north of Astrago, the chief of the city watch, and Gordo Lidi and his deputy Vespasi. The most powerful preachers were here, too: the bishop of Astrago sat next to a black-robed pastor of the New Church. A little way from them were two dwarrows, grey-skinned, massive and alien.

Mavlio sat at the far end, next to Lannato and Carmina. He nodded to Sepello and gestured to a seat.

As Sepello sat down, the prince got to his feet.

"Friends," Mavlio said, "thank you for coming along. Let's get straight to business. There are a lot of rumours going around the city at the moment, and I want you to know the truth. We are facing an enemy the likes of which mankind has not seen since the days of the Grey Ague." He looked across the room. "Right now, a force of about ten thousand revenants is marching on this city."

There was no panic, no sudden babble of outraged voices. The male dwarrow huffed loudly and leaned forward. One of the guard commanders coughed.

"You may wonder where they came from. I want you to be absolutely clear on this, especially you clergymen sitting over there. The undead were raised in secret by an extremely powerful sorcerer. They are not – I repeat, *not* – any sort of divine vengeance or the wrath of God. They are the product of evil magic, and our duty as citizens and good Alexians is to destroy every last one of them. Your lives depend on understanding this."

Sensible, Sepello thought. *The last thing we need people thinking is that the Day of Weighing-Out has come. If people start believing that, some maniac is bound to try to open the city gates to let them in.*

"That brings me onto my second point. If we fight bravely and cleverly, we will win. I have sent for military reinforcements from the four corners of the principality. In the meantime, it is my intention that this undead horde will break against the city walls like water against the shore.

"That means that we must work together, every one of us. Right now, I do not care whether you hear Mass in Quaestan or Alexian, whether you pray to the saints, sing hymns or whether you want to smash every icon in the city – even if you don't worship the Alexian God at all. If I hear of anyone stirring up dissent right now, or turning citizens against each other, they will suffer the judgement of their prince. And believe me, I will make examples."

He paused and took a deep breath. The room seemed to relax a little. "We have two experts with us today. Cosimo Lannato's mastery of siege-craft is well-known." Lannato nodded to the room, and the prince gestured at Sepello. "This here is Master Pietro Sepello, of the Order of Saint Cordelia. He has devoted his life to the destruction of revenants. If you would, sir."

Sepello stood up. "That's right. As Prince Mavlio says, I am a professional revenant-hunter, and a Knight Ordinary of the Order Militant of Saint Cordelia."

Mavlio said, "Perhaps you could tell us exactly what to expect."

"Certainly. Has anyone here fought the living dead before?"

Two hands went up; both men looked like hardened captains. The bishop said, "I've blessed men who did. Does that count?"

Sepello said, "No doubt you've heard stories of the old days, of how the Grey Ague made corpses get up and walk around. The things we're facing are different. They're skeletons, not rotting bodies. They're fast and clever: they fight like men. They will be armed with spears, shields and breastplates, although they lack gunpowder. From what we can tell, they will have siege equipment, which makes us think that they'll attempt to storm the city."

His arm was starting to ache again.

"The undead cannot be bought off or scared away. Nor will they stop to eat or sleep, which means that they will continue to fight while our soldiers rest. Therefore, your men will need to work in shifts. In a drawn-out battle, one of the undead will be worth two of you, so you'll need to make preparation for that."

One of the captains made the Sign of the Sword across his chest.

"However," Sepello said, "they can be stopped by bullets, swords or any other method that you'd use against a living man. If you can, you should smash their skulls when they go down, so they can't be brought back to fight."

The female dwarrow nodded. She looked ready to walk out the door and start the killing right now. The New Church preacher was staring intently at Sepello, as if reading his lips.

"The revenants are led by a sorcerer named Constantin Leth. He himself is undead. If he is destroyed, his army won't just stop, but it will be considerably weakened. I will be doing my utmost to kill him. I may need to requisition some of your men to help."

Sepello paused. The soldiers glanced at each other, as if to make sure that they had all heard the same thing. He saw one shake his head in disbelief. Someone smiled uneasily.

"You'll get whatever you need, I'll make sure of that," Mavlio said. Sepello nodded and sat down. "Now, Cosimo. How are the preparations going?"

257

"We are at full readiness, my prince." The philosopher clambered to his feet, oddly eager for such a gentle man. "All the stations along the city walls are fully armed. The five main garrisons have all reported that they are ready. Soldiers are patrolling the walls, with concentration of forces at the west and south gates and the dock. The palace guards have been split in two: one half to guard the palace itself, the other to bolster the central garrison. Should the enemy threaten to overwhelm the defences, the soldiers from the central garrison will be deployed to assist where needed."

A tall, hard-jawed man raised a hand. It was Goodchilde, the mercenary who had trained Mavlio's marines. His accent was soft and unfamiliar to Sepello: perhaps from Northern Anglia or Caladon. "Prince Mavlio, I've spoken to the remaining marines who came here with Sir Francis Vale. Until he returns, they will be under palace command for the duration of the attack."

Mavlio said, "Excellent. How are your machines, Cosimo?"

Lannato smiled. "In perfect order, my prince. There were some teething issues with the rotating battery near the East Gate, but all's well now. The flying machine and the clockwork castle have had their mechanisms rewound. We're all set."

Sepello raised a hand.

"Yes?"

Sepello said, "Will you be sending for help from the other city-states?"

"You've asked me that before," Mavlio replied.

"That was two days ago, Prince Mavlio."

"The answer remains the same. At the moment, I feel that it's not required. However, I will keep an open mind. Should it become necessary, messengers will be sent to

Princess Leonora and the Senate of Averrio, requesting help. I also have longstanding arrangements with the Landsknecht brokers. It would be possible to arrange for a regiment of cavalry to be sent down."

Carefully, Sepello said, "I would strongly recommend that you do so now, Prince Mavlio."

"The point is taken," Mavlio replied.

"It's just that the undead don't work like people. You have to understand that." It was hard to keep his voice level. "Leth's not just marching on you: he's getting stronger every day. He doesn't have to pay his soldiers. They don't need to rest. They won't get scared, or tired, or hungry—"

Gordo Lidi said, "The prince is aware of your concerns." His voice was low and civil, but Sepello sensed the hardness behind it, the willingness to go much further.

"Indeed I am," Mavlio added. He looked across the room. "Now then, let's turn to the details of the defence."

Sepello woke just before dawn. Half-thinking, he lurched out of bed with his arm held across his chest, his heart pounding.

Must've been a dream.

A fist pounded on the door. "Pietro Sepello! Are you in there?"

"What is it?"

"Your presence is required immediately. The prince demands that you join him in the entrance hall."

He glanced at the clock. "What's happened?" he asked. Dread swelled within him; he knew the answer before it came.

"The enemy are here," the voice replied. "Our scouts have seen them."

It took four painful minutes to get dressed. Sepello checked his arm in front of the mirror. The original numbness had faded, and now the damned thing was starting to ache as if it wanted to tear free from his body. He turned away and pulled his coat over his shoulders.

Two palace guards were waiting outside the door. "This way, sir," one said. "I'll take you to the prince."

They headed through the palace and out a side door, into the warm night air. They passed from the palace grounds and crossed the square in front of it. The huge gate on the far side of the square was open. Beyond the gate, the streets seemed much narrower than before, the buildings taller. People emerged from their homes like timid animals and, as they passed, the guards accompanying Sepello ordered them back inside.

Somewhere to the east, deeper into the city, one of Mavlio's criers was shouting to the populace: "All women and children are to remain in their homes. All men capable of bearing arms, between the ages of thirteen and fifty, are to report to their militia captain at the nearest square…"

Sepello stopped to adjust his sling. "Who saw the undead coming?" Sepello asked.

"Riders along the High Road," the soldier explained. "They just got here. They've seen them marching and everything."

Sepello had to swallow to speak clearly. "Many of them?"

"They're saying thousands, sir."

He nodded. He realised that, even now, part of him had thought it would not happen.

Carmina waited at the bottom of the wall with two guards and a lady's maid, next to a row of mortars as big as witches' cauldrons. She wore a cloak with a thick fur collar; her face was smooth and pale. Sepello bowed to Carmina and climbed the ramp up to the battlements, where the prince stood with his bodyguards. Mavlio wore a steel breastplate polished to the shine of a mirror . The dawn sunlight glinted on it as he moved.

A telescope was being passed around. Flags hung loose in the still air. Thin flames rose from a brazier.

"Good morning, Prince," Sepello said.

"Morning. You've heard the news, I assume."

"Yes."

Bread was cooking, and the smell reached him over the usual city smells, making him feel both hungry and unwell. Sepello peered out from the wall, at the empty countryside. Fields stretched away, crossed with roads and blotched with clumps of woodland and little farmhouses. Nothing moved: nobody worked the land.

Further down the battlements, a priest was blessing a row of soldiers. His voice was a low, fast murmur. One man rose and walked away, another stepped forward and knelt.

"Have you seen anything yet?" Sepello asked.

"Nothing," Mavlio replied. "Only what the scouts reported. They saw them on the west road and came straight back."

Sepello nodded. He felt a strange, foolish hope. Maybe the scouts were wrong. Maybe the army was much smaller than they'd expected. Maybe Leth's magic had faded, and the skeletons were already starting to fall apart. "They'll come," he said. "In the Order of Saint Cordelia, the first thing they teach you is never to underestimate the undead."

Mavlio looked down the wall, at the soldiers and the fortifications. "God knows we're not doing that." He lowered his voice. "Sepello, I know this is unusual for you, but if these things attack *en masse*, if what the scouts say is true – what are our chances here?"

"You'll need to defeat them quickly. If he bogs you down into a war of attrition, you're much more likely to lose. They don't tire: people do." He leaned closer. "Mavlio, you've got to send for help. This isn't a dispute between cities."

"I realise that. But I have enemies, both outside and within—"

"It's more than that!" Sepello hissed. He struggled to keep his voice down. "Please, Mavlio, this is more than states trying to get one up on each other. Send men to Sanctus City, to Pontifex Justus. Tell them that a terrible evil is coming."

The prince put his hand on Sepello's shoulder, and gently turned him so that they were both looking out across the fields, so nobody could read their lips.

"Do you know what the Pontifex was called, before he named himself Justus and took the Holy Throne? His name was Ludovico Sciata. Of House Sciata. I killed the tyrant Diello Sciata to take this city. How do you think his blood relations feel about me?"

"Well, what about Princess Leonora of Pagalia? Or General Attelani, in Averrio?"

"Trust me," Mavlio said. "When I need to, I will. You have my word on that."

Footsteps pattered on the battlements. A lad ran down towards them, a sword swinging at his side. He looked like a child playing at soldiers.

"Sir, sir!" The lad pointed, jabbing his arm out to the west. "They're coming, sir! Over there!"

They hurried along the wall. A massive captain of gunners pulled a spyglass from his belt, held it to his eye and cursed. From behind, Sepello heard someone say, "Oh God, watch over us", his voice shivery with dread.

Be calm, Sepello told himself. *You've hunted Leth this far – soon you'll have him. Once his army's broken, you can go in and finish the bastard for the Order. Just think of that.*

But he felt sick with fear.

Mavlio had his own spyglass, Lannato too. "Where are they?" Sepello demanded, and the big captain pointed. Sepello raised his hand, shielded his eyes, and saw something moving on the road, between the trees. It was tiny, nothing more than a red square above a miniature cart – a flag. Then he saw the figures beside it, and slowly the army left the road and spilled out across the land before the city wall.

At first there were only a few of them: the grass was visible through their bodies, so that they looked like a mirage, a trick of the light. But with each minute the enemy swelled, spilling across the landscape like a blight on the crops. They stretched out half a mile either way from the road, wading through corn and grass. Around him, Sepello heard men curse and whisper to God. His hand in its sling had curled into a fist. The knuckles were almost as bloodless as the army outside.

Six yards further down the wall, someone's nerve broke. "Fuck," a man said. It came out as an awed whisper. His voice rose and rose. "Oh God, look! Look at them! Look!"

Another soldier remonstrated with him, his voice low and urgent. Sepello kept watching the enemy, unfolding as steady and inhuman as a pack of ants.

The man was still raving. "Just look at them! It's the fucking Devil, come for us! Look—"

"Shut him up!" the captain barked.

The man was cut off as one of his comrades punched him in the gut. Embarrassed, Sepello glanced to his right. The fellow was clinging onto the battlement as if about to puke over the side. Sepello closed his eyes.

Saint Cordelia, layer of the dead to rest, protect me and this city.

He opened them again, and watched. At first it was just skeletons, marching by the hundred like some miraculous bit of puppeteering. They had short spears and shields the size of doors, curved to cover their bodies.

Then came the carts, drawn by oxen either nearly or already dead. They stopped on the far side of the fields, and the revenants worked to unload them. Sepello saw bolt-throwers pushed onto tripods, bundles of javelin-sized quarrels stacked beside them, and pavises racked up. The wagons sat in the sea of skeletons like pebbles in the ashes of a fire. The army of the dead stretched on and on, rank after rank of skeletons broken only by siege machines and flags.

Sepello stared at the undead. His head spun; he gripped the parapet and clenched his fingers on the stone. *Now what?* cried a voice in his head. *Now what do we do? Why aren't we shooting yet?*

Fear began to rise, to turn to panic. He turned to the prince. "Are they close enough to hit?"

Mavlio said, "Nearly. They're approaching the first flag. It's a long shot, but within range."

"Shouldn't we start shooting?"

"Let them get a little closer, so they're comfortably in range. We don't want to waste our powder."

Sepello swallowed. "But, ah, won't we be in range of them?"

"Yes." Mavlio smiled grimly. "But our cannons are better than anything they've got."

*

Mavlio heard the fear in Sepello's voice. He felt a brief stab of contempt. But of course, defending the city was not Sepello's business. It was his. He looked out across the revenants, and felt a strange calm. He had not expected this, yet somehow it seemed inevitable.

"Lannato," he said, not looking around.

"Prince?"

"Get ready to fire."

"Yes, my prince."

Lannato nodded to one of the sergeants. Men lit tapers. Crossbows were cranked and loaded, matchlocks cocked. Engineers grimaced as they loaded powder and balls into the mortars.

"Just give the order," Lannato said.

Sepello had borrowed a spyglass, and was looking over the enemy. He lowered it and turned to the prince. Their eyes met. "Prince Mavlio, one of them is coming forward. I think it's a messenger."

Mavlio said, "Leth wants to talk?"

"I don't know if it's him."

"Give me that." Mavlio took the spyglass and looked across the enemy ranks. He saw the pale blur of bones, the endless rectangular shields – and two horsemen approaching at a lumbering trot. They wore breastplates and helmets, and their horses were barded with leather strips. The first horseman carried a standard and a massive shield. The second was unarmed. A white flag hung from the standard.

"It's a revenant," Sepello said quietly.

Mavlio said, "Leth?"

"One of Leth's followers."

The revenant rode well; the little of his skin that Mavlio could see was pale grey, like ash.

"That's a flag of parley," Mavlio said. "You ever hear of the undead doing that before?"

"I've never heard of them having an army before. Be careful," Sepello said. "Never trust the living dead."

The riders halted thirty yards from the walls. The unarmed man raised a hand. As one, the army of the dead pulled their shields in close and hit them with their javelins – once, twice, three times, three peals of thunder. The city stood in the silence that followed, as tense as a beaten gong.

Behind Mavlio, a voice muttered, "God in Heaven."

"Mavlio!" the man called up. His voice was rich and deep, loud without shouting. "My name is Tarrus, and I speak on behalf of Constantin Leth! By the known laws of siege, my lord calls for your surrender. As is the custom, your terms shall be far kinder now than later! Give this city to its rightful lord and nobody need die. Renounce your stolen throne and all will live!"

"Horse-shit," Mavlio said quietly.

The orator threw his arms open, as if calling upon Heaven. "Open the gate, Mavlio! You have our word that you will be granted mercy and the city spared. This army cannot rape or steal. What have you to fear?"

Mavlio turned to Lannato. "Shut this prick up," he said. "Flatten him."

Lannato nodded. "I will."

"After all, Mavlio," Tarrus called, and there was a knowing, mocking edge to his voice now, "if you fall, you'll be leaving your throne to one much—"

"You want an answer?" Mavlio yelled over the battlements. Behind him, men raised guns and

266

crossbows and held fizzing match-cords out to the mortars. "Here's your answer, you son of a bitch!"

*

There was a moment's pause, and the mortars roared and spat their load into the air. The bombs soared past like a storm of birds, and then they dropped onto the undead. Bombs burst and lead balls crashed down; fire blasted through the enemy ranks. Tarrus turned his horse and rode, his standard-bearer holding up his shield to protect him.

Half a dozen bullets and bolts hit the shield and horse. The horse fell; the standard-bearer dropped his flag and stumbled upright.

On the walls, the soldiers whooped and cheered. But Sepello saw the way that the standard bearer raised the shield – not covering itself, but protecting Tarrus. As Tarrus fled back to his lines, the standard bearer buckled and collapsed, its job done.

One body lay outside the wall. *First blood*, Sepello thought. *If they had any blood.*

"Reload!" Lannato called, and a sergeant of gunnery took up his call, yelling it at the men, and the crews grabbed winches and ramrods and got to work.

Something twitched in the ranks of the undead, the air blurred, and a second later a steel-tipped bolt the length of an oar hit one of the wooden guardposts further down the wall and drove straight through it in a shower of broken timber. "Is anyone hurt?" a voice cried. It sounded like a woman. "Is anyone hurt?"

A fat militiaman leaned over the battlement and yelled "Fuck off!" at Leth's army. Around him, soldiers laughed.

A second bolt shot out, its tail blazing with flames. It hit the parapet with a loud flat bang. Liquid splashed the battlements. A rough clay shard landed at Sepello's feet. Below, Lannato was checking the mortars; now he looked up and shouted, "Get away from there! Run!"

There was a sudden low roar and the battlement burst into flame. Soldiers grabbed blankets and cloaks and battered at the fire. The fat man lurched away, flames licking up his forearms. Sepello stared at him for a moment, as though he were some new kind of juggler. Instinctively, he tried to pull his coat off, to throw over the burning man. His own arm screamed as he struggled with the coat: pain shot down Sepello's arm and he flopped against a clear stretch of battlement, panting.

His ear and head hurt as if the pain was screeching at him. *You tore the wound open*, he thought, clutching his bandaged arm to his chest. *You stupid, stupid bastard.*

Three soldiers smothered the fire on the fat man's arms with a blanket. Grimacing with pain, he was escorted to the ramp that led down from the wall.

"Here now," a voice said, and Sepello turned and saw a bearded soldier standing next to him. The man helped Sepello upright and guided him towards the ramp. At the top of the slope, a boy stepped to Sepello's side. "Here we go, my lord, careful now, it's dangerous up here…"

Sepello felt like hitting him. As they reached the bottom of the ramp, the mortars roared again. Sepello saw Lannato turn away from the guns, his hands clamped over his ears. The fat man was led away, to take his pick of the pallets in the apothecary station.

It occurred to Sepello that the burned man was the first casualty of the siege, and that he had just become the second.

Well done, monster hunter.

268

*

Slowly, the siege began. Mavlio was surprised how long it took for the combat to begin in earnest: it was like a battle between two huge galleons. The undead advanced behind their shields, and Mavlio's men rained bullets and cannonballs down on them. A column of skeletons marched out, holding their shields over their heads so that they looked like the scales on a serpent's back. They were carrying some kind of ram between them, hidden from view, but the guns soon blew holes in their formation. The undead got within thirty yards of the base of the wall, at which point they were pelted with rocks as well as lead shot. The column fell apart, and the surviving revenants abandoned their ram and retreated. They strode back to their own lines, long-legged and jerky like puppets.

Men cheered. Mavlio leaned over to Lannato. "That wasn't so hard."

The engineer was not smiling. "They're probably just testing our defences, my prince."

Dusk was drawing in. A heap of bones and armour lay below the parapet. The abandoned shields looked like broken tiles. Mavlio shuddered. "Don't let them get those bones back, Cosimo. Leth might be able to bring them back to life."

Lannato nodded. "I'll make sure of it."

The mortars boomed. Further down the wall, one of the turret batteries fired. Three cannons roared and, slowly, the gun-house at the top of the turret turned ninety degrees. Fresh guns faced the enemy: they aimed and fired as the previous cannons were reloaded.

"So," said the prince. "This is it."

"Indeed." Along the wall, men were lighting lanterns. "My prince, why don't you rest for a little while? It might be better if we staggered our time out here. That way, there'll be always one of us out here to encourage the men."

Mavlio felt a brief burst of resentment. Then he realised that it was a good idea: if they both tired at once, there would be nobody here to stiffen the defenders' resolve. "I'll take a few hours' rest. Will you be all right without me?"

Lannato nodded. "I'll be fine. We can keep sniping at these things all night." His expression became more sober. "To be honest, the real attack hasn't started yet."

Mavlio walked down from the wall, flanked by soldiers, and returned to the palace. He retired to bed, leaving strict instructions that he be woken in four hours' time.

He didn't reach his bedroom. A small man in dark clothes was waiting for him on the staircase.

The prince stopped humming and rubbed his eyes. "Problem, Gordo?"

Gordo Lidi nodded. "Yes, my prince. The rotating battery on the East Gate has stopped working."

"Has Lannato been informed?"

"Runners have been sent to the workshop, Prince."

"Lannato's on the wall. Tell them to find him there," Mavlio said, and he took another step.

"Prince, the gunners suspect sabotage. They'll only speak to you or Master Lannato: they wouldn't tell me any more than that."

"Oh." Mavlio rubbed his chin. *I wondered when this would come. Who will it be: Purists, fey folk, men Leth's bribed into helping him?* "Very well," he said. "Let's go and see what they've got to say."

As they walked back downstairs, Mavlio thought, *I need a crew.* His boots were loud on the wooden steps.

Candles threw little patches of light along the walls. *If Lidi thinks there's a traitor in the city, I need people I can trust.* "Lidi," he said as they reached the bottom, "fetch Carmina. Get Sepello too. Tell him to bring his pistol."

"Yes, sir." Lidi bowed and strode away.

Mavlio armed himself and waited in the hall. Lidi returned ten minutes later, followed by Carmina and Sepello. Carmina looked tired: she had spent the afternoon meeting the common people, the teams of civilians who supported the Citizen Guard. She had donated ale to the Northern District militia, and toured the requisitioned inns now used by the local apothecaries. The citizens were starting to know their little princess, and before long they would love her. Carmina had earned a good night's rest.

Sepello just looked tough. His arm was bound more tightly in its sling, and Mavlio could see his pistol under his open coat.

Lidi led them out one of the servants' entrances, through the streets.

"Who told you about this?" Mavlio asked.

"The head of the battery," Lidi replied. "One Captain Meristi."

"I don't know him."

"He's a loyal man. Well-respected."

They passed a fierce-looking woman sitting on a barrel under the eaves. Lidi stepped in, said something, and their hands met as he slipped her a coin. "One of my watchers," he said, coming back.

"I know," Mavlio replied. "Angry Sal, I believe."

The battery tower bulged above the city wall. The stone base of the tower housed the powerful winding gear required to make the upper section rotate. The upper section was drum-shaped, built out of wood reinforced with metal plates. Cannon barrels protruded from the drum, spaced around its edge.

Lidi's bald head shone as he led them up the ramp. A man with a halberd saluted them, turned and continued his patrol. Lidi opened a heavy door. "This way."

They climbed. The stairs wound their way round a central pole thicker than a ship's mast. It disappeared into the wooden floor above. At the top of the steps, Lidi opened the door and walked inside.

The inside of the tower was full of cannons, set into runners on the floor. The guns could be pulled back and reloaded as the room rotated, enabling a loaded gun to permanently face the enemy. Mavlio had approved the drawings himself.

Four men stood around one of the guns, rubbing their chins and shaking their heads. They looked like actors expressing surprise, Mavlio thought, and as soon as he did he realised that something was wrong.

He turned, and the sharp tip of a knife met his neck.

"Nobody moves," a voice said from behind. Someone closed the door. Mavlio heard the bolts bang home. "Hold your hands up," said the voice. "Nobody say anything."

Mavlio's stomach shuddered. He felt tired and angry. *A cheap, shitty trick like this.* His stomach quivered: he suddenly needed to crap.

Carmina turned to look at him. Her face was white under her red hair. Mavlio was struck by how much she resembled her mother.

At the end, we all fail each other.

The four men stood up from the cannon. The youngest took a step into the centre of the room, beneath the lantern. "Well fucking well," he said. It was Rinalto Sciata. "Mavlio DeFalci, prince of shit."

Sepello was staring at the men, his face grim and set. Lidi's breath came out in a shudder. "I didn't know," he said quickly. "I swear, Mavlio, I didn't know anything about this."

Sciata glanced at Lidi, then to the right of him. He nodded.

There was sudden movement and Lidi jerked forward. He made a high, choking sound, his hands tensed into claws. Lidi gasped and fell onto all fours. His hand reached weakly, blindly, towards the hole in his lower back.

"You were told to be quiet," Rinalto Sciata said. "It's time you learned how to take orders, my prince." He stepped over to Lidi's side, raised his boot and shoved the servant onto his back. Lidi moaned.

"He understands," Sciata said. He stamped on Lidi's stomach. Lidi and Carmina screamed.

Lidi rolled about on the floor, as if to shake off the pain. *He's finished*, Mavlio thought. *Nothing you can do for him now.*

"Stop it!" Carmina cried.

"Shall I stop hurting him?" Sciata asked. "Would you like that?" He smiled and stepped back. Mavlio imagined driving his fist into Sciata's pouty mouth, knocking out his teeth, ruining his sulky, handsome face. "As you wish, milady."

Sciata pulled a knife and dropped. The blade went straight into Lidi's neck, up to the hilt. Lidi twitched and was still. Sciata wiped the knife on Lidi's shoulder and stood up. "Quicker than my uncle got," he said.

Mavlio's throat had become stiff, like a hinge that had begun to rust. "What do you want?" he asked.

273

Sciata glanced at his men. He opened his hands and gave a big, fake shrug. "I don't know. My throne, perhaps? How about my city? Or my uncle, who you fucking murdered? There's a good idea. A challenge for you, my prince: Uncle Diello in return for your life. How about that?"

"He was a tyrant," Mavlio said.

"He was the rightful prince." Sciata glanced away, as though he had forgotten where he was. Then he said, "I suppose you'd like me to let your people go. Well, fuck that. I don't want to lose them, not when they bring me presents like this." He stepped over to Sepello and plucked the pistol from his coat. "Shit," Sciata said, raising the gun. "Just look at this thing."

One of his men took the pistol, and they admired it. They looked like lesser versions of Sciata himself: all young, like a street gang, dressed in Guard tunics that did not look quite right. Mavlio found himself wondering if they had made the tunics themselves or whether they had stolen them, as if his thoughts wanted any excuse to creep away from the here-and-now.

Clearly and slowly, Sepello said: "I am a member of the Order of Saint Cordelia. Believe me, you would be best advised—"

"To let you go? I don't think so. You're part of the deal."

Mavlio said, "What deal?"

"The deal that makes me prince." Sciata smiled. "I've got friends, Mavlio. Powerful friends."

Suddenly, Mavlio realised. *My God, Sciata's with Leth. Sciata is in league with the undead. He's insane. He must be.*

Sciata passed the gun to the man on his right. "Listen," he announced, "here's how it's going to be. You, Mavlio, are going to give the order to open the gate.

The army outside is going to take control, and in return, I will be getting a new throne and a lovely new wife." He gestured at Carmina. "Milady."

"Leave her be," Mavlio said. "This isn't to do with her."

"Not likely." Sciata took Carmina's wrist and tugged her into the centre of the room. She did not resist. Her eyes were distant. Mavlio hoped that her mind was a long way away. "You made her part of this, Mavlio. You made this about her. Remember that when you give her away to me. Remember it on my wedding night, too."

"Let her go or you'll die," Mavlio said. "I mean it."

Very carefully, Sepello said, "You are entering an alliance with a revenant and a murderer," he said. "Constantin Leth has killed thousands of people: men, women and children, his own followers as well as his enemies. He won't spare you."

"Constantin Leth knows what the martial virtues are," Sciata said. "Which is more than can be said for the bastard who drove my family out. Strength, honour, loyalty!" he barked, like an Inquisition soldier on the parade ground. "You don't know what those words mean. Get him down!" he cried. "Get our glorious leader down where he belongs!"

Hands grabbed Mavlio. He thrashed, and a boot stamped into the back of his knee, folding it. Carmina cried out and the prince hit the ground beside Lidi's corpse. A kick caught him in the elbow and pain jolted like lightning up his arm. A dull weight dropped onto his back and he collapsed onto the ground, suddenly small and helpless, his face flat against the boards.

Sciata was beaming now, giddy with triumph. He looped one arm around Carmina's neck, and hooked the thumb of his free hand into his belt. "I don't know whether to kill you, Mavlio, or to keep you around to watch," he said.

Carmina made a low, moaning noise. She shuddered and took in a great gulp of air. Her eyes had rolled back in their sockets.

"Do it," Mavlio said.

"Really?" Sciata asked. "Well, that was easy! But what first, though? What do you think, boys?"

Carmina grunted in Sciata's grip. Her pallor had deepened: her eyes were sunken and red, like an angry drunk's.

"Do it, girl!" Mavlio cried.

Carmina twisted in Sciata's grip and grabbed the young man's neck. For a second they were locked together, Sciata struggling to stay upright, and then Carmina ripped his throat out.

Blood sprayed. Sciata gurgled and fell, and Mavlio pulled a stiletto from his sleeve. Carmina snarled like a mastiff, her face striped red. Horror slowed Sciata's gang: Mavlio leaped up like a sprinter, ran into the nearest man and stabbed him in the thigh, then the gut, tore the knife up, twisting it.

One of Sciata's men raised Sepello's pistol. Carmina grabbed his arm and yanked it. He screamed and she tripped him and slammed the back of his head into the wall.

Sepello rushed across the floor in Carmina's wake and snatched his pistol from the ground. A young thug lunged at Mavlio with a dagger. Sepello fired and the lad fell back, clutching his chest. Someone shrieked from the far side of the room: Carmina dragged a man up from the floor and smashed his brow into one of the cannons, pulled him back and did it again. She stepped back, her face and neck smeared with blood, and tripped over one of the bodies.

Rinalto Sciata stared up at them from the floor. His hand clutched his neck: blood pumped between his fingers. His eyes faded, and his head fell forward.

The room was hot and bloody as a fresh wound. The three survivors stood in the sudden silence, panting.

"Easy," Mavlio said. "It's all right, Sepello."

"I'm fine," Sepello replied. He stepped away and put his back against the wall. Very carefully, he slid his gun back under his coat. His eyes rolled; Mavlio thought that he was going to collapse. Then Sepello blinked, and focused on the prince again.

"Stay there, Sepello," Mavlio said. He smoothed down his jacket. "Carmina, I'm going to come over now," he announced. "Are you happy with that?"

Carmina was sitting up where she had fallen, legs sticking out in front of her. Her voice was choked and sniffly. "Yes."

Mavlio pulled out a handkerchief and spat on it. Carmina got off the floor and sat on one of the gun carriages, and her father helped her wipe her face.

Mavlio looked over his shoulder. "You don't tell anyone about this, understand?"

Sepello rubbed his head. "I understand."

"Never. Not when you get back to your chapter-house or whatever you call it, not ever."

"Can you control her?"

"They give me a potion," Carmina said. "It makes it better, but it doesn't cure it."

Mavlio took a step towards the door. "You owe her, you know. These men would have killed you if Carmina hadn't stepped in. Remember that."

Sepello said nothing. He closed his eyes and his head drooped.

"Are you hurt?"

Sepello looked up. "One of those bastards cracked me across the skull. I'm a bit dazed, that's all."

"Good. Can I trust you, Sepello?"

The hunter looked around the room, from one corpse to another. He seemed to make a sudden decision. "Yes," he said. "You have my word. I take it that Lannato knows about this as well, then?"

"Yes," Carmina said. "It's him who makes the potion."

Sepello pointed at her face. "You've missed a bit. There's some blood on your cheek, just under your eye."

"Thank you."

Mavlio shivered: he gritted his teeth and forced down his fear. The first step in ruling the city was, after all, ruling himself. "So," he said. "It appears that Leth made a deal with Rinalto Sciata, that his family would murder me and Leth would put him on the throne as a reward." Anger flared up in him. "Well, I'm still the prince, and another dead Sciata suits me fine." He stood up. "We'll need to tell the others what happened here. It's lucky that you're such a good fighter, Sepello."

Sepello opened his mouth, then seemed to realise what the prince meant. "We killed them all between us, Mavlio. You and me and Lidi here."

"With a little help from my daughter," Mavlio added. "But nothing unladylike. I'll explain how it happened. Now, let's go."

He got up and held out his arm. Carmina took his hand and got to her feet. Sepello followed, slow and careful as if fighting off the effects of drink. They left the bodies behind them.

Chapter 10

There was a dream of movement through the trees; of being helped along by hands and voices. Giulia felt as if her head and belly were pendulums, swinging with every step she took. She stopped, panting, and threw up.

Time came and went, and she trudged on. More faces melted out of the dark, more large eyes peered at her. Lanterns were smudges of yellow in the night. At last, she was led into a building with a bed. She collapsed onto the sheets. Someone tugged at her boots, and she passed out.

Giulia woke with a foul taste in her mouth. She rolled over, her brain and gut following. She could think of nothing without spikes seeming to punch into her head. Fever churned in her guts, crackled through her legs and arms.

She dragged herself to the edge of the bed. There was a bucket and a chamber-pot below. She leaned over the edge and was loudly and violently sick. She pushed herself back onto the bed and fell asleep.

Wake up, lean over, spew, get up to piss, and then back to bed. Soon there was nothing left to throw up, but the retching continued. She would sit on the edge of the bed, cradling the bucket, yelling into it until her eyes were wet and every muscle from gut to throat burned from the effort of getting the fever out. Then there would be a period of rest, never long enough, where she would lie on top of the sheets, dizzy and exhausted, waiting for the next set of spasms.

Once Giulia woke and her veins were great black cracks in the marble of her arms: the next time she came around, she did not know whether she had dreamed it or not. She slept and someone changed the pots, opened the window and let in air. A hand sometimes stroked her head. She saw one of the noxi squatting on the ceiling like a huge grey frog, and she sat upright and screamed. People came and went in the night: none of them was real.

After days, as if learning how to use her mind for the first time, she began to think straight again.

Giulia could move about now. Not for long, and not without the bucket, but she was able to cross the room. A cup appeared on the bedside table. It contained a mix of water and milk, mixed with something that smelled a little like mint. It stayed down for most of the day, as far as she could tell.

Soon I'll be ready to go on a great adventure – like walking down the hall.

Her head hurt terribly, and her insides ached as if something in her stomach had torn, but she was much better than before. The sense of fever and madness had faded. She didn't sweat so much, and she slept under the covers now.

The room was neat and well-kept, she saw, with large potted plants in the corners that she did not recognise. A strange room, plush enough for a nobleman but much too small.

Giulia woke to find a slim figure changing the bucket. At first she thought it was a woman: it wore a loose man's shirt, but also had a length of cloth wound around the waist to make a skirt, long enough to reach the ankles. She grunted and, as the figure turned toward her, she saw spectacles and kind, shrewd eyes.

"Sethis?"

He smiled. Her mind wanted to hang on to that smile, to bathe in it and let it heal her. "Hello there. I wasn't expecting you to be awake. Don't get out of bed. You've been very sick. You still are."

Giulia groaned. "What happened to me?"

He paused. "Honestly? You were poisoned. You nearly died. Worse than that: you were changing, turning undead. We had to bring you back again."

"Turning undead? God, how? That's impossible. Am I—" She stopped, not sure how to finish it.

"You're not changing any more, no. Lie back. You're still very weak."

"How did it happen? Did they bite me?"

"It doesn't look like it. I'm no expert on these things, but I think you'd normally have to drink their blood for that to happen. But if you'd done that, you'd know."

"Yes. I don't see how—" And suddenly she did see how. She remembered a darkened room, a fight with a spindly creature with flailing white arms, blood gushing from a cut throat, spattering her. "I killed one of them with a knife. Some of its blood went on me. I spat it out, but—"

"You must have swallowed some of it."

She felt disgusted and very weak. "Sepello gave me a potion. He said it would stop me being brought back from the dead."

The dryad leaned against the windowsill and folded his arms. "Perhaps it would have done, but I'd rather that you stayed alive in the first place. At best it would have left you as a corpse. Not much use to us, I'm afraid. Or to you."

"How long have I been like this?"

"Six days."

Six days. Now, why was that a bad thing? There had been something she'd had to do, something she had to do soon…

Two weeks, Leth had said! "Shit! I've got to go!" She sat up, holding the covers across her chest. Her head swam, and a moment after, cold ran through her body like lightning. "I've got to get back to the city, Sethis. It's vital."

He shook his head. "Oh, no. You can't be running around yet. You're still very weak, for one thing—"

"Sethis, I have to go. Please—"

"*No.* You're not better yet, not even close. You won't die now, not if you rest, but you're still very sick. There's a tincture Arashina says you've got to take, to put some life back into you. She says it's vital that you drink it, but it'll make you feel strange."

Her stomach rumbled. "I feel fucking strange already."

"We'll see how you're doing tomorrow morning."

Seven days. She'd still have a week. "All right. I'll stay tonight. But then I've got to go."

Sethis smiled, as if the idea of her thinking she had a choice amused him.

She said, "Have you been looking after me all this time?"

"A few of us. It was me to begin with, but then I had to get some help. You really were in a bad way, Giulia." Sethis stepped towards the door. "I'll bring the potion in to you with some food. Then you've got to go to sleep."

She nodded. "Thanks."

"Glad to have you back," he replied, and he opened the door.

Giulia woke in the warm dark. The moon filled the whole room with dim light, as if everything was starting to glow. The air smelled rich and heavy with rain. Slowly, not trusting her body, she sat up.

She had been sweating. That was a good thing: it meant that the disease was coming out of her pores. Giulia waited, trying to work out what it was that she felt. She didn't feel sick now – not about to puke, anyhow. But there was an odd ache in her stomach: not a pain as such, but a kind of hunger she couldn't quite place.

As she shifted in bed, she could feel the sheet very clearly beneath her legs and feet, as though her skin had become thinner overnight. Yes, she realised, that was it: she could feel everything much more sharply than before. It was not just that the pain in her skull had gone, or that her senses had improved – she could feel her hair brushing her neck as she breathed, feel the covers moving over her chest as her ribcage rose and fell.

The room breathed with her. She imagined her breath sucking the clean air in from outside, setting the leaves groping towards the window-frame. Giulia felt raw and powerful, as though she was the heart of the room, making it live.

She pushed off the covers and lay down again, lay flat on her back.

I know what I need.

How long had it been? Months, years – to hell with that: she felt too good and too strong to be counting up her failures when here she was, ready to take. The lust she felt was more than hunger now – it was a sort of fury that there was no-one here to seize, to press down on the bed and kiss and bite and fuck. The men she'd known and wanted blurred together: Marcellus van Auer mixed into Giovanni of Pagalia.

Giulia climbed out of bed. She stood in the centre of the room, breathing slowly and heavily, ready for sex or violence, or both. She raised her hands and stared at the fingers, as if she'd never realised how strong they were. *Sethis*, she thought, and grinned.

She imagined him walking in, what his expression would be like. That made her chuckle, but it also aroused her: she thought about the dirty stuff the pixies were said to do, how she'd throw him onto the bed and screw the poor little creature half to death.

"Sethis?" she called. "Sethis, are you there?"

She heard nothing, just the small nocturnal sounds of the house. Suddenly, as if all the strength had drained from her body, fatigue washed over her, and she thought her legs would buckle. Half-exhausted, half-aroused, Giulia stumbled back to bed.

Clothes had been left out for her. Giulia wondered if they had belonged to Arashina. She pulled the shirt on, and tried to work out how to wear what seemed to be a skirt. It was a confusing wrap-around affair, and even when she had worked out how to put it on, it showed an embarrassing amount of ankle and shin. The shirt was weirdly short – when she leaned forward it exposed the small of her back – but at least it wasn't cut low at the front. Dryad women didn't have a lot to put on show.

The shoes were wooden-soled sandals, with a strap across the front that went between the toes. They felt as if they were permanently about to fall off. She decided to go without. Giulia opened the door and left the bedroom.

She stepped into a corridor. She had expected something wild, half-overgrown and full of nesting birds: instead it reminded her of the home of a wealthy merchant, albeit smaller. She walked down the passage and headed down the stairs.

"Hello?"

She passed through a neat kitchen, into a pleasant sitting-room. A painting of a horse hung on the far wall. The floorboards were warm, and a small fire burned in the grate.

This must be where Sethis lives, she thought. *A bit fancy, but not bad at all.*

Four books were stacked on the far end of the table. Several bookmarks protruded from each. She wondered if he had borrowed the books from the Scola san Cornelio back in Averrio. In the corner of the room, a pistol lay dismantled on a small table, abandoned mid-repair: Sethis clearly followed the modern belief that a man should be able to turn his hand to almost anything.

As she picked up a book from the table, the door opened and Sethis came in. He wore tough-looking clothes, like a farmer, and his sleeves were rolled up.

"Morning!" the dryad said, dumping a bag on the tabletop. "So, how are you feeling today?"

"A bit better, thanks."

He poked his glasses up his nose with one long finger. "I'm glad to hear it. You look much improved. I'm afraid last night's mixture was some pretty strong stuff, but I gather it'll be the last."

"Yes," she replied, "it, er, had an effect. What was in it?"

"I'm not sure: I didn't mix it. Meadowsweet, probably, mandrake, saffron, foxglove—"

"Foxglove? That's a poison."

"And probably bull's blood and amphisbaena venom. We had to get some life back into you. I'm sorry if it made you feel bad, but it hard to be done."

"It didn't make me feel bad." *Quite the opposite.* "Where are my clothes?"

"They had to be washed, I'm afraid. You were, er, pretty unwell. They'll be dry soon. Your knives are in the box down there."

"What about my boots?"

"Also drying."

Giulia shook her head, wondering how she had managed to vomit into her own boots. She pulled back a chair and sat down. "I like your house."

"Thank you. We're on the edge of the woodland, where the overlap begins. Part Faery, part not."

Giulia nodded. *Part Faery...* It was easy to forget that Sethis was not human. He seemed far more like a man than the other dryads she had briefly met: less cryptic, easier to trust.

"You keep seeing me in a bad state," she said. "One day we'll meet and I won't be puking or half-dead."

He smiled. "I look forward to it."

"Don't hold your breath, though." She felt grim again. She had work to do. "I almost got Leth," she said. "I got really close, but—" She stopped, wanting to say more and not knowing whether it was safe to say it. "He was six feet away. I got so bloody close. I know I can do it," she added, in case he thought that she'd missed her chance for good. "I know all about him now. Look, this is going to sound insane, but he's got a city down there, under the ground. The city's partly in ruins, but... he's using it to make an army. It's in a huge cavern, with all these revenants guarding it. He controls them. I saw these rooms full of equipment: huge crossbows, all sorts of things. He's planning something big."

Sethis opened one of the books and flicked through the various bookmarks. "Crossbows? Like this?" He slid the book across the table. She looked at a diagram of an oversized bow mounted on a wooden frame.

"Yes, just like that. How did you know?"

"He's marched on Astrago."

"What? What do you mean?"

The dryad nodded solemnly. "I heard about it yesterday. I would have told you, but you weren't in a state to think very clearly. I was told he's got an army of several thousand revenants, armed like Quaestan legionaries."

"Who told you this?"

"Arashina. We've got sources in the city: not just the dwarrows, but others, human friends. The revenants came out of the ground, apparently, and they've marched to Astrago and are trying to break down the city walls."

"My God." Even now, after all the things she'd heard, it sounded wild. "Do you think Leth will do it?"

"I don't know. It won't be easy, that's for sure. You've seen what Astrago's like. It must be the best-defended city on the Peninsula."

Giulia remembered Cosimo Lannato and the prince sitting at the far side of the table to her, making their plans. She thought of the ramparts and the cannons jutting from the gun towers, the embrasures and fire-pits. The defences were truly impressive: they marked the place where Lannato's genius and Mavlio's cunning had merged and taken solid form. "Shit, I don't know. This changes everything, Sethis. The city's like a fortress, but this is Leth we're talking about. God only knows how long he's been planning this."

Sethis gently took the book from her. "I know. No doubt he's got more tricks up his sleeve. That evil old bastard's too smart to just charge at the walls." The dryad ran a hand through his thick hair. As usual, it looked as if he had just woken up. "Arashina wants to call a meeting. She thinks this could be our great chance to hit him, while he's out in the open. All this time we've been waiting for him to play his cards. Now we know what he's doing, we can get the jump on him."

Arashina had her flaws, but she was cunning and tough. "Sounds good to me. When can I talk to her?"

"Very soon." He smiled. "Now, can you manage some food? I've got some bread and soup. You ought to eat something."

"That sounds fine. I'm going to get some air."

She stood up and crossed the room. The front door opened easily.

She stepped outside warily, feeling the thick, soft grass under her bare soles. Her body was still a little sensitive, as if her skin was too thin, and she wondered if the effect of the life-potion had fully gone. Giulia glanced over her shoulder, at the house with Sethis in it, and consciously admitted what she had known for some time: she was attracted to him. It was not the giddy sexual thirst of the night before, but a kind of affection made stronger by shared experience. It surprised her that she could feel that way, towards a creature like that.

He's kind to me, she thought, and she pushed the thought away.

She walked across the grass with her arms folded. Trees rose up in an arc ahead of her, as if keeping a wary distance from the house.

So, Leth had made his move. Giulia imagined him sitting in a tent, surrounded by an honour-guard of revenants, poring over a map. It would be harder than ever to get at him now. If she could sneak close enough, she could finish him for good. Then she'd just have to rescue Hugh.

But I don't know how to make Hugh better. What if he can't be made better at all? Giulia's head began to ache, and she rubbed her eyes. *I have to try. I can't leave him there.*

Perhaps destroying Leth would wake him, as though lifting him from a curse – but it was just as likely that it would leave Hugh helpless and undead.

Sethis made me better. Maybe I could do the same for Hugh. Sethis could show me how.

She paced towards the trees, trying to remember the ingredients he had mentioned as she went. He'd said that Arashina had helped to make the potion. She'd know how to brew up a batch for Hugh.

Would Arashina trust me to get the job done? If she knew that Hugh was down there, she'd think Leth had a hold over me. My God, what if Hugh's marching to Astrago right now?

Her head swam: she gritted her teeth and tried to concentrate. *I could kill Mavlio, like Leth said. And Lannato. And then I'd have to hope that Mavlio's men didn't cut me down, that I could escape once I'd murdered them, that Sepello didn't come after me and – most unlikely of all – that Leth decided to keep his word.*

"Giulia!" She turned. Sethis stood in the doorway of the house. "Food!"

The smell of the soup made her ravenous. She got to work quickly: it seemed perverse to sit and eat while the dead were marching on Astrago. *I ought to be getting ready*, she thought, *not sitting around, dressed like this.* She was well enough to walk, to run, probably to fight: she needed to get going right now.

"Easy there," Sethis said. "There's no rush."

"I've not eaten anything for days," she replied. "I'm hungry."

"You might not be able to keep it down."

"It's bloody good. What's in the soup?"

"Venison. We get a lot of deer in the woods."

Something brushed Giulia's ankle and she flinched. Glancing down, she saw a dark, solid creature below: a tame badger. She had seen it once before, at a meeting Sethis had called in Averrio. Sethis clicked his fingers, and it scurried to his side.

"When do we meet Arashina? I need to get going."

"Tomorrow, at noon. The meeting-place isn't too far from here, but it is a bit of a walk. We'll have to go a bit slower than normal—"

"I can walk fine. I'm feeling much better now."

"It's not that." Sethis helped himself to more stew. "The journey will be longer if it's an outsider making it." He shrugged. "It's hard to explain. Paths and things change out here, depending on how... how the forest sees you, in a way. Arashina would find it much easier to get around than I would, and some of the *real* elders would hardly have to move at all to get to where they want to go."

She wasn't quite sure what he meant. *Fey stuff.* "Well, the best thing would be to head off soon, then."

"That's what I thought. If we set off today, we'll easily get there by midday tomorrow. Your gear's all dried, by the way. I've got a spare bedroll you can use on the journey. The weather should be fine: it stays pretty warm at night."

"Thanks." She realised that she would miss this house. It would have been good to sit here all day, perhaps dressed as she was now, reading Sethis' books.

Sethis stood up and Giulia followed him. Her stomach rumbled, loudly enough for them both to hear. He smiled. "Need more soup?"

"Perhaps less would have been a good idea," Giulia replied, and she followed him into the kitchen.

Her clothes hung on a rack before the fire. The stone floor was warm underfoot. "There you go," Sethis said, "all clean and dry. They'd have been ready earlier, but it wasn't just washing them: we had to be sure the undeath was out of them too."

Giulia nodded. Sepello had said something about undeath being a magical disease. She wondered what had happened to him. She remembered Sepello sitting in the afternoon shade, telling her about the noblewoman he hoped to marry. Giulia hoped that he was safe: he was a good man, and he'd been kind to her.

She took her shirt and britches down from the rack, and scooped up her boots from the floor. "I'll get changed in the bedroom," she said.

"Go ahead. But I was just getting used to you like that."

"So was I," Giulia said, and she left the room.

Putting on her thieving gear usually made her feel strong: as she unlaced the skirt it just made her sad. *Here we go*, she thought, fastening her belt and tucking it back in on itself. *You've had your time as a woman: now you're back to being a shadow again.* She left the dryad clothes on the bed, stood back and threw an experimental punch. Giulia bent her legs, drove her hand out cupped, in a technique meant to break the jaw, then sidestepped and blocked. Her head did not ache as she moved.

She tied her hair back and returned to the living room. Sethis was bent over a small chest, and as she approached he came up with a handful of belts and knives. "Here."

"Thanks." Giulia dumped the gear on the tabletop, beside the books and bowls. She slid her leather bracers onto her forearms, buckled them up and slipped the picks into the loops on the right bracer, her stiletto into the left.

"You've got a lot of knives," Sethis said. He picked up the pistol from the table, and quickly assembled it.

Giulia put her foot on the chair and pushed a sheathed dagger into her boot. "I've got a lot of enemies."

"Which did you have first?" The dryad pushed his pistol into his belt. The smile faded out of his eyes. "Are you sure you're up to this?"

"Yes. I'm certain."

"Good. Let's get ready, then."

Giulia raised her hand. "Wait," she said. "I just want to say thank you. I'd be dead if you hadn't fixed me up. I owe you, Sethis."

He glanced away. "Well, you saved me back in Averrio. I suppose that makes us equal now."

"You're a good friend." *Better than I am*, she thought, remembering Hugh. Leth seemed so far away from this pleasant little house, but there the revenant was again, nestled in her mind like a worm in an apple.

"Well," Sethis said, holstering his pistol, "I wouldn't have done it for just anyone." She smiled, flattered. "I'd expect anybody else to clear up their own puke." Sethis chuckled and turned away, looking for something. He came up with a sword. "That's it," he said, buckling it on. "Are you all set?"

"Fine. Ready when you are."

She waited as he disappeared into the back room. He returned wearing a pack. "Your cloak and bag are in here."

Sethis walked straight out. He left the front door open. Giulia thought of the books and the furniture inside. "Hey," she called. "Shouldn't you lock up?"

He looked back. "Oh, I'll leave it. The badger needs to go in and out. Besides, I needn't worry about thieves, need I? The only thief within thirty miles is standing right next to me."

Outside, the air was warm and still, slightly humid. "The path's this way," Sethis said, pointing at the trees. Giulia saw nothing except foliage. It was only as they approached that the route became clear. The path had not been cut back, but the long grass was beaten down as though a wind had swept between the trees, a single gust to mark their way.

Looking from the right angle, the route was obvious, the way you could turn your head at the playhouse and see the stagehands scurrying about in the wings.

Giulia peered into the forest and wondered what lived in there. It was not a normal forest, not natural – or perhaps a different kind of natural. She could make out almost every sort of tree she knew, from neat, upright spruce to a sprawling elm, as though they had all gathered to see the strange woman from outside. Shafts of light slipped between the trunks. She stopped and looked back the way they had come.

It was just possible to see the little house. She took a last look at it, then she walked on, picking up speed.

"You've got a lovely home," Giulia said, ducking under an overhanging branch. "I'd like a house like that: in the country, somewhere quiet. Do you own it properly?"

"I didn't buy it, if that's what you mean." Sethis was quiet for a moment. "Nobody else wanted it," he replied. "Too close to the border."

Giulia wondered whether to ask the question that came to her mind. *What the hell.* "Did the other dryads make you go there?"

"Banish me? Oh no. I pretty much banished myself. The thing is," he added, "I rather like you people. Arashina does too, believe it or not. But some of the older ones just want us all to go back to Faery and lock the doors. They think you're all biding your time to try to murder us. The last Inquisition failed, but the next one won't. That's how they see it."

"That sounds more like a reason for making friends instead of hiding."

"My thoughts entirely. If we leave the world, the wrong people will have won."

They walked on. Giulia had no idea where they were going; her head felt a little light, as though she'd drunk a couple of cups of wine in the sun, but she didn't feel sick anymore.

"So these elders who don't like people – are they the ones we're going to see?"

"More or less." Sethis sighed. "I just hope they're willing to listen to reason. This is the best chance we've had to get at Leth for years – forever, probably. I'm all for taking it, and so's Arashina. If we can get some people together and make a move…"

"An army, you mean?"

"I wish! Lord, it's hard enough to get twenty dryads in the same place, let alone to form a regiment. That's part of the reason the Inquis Impugnans were able to do what they did. In little groups we're hard as nails, and in the forest, well, we're just death – but out on the battlefields, against an organised enemy, we wouldn't have a chance. There's not enough of us, for one thing. We say that the Lord and Lady made the dwarrows for the stone, us for the forest, and you lot for the grass. Put any of them in the wrong place and, well, they're done for."

"Not all of them, surely. Arashina seems happy enough. You do pretty well in Averrio, working for the Scola."

"There's some who'd argue that I've spent too much time among humans. To them I'm barely a dryad at all."

"And I'm barely a woman to most of my people." She smiled grimly. "Welcome aboard."

The path began to weave uphill: very gently, between the trees. To the left, birds rose in a curtain of beating wings. Giulia glanced around to see what had frightened them, and fancied she saw something grey and hulking in the distance, turning its back to them. No, just a boulder. She kept on going.

Giulia's boot snagged on a root and she stumbled, lurched and came up standing. She paused beside the path and wiped her brow.

"Careful," Sethis said. "Looks like it's getting a bit difficult ahead." He pointed down the path. Roots stuck out of the ground, formed like hoops and snares.

As they walked, Giulia said, "Sethis?"

"Yes?"

"That medicine you gave me: it burned the undeath out of me, right?"

"Yes, that's right."

"Have you got any more of it?"

He sounded worried, not afraid. "Are you all right? You're not feeling sick, are you? We can go back—"

"No, it's not that." *It could cure Hugh.* The urge to say it out loud was terribly strong. "I – I wondered if it might work like poison on them."

"Ah, good thinking. I don't know, but we could always ask. You could put it on your weapons, perhaps. We'll ask Arashina when we get there."

Giulia passed through a cloud of humming flies that hovered like a curtain across the path. She walked straight through, expecting there to be a dead animal nearby. There was nothing: the flies just seemed to like it there. Perhaps they were guarding the path. A little way back, a small deer stared at them, without fear, then turned and walked away.

"So is Arashina a lady, then?" Giulia asked.

"How do you define 'lady'?"

"A noble, like a lord."

"Oh, I see. Well, no, she isn't really." Sethis fiddled with the shoulder strap of his pack, shrugged it back into place and started walking again. "We don't really have nobles, not in that way. It tends to be age that gets you noticed, rather than title. The problem is that the older they get, the less like you and I they become."

Giulia could hear running water to the left. The warmth of the sun seemed to sink into her, quickening her. She realised that she could have made the walk in the dryad clothes Sethis had lent her, and as soon as she thought it another, more enticing image came to mind: of stripping naked and walking between the trees, undressing before the forest and letting it welcome and swallow her.

She shook her head and blinked herself back to the trail. The trees were just trees again. For a moment she wondered if the place was putting a spell on her, or if being here was making her strange, the way a man might go mad left alone for too long.

That potion he gave me is still doing things to my head. Or maybe this place is.

She felt a sudden urge to be elsewhere – in Astrago, perhaps, and then she remembered that by now, Leth might be well in the city too.

The sun was just starting to sink below the treeline. The whisper of running water became a soft babble, and then the path twisted to the left and Giulia saw a small bridge through the trees, the sort of neat, hump-backed thing a rich man might put in an ornamental garden. "Ah, there's the bridge!" Sethis exclaimed, as if it had crept up on him, and he sped up as though worried that it might escape.

They crossed the bridge and, although it was clearly a landmark, nothing unusual happened – so far as Giulia could tell. "We've made good progress," Sethis said as he stepped back onto the path. "We'll make camp soon. I know a good place."

"Fine," Giulia said. They turned right and followed the river upstream. As they left the bridge behind, she saw that a stick-picture of a woman had been scratched into the bark of a beech a little way ahead. It was childish and crude, the breasts and belly huge and round. It had antlers. She passed it, feeling that somehow it was watching her, a window for the gods of the forest to spy from.

"There!" Sethis said a minute later, pointing ahead. "Up there!"

Giulia squinted – her eyes had seemed to work better in the city – and made out a gap between the trees. Rocks glinted, and water danced over them.

"Come on," Sethis said, "Follow me!"

He took the lead, almost running, and Giulia had to stride to keep up. The tree roots avoided the path, and their footsteps were lost in the sound of the river.

The trees parted and suddenly they stood under the sky before a pool thirty feet across, before a cliff five times Giulia's height. Water fell noisily from the cliffs into the pool. A bird screamed out across the water's edge. Fish danced in the depths. "That way," Sethis said, and she saw that the path wound behind the pool and up the rocks. "That's where we're staying," the dryad added, and he pointed to an opening to the side of the waterfall, a little way back.

"Will it be safe?" The cave did not look big enough for a wyvern, but a bear could have fitted in there quite comfortably, perhaps with a couple of friends.

Sethis paused, looked over his shoulder, and nodded. "It'll be fine. The journey's been good so far."

Giulia wondered what the hell their journey had to do with bears living in the cave. She sighed and walked up the slope behind him.

The cave was fairly narrow, but it stretched back some way: Giulia was surprised to see no sign of anything larger than bats inside. It was strangely quiet, as though someone had drawn a heavy curtain across the entrance. A firepit stood a few feet back, away from wind and rain. A pile of dry sticks lay nearby, as if left for them to use.

As dusk began to turn into night, Sethis lit a fire and laid out the bedrolls, one either side of the pit. He had brought a lantern, and its light made the cavern quite pleasant.

Giulia was surprised at how dry the place was. She would have expected a cave by a river to be as damp as a frog's back and infested with biting flies. As Sethis unpacked his bag, she wondered if somehow the forest was responding to them, judging them before letting them through.

"Are you hungry?" he asked, taking out a small pot.

"Not very."

"That's probably good. I've only got dried stuff." He fished out several strips of cured meat. "I never was much of a cook." Sethis took out a tiny bag and tipped dried herbs into the pot. "Purely for flavouring. Otherwise you might as well boil your belt and eat it instead. On the plus side, I *do* have this," he added, pulling a wineskin out of his bag. "And a spare."

"I wish I'd brought something," Giulia said as he passed her the wineskin and a pair of small cups.

"You are bringing something – knowledge. You've seen inside Leth's hiding-place. I doubt anyone's ever got that close to him and survived." Sethis took a cup from her. "I just hope they care enough. I hate to say it, but there's a few of the elders who would really like to see Astrago get levelled to the ground."

"Surely they'd want to have Leth killed, after all he's done."

"Some of them think nothing good can come out of you people. They say the Inquisition was humanity as it really is. Seeing mankind take a good beating would be like poetic justice to them."

"That's stupid. If they want justice, they should help me to find Leth and kill the son of a bitch." Giulia finished her wine and poured them out new measures. "I'll tell them that, if you like."

"I doubt it'll be necessary. But thanks."

Giulia settled back, shaking her head. The fey were fools if they thought that there was something to be gained by allowing Leth to run amok. Letting their own grievances get in the way... She stared into the fire. *Save Hugh and kill Leth. One would be hard enough – doing both is going to be damn near impossible. Perhaps if I took Leth captive, I could force him to make Hugh normal again. But how do you force a monster like that to do anything? Would he even feel pain?* *Bastard*, she thought, fury rising in her along with the Melancholia, *he's got me trapped. Even if I could get near him, he'd still have Hugh. God, when I get the chance, I'll fucking teach Leth what pain is. I'll—*

"More wine?" Sethis asked.

She glanced up, wondering what her face had looked like a moment ago. She felt guilty. "Yes, please. I think I need it." She held out her cup for more.

I can't do this. The thought dropped onto her from nowhere, as she was spooning dinner into her mouth. As soon as it was in her head, she knew that it was completely, unarguably true. She'd only been able to get close to Leth because he had wanted to speak to her. He would be wise to her now and, if Sethis was right, he wouldn't even be in Oppidium anymore. He'd be somewhere on the march, surrounded by thousands of soldiers. She felt empty.

I can't do this alone.

Sethis leaned around the fire to look at her. "Are you feeling well?"

"Fine, thanks."

"It's not the food, is it? Because I thought I made a pretty decent job of it, given the materials."

"No," she said, "it's good. I really appreciate it." *It has to be said.* "Sethis? Can I ask you something?"

He looked up from mopping his bowl with a crust. "Of course."

300

"I need your word that this will go no further than the two of us. On your gods, or your honour or whatever it is."

"It won't go any further. You have my word."

"Good. You remember I asked if you had more of that stuff you used on me, the medicine?"

"Yes?"

"It's not Leth I want it for. It's Hugh. He's alive. I mean" – the word sounded awkward, ugly to say – "undead. Leth's got him trapped in his city. I reckon I could get him out."

"Oh." Sethis looked alien, as if he had always lived in this cave and was gazing in wonder at his first human being. "I see. That's… well, that's difficult. Are you sure it's him?"

"Certain. Leth showed me it was Hugh."

"He showed you?"

"Yes. Hugh was under Leth's control, as if he was in a dream. It was horrible. Leth said it would take more time for Hugh to change – for it to be impossible to reverse, that is. He said it could be possible to make him come back, but if he died – if Leth died – I'd never be able to fix Hugh." When Sethis said nothing, she put it more simply. "I thought we could use that potion you gave me to make Hugh better."

Make him better? Once spoken out loud it sounded like child's talk, nothing more than a stack of wishes heaped up on one another.

Sethis said, "Maybe it would work. I don't know for sure – I doubt anyone would. And even if it did work, you'd have to give it to him somehow. Why did Leth talk to you, anyway? What did he want from you?"

Say it. Just say it. "He wanted me to kill Prince Mavlio and Cosimo Lannato. In return, he'd give me Hugh."

301

Sethis gave a low, soft whistle. "Well, that's… that's quite a thing."

"I'm not going to do it, in case you're wondering. For one thing, Lannato's an innocent man. Mavlio – well, I wouldn't call him innocent, but he's played fair with me."

"He's always been fair with the fey folk, too. To be honest, I did wonder if Leth had spoken to you."

"Really?"

The dryad smiled. "You talk in your sleep." He passed her the wineskin, and she poured a little more into her cup.

"The thing is," she said, her voice tightening a little, "I still want Leth dead, and I'll get him. It's just that— Well, you shouldn't lie to your allies. I owe you the truth, after all you've done for me." Suddenly she felt terribly weary, sick of everything. "I just can't leave Hugh there, not like that. Even if I go there and finish him off, kill him for good, it's got to be better than *that*." She leaned back against the cave wall. "Grodrin said a man was known by the debts he honours. I don't know about that, but, well, I've got a debt to Hugh. I ought to at least try."

"I suppose it's pointless me saying that Leth was almost certainly lying to you."

"Yes. But he might not have been. That's the damn thing."

She sat there watching the fire, feeling a sadness as deep and dark as the ocean.

"It's never easy, trying to do the right thing," Sethis said.

"No, it isn't."

He looked at her, and she wondered what it would be like to sleep with him. He'd have the right stuff – at least, there were stories and songs about men and fey folk interbreeding – but…

She stood up quickly and fetched the pack. She unfolded her cloak and took out Hugh's book.

"This belongs to Hugh," Giulia said. *"The Death of King Alba.* He used to read it all the time, like it was holy. To be honest, I think it was the only book he'd ever read." She handed it over. Sethis took the volume and opened it carefully. "Not that it did him a lot of good."

"Hmm," the dryad said. He seemed very interested in the book: not so much in reading it as just holding it, as if he had never thought that such a thing could exist. Sethis passed it back to her.

"You're a good man, Sethis."

He smiled. "I'm not a man and I'm not especially good. Otherwise, I completely agree."

"To me, you're a man." She realised what she'd said, and added, "I mean, you aren't a *man*, not a human being – but you are a man, if you see what I mean."

"I think I do. And I'll take it as a compliment."

Giulia woke up with the dawn and the sound of water. She got up slowly, slightly unsure of how she'd got here and why. She remembered Hugh, and Leth, and it was like a weight dropping onto her. *I've got to go!* Then she saw Sethis, stretched out on the other side of the dead fire. She felt vaguely guilty, as if she'd insulted him the night before.

He stirred and opened his eyes. "Hello, Giulia. Did you sleep well?"

"Yes, thanks. We'd better get going."

They packed up their things. "I'll take the pack," Giulia said. "It's my turn."

Sethis pulled Giulia's bag and her cloak out of the pack and tossed them over. "You could carry these." He looked at her as if he was trying to make his mind up

303

about something. He took a deep breath. "Giulia, when this is over, you could come and live in my house, if you liked."

"Your house?"

"Yes, the one you stayed in just now. You could come and live there. It's not huge, admittedly, but there's plenty of room, and— Well, it gets a bit lonely."

"Really?"

"Well, it's just a thought, but you're welcome to stay if you'd like. There are other houses nearby, in the forest, that you could use."

The offer confused her. There was too much to think about for her to consider it properly. "Well, um, I don't know. It's very kind of you. Look, let's get this done, and then I'll think it over. I appreciate the offer, though. I really do."

She filled the empty wineskin at the pool. As Sethis started off down the path, she pushed her head under the waterfall. It was icy cold. When she stood back, water running down her face, she felt ready and alert.

Chapter 11

The air was warm and a little muggy. To the left, the lower branches of a young oak had been decorated with coloured string. A bird sat in the tree, watching them. It was a type Giulia had never seen before, a sort of long-tailed woodpecker whose feathers caught the morning sun like stained glass.

"Look," Sethis said. "There."

Two statues flanked the path, nestled in the undergrowth like eggs in a nest. They were the Lord and Lady, or at least some form of them, but they were ugly and crude. The faces were round and lumpy, the arms fixed onto their bodies. Holes had been drilled into their heads, and stag's antlers pushed into them. They looked like a couple of monsters.

Pagan things, Giulia thought. *Blessed Senobina, watch over me.*

"These are very old," Sethis said.

"Who made them?" Giulia did not want to get any closer to the statues.

"Nobody knows for certain. Maybe primitive men. Once, humans worshipped the Lord and Lady, as well as your god. Let's keep moving," he added. "We're almost there."

They passed between the statues. The trees grew closer to the path, their branches arcing overhead to form a tunnel. *Here we go*, she thought, and she followed him through.

Sethis stopped and turned back to her. She could see grass between the trees behind him. They were near some kind of clearing. "We're almost there," he said. "It's just through here."

"Wait. Sethis, what I told you last night, about Hugh—"

"It's private. I know."

"Good. Let's go."

They emerged into bright sunshine. The grass was thick and soft. To the right, a cliff rose up. There were holes and cracks in the cliff face, and moss had settled in the fissures. Sixty feet up, at the top of the cliff, stood a round, dumpy watchtower like a stone barrel. On the far left, a lake stretched away as far as Giulia could see. She doubted it would appear on any map of the peninsula. She could smell salt on the air.

A table stood thirty feet away. It looked big enough for a banquet. People sat around the table: mainly dryads, but there were a few dwarrows as well. Nobody seemed to have noticed Sethis and Giulia. The scene felt unreal, like a stage backdrop.

"Are you ready?" Sethis asked.

She nodded. "All set."

As they approached, she saw that, instead of a wooden tabletop, a huge mirror had been set into the wood. In the greenness of the clearing, it seemed as if the sky had been trapped inside the table, as if Giulia could climb onto it and dive into the reflected sky.

A stone statue of a dwarrow sat at the near end of the table. It had that stylised, rounded quality of dwarrow sculpture, as if made by running water, not hands. On the far end of the table was something which was either a wooden statue or a small birch tree induced to grow into the rough shape of a sitting man. The face was a simple wooden plate roughly modelled on a dryad's face, with two diamond-shaped holes for eyes and a little scar in the wood for a mouth and lips. Green twigs rose up behind it, like hair or the peaks of a crown.

306

A dryad saw them and raised a hand in greeting. As they got closer, Giulia realised that it was Arashina.

One of the dwarrows stood up and turned to face her. A huge smile spread across his wide, grey-tinted face. "Giulia!"

Relief seemed to burst inside her, to shoot through her limbs. She laughed. "Grodrin? Is that you?"

"The very same!" Grodrin strode over and threw his arms around her. She had forgotten how strong he was, how tightly he could hold her.

"God, it's good to see you," Giulia said. "How are things in Pagalia?"

"Better than they are here, from what I'm told." He stepped back and looked her over. "You still look unwell, though. Stick thin."

"I was sick. Poisoned. Look, Grodrin, we have to talk."

"Of course." His smile was gone. The dwarrow turned back to the table and said something in Darvin.

There were nods around the table, and Grodrin took Giulia's arm and led her a little way off. "I heard that things have been hard," he said.

"You heard right. But nothing like this." Sethis was at the table now, talking to his people. Giulia leaned closer to Grodrin and lowered her voice. "You remember that knight, Hugh of Kenton, that I left Pagalia with?"

"Yes, I remember him. A good man, I thought."

"He was. Is. Do you know Arashina?"

The dwarrow nodded. "Of course. She's been telling me about what you did in Averrio. Impressive work."

"Right. Good. This is between you and me and nobody else – including them. I thought Hugh was dead, but he isn't. Leth's got him, down in this underground lair… it's like a city he's got down there, full of these old buildings. He's holding him prisoner in there."

"Hugh's alive?"

"Not exactly, but he's not properly undead either." Grodrin's expression changed – the beginnings of fear, and perhaps disgust – and she pressed on. She had to make him listen. "Look, I've got a week to rescue him, before he turns revenant for good. Leth thinks he can use Hugh to force me do what he wants, but, well, to hell with that."

"Nobody can make you do what they want. Believe me, I've tried."

"Sethis says that Leth's marched on Astrago. His base will be nearly empty. If you could get enough people together, we could break in and rescue Hugh—" The dwarrow's expression had changed. "What's the problem?"

"They won't go for it," he said. "It's about the only thing they agree on. No army for Mavlio."

"Fuck. Why not? He's hardly perfect, God knows, but he's not exactly the Inquis Impugnans, is he? He's always been fair with you people."

At the table, Arashina stood up.

"We'd better go," Grodrin said. "There's a lot to discuss."

Arashina gestured at the two newcomers. "Everybody, this is Giulia Degarno, who I told you about. A friend. And this is Sethis of Averrio, who deals with the good people there."

Giulia sat down beside Grodrin. Sethis took a seat opposite. She looked left and right, and felt only nervous and alone. The fey folk all looked so damned similar, as if two faces had been copied half a dozen times. She felt instinctively drawn to the dwarrows – she had spent time in their temple, back in Pagalia – but right now, they looked no more friendly than any of the others.

"We have been talking," Arashina said. "It appears that Leth has played his hand, and the chance to settle with him approaches. At the moment, his army is preparing to attack Astrago. The last I'd heard, they had yet to breach the walls. But it remains close."

Giulia said, "When you say 'attack', do you mean he'll storm the city or try to starve them out?"

"We think he will have to break through the walls. Leth has one very large advantage: if he kills a man, he can raise him from the dead as a revenant, and use him as a soldier. So, for every enemy that Leth kills, he gains a man. In that way, his army could increase hugely over a short space of time."

Fuck, she thought. "So every man we lose, he gains one?"

"Quite possibly, yes."

Grodrin added, "We don't know for sure. It may not be that easy for him: he might become exhausted, or run out of whatever he needs to raise the dead. But yes, that's the worst that could happen. His army would spread like a plague."

"However," Arashina continued, "if Leth's army loses its… what's your word for it? Like a rock rolling."

Sethis said, "Momentum?"

"If it loses momentum, he loses the advantage. If Leth cannot break into the city, Mavlio could pin his army in place and seek help from allies to destroy it for good. If Mavlio has any sense at all, he will have sent for aid from the neighbouring states, or perhaps even from the Church."

One of the dryads said something, a long, liquid set of syllables. It was a male, Giulia supposed: at any rate, it seemed slightly bigger than the ones that she reckoned were female.

Arashina raised a hand. "Please, so Giulia can understand."

The dryad nodded. "Apologies. I said that the Pontifex will not rush to help the city. He will recognise a fellow inquisitor in Leth. They are brothers in their hatred of us."

"Then what of the other states?" Arashina asked.

Grodrin put his big hands on the tabletop and leaned forward. "Pagalia is Mavlio's ally, but also its rival. Princess Leonora will help, eventually, once Astrago has been weakened. And she may not understand the nature of the threat – if someone told me that an army of skeletons was approaching, I probably wouldn't believe them. By then, Leth may have taken the city. As for Averrio and Montalius, they have their own problems. Montalius certainly has other things to think about, not least the Archduke of Vorland threatening it from the north." He looked down the table. "Does that sound right to you, Giulia?"

"Yes," she said, grateful to have been asked. "That's about right, as far as I know. Mavlio's very clever, but I never heard of anyone who *likes* him much."

A dwarrow woman coughed further down the table. She had pleasant, even features, and the grey tint to her skin made her look like a sculpture. She chose her words carefully, as if she did not trust them. "What will happen if Leth captures Astrago? Will he be the king? Will he seek peace with the other states, or try to capture them? I don't know how men are in this thing."

"May I?" Sethis asked. Heads turned to him. "As far as I can see, Leth has to keep going until he's too powerful to defeat. If he takes Astrago, he has to try to conquer Pagalia. No-one, not even the Pontifex, would allow an undead monster to stay in charge of a city. If he stops, he runs the risk of an alliance being declared between the other states – or worse still, the Pontifex calling a crusade. He needs to keep going, and he *has* to replenish his army. Now is the right time to make a move, before enough people have died to make his army unstoppable. We need to gather our forces—"

The tree at the end of the table moved. The blank face turned, and a creaking sound came out of it. Giulia started and clenched her fists under the table.

Easy, easy. They're on your side.

The creaking continued. The tree-thing stopped talking, and was still.

The dryad closest to it said, "We will send no soldiers. That is the word of the Oldest."

Sethis folded his arms.

The tree-thing creaked again. "None of our lives are worth losing over this," the dryad beside it said, and Giulia realised that she was translating. She felt queasy. "Leth has taken too many fey lives already. He was once a human: let men spill their blood destroying him."

"I disagree," Grodrin said, and the dwarrow woman began to nod. "There are over a hundred dwarrows living in Astrago. If we send no help, we will be seen to have abandoned them. I can speak for us at the court of Pagalia—"

The tree-thing creaked. As though worked by a puppeteer, it raised one of its branch-hands.

"The decision has been taken," said the interpreter.

"For you, at least," Grodrin replied.

The Oldest made its low, scratching noise again. It was not a beautiful sound: Giulia would have expected an ancient dryad to sing, like a bird, or perhaps babble like a stream. It sounded like two branches rubbing together in a breeze, and it made her skin crawl.

"No, we have *not* forgotten!" Grodrin snapped back, and Giulia's hand twitched towards the knife on her belt. Grodrin's colleague muttered something, apparently in support. "The entire reason we have given Prince Mavlio our help," Grodrin continued, "is that he and Leonora are about the closest thing to friends that we have. We have to face the truth. Outside Faery, people like them control the world. If we want to be in their cities, to live with them – to do anything that doesn't involve running and hiding – we need to work with them. Together we can kill Leth, once and for all."

For a few seconds, nobody spoke. A bird called out, long and high. Giulia didn't recognise it.

The female dwarrow said, "If we don't work with the human people, they will say we work against them."

Silence again.

Giulia raised a hand. "I just want to be sure about this. You're not sending any help to Astrago, are you?"

"Correct," Arashina replied.

"And they can just die?"

"They can manage without us."

Giulia licked her lips. "Fine. I'll kill Leth myself."

The female dwarrow peered at Giulia. She leaned over and said something softly to Grodrin.

Grodrin said, "Tell them exactly who you are, Giulia. Tell them what you've done."

"If you wish. Here's who I am. I'm the woman who killed Publius Severra," she said, "the most powerful criminal in Pagalia. Grodrin knows all about that. Then, last winter, I broke up a conspiracy of former Inquisitors in Averrio, trying to smuggle gold into the city. I killed their leader, Ramon Azul. Sethis and Arashina can tell you more about that. In Astrago, I've been working with Pietro Sepello, Mavlio's pet revenant-hunter. I can get close to people the way you can't. Basically," she said, looking down the table, "if you need Leth killed, I'm the one to do it."

"She's right," Grodrin replied.

A murmur of conversation at the far end of the table. Heads nodded.

Arashina said, "Much as I would like it to be one of us who strikes the killing blow, Giulia has a good point. Giulia, you need to be able to get back into the city of Astrago, yes?"

"Yes."

"We can help you to get there quickly. In return, I would ask you to take something to Cosimo Lannato: a formula like the one we used to heal you. If he is the alchemist that he's said to be, he may be able to use it to make a weapon against the undead."

"So, I'll bring this formula to Lannato, in exchange for your help killing Leth."

Arashina looked pointedly down the table, at the Oldest and its interpreter. They did not respond. She looked back at Giulia. "Exactly," she said.

"Good. But I can't just walk back into Astrago. The city will be sealed shut. Even if they let me in the gates, there's no guarantee they'll let me see the prince. They probably think I'm some kind of revenant, given how long I've been away."

Arashina looked surprised. "Then sneak in. That's what you do, isn't it?"

"It is. But I'll need to be able to get past the defences. The city's got ramparts and high walls, not to mention towers with guns in them. Lannato designed it to be damned near impregnable."

Grodrin said, "Could you get over the walls by night?"

"Not a hope. Maybe if someone dropped a rope down from the battlements, maybe I could climb up…"

"We can deal with that," the dwarrow replied. He sounded so certain that Giulia was rather taken aback. "We have a grapple you could fire out of your crossbow, like a bolt. It's heavy compared to the usual sort, but it would do the job."

"All right," she said. "I like the sound of that." She smiled at him, and he smiled back. She remembered how they had worked together in Pagalia, fighting off Publius Severra's thugs. *Back in business.* "It sounds as if we're done here," Giulia said. "The sooner I can get started, the sooner I can take care of Leth."

Six days left, she thought, and her smile faded. *Six days until Hugh is a revenant for good.*

"Well said," Arashina replied. She gestured, and one of the dryads stood up and brought her a canvas bag. She took something out and held it out to Giulia. "Take this."

Giulia took the object. It was a slim flask, wrapped in a piece of paper.

"That is the elixir we used on you, to purge you of undeath. Put some of it on your knife and your crossbow bolts. The paper has a list of ingredients to make more – give the paper to Lannato. The elixir will be sure poison to any of the lesser undead – to an old revenant like Leth, it'll weaken him considerably. Then you can close in and finish him."

Giulia opened her bag and slipped the flask inside. "Are you sure it'll work on Leth?"

"Yes. When Sethis used it on you, it cured the undeath in you and left that which was living. But on the undead, there is nothing living. Cure the undeath in them, and they are nothing."

Cure the undeath, eh? It brought me back from the edge of death. And perhaps it will cure Hugh.

Sethis was watching her. It made her feel guilty. Giulia put the flask into her bag and closed it.

"Good luck." Arashina leaned across the table and held out her hand for Giulia to shake.

Giulia stood up, took her pack and walked to the edge of the clearing. The meeting was dissolving, the various attendees standing up in twos and threes. The interpreter and another dryad were talking beside the Oldest, which seemed to have frozen solid again. A male dryad with long grey hair was addressing a female at the far end of the table. It made a grand gesture, taking in the whole lakeside, and Giulia thought of a drunken aristocrat at a party.

She felt a sudden stab of anger, a sense that these creatures could never understand what she felt or had to do, and put it aside. They had their own reasons for hating Leth. And now Giulia had work to do and a monster to destroy.

"Giulia."

She looked around: Grodrin stood there, calm and strong.

"It's time for me to go," she said.

"I know. We'll walk you to the edge of the forest. Oh – this is for you." He held out a metal rod. It looked like a piece of a clockwork machine: splines were folded against the main body of the rod. She took it from him: it felt light, perhaps hollow. "Give it a shake."

Giulia flicked the rod down as if to knock someone out. Three spines snapped out at right-angles. She understood what it was for, and grinned at the dwarrow. "It's a grappling hook."

"Exactly," he replied. ". When I heard you were here, I thought it might be the kind of thing you could use. It arcs in flight, so you'll need to aim high."

"You know me too well," Giulia said. "Look, I'm sorry I didn't keep in touch. I've— I've not been myself lately."

"So I gather. You should have come and found me," Grodrin said. "But a person doesn't always think straight, when they grieve."

Giulia suddenly felt terribly sad, then ashamed. She wondered how she must have seemed while the Melancholia was in control of her. She felt like a drunkard wondering if he had disgraced himself the night before. "You're a good friend," she said. "Better than I deserve."

"Rubbish," he replied. "You've been sick, and not just while you were throwing up in his house." He nodded at Sethis. "Come on. I've got one more gift for you. Or rather my friend here has."

Giulia looked at the female dwarrow. She smiled. She looked shy.

"Away from here," Grodrin said. "Sethis, you lead the way. We will follow you."

They walked up a narrow track. Giulia could hardly fit through: behind her, the two dwarrows stomped and shoved their way through the undergrowth. At last the path widened, as if it was getting the hang of their size.

She wondered why they were going out of sight of the others: she had a strong, vague feeling that the dryads would be able to find them no matter what, thanks to whatever magic controlled this place.

They reached a small clearing. The female dwarrow said something and Grodrin said, "We'll stop here."

Giulia turned to him. "What is this gift?"

"It's about Hugh," Grodrin said. "May I speak about him in front of Ardva here?"

The female dwarrow was staring along the track. Quietly, Giulia said, "What is it?"

Grodrin lowered his voice. "There's a way of … not bringing him back, but making sure that he is still alive. A sort of spell."

Giulia felt a stab of hope; she pushed it aside. "Make me see him? How?"

"A thought is a real thing," Grodrin explained. "If a person thinks of something hard enough, it is said that that idea can take on a form of its own. A kind of dreaming, if you like. If you have a thing that Hugh owned, or liked, my friend Ardva can put a glamour on it – a sort of magic – that will enable you to see him. You'll be able to tell whether he is still alive."

"Will I be able to know where he is?"

"You could ask him."

"Ask him? I can talk to him?"

Grodrin paused. Sethis watched closely from the far side of the little clearing, as if he thought one of them might collapse at any moment.

"You could talk to your memory of him," Grodrin replied.

Giulia had no idea what that meant. But the thought of seeing Hugh, of talking to him again, even through some strange magical trickery… *Careful*, she thought. *It can't be him. Don't get your hopes up.* "All right," she said. "Tell her she can. I've got his book. You can use that."

She shrugged her pack off and delved inside. Her fingers touched paper and she pulled out the battered copy of *The Death of King Alba.* "He loved this thing," she said. "He never read anything else."

Grodrin stepped over to the dwarrow-woman and they spoke. Ardva nodded. They returned.

"It is good, then," Ardva said. She held out her hand. "Please."

Giulia passed the book over. She felt nervous; she didn't want to watch the dwarrow-woman preparing whatever she was about to do. "You know," she said, "Leth must have had Hugh down there for months, not quite dead. I reckon he was waiting for me to find him. Otherwise, he just would have made Hugh properly undead. He must have thought he could keep Hugh alive and use him against me."

Sethis said, "Maybe not just against you, but anyone who came looking for him. Perhaps he thought Hugh was an important nobleman. That he could use him as a bargaining tool."

Giulia had a sudden, bleak sense of how cunning Leth was. He had been preparing for this for centuries. Whatever she came up with, he had a response. How could you compete with that?

Ardva put the book into Giulia's hand and closed her fingers around it. "You should shut your eyes."

Slowly, Giulia closed her eyes. She disliked hearing without seeing, the sense of vulnerability that came from knowing that people were surrounding her. Even among friends, it was there.

"Remember him," Ardva said.

Giulia remembered Hugh. She thought of him sitting in the shabby inn the night before his death. Of the weight of his body as she'd helped him stagger away from the Tower of Glass in Averrio. And all the way back: to the mild, befuddled man she had met in the House of Good Cheer in Pagalia, who'd cadged drinks off her and saved her life.

"Open your eyes."

She opened her eyes and there he was. He stood a little way from her, just before the trees. He wore the cuirass that she'd bought for him and his hand rested on the sword on his belt. His moustaches hung down, giving him the look of an old mastiff. His eyes focussed on her as if it was Giulia who had just appeared.

"Hello, Giulia."

"My God," she managed. "Hugh? Is that you?"

"I think so," he said. "How are you?"

"I'm... fine. I think I am." Astonishment was giving way to delight. She felt a prickling behind her eyes.

"Can you see him?" Ardva asked.

"Can't you?"

Ardva said, "Only you."

"My God." Giulia wanted to touch Hugh. She put *The Death of King Alba* on a rock and stepped towards him. Hugh vanished. "He's gone!"

"Hold the book."

She reached out for it. Her fingers touched the cover and Hugh was there again. There was no process of coming to life: he was simply present, the way he'd been absent a second before. He frowned. "Nearly lost you there, old girl."

"You're alive."

"Well, yes, I am." He looked down at himself. "Yes, I think so." He smiled.

"What you see is your memory," Ardva said. "He is like... how to say it... like a ghost. While he lives, you can see him."

She was right, Giulia thought. This version of Hugh wasn't quite right. He was thinner than he'd really been, longer in the face, with larger, sadder eyes. She was looking at her memory of him, not the man himself. "Hugh," she said, "where are you?"

He frowned, as if he'd forgotten something. "Well," he said, "I'm not really sure, you know. I wondered if you could help me there. Or maybe Grodrin or that dryad fellow – what's his name again?"

"Sethis," Giulia said.

Sethis said, "Yes, Giulia? What is it?"

"That's the one." Hugh still looked puzzled. "They can't see me, can they?"

Giulia shook her head. "No."

"Say hello to everyone, would you? Look, ah, Giulia, could I talk to you for a moment? I think I need to, er, catch up with things, yes?"

"I think you do," she replied.

"Good lord," said Hugh's ghost. Except it wasn't a ghost, she told herself. To be a ghost, you had to be dead. "So you've got six days?"

"More or less." She kept wanting to touch him: a few minutes ago, she'd started laughing like a crazy person. She'd had to stop, to remind herself that her friend was not truly here. She was only seeing a memory, a piece of her imagination.

"We need to get on with this, Giulia."

"That's no lie."

"And you're all set to do this?"

"Pretty much. As ready as I'll ever be."

He was sitting on a fallen log. Her memory of him had made his arms and legs rather spindly: his legs stuck out in front of him, as clumsy as a foal's. "Who can we trust, beyond Grodrin and Sethis?"

"Arashina's on our side. Sepello as well – to an extent, anyway. Carmina and Lannato seem fairly decent, but Mavlio holds the reins in the palace. Anything they want goes through him."

"I see. I never liked the sounds of Mavlio DeFalci. Though the fellow he overthrew sounded even worse." Hugh stood up, quick and jerky like a marionette. "Well then, better get going. I don't mind if you want to let go of the book – you'll need both hands for what you've got to do. I'll remember everything you told me when I'm next here – well, I'll remember as much as I ever did…"

She put the book into her pack. Hugh vanished. Giulia hurried back down the path.

Grodrin, Sethis and Ardva were waiting up ahead. "What did he say?" Sethis asked.

"I'll tell you on the way," Giulia replied. "Let's go."

They walked for several hours. They stopped briefly to eat, but Giulia wasn't hungry. She chewed the bread and sausage that Grodrin had brought, fighting the urge to pull *The Death of King Alba* out of her pack and see Hugh again. That was the thing about magic, she thought: the moment it was gone, it was hard to credit that it had existed at all. She wondered how much more she'd have to see to go completely mad.

Sethis acted as their guide. He was quieter around the dwarrows than he had been with just Giulia. "We're making decent progress," he announced, in what seemed to be the late afternoon.

"Good," Giulia said. "I suppose Leth will have surrounded the city. It's going to be hard to get through his lines."

"True," Grodrin replied, "but if he wants to break through the walls, he'll have to concentrate his forces on one or two points. If I was him, I'd block off the main roads out, to stop anyone escaping, and attack the weakest parts of the wall. That means that there'll be places where his forces are more spread-out than in others."

"Then I'll go in there."

"So, given Leth's army approached from the south-west, if we come out of the forest to the north-east of the city, that should keep us away from the bulk of his forces."

"Can we do that?"

Sethis nodded. "I think the forest will allow it."

Giulia looked through the trees. The light was fading now, and the thought of being left in here at night was not entirely pleasant. Sethis seemed to know the way, but she would never feel at home in the deep forest. She suspected that, without a guide, it would regard her as a parasite rather than a guest.

They walked ten yards up the path. The night air was warm and close. Giulia could hear something now, very faintly: the flat banging of guns and the boom of falling stone. Sethis turned left and pulled back the branches, and Giulia saw Astrago again.

Astrago glowed. It looked as if the whole city was being cooked, like a pot on hot coals. There were lanterns on the walls, and great torches burned on the battlements. Smaller fires glowed at the base of the walls: perhaps put there to hinder the undead, perhaps the burning remains of things that had fallen from the parapet. Worse, an evil orange light hung above the city, as if dawn was about to rise within it. She wondered if it came from Leth's army – or whether Astrago was in flames.

"My God," she said. "Look at it."

A ball of fire arced out, streaked through the air. It hit something and burst like a chunk of ice; lumps of fire fell down.

They were looking at Astrago from the east. The walls on that side were straight stone things, without the earthworks of the western wall: Mavlio's redesign of the defences hadn't reached this part yet.

Good. Less chance of being seen as I climb them. It occurred to her that, in the darkness between her and the city wall, Leth's soldiers waited. Giulia shuddered.

"This is it," she said. "Time to go. I'll see you soon, Grodrin."

"Make damn sure that you do, girl." Grodrin reached out and hugged her. His body was too massive for her hands to meet around him. He patted her back with his broad hand and stepped away. "May the Lord and Lady watch over you."

"You too." She bowed to Ardva. "Thank you."

"A pleasure to meet you," Ardva said carefully, and she smiled.

Sethis stepped in. "Good luck, Giulia."

For a moment it seemed as if they wouldn't embrace; that, at most, they might shake hands. But Giulia grabbed him, held him tight, felt the slim strength of his body against her own.

At last, she let him go. "Thank you," she said. "For everything."

"I could come with you," Sethis said.

"No. Stay here. Get your people ready. I'll do what I can, but I may need help."

"Just give us the word," Grodrin replied.

Sethis peered between the trees, at the glowing city. "You could do with another pair of eyes," he said. "Someone to watch out for you."

Giulia took her pack off and rooted about in it. Her fingers brushed the leather cover of *The Death of King Alba*, and Hugh of Kenton stood beside her.

"I'll be fine," she replied, and she pulled the pack onto her back.

Chapter 12

She walked out of the trees. Her left hand was open; the book was in her right. The ghost of Hugh – her memory of him – paced along beside her, a few yards to her left.

The city walls stood about half a mile away. Bonfires burned at intervals beyond the walls, to warn the defenders against night attacks. She could see nothing of Leth's army.

Oh, they'll be there, all right. Waiting, in the dark.

From the far side of the city came the steady popping of guns. It might be quiet here, but the fight was going on. The undead didn't sleep.

The ground was open and flat. It rose slightly at the edge of a road and she walked quickly and carefully over the ruts.

The sounds of violence grew louder. She could just about hear voices now, as well as gunshots. She wondered why she hadn't seen Leth's army yet. Perhaps he had concentrated his forces on a small area, trying to punch through in just one place.

Then she saw that one of the bonfires wasn't just a fire: it was burning around a massive gate. The gate loomed out of the dark, three times taller than a man, glowing with the flames of a hundred torches. She saw carts and low mounds before the gate – tents, perhaps, protected by wooden pavises . Something spindly moved in front of the lights, and for a moment it looked like branches arranged in the shape of a skeleton. They weren't branches, though. They were bones.

Fuck.

The undead weren't trying to bash their way in. They were just standing outside the East Gate. Waiting. Giulia shuddered. There was something horrible about the patience of the dead.

Hugh stopped and folded his arms. "Be careful, Giulia."

"I've got to go now." She let go of the book and he vanished. She was alone.

There could be a hundred skeletons, a thousand, just standing there in the dark around her, silent and still.

She turned right and headed north. She'd climb the wall somewhere between the east and north gates, where the undead would be thinner.

Getting in would be best done quietly. If she called out for assistance, she would be more likely to get a bullet in the chest than a helping hand: no doubt the soldiers had been instructed to kill anything that tried to climb or trick its way inside. She recalled the noxi, with their masks and scars, and realised that the defenders would probably fire on anybody that came out of the night.

The walls loomed up ahead. Soon she'd be in range of the guns. She could hear the crackling of the bonfires, each thirty yards from the walls and fifty yards apart. They weren't enough to light up the area. There was enough darkness to let her through.

Giulia dropped down and checked her kit. She tied the grapple onto the end of her rope, tugged it a few times and felt the weight. It would fly terribly: she'd have to compensate for its weight by aiming high.

Something lurched out of the darkness. Stopped.

She froze, head lowered. She looked up, not raising her head, and saw what looked like four white sticks driven into the earth. They were leg bones. They moved, and Giulia saw the pale complexity of the skeleton's feet. They stepped aside, turned from her. It was looking the other way.

She stood up. The revenant was armed like an ancient Quaestan legionary, in a tunic and banded armour. Firelight glowed on the metal strips, on the reinforcements fastened to its massive shield. The skeleton faced the East Gate, watching for something.

I'll have to kill it.

Giulia put the crossbow down and drew her long knife. Stabbing had worked before: what would kill a living man seemed to break the magic holding the undead together. She crept towards its back. Fires glowed at the edge of her vision.

Grab it from behind, stab it in the neck—

It spun around and belted her with the shield. She cried out, fell, rolled, and the skeleton slammed the edge of the shield down where her head had just been. Giulia scrambled to her feet and it was striding towards her, sword glimmering with firelight.

She sidestepped, jumped up and slammed her heel into the shield as if to kick down a door. The skeleton stumbled back, righted itself and strode towards her again.

It bore down on her, the sword blade held out around the edge of the shield. The eye sockets were two caves, the old bones as pale and hard as sandstone. Giulia braced herself to dart to the left, past the shield.

There was a sharp crack and the skull burst. The helmet rolled down its body, and the bones broke apart. Armour clattered onto the ground.

They shot it.

Giulia turned and saw tiny figures on the battlements, lit by the glow of flames.

Another shot cracked out. Dirt burst a yard from her feet.

"Shit!" Giulia grabbed the crossbow and ran into the dark. She dropped into a crouch, waited for the shadows on the battlements to stop moving.

Fucking idiots.

She pulled her hood up and began to creep forward again, her head down, the crossbow in her hands. On top of the wall, people were gathering, moving towards the East Gate. She could hear voices, but couldn't make out words.

One person stepped away from the others, to a torch blazing on the battlement. The torch sailed out from the wall, drew a long arc across the sky and landed twenty yards away. The men hurried along the wall, and she saw a hand pointing. For half a second something was illuminated in the torchlight, something thin and pale.

She kept absolutely still, her heart suddenly drumming in her chest.

It could have been a dead sapling, or a scarecrow – or an upright skeleton. A second torch flew out, landing closer to the wall. It revealed nothing but grass. On the wall, the men argued. Giulia scuttled closer, bent double.

There was a tower at the corner of the wall, covering a weak point. A structure protruded from the tower. It was a crane, perhaps, or some mechanism for dropping rocks on enemies, but from below it looked like a gallows arm. *That's it,* she thought, *that's where I get in.*

The wall was ten yards away. Giulia stood up and ran.

She reached the wall with her calf muscles aching. She dropped down and allowed herself to sigh. Above her and to the right, the soldiers were still scanning the night for the undead. Giulia loaded the grapple into her bow.

It was too heavy and it sat awkwardly in the groove. She pulled the rope from her shoulder and laid it to the side. Very carefully, she raised the bow and tried to work out how the grapple would fly. The angle was tight: with a bit of luck the grapple would drive straight into the workings of the crane and lodge there.

Here we go.

Giulia lifted the bow and fired. The bolt shot upwards, dragging the rope behind it, over the arm of the crane, so high that surely everyone on the wall must have seen it. It reached the top of its arc and dropped swiftly. Giulia trod on the rope. She felt the rope snap taut beneath her boot, saw the grapple stop and swing back. It struck the wall: *tink*.

The grapple was still. Above her, someone called out "Hey, Rolli! Rolli!"

Boots moved on the parapet above her head. Giulia heard a voice, rough and worn-out, saying "What now?" The boots kept going on the battlements, past her. She bent down and, very slowly, began to pull in the rope.

The grapple rose and she hauled it in, hand over hand. She saw it disappear into the dark mass of the crane and she slowed down, pulling very carefully now. It hit something and stopped.

Giulia pulled it again. It didn't move. She wiped her palms on her thighs and began to climb.

She'd always hated climbing. The constant strain on the muscles, no matter how you did it, the feeling of swaying on the rope, the sense of vulnerability; it was one of the last things she'd learned as a thief, and it had never quite come easily. She gritted her teeth and climbed up, one hand over another, catching the rope between her boots. She was fifteen feet off the ground now, enough to break her ankle if she fell. Soon she'd be high enough to break her leg, then her neck... The arm of the crane was directly above her. Giulia climbed as high as she could go, then pulled her legs up and pushed them into the gap between the beams of the crane. She grabbed the wooden struts with one hand, then the other, and pulled herself onto the arm of the crane. She paused a moment, catching her breath. She felt giddy: her palms were beginning to sweat. Her arms and back ached as if poison was in the muscles. Everything seemed precarious, as though any movement would make her fall.

Nearly there.

She crawled down the arm of the crane on all fours, and dropped onto the battlements.

Her boots struck the stone. Nobody seemed to have heard. She stood up and brushed her hands together.

A young man leaned out of the darkness, a crossbow in his hands. Giulia ducked back. The bow clacked and a bolt thumped into the crane behind her. "Help!" the young man shouted. "There's one up here!"

Boots pounded the stone. Men called to each other. A skinny man ran into view, holding a musket. He jabbed it towards her.

Giulia raised her hands. "Don't shoot!" she cried. "I'm alive – don't shoot!"

The crossbowman held up his empty bow. His face was pale and young. His hands fumbled to reload the bow. "Sergeant! There's one down here, by the crane," he called. "It's trying to get in!"

A third man appeared, carrying a halberd. The three soldiers glared at her, their faces lined and grotesque in the torchlight.

"Easy, easy!" Giulia said. "Don't shoot. I'm on your side." The musket made her feel queasy: her head was spinning, her guts churned. "I'm alive: I work for Prince Mavlio. I've got a message for him, from the fey folk. It's all right."

The halberdier tried to level his weapon at her, but the blade caught on the battlements. He cursed.

"It's all right," Giulia said. "I'm not one of them. I'm not undead, I promise."

"It's one of those things," said the pale-faced youth. He was loading the crossbow slowly now.

"I work for Pietro Sepello," Giulia said. "You know him? He's a revenant-hunter. I was sent to kill Constantin Leth. He's their leader. I've come back." She couldn't explain herself fast enough, not with that bloody gun aimed at her chest.

A fourth man appeared from the dark. He was older, bearded, with an ugly scar at the corner of his mouth. "What's going on?" There was a sword and a pistol on his belt.

"We caught one," said the halberdier. "Came over the wall. Says it's come here with some kind of message."

"She's one of 'em," the youth explained. "Just look at her face."

"Bring that torch closer," said the older man. He peered at Giulia, like a farmer checking an animal for disease. "God have mercy," he said, "that's a woman. How'd you get up here?"

"I used a rope," Giulia replied. "It's on that crane. Now, will you stop pointing that fucking gun at me?"

The sergeant said, "Keep it on her, Rolli. Until we know what she is."

"I just told you. I'm with the prince. I've got a message for him. I work for Pietro Sepello. Go and find him. He'll tell you."

The pale young man swallowed hard. Only the sergeant and the halberdier seemed like professionals, although the man with the musket had a quick, mean look to him, like some of the criminals she'd known in

331

the old days. Giulia stayed quiet and still. They would be dangerous if they panicked.

"Disarm her," the sergeant said.

The musketeer looked her over. "Shit," he said, "where do I start?"

They took the crossbow and the knives in her belt and boot – but they missed the stiletto in her left sleeve. "And that," said the sergeant, pointing, and the halberdier used his polearm to pull the grapple from the crane. He hauled in the rope, wrapped it into a coil.

The sergeant cleared his throat. "You are my captive," he announced. "You will be held down the wall there, in the tower room."

"Listen, I need to see the prince," Giulia said. "Please. We can sort this out."

"*Everyone* needs to see the prince," said the musketeer. "Too bad that arsehole's always hiding."

The sergeant barked "That's enough! You'll show some fucking respect!"

The musketeer smirked and glanced away.

"Now," said the sergeant, turning to Giulia, "you will go inside and these two men will guard you. Rolli, Tomas – *watch her*. Alonzo, you keep walking the walls. Three blasts on the horn if you need help."

The halberdier patted the horn hanging on his belt. "Yes, sir."

"I'll go down and see if anyone's heard of this woman. What did you say your name was?"

"Giulia Degarno. I work for Pietro Sepello."

"I see. Take her away, men," the sergeant commanded, and he turned and walked away.

The pale youth lifted his crossbow. He'd managed to reload it, at last. "Go on, then. It's down the wall. That way." He nodded at the battlements. Giulia turned, her hands still raised, and walked.

They walked the few yards to the guard-tower. Giulia hesitated, thought about running off, jumping from the wall.

It was too risky. These twitchy arseholes would put a bullet straight through her.

The musketeer opened a narrow door and gestured to the dark room beyond.

"Ladies first," he said, and they followed her inside.

The roof was small and the walls were made of hefty stone bricks. A few stools stood around a battered table. A lamp seemed to throw out more shadows than light.

"Over there," the youth with the crossbow said, pointing to the far side of the room. He seemed to be called Tommo. Giulia picked up one of the stools and carried it to the wall. She sat down next to a small, barred window.

The sun was coming up, and the horizon glowed as if about to catch on fire. Tommo covered her with the crossbow while the musketeer – Rolli, the sergeant had called him – dumped Giulia's bow, rope, grapple and knives on the table, next to a bottle of wine.

Tommo didn't hold the crossbow easily. His lack of confidence unnerved her. She made herself keep still, so as not to panic him. She tried not to look as angry as she felt.

I should have been more careful. All that effort, to end up getting captured by these bloody fools. God damn it, this is wasting my time!

She wondered how long it would be before Hugh was irreparably undead, and then whether Leth had simply lied about it. She thought of Mavlio, then Sepello, hunkered in the palace. And then of Hugh himself, trapped in that strange armour, bewitched into obedience. She wanted to hold his book again, to see his face.

"The sergeant reckons you might be dead," Rolli said. "Dead but still walking, like the other ones outside."

"He's wrong. I'm as alive as you are."

"That's what I think," Rolli said. "He may be the boss, but he says some stupid stuff at times." Rolli was broad across the shoulders, with a face that was nearly handsome. Right now, he looked grimy and tough. "What about you, Tommo?"

The youth shook his head. "I don't know. She's got the scars, Rolli. I heard that one of them climbed up the wall by the North Gate. I heard it was naked except for a mask. They took its mask off, and the face was all scars underneath. Like its face came off and they stitched it back on again."

"Well, she's not wearing a mask, is she? And she's not naked, as far as I can tell. Very well dressed – for a man. Excuse my friend here. A little slow," Rolli said, tapping the side of his head.

"Leave it, Rolli," Tommo replied. His hands gripped the crossbow tightly.

"Where's the sergeant gone?" Giulia asked.

"Gone to see the north-east captain," Rolli said. "They do it by quarters, see. It's well-organised, but it doesn't leave us lads with much to do. He'll be gone a long time. You're stuck with us. Sorry."

He wasn't sorry. He smiled. Fear began to settle in Giulia's gut, fear of something more than just the crossbow-bolt.

"You ought to be watching the walls," she said.

"The sergeant wants me watching you," Rolli replied. "What happened to your face?"

"Knife fight," Giulia replied. "I won."

Rolli smiled and glanced at Tommo. "You should see the other fellow, eh?"

Tommo said nothing. He looked down and frowned at his bow, as if it was a musical instrument he didn't know how to play.

"Tommo here's our knife man," Rolli said. "Cutpurse, that's what he is. He'd swipe your money before you knew – hell, he'd swipe the britches off a man's arse, crafty little beggar that he is." Giulia looked at Tommo. He looked away. Rolli said, "Young Tommo cut a purse too many, finds himself in jail. They were going to burn his palms when Mavlio offers the crims a pardon, if they helped the militia man the wall."

"That's not true," Tommo said. "You're talking about yourself." But his voice was very quiet now.

"I used to be a thief," Giulia said, and she stared at Tommo until she caught his eye. He glanced away, as if her gaze frightened him. "Just like you."

Rolli said, "Me, I'm an honest soldier. I've got no time for criminals." He grinned. His teeth were very regular and white. He tilted his head left and right, as if appraising workmanship. "You know, you're not bad looking, except for the scars."

Tommo stood up. "Come on, Rolli. We've got to walk the walls."

"You walk the walls. I'm guarding the prisoner."

"We can lock her in here." His face was pale. "I think she's one of them. A mort."

Rolli snorted. "She's no mort! She's alive. I bet she's as warm as you are. Here." He grabbed Tommo's wrist and pushed his arm out. "Feel her cheek."

"Don't touch me," Giulia said. She raised her hands, palms out – partly as a gesture of surrender, and partly ready to strike. Tommo paused, glanced around for reassurance, for some fourth person who was not in the room. "There's no need for any trouble. I'm the prince's messenger, remember?"

Quietly, as if it solved everything, Rolli said, "That's what you say. Let Tommo here touch your cheek. The boy needs putting at ease."

Tommo said, "We should lock her in."

"Let me out," Giulia said.

Rolli shook his head. "Good try. You'll have to ask a hell of a lot better than that."

"Open the door," she said.

He grinned. "Giving the orders now, are you? Now, why would I do something like that?"

Something broke in Giulia. She stood up. "How's about this? Open the door or I'll kill you."

"Bull-shit you will!" Rolli said, almost shouting.

"Rolli," Tommo said. Now it was his hand pulling Rolli's sleeve. "Look at her, man. She's all wrong. Let's just leave her here."

Rolli took a step forward. He was close, much too close.

Giulia put her hands together and slid the knife from her left sleeve. She held it up, knowing how the sight of steel could change a man's mind.

"I'm warning you," she said, and his hand flicked out and snapped around her wrist. It was the oldest move in the book, but he was fast – he sidestepped and twisted the hand back and up. Her wrist locked and pain shot through her arm. Rolli yanked her off balance. Arm outstretched, legs bent to compensate as best she could,

Giulia dropped the knife and tried not to let him break her wrist.

"I learned that with the Landsknecht," Rolli said. "Four years on the field, messenger girl." He put his free hand on her elbow, and pressed her down. Pain rushed up her arm, and she hissed. She was almost squatting now, her head level with his waist. "You still think she's undead?" he asked, not looking round. "Undead don't feel pain—"

"Stop it!" Tommo barked.

Rolli looked at him. "Leave us to it," he said. "You can walk the walls now."

Giulia's free hand found the table edge. Her fingers wrapped around iron, and she felt the cold stripe of metal in her palm.

Giulia swung the grappling hook into Rolli's shin.

His leg buckled and she jerked her arm free. Tommo gasped and Giulia came in from the side, chopped her left fist down onto his crossbow and it went off in his hands. The bolt hit the far wall and Giulia barged into him with her shoulder. He stumbled.

Giulia held the grapple in her left hand. Slowly, she flexed the fingers of her right. The bones seemed to grind together, but nothing was broken. Tommo cringed against the wall, hands raised in surrender. Rolli lay on the floor. One of the hooks on the grapple had torn the flesh of his calf open. His fingers were bloody.

Giulia flexed her right arm to get the pain out of the joint. She picked up her gear from the table and pulled her rucksack on. "Keys, now," she said.

Tommo blinked, glanced around.

"Give her the fucking keys!" Rolli snapped.

Tommo held them out. His hand was shaking.

Giulia slung her crossbow over her shoulder. She picked her knife up from the floor and slid it back into her sleeve. Rolli sat propped against the wall, silently gripping his leg. His calf was soggy with blood. Giulia wondered what he had been trying to do – beat her, goad her into attacking him, work himself up to molest her? – and realised that now she didn't much care. He was like a lamed dog.

She looked at Tommo. "Keep quiet, both of you. Your sergeant'll let you out." Rolli gritted his teeth. *I hope that stings, you arsehole*, she thought.

She opened the door, slipped out and locked it behind her. The halberdier stood ten yards further along the battlements, staring out over the wall and watching for the enemy. Giulia saw the stairs that would lead to ground level. As she stepped onto the staircase, a man in a big helmet started to ascend. Two swordsmen followed him.

The man looked up. It was the sergeant. He stared at her as if he could kill her with his eyes alone.

"Giulia Degarno, believed dead these last six days," he announced, "I am taking you into trial for criminal necromancy. Men, secure her!"

You fucking imbecile, she thought.

On the far side of the city, the cannons thundered. As if to answer them, hands beat on the tower door. Tommo's face appeared. "Help!"

Giulia glanced down the wall and saw the halberdier approaching, his weapon lowered. The sergeant stepped aside and his swordsmen drew their weapons.

Three against one was bad, long blades against knives doubly so. She glanced left, then right, and felt the desperate energy that came from being trapped. The battlement was thirty feet above the town. The rooftops stretched away like scales on a monster's back.

I can do it, she thought. *Do it now. Go!*

The soldiers were almost on her now. Giulia ran to the edge and jumped.

She threw herself through the air, felt it rush past her face, felt her stomach seem to drop away from her, and her feet hit tiles and she rolled. Giulia leaped up, heard screams and yells beneath her, and ran along the spine of the roof. "There's one of them up there!" a man shouted, and she heard the sergeant bellowing orders to his men. *They'll kill me*, she thought, and a gun cracked out behind her.

The road was twenty feet below. Giulia stopped, took a deep breath, and raced towards the edge of the roof. She drove off from both legs, and for a weird frozen second a girl below gawped up at her, and Giulia hit the edge of the roof across the street. She slipped and dropped onto her front, hands clinging to the edge of the roof, legs dangling below her. Someone shouted for the guards. Giulia saw figures running in from the edges of her vision, spears wobbling above their heads. Her toes caught on a windowsill, giving her the foothold that she needed. She hauled herself onto the roof. Panting, she crawled across the tiles, astonished by the weakness of her body. She wanted to lie there forever, getting her breath back and feeling the morning sun on her face. Giulia gritted her teeth and lurched upright.

She looked west, away from the dawn, and saw the Quincunx Palace rising over the city. Further away, on the south-western wall, the guns and shouts seemed to be getting louder. A fresh attack had come with the sunrise, and from the sounds of it the fight was wild.

People were shouting down below. *Of all the bloody luck.* Giulia jogged along the roof, her right arm aching, trying to run quietly. If she could get to the palace she could find someone who would understand that she wasn't the enemy. *Can't let the militia get me*, she thought, and for a moment she understood the horror of the siege, the breeding-ground for fear that a city could become.

She ducked down beside a chimney and tried to think. She peered across the city, across the sea of roofs. Why had Mavlio decided to widen so many streets? To get to the palace she'd have to climb down, and then it would get nasty.

At the meeting of four streets there was a statue of an orator, twice life size. His hand was outstretched towards the palace. *If I could get onto him, I could climb onto the houses beyond, maybe hide in there...*

"Hey!"

She turned. A soldier in palace livery stood on the roof behind her. He'd scrambled out of a hatch in the roof: there was a little dovecote next to him. He pointed a pistol at her. "Raise your hands," he said.

"Take me to the palace," Giulia replied.

"I said *raise your hands*."

She lifted her hands. "I surrender," she replied.

In the street, a woman screamed. A man pointed towards the south side of the town, shouting. Others followed, yelling and starting to run. Had the revenants broken in? Giulia looked along the walls, trying to spot the undead. She saw nothing. Then one of the spires on the horizon began to tilt.

It was Saint Allomar's church. Surely not. It was just her head spinning. The spire shuddered, and the great iron sword that topped the steeple shook. For an instant the church stood still, as if it had taken the blow but weathered it, and then the tower twisted like a withering plant and collapsed.

The sound was like an avalanche. Tenement blocks fell apart; the fronts of apartments were wiped out by waterfalls of brick. The guns were silent, suddenly.

"Oh God no," the soldier said.

A vast cloud of dust rose from the wreckage. Giulia stared at the space where the great church had been. *A spell*, she thought, *or some new kind of catapult—*

Something stirred in the dust-cloud. It looked like a frond, whipping around in a storm, but it was taller than a tree and as thick as a man's waist. *It's a snake*, she thought, and the dust parted enough to show a head at the end of the neck, a huge skull plated with steel.

It was part mechanical, part undead. The thing's body, made of massive bones and sheets of leather, crawled out of the ruins of the church. It raised its neck like a dragon in a painting. Great studded wheels spun in place of jaws, spewing out earth. For a moment, the monster just stood there, as if to get its bearings. Then it smashed its head into the city gates.

*

"Turn the guns!" Lannato cupped his hands around his mouth. "Turn the cannons round and shoot that thing!"

The monster was heaving its patchwork bulk out of the ground. Citizens scattered like mice before a viper. The front part of the beast slammed into the West Gate, throwing out chunks of wood the length of a man's arm.

"Shoot it, shoot it!"

Soldiers turned on the battlement and let rip with crossbows, muskets and organ guns. A wide-bore culverin tore a hole in the side of the worm, smashing metal and bone. It reared up, the cogs and blades of its head shining in the morning sun.

Lannato cheered and ran to the culverin team. Excitement gripped him like fever, filled him with wild courage. "That's it," he said, watching the gunners upend the culverin and pour more powder in. "Good lads. Pack it down hard—"

Prince Mavlio ran along the road that led to the palace, surrounded by guards in DeFalci heraldry. People dashed out of their homes, away from the monster at the gates, and for a moment the prince had to shove through his own fleeing citizens to get close. "Lannato!" he yelled. "What the hell is that thing?"

The burrowing creature lurched forward. A statue of the prince on horseback vanished under its weight. It slammed its head into the cannon-tower beside the gate. Wood and stone rained down: chunks of masonry fell into the courtyard. All Lannato could hear was the racket of collapsing stone, and then a fresh row of gunfire burst from the walls. New wounds appeared in the monster's flank: some just holes in taut leather, others belching oil like insect blood.

A mob of citizens ran up the road, yelling and howling. Mavlio's guards tried to shove people back. A woman fell over and somebody stamped on her hand. Lannato saw Mavlio point at her and snap something at one of the guards. Two men pulled her to her feet. Then the prince ran up the ramp, to shout into Lannato's ear.

"What the fucking hell is that?" Mavlio demanded.

"I don't know," Lannato cried. "It's some kind of digging thing. Bones, I think, mixed with a mechanism—" The guns roared again, and one of the abomination's legs buckled and flopped. "We can destroy it," Lannato said, "but the big cannons all face outward—"

"My lord, look out!"

Lannato looked around and saw grey, masked figures crawling over the battlements. One of the culverin team screamed and fell, a trident sticking out of his back. A net sailed out onto two militiamen below, and a moment later one of the noxi had sprung down after it. A fresh column of guards reached the bottom of the ramp, reinforcements from the central armoury. Half a dozen dwarrows followed them, clutching hammers and sharpened picks. The noxi went down under dozens of blows. Scrawny bodies were thrown back over the parapet.

The monster slammed its drill-head into the gates again. Men poured lamp-oil onto its back. A hail of burning arrows followed. Flame erupted down the monster's spine.

"That's it!" Lannato cried. "Burn it, men!"

One of Mavlio's guards grabbed the prince's arm. His face was a mask of horror. "Prince, *look!*"

Behind the monster, in the wreckage of St Allomar's church, bulky figures were emerging from the hole. They clambered out slowly, awkwardly. Lannato saw sunlight catch on short swords and heavy, armoured heads.

"Get some people over there," Mavlio snapped. "Kill those things. Now!"

With a huge spasm, the drill-beast threw itself against the gates again. This time, they broke. The monster flopped forwards, shoving the gates apart. Lannato saw a stripe of green grass in the gap, widening as the gates were forced open. Figures moved on the green: the morning light caught a sea of armour and long red shields.

Burning, quivering, the monster had started to fall apart. Skin tore open like stretched parchment, beams and tendons twisted free, alchemical blood slopped across the stones. The remains fell apart and in places it was hollow, like something players would animate at a festival. It crackled and burned. Behind it, in the open gates, stood endless rows of skeletons.

Mavlio turned to his guards. "Get everybody back and close the gates to the other quarters. The south-west quarter's gone," he said. "Get everybody out."

*

Giulia stood on the rooftop, too shocked to do anything but watch. The burrowing thing hurled its weight against the gates and pushed them open, the flames covering its back like fur. It flailed and thrashed, and she saw that it was splitting at the seams, like a costume after a wild party. It was dying. Giulia wondered what it had ever been: some overgrown burrowing animal, perhaps, or the mutilated corpse of a sea serpent. It was impossible to tell. She blinked – and saw Hugh.

Her breath caught. She leaned forward, struggling to keep him in view: it was Hugh, encased in that strange armour and massive helmet, the way he'd been in Leth's city. Wait – something else moved behind him. A similar figure jogged in his wake, a massive shield on one arm and a shortsword in the other, and panic rose in her as she looked from the first two, to a third, then a fourth, clambering from the hole in the ground.

He wasn't the only one! The blood pounded sickeningly in her skull. Below her, people ran and called and shrieked. Giulia realised that, from here, she would never be able to tell which one of the armoured revenants was Hugh.

Got to get closer.

Beside her, someone cried "Oh God!" Giulia glanced around and saw the soldier there, his arrest of her forgotten.

"Take me to the prince," she said.

"Come on." He turned and ran to the hatch. He holstered his pistol and scrambled down.

Giulia followed him . She clambered down a rickety ladder, into a little bedroom. She raced to the stairs, bounded down them, and reached the front door. The soldier threw it open and they ran into the sunlight and the chaos.

Citizens swarmed around her, a constant flow of bodies, a jumble of frightened voices. At once the soldier was pushed away and lost to view. Giulia saw her chance. She slipped past the citizens, turning and ducking, shoving where shoulders met. As she reached the street corner, she heard a ragged salvo of cannon-fire and turned left. She ran past a row of women carrying buckets full of lead shot. She had to get to the hole, to where Hugh might be. Giulia glanced around, looking for the best route.

The partition wall was up ahead, the cross-shaped fortification that divided Astrago into its four quarters. The gate was three times Giulia's height, opened and closed by clockwork. It was still open, thank God, and she ran straight through and kept going, ignoring the guards on the battlements, calling her back.

A soldier rushed around the corner and knocked her sprawling. He grabbed her, weirdly clownish in his striped uniform, and yelled into her face. "They've broken the gates open – run!"

She wanted to find out more, but he was tearing away behind her now. She had to find Hugh, to rescue him before the defenders could kill him themselves. She quickened her pace.

Giulia turned left into Millers' Street, then right into the main avenue, and ran into a flock of citizens, women and men of all ages, rushing away from the enemy. The road was clogged with them: further back, four soldiers tried to manhandle an organ gun through the crowd. Someone fell over and screamed, and there was shoving and kicking among the bodies. Three men pulled a woman upright. She cradled a bloody arm like a baby against her chest.

Fuck. I can't get through.

Giulia darted back into a doorway. To the right was a shop with a broad awning: inside, two men and a girl were frantically searching it. Looters, perhaps, or a family hunting for a missing relative. Giulia looked at the wide poles that supported the awning, the rolls of cloth outside the door, stacked into little pyramids.

Up.

She grabbed hold of an awning pole, yanked herself up, leaned across and put her hands on the windowsill. Then, too fast to let herself think about falling, she clambered hand over hand. Above the door was a little carved saint. She put her boot on his head, shoved and scrambled up, caught hold of the next windowsill and hauled herself onto the roof.

Below lay the square and the open gates. It was like a scene from Hell – no, she thought, like the spilling out of Hell onto the Earth. The undead had climbed onto the city walls, and were butchering men on the parapet. Two of the noxi jabbed a man caught under a net with tridents. A corpse dangled from the battlements on bloodstained ropes.

Little groups of men fought together, holding back the dead. One of the armoured revenants charged into a spearman, ran him through with a shortsword and tossed the man over its shoulder. Giulia hoped that it was not Hugh under that helmet.

She hurried down the roof. The drill-beast lay smouldering in the centre of the square, a blackened shell. Behind it, through the gates, marched the skeletons.

Shoulder to shoulder they poured into the city, as inexorable as a rising tide. Some of them put their spindly hands on the city gates and pushed them wider still. The rows of long shields were like bricks in a moving wall.

The undead started to split up, jogging into the narrow city streets, filling the alleys like a flood. Giulia had minutes before they overwhelmed her, at best.

Hugh was nowhere. Giulia crouched down, surveying the heavily-armoured revenants as they clambered from the hole. By now, there were at least twenty down there. A couple had no armour on their chests, just bare, dead skin, and she could see the traces of the improvements Leth had made to them. She clenched her eyes, and for a second prayed that none of those doctored bodies was Hugh. Not seeing him was a relief – and yet she wanted to see him, to know that there was something left to save.

Where the fuck is he?

Give up, she thought. *Hugh's not there. He's – somewhere else.* Panic began to creep its way into her head. *He's not there. They've killed him, they've taken him away and murdered him for good—*

The book!

She yanked her pack off and rummaged inside. Her fingertips brushed the cover and he flicked into life at her side.

He pointed. "Giulia, look out!"

She whipped around. She was almost too late: a grinning plaster face appeared at the side of the roof, and hands scrabbled on the tiles. Blood had spattered the front of the mask.

The noxi crawled onto the edge of the roof, quicker on all fours than upright, and Giulia ran down the roof and kicked it. The mask broke and the revenant twisted away, blood leaking through the crack in its plaster face. Giulia drove her heel into its thigh and it fell into the street below.

She grabbed the book, and Hugh was beside her again.

"Bloody hell," he said.

"Hugh, are you down there?"

"Down there?"

"Where are you? Where's your body?"

He frowned, as if trying to remember. She gritted her teeth. *Come on, damn it...*

"I'm in the dark," he said. "In a cave, I think—"

Someone screamed, and she let go of the book. It was time to go: way past time. Her fear growing, swelling, Giulia turned and saw that the streets behind her were full of the living dead.

Cut off. Shit!

They were scrabbling at the walls now. In moments the noxi would be up with her. She doubted they knew anything of her deal with Leth, or that they would care. She paused a second to line herself up, ran and leaped across the narrow road, onto the next roof down. The

348

tiles slid from under her feet. Giulia stumbled and staggered, catching her balance.

She stood on one end of a long tenement building, three stories high. At the far end, the building was covered in scaffolding. Four people stood on the scaffolding, surrounded by sacks of mortar, battering the undead as they tried to climb up. A musketeer lay sprawled over the peak of the roof.

Giulia ran down to meet them. An old man heard her coming and stumbled around, raising a shovel in both hands. "I'm a friend," Giulia said, but he did not put it down.

A woman, red-faced and thick-armed like a farmer's wife, turned to look at her. "Then *help*," she said. She nodded at the gates to the north, which would seal the fallen quarter off from the rest of the city. "They'll be closing those soon. We've got to get down from here."

Beside her, a lad in Citizen Guard uniform swung a mason's hammer onto an upraised shield. The sound was like a door being broken down. The skeleton dropped from the scaffolding, landed and began to climb again.

The woman was right, Giulia realised. Mavlio would close the gates: he had to. "You've got to get down from here," she said.

"Do you think so?" the man with the shovel demanded. "And how do you suggest we do that?" A helmeted skull appeared at the edge of the roof, as if poked up on a stick. The man bellowed and swung the shovel's edge into a skeletal neck. A javelin flew overhead, missing them by a yard.

Giulia looked down at the dead musketeer: a militiaman, by the looks of it, with a belt of cartridges and a powder-horn at his waist. His gun lay beside him like a length of pipe. Cannons boomed to the north.

We need to clear the road. If we can get off this roof…

Giulia reached into her bag and found the thieves' tinder there. She ducked down and cut the musketeer's belt. Keeping low, she scurried to the edge of the building and looked down onto a row of skulls.

It was still impossible to quite believe. Part of her mind still thought that, if she closed her eyes and ignored the chaos, the undead would disappear.

One of them hurled a spear and she flinched back. Giulia drew her fighting knife and drove it into one of the mortar sacks. The hessian ripped, and white dust spilled out: powdered lime, the mason's friend. *And mine, God willing*, she thought, and her knife gouged out a hole in the dust. She ducked down and twisted the cartridges out of the dead musketeer's belt. They were little tubes of greased paper, each holding a ball and enough gunpowder for a single shot. Giulia pushed them into the lime, one after another. Then she tossed in the dead man's powder-flask.

"What are you doing?" the big woman cried. "They're getting up!"

"I'm getting us out of here," Giulia replied. "Help me with this."

She took the thieves' tinder from her bag and pushed it into the end of the powder-flask. "When it explodes, climb down and run for the gates," she said. "Don't breathe it in. Now, help me with this."

She took one end of the sack, and the big woman picked up the other end. With a grunt, they picked up the sack and struggled to the edge of the roof. Giulia leaned forward and spat onto the thieves' tinder. It sparked into life, fizzing above the powder-flask.

"Throw it into the road!"

Together, they hurled the bag into the street.

350

It hit the road and the sack burst. With a loud crack, the powder fired. White dust billowed up, and Giulia called out, "Everybody, climb down now!"

She scrambled down the scaffolding, felt it shake under her, and dropped into the road. She threw her hand up to shield her eyes. A skeleton stood to her right, bolt upright, stupidly looking at the wall. Giulia stabbed it in the side, felt her knife pass through thick resistance like mud, and it collapsed.

The boy from the roof was beside her now, holding a sword that looked better suited to a parade ground than a fight. "That way," Giulia said, pointing. He nodded and moved. "Not yet," she said, grabbing his arm, but he twisted free and ran.

The big woman pulled the old man down. He was frantic with fear, shaking and muttering. He'd be useless to anyone, Giulia realised, but what else could you do? Leave him here? She led the way, out of the dust cloud and down the alley into the avenue that would take them to the gates.

Men fought down the length of the avenue. Little groups of gunners and crossbowmen covered the retreat, firing and moving back in turns. The last few civilians ran past the marksmen, towards the gates. A trumpet blared at the far end of the wall, hard fast blasts to signal the retreat.

The undead filled the far end of the road, their shields held out before them. They strode forward, completely confident. It looked like the end of the world.

Giulia jogged out of the alleyway, into the road. A woman nearly ran into her, leading a child by either hand. Giulia cursed and ducked aside. An armed dwarrow waved them on. "Keep going, keep going!" the dwarrow called.

The gates were thirty yards away. The boy from the roof had disappeared. The big woman pulled the old man along. Guns burst into life along the wall and a dozen undead fell apart. The old man burst into tears.

At last Giulia reached the gates. She helped the big woman drag the old man through. Soldiers hustled them on, into the palace square and through to the roads beyond. Up ahead, people sat on the ground and slumped in doorways, dirty and spattered with blood. They looked like gangs after a fight. Giulia stopped running and leaned against the wall. Beside her, a small, bearded man looked round and gave her a meaningless grin, as if to welcome her to the fun. She looked at the filthy, exhausted people around her, and realised that she looked no better than they did.

*

Mavlio stood on the battlements, watching the undead columns grow closer. There could be few people left in the south-western quarter now. Only the weak and slow would remain, and those who refused to leave them behind. *Women, children and brave men*, Mavlio thought. *That's who I will kill when I close the gates.*

One of the captains ran to his side. "My prince. The gatehouse awaits your order."

"I know," he said. He took a deep breath. For a few seconds he was silent, and in that time six more people ran through the gates, and the undead advanced three yards closer. "Shut the gates."

"My prince, look over there." The captain pointed: on top of a church, a dozen citizens had clustered for a final stand. In the centre, a militiaman waved a flag.

"It's too dangerous," Mavlio replied. He turned to the captain. "Close them."

"Yes, my prince."

The captain turned away and hurried back to the gatehouse. Mavlio heard him relaying the order to his comrades. Slowly, the gates began to close.

Well, that's done now.

Muskets fired from the gatehouse, down the avenue. Holes appeared in the undead ranks and were filled again. Mavlio watched as some of the revenants dispersed into alleyways, working their way forward out of view of the guns.

They're getting clever, trying to keep out of sight.

Mavlio turned and walked towards the steps. A soldier stood by the wall, reloading his musket. He stood to attention as the prince approached.

"Carry on," Mavlio said. He made himself smile. "Shoot one for me, son."

The square behind the gates was full of refugees. Soldiers were trying to move them back, but many were wounded or too weary to go. As Mavlio reached the bottom of the steps, someone called "Make way for the prince!" and his guards shoved citizens out the way. The last people to have escaped stood around the bottom of the wall, like ghosts haunting the square.

Women, children, old men: useless mouths. The undead have no families to slow them down.

"Move back, move back!" Soldiers hurried the citizens into the narrow streets, trying to clear the square. Carts loaded with shortbows and gunpowder crawled towards the gates. "Move it, God damn you!" a young militiaman yelled, waving a stick above his head. An old couple stumbled away from him as though he was one of the undead.

Mavlio watched him, knowing someone ought to stop the lad before he began beating people. The prince was too tired to intervene.

The townsfolk struggled along, dispersing into the city: to pray, perhaps, or to further burden the apothecaries with their wounds, or to try to find a place to rest.

A fourth of my city gone. No – don't think that. Three quarters left. We can still fight.

"Get back," the young militiaman bawled, and his stick cracked down on dirty hair. "Clear the square!"

Mavlio hardly knew that he was moving. Suddenly his legs were striding forward and he was in the press of people, shoving dirty bodies out of the way. In a second his guards were pushing after him, shouting to the frightened people to move aside, but Mavlio was too quick. He burst free from the press of bodies and snatched the stick from the young soldier's hand.

"Stop that!" he barked. "Those people belong to me. I won't have you beating them, you hear?"

The man turned, ready to shout back. The fury dropped off his face like water. "My prince, forgive me, I didn't know—"

"You do now," Mavlio heard himself say. He stood there as if waking from a dream, his guards gathering around him. Quietly, he held out the stick. "These people are scared," he said. "Save your anger for the skeletons."

The soldier was little more than a boy. He took the stick back. "Yes, my prince. Of course. I'll do as you say, I promise."

"Good man." Mavlio looked around, unsure what to do. He had never felt lost in his own city before. Everything seemed to be happening without him.

Further back, Cosimo Lannato stood in the middle of a group of oddly-dressed soldiers, pointing towards the walls. They looked like armoured smiths, equipped with heavy pistols and long-barrelled muskets custom-made for sharpshooting. The scholar jabbed his hand out, and the men around him nodded.

Mavlio approached. Lannato did not see him, and continued to give his orders. "— need to demolish a section of the outer wall," he was saying, "to stop them making sallies along the battlements—"

"Cosimo," said the prince. "I had to close the gates. I couldn't have left it any later."

"I know."

"I want you to get the flying machine ready. Have Carmina's maids pack her things. You do the same, understand?"

Lannato leaned forward. "If you wish, but—"

"If the city falls, you're to get away, you hear? You and Carmina. Take Sepello with you, tell his order what's happened. If Leth was to capture—"

"My prince!"

Both men turned. One of the runners from the gatehouse stood to attention and flicked them a quick, hard salute. "Pardon me for interrupting you. I have news from the walls."

Mavlio glanced at Lannato. He looked grim. "What's happened?"

"My prince, a messenger approaches under a flag of parley. He says Constantin Leth wants to talk terms with you."

"Tell Leth I can't hear him from here. Tell him to come closer, preferably within musket-range."

The runner looked perturbed. "My prince, it isn't Leth who's carrying the flag. It's Sir Francis Vale."

355

Chapter 13

S epello gasped and was awake. The shock of it was like being thrown into cold water. He panted, his nose and mouth full of the stink of alchemy, gulped down air. Slowly, his breathing calmed itself. He was alive.

He was looking at a wall, but it felt wrong. No, Sepello realised – he was on his back, looking at the ceiling.

And someone else was in here with him.

He turned his head carefully, as if afraid that it might roll off his shoulders. He saw a white room without windows. Something, perhaps the quality of the air, made him realise that he was underground. The walls were lined with alchemical equipment: condensers, flasks, weird lengths of coiled brass tube. Half a dozen pieces of paper were pinned to a large wooden board. Most were just scribble – alchemical formulae, perhaps – but one was a diagram of a naked man, his body covered in veins.

A figure detached itself from the shadows at the rear of the room. It was small, somehow meek, but he drew back as if it was a ghost.

"Hello," Carmina said.

Sepello slipped his right hand inside his coat. His pistol had gone. "Hello," he said.

"It was me who woke you up." Even now, she sounded apologetic. "I wanted to talk to you. Alone."

"Go ahead." He sat up, slowly and carefully. Sepello thought: *What happens now?* Carmina could have killed him easily enough, and Prince Mavlio could have arranged for his body to disappear. Who knew how many people were already missing in the siege, gathering flies in whatever place they'd crawled into to die, or now marching among the ranks of the dead?

Saint Cordelia, guide my hand.

"You saw what happened," she said.

His mouth was dry. "Yes."

"Cosimo gives me medicine," she said. "It stops anyone finding out. Most of the time. Some things bring it on. Like when I'm worried."

He moved his left hand onto his belt, felt for his knife. "I see."

"I took your gun away. But you can have it back soon. Just after we've finished talking." Carmina gestured at the door. "There are men outside," she said, as if it helped. "I don't want to hurt you, honestly I don't."

"Well, I, ah, don't want to hurt you either. You probably saved my life back there. And your father's."

"I think so," Carmina said. "This is where Cosimo makes the potions. They mean that I don't have to hurt anyone to stay alive. To stay moving, I mean."

"Really? He can do that?"

She smiled. "He can do almost anything. He's the cleverest man alive. Father thinks the cleverest man ever. Even more than the Quaestans."

"Yes, that's pretty clever," Sepello said, and he thought, *Are you telling me that Lannato has cured undeath?*

"It's not permanent," Carmina said. "It just delays it. But Father says that Constantin Leth knows how to cure me for good. He's one of the oldest revenants there is, and he used to be an alchemist. He has books about it. That's what Father thinks, anyway."

"What do you think?"

"I don't know. I hope so. You know, I don't *feel* dead. I have a pulse, I get hungry, I can see myself in mirrors—"

"The stuff about mirrors is just old wives' tales," Sepello replied. "It's about having a soul. It's a – what's the word? – a metaphor." He realised what he'd said, and added, "I'm sure you do have a soul. Look, Carmina, I didn't come here to kill you. Leth is my target. He's the one I've been hunting all this time. He's a monster. You're not. You're just… unlucky."

"Yes."

"And it sounds as if Lannato can, er, help you keep it under control. Am I right?"

She nodded.

Sepello took a deep breath. "Then you have my word that, provided your father leaves me be, and you stay… healthy, I won't come after you."

"What about the other people in your order?"

"They won't know."

"You promise that?"

"On my life. No, on Saint Cordelia's life. You have my word."

She stepped forward and held out her hand. He hesitated.

"Your father's a clever man, Carmina. Ruthless, too. You'll make sure he doesn't try to do anything against me, yes? That he knows he can rely on me to keep my word?"

"Yes."

Sepello got up and shook her hand. It was warm and dry, fairly soft; the hand of a living person.

Carmina pointed at a row of shelves. "Your gun is up here."

"Thanks." As he reached for it, he felt a little rush of fear. She could grab his wrist, leap on him, tear out his throat. His fingers closed around the handle, and he felt stronger. Stupid, really. It wouldn't be loaded.

And suddenly Sepello realised how weak he was, how dependent he was on Mavlio's goodwill, on Carmina's, on how few allies he had here. He missed Giulia.

Sepello looked at the door. "How long have I been unconscious?"

"A few hours. You were feeling bad after – one of the Sciata men hit you on the head."

He grimaced. "I remember."

"The undead have broken open the western gate . They had some kind of tunnelling creature. It's dead, but they got inside."

"The south-west quarter 's fallen?"

"I'm afraid so."

God almighty. She saw the horror in his face, so he said, "Don't worry: we'll fight them off. Your father's men are real tigers, you know."

Carmina looked at him thoughtfully. "Are there other ones like me?"

"Not that I know of," Sepello said. "Most revenants are, well, not like you."

"They're mad, you mean."

"Well, yes. You're different. Exceptional." Sepello said, "Carmina, how did it happen?"

"No-one knows. Not even Father. I was about twelve years old. There was a tournament on the border with Montalius – a bit old-fashioned, but they're like that up there. Father took me there to see all the knights. I suppose he was looking for a husband for me. I got sick a little while afterwards and, well, that was that. Father says that one of our enemies might have poisoned me.

But why would you turn someone undead when you could just kill them instead?"

"Good point."

"That woman who worked for you – the one with the scars on her face. What happened to her?"

"We lost her," Sepello said. "She was on the flying machine that didn't come back."

"I liked her," Carmina said.

Someone knocked on the door. "Come in," Carmina said.

A tubby guard looked into the room. He had drowsy eyes, like an old horse. "You're awake, sir."

"I am."

"I just came to make sure everything was all right. The prince says you're needed up above, sir."

"Please, lead the way."

Sepello slid his gun into his coat. "Thank you for waking me, Princess."

"Happy to help," she said.

"It's been a pleasure," Sepello said, and he bowed to her. "Remember what I said."

"Likewise. Go with God, Master Sepello."

"You too."

Sepello followed the guard down a stone corridor like an unusually well-lit dungeon. This had to be part of the workshops, part of Lannato's little kingdom underneath the palace.

He heard noise up ahead, the clanking of chains and the call of rough voices. They turned a corner, and they were in a brick-lined cavern. The prince's clockwork castle stood in the centre, like a fort on wheels. A dozen men worked around it, checking the axles and attaching metal plates to the wheels. Chains clinked and a small cannon descended from the roof. Two engineers manoeuvred it into a hole in the front of the machine.

The tubby guard led Sepello past the workers. "How's the princess, sir, if you don't mind me asking?"

"She seems fine," Sepello said.

The fat face smiled. "Ah, that's good news, sir. Served the family all my life, I have. A lot of us have. I'd hate to see her come to harm. Best hurry along now, sir."

The man was too familiar: Sepello would have expected Mavlio's servants to be tight-lipped, ruthless men. They reached a narrow set of stairs, and climbed back up into the palace.

'Served her all my life', eh? Maybe he knows. How many of them know? And how many realise that I do, too?

*

Lannato bent over the man in the chair and touched a scalpel to his fingertip. Vale did not flinch, but he grimaced as the doctor squeezed a little blood from the wound and collected it in a tiny metal cup.

Mavlio watched the scholar take the sample to the rack of glass phials that he had set up by the fireplace. Lannato tilted the cup so that a few droplets of blood fell into each phial. The water changed colour, turned red, then purple.

Lannato stepped back. "Hmm. Well, yes, he's alive."

"Pleased to hear it," Mavlio said. Lannato had spent the last ten minutes making tests: feeling for Vale's pulse, making him breathe onto mirrors, peering into his eyes.

"Of course I'm alive." Vale held his hand out while Lannato applied a tincture to his finger. Lannato squeezed the wound and held it there, to seal it.

The ambassador still wore the tough clothes that he had put on to explore Oppidium, although his armour and weapons were gone. "Leth kept me as a hostage. He probably thought I'd make a good trade. I was going to warn you that he had an army down in Oppidium, but I suppose you've realised that now."

"Oddly enough, yes," Mavlio replied.

"Leth says you've got until sunset to come up to meet him on the battlements."

"And what happens if I don't?"

The Anglian looked around, as if for eavesdroppers. "Leth claims to have created a new disease, a mixture of plague and the Grey Ague. It kills swiftly, and those it kills rise within the hour. If you fail to surrender, he promises that the next things he throws over your walls will be baskets of infected rats."

"And do you believe that?"

"Yes," Vale admitted. "I've seen what he can do: he knows how to mix animals together, to create monsters. That burrowing thing was one of his creations; so are those things with masks." Vale frowned, and the shadow seemed to sink into his face. "I'm no alchemist, but I think he could do the same with a disease."

"My God," Lannato said, "to create a special disease… I don't think anyone's ever done that before. He must be an exceptional alchemist."

"If he's that clever," Mavlio replied, "why hasn't he used it on us already?"

"That's a good point," Vale said. "If Leth wants to parley with you on the battlements, he must think there's something more he can get out of you. Either that or he wants a good clean shot for those ballistae of his. Whatever it is, he wants something – something he can't get through force alone."

Mavlio nodded. "My thoughts entirely."

Vale smoothed his beard down into a point. "Whatever happens, I say we keep on fighting. If you ask me, we can break this army of his."

Mavlio smiled. "Trust me, we'll keep fighting. And then we'll put his head on a spike, where it belongs."

"Something like that," Vale replied.

"Thank you, Sir Francis. You've been very helpful. It's good to have you back."

"Thank you, Prince Mavlio. You can rest assured of our support. My marines remain at your command."

Lannato started to pack up his tools. "You should rest a little while, Sir Francis. I'll have the servants bring you up some beef and tonic wine."

Mavlio tapped the scholar's arm. "Cosimo," said the prince, "would you come with me?"

They left Vale in the care of two loyal guards, and headed to the square in front of the palace. It had become the centre of resistance, the new front line in the siege now that the docks had fallen.

Men and mules pushed carts full of spare weapons and ammunition. Messengers ran in and out of the square, carrying reports and orders. Behind the battlements, soldiers loaded the artillery and tried to rest. The palace cooks were handing out bread and cheese. Those who could fight – anyone between twelve and sixty with more than one arm – was given a weapon and sent to bolster the second row of defenders.

To the right of the palacial square, the Church of the Archangel Ascended had been thrown open as a makeshift hospital. Mavlio looked into the double doors, and saw robed men at work like busy ghosts. Priests wore black, doctors red: you could tell the state of a patient by the colour of the man by their side. It occurred to Mavlio that, if Leth's forces broke into this quarter as well, the church would be the site of the first massacre, and probably the first recruiting centre for the undead.

"Is that possible?" Mavlio asked. "About Leth making a disease to use against us?"

"I don't know, Mavlio. But right now, I wouldn't rule it out. I wouldn't rule out anything, to be honest," Lannato added.

Mavlio nodded. He'd thought that he had a tight grip on the defences, and then that burrowing thing had burst out of the ground. It was one thing to raise the dead, to arm them and send them out in legions – but that was something else. To attack in such a way that the defences meant nothing, to take the enemy entirely by surprise: it was hard to even respond.

"My prince," Lannato said, "the men are bringing up the clockwork castle. I'd like to go down there. To make sure it's done right."

Mavlio smiled. He'd loved the castle from the day that it had first rolled out of the workshops: loved the ingenuity and power of it all. For Lannato, it was just the application of old principles on a grander scale, but for Mavlio it was a demonstration of his might. "Do it, Cosimo. I've got a mind to give these undead bastards a little surprise."

He looked at the gates. Fifty yards behind them, hundreds of the risen dead waited to attack.

*

Lannato hurried down a narrow staircase that corkscrewed into the earth like a drill. Shadow fell over him like cool water, and the sounds of the siege faded behind the walls. He had never liked rough men, loud voices and violence. The smell of sawdust and burned metal reassured him.

He walked through a service tunnel, past the tiny old cells built by Diello Sciata, and turned towards the storerooms. Lannato entered the long white room where he kept his tools.

The workshop stretched away like a dining-hall, diagrams and half-finished machines attached to the walls instead of swords and trophies. A clockwork lion bared its fangs at the roof; he'd built it for a celebration several years ago. The skylights were closed, and the light was bad. Lannato stepped forward, reaching for the rope that would open the skylights.

A figure stepped out from behind the lion. "Lannato," it said.

He froze, then slowly lowered his hand. "Hello?"

"Go ahead," said the voice, and he realised it was too high to be a man's. "We could do with some light in here."

I know you, Lannato thought. *It's Sepello's apprentice. The one we thought had died.* And then, with real fear, *Perhaps she did.* He reached up and pulled the rope. Shutters dropped open.

She didn't flinch when the light hit her. She stood there in the sunlight, with a leather satchel in one hand and her other hand resting on the workbench. Her crossbow lay beside her hand. It was not loaded.

"Giulia," he said. "Giulia Degarno." One of the shutters was out of shape, as though someone had prised it open. She must have climbed in that way.

"Sorry to get the drop on you. But I need to talk, and, well, I reckon the prince would be just as likely to throw me over the wall as speak to me. I thought I'd get a better response from you."

"We thought you were dead," Lannato said.

"I'm not. You can check if you like. Go on." She pulled her sleeve back and held it out. She wore leather bracers that buckled under her arm. They wrapped around to protect her wrists, and she had to undo the lacing to let Lannato see.

He pressed his finger to her wrist. The skin was pale, but warm. She had a pulse – but then, he thought, so did Carmina. If Giulia had been changed, it had happened when she was still alive.

"If it makes you feel any better," Giulia said, "if I wanted to hurt you, I would have done so by now."

"Actually, it doesn't." Lannato glanced at the crossbow. It was a custom piece, ratcheted under the body with a little lever to draw back the spring. The workmanship was decent. A good weapon for a huntress. "What happened to you?"

"I got caught in Oppidium. Francis Vale sent me to scout out the tombs. The revenants jumped his men while they were waiting for me to come back. Leth's got a whole city down there, full of the living dead. It's where he must have got his army from."

Lannato nodded. "We suspected something like that."

She said, "Where's Sepello?"

"He was hurt. He's resting. But he'll be fine."

"Good," Giulia replied. "The Anglians I went in with are all dead."

"Not all of them. Vale was sent back by Leth, as a gesture of goodwill."

Giulia snorted. "Goodwill? From Leth? Horseshit."

Lannato nodded. "My thoughts entirely," he said.

"You should keep an eye on him. Leth might have turned him."

"I checked. He's alive."

"Listen," Giulia said. "I went to the fey folk after I got away. They gave me something to pass on to you. Here." She opened her bag, rooted about and took out a piece of folded paper. "It's a list of ingredients for a potion. It's a poison to use against the undead."

She passed him the paper and he opened it. Lannato ran his eyes down the list. "Let's see… saffron, mandrake, Maggorian pine… This looks like an aphrodisiac, not a poison."

"On a person, maybe," Giulia replied. "But on the undead, I'm told it's lethal. If you could mix it up and put it on an arrow, or a knife—"

The philosopher frowned. "Well, the ingredients wouldn't be too hard to find. Between the spice stores in the palace kitchen and the alchemical equipment I've got down here, I can't see why not. The question is: will it do anything? We need to test it."

Giulia took a little bottle out of her bag. "I've got a sample. We could catch one of the skeletons, pour this stuff onto it, maybe." She sounded uncertain.

"Testing it won't be a problem. I can deal with that. But you're sure the fey say that this will work?"

"That's what they told me." She glanced around the room. "We could paint it onto a bolt and shoot Constantin Leth with it."

"Maybe. I suspect that you'd need a much stronger dose for him than for his minions. Sepello would probably know."

At the far end of the room, a little bell jangled on its chain. One of the side doors opened and a palace servant entered. He saw Giulia, stopped and said, "My apologies, Master Lannato. I didn't realise that you had guests." He looked nervous. Seeing Giulia seemed to have worried him.

367

"Come in," the philosopher replied.

"The prince wants to see you in council in one hour, Master Lannato. It's a matter of urgency."

"Everything is," Lannato replied. "Tell him I'll be there. Oh— and could you run down to the kitchens and check the traps, please? I need three dead rats. Freshly dead, if you can get them."

"Freshly dead, sir," the servant said. "Is that a matter of urgency as well?"

"Absolutely."

Emotionless, the servant said, "Right away, sir. I'll send the boy up with them." He bowed and closed the door.

Lannato turned to Giulia. "We've got an hour – no, less than that. You can help me with this, if you want." A thought seemed to strike him. He looked at her. "What *do* you want? I mean, you came back. It must have been a hell of a thing, getting back here. You could have just run away…"

She shook her head. "I want the same thing as you," she said. "To kill Leth and save the city. And right now, you and I are the only people who can do it."

Half a suit of armour lay on one of the workbenches. Part of a wooden frame protruded from the torso, trailing thin ropes across the bench. It looked familiar. *It's the suit that was at that party*, Giulia realised. *The one that moved by itself. It's some kind of puppet…*

Lannato unclipped the metal gauntlets. "I'll need some of your potion," he said, pulling one of the gauntlets on. His hand looked bizarre encased in steel.

"All right," she replied. "I can spare a little of it." The stuff was precious – doubly so if it could cure Hugh –

but if anyone knew how to make the best of it, it would be Cosimo Lannato.

"That's all I need. Can you get a fire going?"

"Of course."

The stove was complex: it took as much time to work out how to open the doors as to find the wood and get the flames burning. Giulia glanced over her shoulder and saw the philosopher unlocking a massive chest. He lifted the lid, and a shelf rose up on some kind of weighted mechanism. There were bottles on the shelf, rows of them, neatly arranged and lettered A to F. With immense care, Lannato lifted out a little black bottle.

"There's water over there," he said. "Could you boil a pan?"

Giulia dipped a battered pan into a barrel near the door. The fire was crackling now. She wondered what Lannato had in mind. Was he making a spell?

"Bring that condenser over," he said.

She looked around, having no idea what he meant.

"The big glass tube, on its side. We'll need to pour the water into it."

"Right," she said. She liked him: he had that businesslike quality you saw in craftsmen and mercenaries, the willingness to get to work.

The bell jangled and a child entered, holding a wad of dirty fur in one hand. "Sir? Rats for you, sir."

"Just in time," Lannato replied, and he smiled fiercely and tossed the boy a coin. He looked like a hunter who had just got a clean shot on his prey.

Giulia watched him lay out the dead rats in a row. They were fat, ugly animals, long of body and tail, and they'd been dead for a while. She wanted to hold *The Death of King Alba* again, to ask Hugh what the hell was going to happen. Not that he would have known. "Why do we need three rats?"

"Because two isn't enough." Lannato opened a cabinet on the wall and took out a roll of tools, like a carpenter's chisels. "It's part of the testing process. One to test, one to check, and one to make sure. Here we are." He took out a metal implement that she didn't recognise: a short brass tube with a handle at one end and a thin metal spike at the other. It looked too clean for a torture device, but still worryingly medical. "It's called a syringe."

The philosopher pointed to a wooden box on a high shelf. "Could you bring me that, please?"

Giulia stood on tiptoe and passed it down. Lannato took the nearest rat in his armoured hand, held it steady on the bench.

Very carefully, he unstoppered the black bottle and tilted it. Giulia saw dark liquid move inside, sludgy and thick.

"What is that?" Giulia asked.

"Revenant blood. Taken from the fellow you disposed of at the docks." The scholar put the tip of the metal spike into the bottle and pulled the tube a little. "Look." He put the tip of the spike against the rat's side, then pushed it into its body. Giulia watched, disgusted but intrigued. "Now then," Lannato said. "Let's see…"

Under his gauntlet, the dead rat twitched.

"Shit!" Giulia stepped back and drew her knife.

Lannato shook his head. "Wait." In his fist, the long pink tail began to stir.

"God almighty," Giulia said, and she made the Sign of the Sword across her chest.

The rat shuddered violently, then thrashed. The head, little more than a tiny skull covered in papery skin, shook from side to side. "Box," Lannato said. "Keep your hands back."

Giulia pushed the wooden box over and stepped away. Lannato dropped the rat into the box, and she heard it hit the bottom. The paws pattered on the wood as the creature did a slow tour of its new home. Then it stopped.

Lannato turned to the second rat. "The lesser undead are powered by magic," he said to the specimen, "much the same way you or I are powered by food. It keeps them going. If they suffer too much harm, the magic breaks and they fall apart."

"Like the skeletons," Giulia replied.

"Exactly."

Lannato jabbed the second rat with the syringe. It stirred in his armoured fist, and he dumped it in the box with its comrade.

"Leave them together long enough and they'll turn on one another," Lannato said. "Sepello told me that human revenants are like that too. Naturally vain and self-obsessed, he says. Time for number three."

Giulia glanced at the stove. She didn't like taking her eyes off the box: the thought of those things running around made her skin itch. "The pot's nearly boiling."

"Good." Lannato got to work on the third rat. His voice was fast and slightly nervous. "Revenancy is, in a sense, a disorder of the humours. So, if the illness disorders the humours, perhaps the right alchemy can restore them – or poison them? Why not indeed?" he demanded, dropping the third rat into the box. "Could you put the condenser onto the stove, please?"

Giulia obliged and Lannato brought the box over. She wondered what the philosopher was doing. Surely he intended to destroy the undead rats that he'd just created.

But why not just pour the potion over a knife and stab the horrible things?

"Potion goes in there," Lannato said, tapping a shallow glass bowl on top of the condenser. "Only a few drops."

"I can't spare much more than that," Giulia replied. She took out the bottle, carefully eased the stopper out and tapped three droplets into the bowl. The elixir was almost clear, with a faint blue-green tint.

"Now," he said, "get the water. Careful of the handle."

Giulia wrapped her cloak around her hand and picked up the pan. The water bubbled: she could feel it shaking in her grip. Lannato plucked one of the rats from the box, and it went into a frenzy of kicking. Giulia saw the long yellow teeth scrape across the armoured gauntlet, searching for a way in. Then Lannato nodded to her, and she poured the boiling water into the condenser.

Water ran through the glass tubes like drink through a man's guts. The hot water touched the bottom of the glass bowl, and the sample of elixir began to steam. Lannato turned his hand upside-down and shoved the rat into the vapour.

It burst in his fist like old plaster.

Giulia jumped back. "Shit!"

Dust and fluff trickled between Lannato's metal fingers, onto the floor.

"Shall we try another?" Lannato grinned at Giulia and snatched the next rat out of the box. It thrashed in his grip, teeth bared in undead rage. Lannato held it out. The fumes were thinning now, and it took a whole second before the creature drooped. Its lower body crumbled and fell apart in a little rain of bones and dirt.

"Once more," the scholar said. There was almost no potion left in the bowl now. Giulia could smell the elixir, a scent like sap and cut grass. It made her think of Sethis, and she felt a pang of sadness that he was not here.

But then Lannato held up the last of his test subjects. In Lannato's hand, the rat went berserk. It must have realised what was coming, for it arched its back and struggled furiously. "He knows what's coming," Lannato said.

The rat squirmed free.

It raced up Lannato's arm as quick as a snake. The rat caught the scholar's shirt, scrabbling at his neck.

Giulia's arm shot out, grabbed the rat and tore it off his shoulder. She felt its matted fur, its hard little bones grinding against her palm, and she shoved it into the fumes.

The rat simply fell apart. Its head dropped off: in a moment the rest of the limbs peeled away like wilting petals. She opened her hand, and in her palm were tiny bones. They crumbled against her fingers.

Giulia held her hand in the smoke to make sure that all the undeath was gone.

Cosimo Lannato was shaking. He smoothed down his jacket and swallowed hard. Then he began to chuckle.

Giulia smiled back. "Looks like it works," she said.

*

A weird quiet had settled over the city. On one side of the gates, the living worked. They moved their wounded back, hurried civilians out of sight, and carried ammunition up to the walls. Nobody shouted; men worked swiftly and grimly. Hooves and wheels clattered on the cobblestones.

373

On the other side of the gates, the undead waited. Mavlio knew that he shouldn't look, that they would have archers ready, but he put on a common soldier's helmet and peeked over the battlements.

The skeletons stood in the streets – his streets – waiting for the order to move. They were ten deep, lined up like rows of corn. They all faced towards the gates, their shields held across their bodies. Looking at them, Mavlio wondered if his mind had broken, whether he would ever see the world properly again even if he survived. He had never had much time for magic. Wizards and sorcerers were either puny or outright charlatans: the Old and New Churches demanded obedience without proof. And yet there was real magic, come to murder him.

He walked back down, unfastening his helmet as he went. Half a dozen soldiers waited for him at the bottom. They were marksmen, equipped with crossbows and muskets, and at their head was Goodchilde, the former mercenary who worked as his military advisor.

The sun seemed hotter than before: Mavlio's shirt was slick with sweat. Maybe it wasn't the heat, but the thought of what he had to do. He pointed at a tall townhouse overlooking the street. "Right there, near the gates."

Goodchilde shielded his eyes. "Aye," he said. "I think we could manage that. How about that church tower, over there?"

"I could do that, sir," said one of the musketeers.

"And the palace window," Mavlio said. "At the top of the south-west corner. Put a couple of men there."

Goodchilde squinted back at the palace. "Yes, that's good. Think you'd get a decent shot from there?"

The crossbowman looked back. "Easily, milord. It's well within range."

Goodchilde said, "Between the two of them, they'd have Leth well covered."

"All right, then," Mavlio said. "When I make this gesture, you fire." He reached up and rubbed the right side of his face, as if to check the quality of his shaving. "Yes?"

"Yes, milord."

"Yes, my prince."

"Good," Mavlio replied. "And go for the head. I don't want him injured. Then we're all ready." *All ready? That's a joke. I'll never be ready. Not for this.*

A figure was walking across the square towards him. It was Vale. Two of the ambassador's soldiers followed him: big solid men in breastplates and dark clothes. Goodchilde took a step forward, putting himself slightly between Vale and the prince. The marksmen turned to face the newcomers.

"Ah, Prince Mavlio. Instructing your sharpshooters, are you?" Vale was surprisingly sprightly. "It seems that we think alike, Prince. May I have a word in private, please?"

"Be quick. I want to talk to my daughter."

"Of course. I'll walk with you."

They set off towards the palace. Behind them, men, weapons and food were moving towards the walls. A soldier rested against one of the big houses, his face striped with grime. His eyes followed them as they walked. There was no emotion in them.

"You're planning to shoot Leth when he comes up for his parley," Vale said.

"It's crossed my mind."

"That's sensible," the Anglian replied. "Look, I've got a man who can take the shot. He's a bowman: an archer from Plennyd. It's a place near Anglia – a separate country, in fact, but part of Albion – known for the skill of its marksmen—"

"Thank you for the offer, but I don't see the need. I'll cover this."

Vale shook his head. "With respect, my man is much more experienced than anyone you have here," he said. "It'll be a difficult shot."

Mavlio stopped. In the open door of a baker's shop, a man was cutting sheets into bandage strips. "No," he said.

"Prince, my man has more than sixty kills to his name. You'll never find someone as skilled as him, I promise you." Vale glanced around. He leaned in and lowered his voice. "I'll make it worth your while. Mavlio, when all this is done, this city is going to need a lot of repairs. You're going to have to rebuild it – quickly, too. None of the other states has sent any help – perhaps they will, when there's no danger to them, but not before. You need money and backing."

"At the moment, Vale, I'm more concerned with not being murdered. We all should be."

"I realise that. But once this is done, you'll need money to rebuild your defences, to feed all the people whose land these revenants have marched through. And Albion needs an ally on the Peninsula. If you keep with us, Mavlio, we can give you everything that you'll need. But we'd both have to be marching under the same flag."

"Your flag."

"I'm offering you fifty thousand saviours for one shot. Your choice."

Chapter 14

Everything was quiet in the city. The living cowered behind their wall, waiting for the attack. The dead hung back, waiting for their command. Not needing food or rest, the skeletons stood in their lines. The noxi and the myrmex moved up through the empty buildings, through homes and shops, staying out of sight of the soldiers on the walls.

Leth walked through the streets, slow and thoughtful. Eight myrmex surrounded him, carrying reinforced shields. A light wind came in from the bay and stirred the banners on Mavlio's walls. The whole quarter was quiet, pleasantly empty of life: a taste of how the whole principality would be, once it had fallen.

His guards turned onto the main thoroughfare. Eight ranks of armoured skeletons stood before them, an insulation from the living. At the far end of the road stood the great gates that would let him into the north-west quarter. Behind the gates would be a mass of frightened soldiers, ready to defend the palace of the prince. He briefly wondered what he would find there, what chemicals and war machines he could take from Lannato's workshops.

Metal glinted on the walls. Leth paused and squinted at the gates, wondering whether to move closer to get a better look. Men suddenly moved on the battlements. Were the living going to risk a counter-attack? Brass funnels appeared above the gates, and as Leth realised that they were trumpets, a fanfare burst out across the city. It sounded crass and optimistic. The sound rose to a peak and stopped.

The silence that followed was not the kind that he liked. It felt like a threat.

"In the name of Astrago, listen well!"

Leth glimpsed a stout man, built like a blacksmith, with a tube to his mouth and a piece of paper in one hand. It would have been amusing to have one of the ballistae knock the wind out of his lungs, to see the bolt puncture him like a skewer through a ripe fruit. But that could wait.

"In the name of ancient liberty, following the customs of chivalry and the honourable traditions of the Quaestan Imperators, Prince Mavlio DeFalci, rightful sovereign of Astrago, addresses the enemy! Notwithstanding the cruel and unnatural host, nor the acts of criminal necromancy perpetrated by their master, Prince Mavlio will speak with Constantin Leth tonight, at the hour of seven, on the battlements. In accordance with the known laws of combat, all traditional pledges of safety shall be granted by either side, on pain of forfeiting all privileges of surrender and rank. So says the prince – long live Prince Mavlio!"

The honour of the Quaestans – a nice touch. Too bad they've all been dead a thousand years. Too bad I never was a true Quaestan, just a wanderer who found them useful for a while.

"Do you accept this offer?" the man on the battlements yelled. Leth imagined Mavlio crouching behind the parapet, rubbing his hands together and smiling his wide, tight smile.

Tonight he will try to murder me. And tonight I will crush him. Not with weapons, for now, but with the truth.

Leth stepped back and cupped his hands around his mouth. "I accept!"

*

Lannato and Giulia walked back up into the palace. They passed through the kitchens, between walls that seemed

378

to be soaked with the smell of roasting meat. Men and women worked around a fireplace. A bizarre apparatus had been built in front of the fire, and for a moment Giulia thought it was some horrible implement of torture. Then she saw the chunks of pork and mutton skewered on slowly-turning spikes, and realised that it was a mechanism for cooking dozens of joints at once. Meat glistened; fat dripped into huge trays.

"Hungry?" Lannato asked.

She shook her head. "I'm fine. Besides, the soldiers need it more than me."

They emerged in a small dining hall, clearly intended for the staff. Half a dozen men were eating and drinking at a table. They didn't talk, and their hands moved steadily, mechanically. As Giulia entered, one of the men lurched upright, and she saw the sling on his left arm.

"Sepello?"

His tired face came alive. He walked towards her, caught his leg on a chair and staggered. Giulia lunged to grab him, but Sepello caught his footing and righted himself like a boxer too stubborn to fall.

"Giulia! My God. Saints be praised! You're back."

She grinned. "Back from the dead." She stopped grinning. "Not like that, though."

He smiled. "I didn't think so." Sepello embraced her, patted her back with his good arm. Giulia tried not to hug him too tightly. "I thought you'd been killed."

"I nearly was."

Lannato coughed politely. "I'm going up to see the prince. I'll need you to come up, too. He's up in the map room."

Sepello said, "Give us two minutes." He turned back to Giulia. "What happened to you?"

"What didn't?" she replied. "I saw Leth's city. It's under the ground, in this enormous cave. The place is incredible... horrible, too. I tried to kill him, but he was too good. I got bloody close, though. Then I got knocked out. The fey folk found me passed out and... well, I came back here. They gave me something, though, a poison to use on the undead."

"A poison?"

"A potion. Lannato's looking into it. I gave him the recipe."

"Let's hope it works." Sepello said, "You know, I always thought you were tough."

"I had a lot of help. What happened to you?"

He hesitated. She knew that he was choosing what to say. "Turns out Leth had some men in the city – living ones, I mean. They tried to get the jump on the prince. I helped him fight them off, but it was close. We could have done with you there."

"I could've done with you, too. I'm glad you're all right."

"You too." He looked at her for a long, strange second, and looked away. "Mavlio's got something big planned, some kind of counter-attack. We'd best go up and see him." Sepello paused, and lowered his voice, so the men behind him wouldn't hear. "Look, Giulia, you know that the undead have captured the south-west?"

"Yes. I saw it happen."

"Then you know this is going to be a close-run thing."

"Yes."

"If things carry on the way they have been, if this counter-attack doesn't work, the city's going to fall."

The pleasure of seeing him again had gone. There was just the grim truth now. "I thought it might."

"It's going to be a hell of a fight," Sepello said. "But I suppose you knew that."

A hard, cold anger rose up in her, like an ice-blue flame. "I'm going to kill Leth. No matter what."

"Me too," he said. "Let's go."

He led her up one staircase and then another, up and up, into a circular room at the very top of the palace. Sepello bowed deeply and Giulia followed suit. Lannato and Carmina stood beside the prince. Francis Vale was a little way apart. On the far side of the table were two soldiers: one tall and gaunt, the other red-faced and slovenly-looking. "These are my advisors," Mavlio said, pointing. "Goodchilde and Hoffman. Gentlemen, these are the people from the Order of Saint Cordelia. Let's get down to business."

The afternoon sunlight streamed in through the window, making the polished tabletop glow. A model of Astrago covered the table. Shadow lay between its towers as though ink flowed through the streets. Giulia stared at it, fascinated by the sheer mad detail of it all.

Mavlio said, "In several hours' time, I am going to meet with Constantin Leth for a parley. I have given him all the guarantees of protection and honourable conduct I can think of. I expect he will trust me about as much as I trust him. Once I have heard what he has to say, I want him killed." He looked left, then right. "I take it nobody objects to that."

The red-faced man – Hoffman – chuckled. Giulia had a feeling that he was the commander of the Citizen Guard. He certainly looked like an old mercenary captain.

Vale nodded. He was no longer the dapper patron Giulia had seen at the prince's dance: the ambassador looked like a man forced to shoot his own dog. But they all seemed worn-out and hard. Lannato's face had become tired and set. Carmina looked half-ashamed, half-ready to fight. *I hardly know these people*, she thought.

Giulia put her hands behind her back, under her cloak. Her fingertips brushed Hugh's book, wedged into her belt out of sight, and the knight flickered into life at the edge of her vision. He looked down at the model city, impressed.

The prince leaned forward and tipped a purse onto the table. Coppers tinkled on the wood. He set them out on the tabletop. "Leth's people, if that's the right word, occupy this area. That means that they also control a quarter of the outer wall. The inner wall" – he traced a cross with his finger through the centre of the city – "holds firm. As yet, Leth hasn't attempted to break through at any of the gates separating the quarters. If he does break through, we run a serious risk of being overwhelmed."

Sepello nodded grimly. Vale frowned and tugged his beard into a point.

"And that," Mavlio added, "is why I intend to open the gates before Leth can. We will counter-attack."

Oh shit, Giulia thought, looking around the room, *he means it*.

"We'll need to work fast. Once we've killed Leth himself, we will immediately take advantage of the surprise and fight back. I suggest a rapid strike into the main avenue of the south-west quarter, with a view to recapturing the gates – here – and the hole that tunnelling thing made. Once the area has been captured, powder can be used to demolish the tenement blocks around the hole, hopefully choking the hole with rubble. Any questions so far?"

Hoffman raised a hand. "How do you propose to kill Leth?"

Mavlio glanced to his left. "Cosimo."

Lannato leaned forward, overshadowing the city. "There are several methods. However, all of them rely on us only having the chance to take one or two shots before Leth's soldiers pull him away. The obvious answer is to use some sort of cannonet. A good hit from something like that would probably blast anyone nearby limb from limb. Unfortunately, given that Prince Mavlio will have to be close in order to talk, that runs the risk of taking the prince with it."

Vale said, "Which is why you need an expert marksman. Such as my man Daffyd."

Lannato shook his head. "With respect, Sir Francis, we have a better option. Giulia Degarno here has brought us a gift from the fey. It's a sort of poison that works on the undead."

They turned and looked at her. *Explain yourself*, their expressions said.

The ghost of Hugh folded his arms. He gave her a little smile.

"That's right," Giulia said. "When the undead attacked us at Oppidium, I managed to get away. I saw what Leth was doing in the caves down there, but I wasn't able to get close enough to kill him. I escaped from Oppidium, into the woods nearby, and the fey folk took me in. I told them what had happened, and they gave me a gift. It's a poison that kills the living dead."

"Why did they give it to *you?*" Vale asked. "Why not bring it to Prince Mavlio himself?"

"Because they couldn't get to the prince, and they trusted me to bring it to him," she replied. "I've worked with them before. The fey want revenge on Leth for the things he did for the Inquisition. They want us to stop him as much as we do."

"Does anyone know if this poison works at all?"

Lannato said, "It works. I've tested it. It rebalances the humours: effectively, it restores life. The stuff is lethal to revenants – at least, the ones that Leth has created."

Mavlio said, "How much have we got?"

"Giulia gave me a list of ingredients," the philosopher replied. "My own supplies are pretty good; I'll send men out to search the alchemists' shops as well. We can probably make several barrels of the stuff."

"We could dip arrows in it," Sepello said. "Pour it off the walls, perhaps. Some sort of spraying-device, maybe—"

Vale looked disgusted. "I've never heard of such a thing."

Hugh rolled his eyes. *For God's sake*, Giulia thought. She raised her voice. "My lords, please."

They looked at her. She pointed at Lannato.

"We can do better than just spraying it," Lannato said. "When heated, the mixture gives off a cloud of vapour, like mist. It could work like a poisonous cloud. But for Leth himself, I'd recommend we use a concentrated dose and a sharpshooter."

The prince put his fingertips together. He loomed over the model city like a hungry giant. "What do you think, Sepello?"

The revenant-hunter rubbed his chin. "I think it's a good idea."

"So that's it, then. Kill Leth, throw the doors open and charge into his men with everything we've got. Between my soldiers and Lannato's alchemical mist, we'll have them."

Giulia looked at the little wooden wall. *So then, Leth climbs onto the battlements, and we shoot him down, just like that. No, he's too clever to die that easily. He might as well be climbing onto a scaffold if he goes up there.*

"I don't like it," she said.

"Excuse me?" Vale looked straight at her, as though staring down a fierce animal. "I thought you were the one proposing that we used this magic potion?"

"Yes, I am. But that's not what I meant. Leth's a thousand years old. He's not just going to climb up onto the wall and let you shoot him. What if he's got armour on, or he sends someone else to do his talking? For that matter, have any of you actually *seen* him before?"

Sepello said, "Fair point."

"I've seen him," Vale said. "I'll be directing my sharpshooter. If you agree, of course, Prince Mavlio."

Giulia said, "You'll get one shot in before all hell breaks loose; two at best."

"I know," Mavlio said. "That's why we're going to use an expert. An armour-piercing arrow fired from a longbow should work. Am I right?"

"Absolutely," Lannato said. "Coated in poison, it shouldn't be too hard at all."

As they nodded their agreement, Giulia raised her hand.

Mavlio looked surprised. "Another question?"

"Yes." Giulia felt absolutely calm, as though nothing that these people might do could affect her. Sepello was watching her carefully. Lannato caught her eye. She could not tell whether he was disapproving or warning her. It didn't matter. "This sharpshooter of yours. I'll do it."

"I doubt you could wield a longbow," Vale replied.

"I wouldn't," she replied. "I'd use a crossbow bolt. The power's much the same."

"A kind offer," Mavlio said. He leaned back, and the low sun turned him into a near silhouette. "But I've already got a man to do it. Two men, in fact."

"You have?" Something sank inside of her. She felt the first stirrings of anger, that familiar sense of being cheated of what she deserved.

It was Vale's turn to lean forward. "One of my marines will take the shot. He's a Plennydri archer. They use him on board ship to shoot the spotters out of crow's nests. He could put a shaft in Leth's head from two hundred yards away."

Giulia tried to hold her tongue. But every word that Vale said made the fury rise up further inside her, and as his long face split into a smile, she knew that there was no point holding back. She said, "Leth killed my friend. I'm owed it."

Hugh looked at her. His voice was a low growl. "You tell 'em, woman."

Mavlio shook his head. "Many people have lost their loved ones. A quarter of this city is overrun. What matters now, madam, is that nobody else dies. And that means killing Leth. And *that* means having the best person take on the job."

"That person is me," she replied. "Prince Mavlio, I've seen him up close: I got as near to him as you are now. I can take him."

"If you got that close," Vale said, "I'd have thought you would have finished the job."

"Hugh of Kenton was a knight, a knight of Albion. He was my best friend. For God's sake, let me kill the bastard who murdered him."

Hugh nodded eagerly.

386

"If your man was from Albion, then he should be avenged by one of his own," Vale replied. "My man should take the shot."

"Giulia should do it," Sepello said.

She glanced around, surprised. The revenant-hunter leaned against the wall, next to the window. He looked almost casual, but his face was set. "She saved my life at Brancanza. She infiltrated Leth's hiding-place. If I could, I'd vote her straight into my order right now. Frankly, my lords, she's a born revenant-hunter."

"Please, my prince," Giulia said. "Let me do this."

Mavlio shook his head. "Sir Francis' marksman will shoot Leth, with an arrow dipped in poison. A poison, I should add, for which we owe you a debt."

Giulia sat down, took a deep breath, looked at the model on the tabletop and slowly shook her head. "As you wish," she said.

"Don't worry," Mavlio said, and he smiled. "There'll be plenty for you to do. You'll both be needed at the gates. Who better to take the fight to the undead than the Order of Saint Cordelia?"

A guard escorted Giulia to her room. "This way, madam," he said, and she followed him across the great hall, her bootsteps echoing on the marble floor.

The palace was nearly empty: everyone who could be spared was manning the defences. She wondered what would happen when Mavlio's men threw the gates open and they rushed forth to alleged victory. She had an image of human bodies hitting a wall of shields, bouncing off as the undead advanced; of the eager soldiers crushed between their comrades and the living dead. She shivered.

"This way," said the guard, ushering her up the grand staircase. Halfway up the stairs, something happened outside, and a cheer went up from the defenders in the square.

"I'm going to need some privacy," she said. "I need to pray."

He nodded. "There's a lot of people praying right now," he said. "Whole city's turned godly all of a sudden."

They said nothing more until they reached her room. Giulia stepped inside and closed the door. She heard the guard's footsteps move away, and she yanked *The Death of King Alba* from her belt.

Hugh was at the window, looking down on the city walls. He turned as if he'd been waiting for her. "Hello, Giulia."

"Hugh." She wanted to embrace him. "How are you?"

"About as good as you are." He looked at the window. "So, this is it, eh?"

"Yes."

"Awful lot of fellows down there. Look, they've got that clockwork thing."

She walked to the window, and he stepped aside. The courtyard behind the gates was full of armed men. About half wore palace livery. Further back, a second wave had gathered. They looked like a mob: she saw apprentices, women, and old men. They carried tools, kitchen knives, broken bottles.

Is that all we've got left?

Just behind the gates stood the clockwork castle. It looked like an exotic fort, like some pagan hut plated in armour and stuck on a set of wheels. A kind of plough had been fitted to the front, presumably to help push through the living dead.

That must be what they were cheering about.

"Are you down there?" she asked. "With Leth, I mean?"

He looked desperately sad. "I don't know for sure. It's dark where I am."

He's out there, she thought, *and so is Leth. I've just got to find him.* Who knew what was going on in the quarter that the undead had captured?

Something moved in her mind. It was half a memory, a sense of having heard something before and being unable to work out quite where. A fresh sense of unease.

Mavlio brought Sepello here, to help him find Leth. He brought Vale here, too. Why does Mavlio want Leth so much? And what does Vale get for helping him?

It didn't make sense. These were dangerous men, men who would never work for nothing. And yet, somehow, someone wasn't getting paid.

"Giulia?"

She looked up. Hugh smiled at her. "You probably ought to get going, you know."

She said, "I want to pray first."

"Of course. Mind if I join you?"

She knelt down. When she put her hands together, Hugh's book was between them. Giulia prayed to Saint Senobina, the way she had always done, that she might go unseen and be granted her revenge. Giulia felt as if she knew the saint well, as if she'd been Senobina's apprentice. But this time she also prayed to Cordelia, the patron of Sepello's order, for victory over the living dead.

If ever my cause was just, it is now.

She got to her feet, and Hugh's image stood up beside her. He frowned and bent his left leg, checking that his knee was all right. It was hard to believe that he was just a memory, a waking dream.

Outside, a deep voice called, "Form up! Come on, form your lines!"

"Hugh," she said, "can you— can you feel your body? Your real body, I mean?"

He shook his head. "I'm what you remember of me, Giulia. I'm still alive – I must be, because you can see me, but – well, otherwise, I don't really know. It's all pretty strange."

"You said it was dark around you. Are you in Oppidium?"

"I don't know. Look, Giulia, I, ah, I can't help wonder if it wouldn't be better if you didn't do this. Safer, I mean. For you. I'm an old man, Giulia, and you've got a lot of years before you—"

"Not if Leth gets through the gates. To hell with safety, Hugh. I'm getting you back."

He shook his head sadly. "You never were much of a one for being safe. I'll watch out for you, as best as I can."

"Thanks. I ought to get ready."

"Good idea," he said. He brightened up. "Right, then. Time for business."

Giulia tossed the book onto her bed, and he was gone. She pulled out her satchel, her crossbow, and her bag of bolts. She put the strap of the satchel over one shoulder, and slung the crossbow across her back.

She stretched, took a deep breath and held it for the count of ten.

"Time to go," she said, and she opened the door.

*

Sepello was waiting in the great hall, flanked by two palace guards. Giulia walked down the stairs, past the place where Mavlio had welcomed his guests. On her right was the gallery where the musicians had played. She half expected to see the ghost of her own self, wearing a hired dress and uncomfortable shoes and trying hard to blend in.

Sepello wore a breastplate over his coat and a high leather collar to protect his neck. He carried his sword on his left hip and his big pistol on his right. The palace soldiers were Mavlio's own personal guard, big men in full armour. They carried massive swords, and their breastplates gleamed like polished silver.

"What's this?" she whispered.

"We're joining the prince's party," Sepello replied. *Where he can keep an eye on us.*

The guard on the right said, "We'd better go now." His voice echoed slightly; it sounded very loud.

Giulia swallowed. "Let's go, then."

They walked towards the doors. Fear lay in her stomach like coals glowing in an oven. She thought about Leth, and Vale, and Mavlio, and tried to put it all together, but she was too nervous to think straight.

The guards opened the doors, and they walked into the entrance hall.

The others were waiting for them, dressed in fine armour like kings in a painting. Mavlio wore a sleek, polished cuirass with its proofing-dent proudly displayed above the heart. It was cleverly made, Giulia saw: the metal was smooth and angled to deflect blows. He carried a helmet. It had no chinstrap for throttling, she saw, nor a plume that could be grabbed. Hugh would have approved.

Her hand wanted to touch the book.

391

Vale was next, flanked by two of his marines. His armour was black, edged in silver, his white collar pulled over the top of his breastplate, Purist-style. He wore a sword and pistol, and held a helmet under his arm in one leather-covered fist. He was more like an officer than an ambassador. As Giulia and Sepello reached the bottom he looked them over and nodded approvingly.

Carmina was last. Giulia had not expected her: perhaps Mavlio had dressed her up to inspire the troops. She wore a cuirass over a red velvet dress. It was proper armour, too, not stage stuff: she was covered from groin to chin, and plates ran down her arms.

"All my generals," Mavlio said, and he smiled his wide lizard's smile. "Now, listen: very soon, I'll go up onto the wall and hear what Leth has to say. Then he'll be shot down. The arrow will be fired by Sir Francis' marksman, and the tip will be poisoned with a potion made up from the formula that Giulia brought for us."

Vale said, "That's right."

"As soon as the arrow goes out, the gates will open, whether Leth dies or not. And then we will launch an attack down the main street." Mavlio looked them over, his eyes flicking from face to face. "Ferocity is our weapon here. Leth expects us to defend, not strike back. It goes without saying that I'm expecting you to set an example. If you fight fiercely, the men around you will as well. So make sure they lift the banners up and go in hard and fast. We'll keep fighting until we're done."

"We're with you, Prince Mavlio," Vale replied. "Once this is over, I'll send word of your bravery to Queen Gloria herself."

"Thank you," said the prince. "And to all of you. Thank you for everything. Without your help, we would never have travelled this far. Now then – we have a hand to play. Let's go."

He turned to the men at the door. They nodded and hauled the doors apart, and the Mavlio led the group into the dusk.

The air was warm and close. As Giulia walked down the front steps of the palace, she made a decision. Let Mavlio and Vale take on Leth's soldiers. She had a friend to rescue – and for all she knew, he might be just behind the gates, among Leth's personal guards. Somehow, she had to get away from this and find Hugh by herself.

Torchlight lit the square. Ranks of men stood on either side. The guards had cleared a path between them from the palace to the gates, and Mavlio's party walked down it like an avenue. The soldiers watched them approvingly, not quite standing to attention. As Giulia passed them, she saw the salvaged weapons, the bandages and dirt. They must be all that Mavlio had. Once the square was empty, there would be few people left to fight except for the gunners on the walls.

She heard men mutter their approval as they walked past. "God bless you, Prince." "Let's take 'em." "Show him, Mavlio!" Their voices made her body tense up, ready to fight. Fear bubbled in her gut. She needed to piss.

"For the city!" a voice yelled from the crowd, and she saw a group of black coats in the rows. A man pushed to the front, dressed in black and white, and barked, "We're with you, Prince Mavlio – all the New Church is with you," before a dwarrow shoved him back into line. To the left, a nobleman in brand new armour raised his clenched fist. "Hail the prince!" She'd seen him before –

at Mavlio's party, making jokes to a gaggle of hangers-on.

The last hand, she thought as she walked. The palace bodyguards flanked them. She felt her fear rise, and exhaled slowly.

To the right, the mass of the clockwork fortress loomed. Its reinforced wheels were as high as she was tall. The sloping sides looked impenetrable. Guns protruded from hatches like cannons on a galleon. A scroll had been painted on the side. It read *Philosopher's Sword*.

Giulia glanced around, at the walls and the buildings behind the men, trying to find some way out and seeing nothing. She wanted to stop, to make a plan, but there was no chance. This must be how the condemned felt, walking to the gallows, wishing to escape and not having the strength or the time to work out how.

They stopped before the gates.

Sepello stood beside her. He looked over and smiled, and raised his eyebrows. "*Dans chaque generation, il y aura une femme comme moi,*" he said.

Giulia didn't speak Heraldique. "What?"

"'In each generation, there will be a woman like me.' Saint Cordelia said that before she died. Perhaps she meant you."

Giulia glanced away. She thought of the undead waiting behind the gates, in silent ranks. Ancient armour and old bone.

Two men brought a box over and set it down in front of the gates. Mavlio climbed onto it. Men leaned forward as the prince began to speak.

"Well, friends, here we are." Mavlio's voice was calm and level. The ranks shuffled towards him to be certain to catch his voice, and at once his audience was guaranteed. "In a few minutes, I will climb the walls to meet with the necromancer, Constantin Leth. I will hear him out, as honour demands. But be clear about this – I will never surrender this city, and I will never betray its people! Astrago will not fall and, so long as I live, I will defend it!"

The listeners cheered. A man to Giulia's right shouted, "You tell it, Mavlio!" Giulia thought, *He's a good actor, but he means it. He has to mean it. There's no other choice now.*

The prince took a deep breath. "At this hour, in my greatest need, I stand before you not as a prince, but as a man. A fellow citizen. Like you, I have my home here, my family and my friends. And like you, I came to these walls to fight for them. I will hear Leth, but I will give him nothing except the chance to walk away.

"Against us are the living dead – enemies not just of our city, and of our faith, but enemies of life itself. Every blow we strike, we strike for mankind, for the very world. So long as we draw breath, we are undefeated!

"So let us advance as brothers today. Today, it does not matter who you are, or who the man is who fights beside you: rich or poor, Old Church or New, man or woman or fey, today we have a greater enemy, and the greatest goal of all. So join me, as I know you will, and in the name of God, of nature, and of life itself – follow your prince!"

The roar that followed sounded like an avalanche. Giulia stood in the centre of the sound, three yards from the prince, and as the fear rose in her, the readiness did as well. Six huge guards approached, pushing massive wheeled shields before them. Mavlio jumped down from the box and let them surround him. They walked to the wall, and began to climb.

*

Mavlio ascended carefully. Two guards preceded him. Another stood at his side, holding a big metal shield towards the occupied part of the city. Mavlio glanced left, and caught a glimpse of the lost quarter. It no longer felt like something he had ever owned.

At the top of the wall, the gunners nodded and bowed. Mavlio walked past. He wondered how many people were watching him. He felt the urge to look left, at the clocktower of Saint Ignatio's, where the marksman waited. It was like an itch, a spasm to be fought down.

Vale's archer had better be good.

A great figure appeared at the far end of the wall, twenty yards away. It was as much like a siege engine as a man, the outline half-hidden under armour plate. The brute lumbered forward with the slow deliberation of a man striding through water, a huge shield held out to its side. The head looked tiny, a last-minute addition.

I should have told them to blast the wall with grapeshot the moment Leth showed up. But then I'd never know for sure.

The monster lifted its shield to one side, and Leth stood behind it.

He was slim and of average height. He wore a black robe, tight around the body and loose at the legs. It made him look like a priest. He had no hair, and his skin was almost completely grey, as if dusted with fine ash.

Leth walked forward, away from his bodyguard. Into the open. Mavlio didn't look at the clocktower.

"Mavlio," Leth said. His voice was flat and strained. He said the prince's name slowly, as if he relished it.

"Leth. You took a risk coming up here."

"I have an offer for you," said Leth. He sounded like an old judge reading out a death sentence. "My terms are as follows: Astrago will surrender and you will step down from the throne. The city will become mine. In return, I will give you safe passage out of the Peninsula."

"And you'll become prince."

"No. Someone loyal to me will take the throne."

Mavlio felt stronger, somehow, now that the talking had started. "Would this someone be of House Sciata, perhaps?"

"Maybe."

"And my citizens? They won't like that."

"People can be controlled," Leth said, and Mavlio remembered that Leth had once worked for the Inquisition. "They can learn to live with anything."

Madness, Mavlio thought, *this is a lunatic's dream*, and then he remembered how the Inquis Impugnans had conquered all of mainland Alexendom, and doubt stirred inside him, like cracks appearing in a castle wall.

"You can't have Astrago," he said. A strange sense of hopelessness was spreading through him. He put his hand on the wall: perhaps to steady himself, perhaps to cling on to his city. "It's mine."

Leth's voice ground on. "I will guarantee the survival of your citizens, provided they remain loyal to me. On death their cadavers will become my property, but not before. I will unite the houses of Sciata and DeFalci, thus preventing any family disputes."

"And how do you intend to do that?"

"Marriage. When my man takes the throne, I will provide him with longevity. In return for your survival, your house will provide him with a bride."

Something crawled up the prince's spine.

"After all," Leth said, "I doubt that Carmina is in a fit state to marry anyone living."

"What?"

397

Leth turned to look at the city. "You have a reputation as a schemer, Mavlio. But I have been playing this game for generations. Oppidium fell to me a thousand years ago, and there were plenty of others before that. I put a claim on this town long before you were born."

Mavlio barely heard him. "What did you say about my daughter?" But he knew already. The pieces were slotting into place.

"You forget who you are dealing with," the revenant added, and his voice became a notch tighter. "I am immortal. Everything you own, you borrowed off me. Now I have come to take what's mine. I want my city, and I want Carmina."

"It was you that poisoned her. You turned her into one of you, didn't you?"

Leth nodded. "I arranged it. Undeath is nothing more than the application of alchemy, after all. She will make an excellent ruler. No doubt she has learned from an expert." He swallowed; his throat twitched as if an animal was trapped inside it. "So, Prince, you have a choice. On the one hand, you abdicate, your people live, and Carmina gains a new benefactor. On the other, your city falls and your daughter will rule over the nation of corpses that is her due. And if that is not enough persuasion, Prince, on her wedding day it will be your dead body that dances at the feast."

"That's enough. I've heard enough."

Leth nodded. "So you see reason, then."

"Yes, I do." Mavlio raised his hand and scratched the side of his head.

"Good. Then go back and tell your men—"

There was a soft whistle, and then the sudden, flat *thwack!* of the arrow punching into Leth's thigh. His leg

398

buckled. He made a small, hard noise, air forced out between his teeth.

Leth's shield-beast came awake. Mavlio's guards ran forward. Mavlio pulled his knife, dashed in and drove it at the revenant's throat.

Leth blocked, shaky on his feet. The blade slid into his bicep.

He snarled and lashed out. His palm hit Mavlio's chest like a battering ram.

Mavlio staggered back into the battlements, slipped and fell. He saw the edge of the wall yawn before him – and a hand grabbed his shoulder and hauled him back. Voices yelled along the battlements.

Leth rose up and pulled the arrow out of his leg. He took a limping step forward – and stopped.

The revenant's hand was turning brown. Veins crawled over his skin like ivy, creeping towards his fingertips, spreading and breaking open. Leth raised his hand and, for a long second, both he and Mavlio stared at it in the lantern-light. It was like watching an apple rot at high speed.

And then, in one quick motion, he drew his sword.

The soldiers grabbed Mavlio. Two of his men dragged their prince back down the battlements. A third – the man who had saved him from falling – ran forward and swung his axe. Leth dodged the blow, grabbed the soldier's head and bit him in the throat. Leth cracked the soldier's skull against the battlements and hurled him off the wall. His face was like a beast's: the eyes wild with rage, the mouth smeared with blood.

Mavlio's guards held their shields up and hauled their prince away. Guns banged and cracked in the city. Chunks of masonry burst around Leth. In a cloud of dust, his undead bodyguard rushed forward, threw a great metal shield over him as if dropping a curtain, and the necromancer was lost to view.

*

Men ran to the gates. *Oh God*, Giulia thought, *this is it.*

Trumpets blared. The gates swung apart.

Guns fired on the walls. Giulia couldn't see what they were aiming at. She craned her neck, past the rows of soldiers, and got a glimpse of the street beyond the gates. She saw the edge of a house, maybe movement behind.

"What's going on?" Sepello demanded. "I can't see a bloody thing!"

"No fucking idea. Come on," she said, and she grabbed his sleeve. "We're going to finish this."

She shoved forward. A soldier turned and barred her way with his arm, shoved her back. "You stay there. Wait for the signal. *Stay* there!"

"I need to get to Leth," she shouted back. "I know how to kill him."

"I said—"

"*Look!*" Sepello yelled.

The gates were completely open now, and she saw. Behind the gate, a wall of shields advanced on them. A terrible noise rose from the dead, like rhythmic thunder: the revenants were beating the backs of their shields.

Guns blew holes in the massive shields, bolts and arrows punched into them, but the dead kept on. She saw a lucky shot clip the skull of one revenant and it fell apart. Another took its place, pressed in between its fellows like a tooth in a jaw. Some kind of organ-gun fired, and half a dozen skeletons burst into showers of bone – and just as quickly their gaps were filled and the wall of walking dead pressed on.

400

From the rear of the square, a vehicle rumbled into view like a fortress on wheels. It was *Philosopher's Sword*, the clockwork castle, and it was pushing a heavy cart before it. A hatch flopped open in the roof and a man stuck his head out. "Everyone clear a path! Get out the way! Move!"

The clockwork castle rolled through the sea of men and weapons like a ship parting waves, and people ran to avoid it.

The cart on the front of it carried some kind of mechanism. As the cart's wheels rolled, a ratchet in the centre turned a thing like a mast, set it spinning as the fortress gathered speed. Blades and chains were nailed to the pole, and they swung out, whipping around like the rotors of a flying machine.

Trumpets blared from the palace. Ten yards from Giulia, the bishop of Astrago raised his staff. "God has struck the hour," he called. "In Heaven's name, advance!"

Men poured onto the walls, taking up positions above the gates. They rained down every kind of shot onto the skeletons: bolts, bullets, arrows, lumps of broken stone. Gunpowder bombs fell into the revenants. Bones shattered in the ranks, and fresh undead trampled those who fell. Some skeletons threw up their long shields to fend off the volley from above – but most rushed forward with that long, hungry stride of the living dead, eating up the distance to the prize.

The clockwork fortress hit Leth's front line. The undead simply burst. The blades and chains whipped through them, shattering the skeletons by the dozen. Scraps of bone flew up like shards of pottery. The armoured wheels rumbled over fallen shields.

The guards on the walls howled with glee. They threw debris onto the revenants. One man slipped in his haste and fell into the ranks of the dead.

Giulia grabbed Sepello's arm. "Help me," she said. "I've got to get to the front."

He looked at her for a long second, and then he rushed forward. Men shoved past them, buffeted them as they followed their priests and officers towards the gate. Sepello was pushed aside and, cursing, he struggled back. Giulia struggled on, surrounded by soldiers.

Someone shoved Giulia in the back and she lurched forward, only just kept her footing and ran into the only place left to run – towards the enemy. The clockwork castle was huge, but the undead lapped around it, past it, and marched at the gates, mindless of the path that it was driving through their comrades.

Suddenly Giulia was in a tide of bodies, pressing forward. There was no chance of going back – she had to find Hugh, had to. The gateway threw an arc of shadow over her and then she pushed forward, into the sun. She looked left and right, her view half-hidden by the heads of the men around her, and saw her chance. To the right, a ramp led up to the battlements. She moved forwards and the ramp was closer. In a few seconds she'd reach it, and then the current of men would push her past—

She threw her weight to the side, shouldered the man on her right out of the way, and shoved herself to the edge of the crowd. Her boot caught on a man's foot and she stumbled, suddenly terrified, lost her footing entirely and fell onto the ramp.

In a second she'd scrambled upright – out of the crowd, thank God – and ran upwards, almost on all fours. She reached the top and was on the battlement, above the soldiers, the clockwork castle and the undead.

The walls were too chaotic for anyone to try to stop her. Men aimed and fired, hurled stones and rubbish onto the revenants and busied themselves with ramrods and windlasses. A man shouted something and Giulia rushed past him. She ran down the parapet, weaving and ducking, struggling to keep pace with *Philosopher's Sword*.

She had to find Hugh, had to. That was the prize, the finishing line that remained just out of reach. He was there, somewhere, in Leth's army and she had to reach him before Mavlio's soldiers did. She could cure him, she knew she could. She just had to get there first.

The front line of soldiers met the undead with a great cheer like a breaking wave, and the sounds of metal on metal followed it. Trumpets blared. She heard screams.

Huge figures pushed through the sea of skeletons, coming up to reinforce the line. They were massive with armour, their faces hidden under crested helmets, their shoulders bulked out with steel. She glanced from one to another, trying to recognise Hugh. Not a chance, not from this height.

"Shit!" Guns popped around her. She didn't have long. She had to get to the front, so that the soldiers couldn't swarm Hugh or run him down. The clockwork castle rumbled under her.

She jumped.

Giulia hung in the air for half a second that went on forever, hit the roof of the clockwork fortress, and slipped. She rolled, the world rushing by, and a flagpole struck her in the midriff. A moment's frantic scrambling and her foot met metal and she grabbed hold of the flagpole and dragged herself onto the roof. She crouched down, riding the machine, hearing the crash and rattle as it ploughed through the skeleton horde.

Bony hands pattered against the hull, swords bounced off the machine's armour. The whirling mechanism at the front was broken now, but that didn't matter.

And then she realised that it was slowing down. *Philosopher's Sword* had punched into the enemy like an arrow, but it was running out of force. The undead were packed in too tight. The clockwork castle couldn't force its way through.

We're going to stop.

"*Puella!*"

She whipped around and saw one of the noxi scrambling up the side of the machine. White eyes like knuckle-bones stared from behind its mask. Giulia drew her knife and its hand grabbed her ankle.

The revenant yanked her off-balance. Giulia fell onto her back and kicked out with her heel. The mask broke; it howled and fell into the mass of its comrades below.

They were almost at a standstill now. She had to get off this thing before the undead swarmed it. Giulia clambered upright and looked across a sea of spears. Skulls and dead faces stared up at her. Where the fucking hell was everyone?

She reached for the copy of *The Death of King Alba*. Hugh appeared beside her. "Where are you?" she cried. "Hugh! Tell me where you are!"

"Look," he said. Giulia turned, but all she saw were the undead. Armour and shields and skulls.

Something huge rose from the Quincunx Palace.

For a moment it seemed as if a tower of the palace had taken flight. The flying machine swung into the air, rotors whirling. Immediately, the undead unleashed catapults and ballistae. Rocks and eight-foot bolts flew over Giulia's head. A great shaft crashed through the bows, shaking the machine.

Something clattered on the roof behind her. Giulia twisted around. A skeleton was climbing onto the clockwork fortress, short sword in hand. She ran over and kicked it in the head, and it fell away.

The flying machine dropped and, as it sank over the undead, white stuff spilled out of its sides. *It's the enchantments breaking*, Giulia thought. *It can't stay up any more.* But a second later she realised what it was: greenish smoke.

The smoke drifted down, and Giulia recognised it: the vapour that Lannato had used to poison the rats. As she made the connection, a thin bank of green smoke wafted over the undead just behind the gate.

They fell apart. The skeletons disintegrated, collapsing into heaps of bone, their skulls falling as if the ground had opened beneath them. One or two lasted a second more, and then they, too, fell, their strings cut in the act of turning. The flying machine banked, throwing out more of the mist. It fell like flour from a leaky sack, and where it touched the living dead, it destroyed them.

Giulia stood on top of the clockwork castle, surrounded by revenants. The flying machine swung down overhead and showered her in green-white dust. She twisted and shook her head to keep the stuff off her face and, as the flying machine let out another burst of alchemical mist, she realised that it was going to hit Hugh.

Where was he? Bolts and arrows sailed into the air, aimed at the flying vessel. A boulder clipped the whirling screw that held the flyer aloft, spun away and smashed into a house. The flying machine turned, sinking as if punctured, and struggled back towards Mavlio's line.

The clockwork castle lurched forward and Giulia nearly slipped. It picked up speed beneath her, and the wheels rolled over piles of bone. She dropped onto all fours, so as not to lose her footing.

Bones covered the ground as if the whole city was a monster's lair. Long shields lay scattered like fallen rooftiles. The fortress crunched and rumbled over them. Giulia looked back and saw Mavlio's banner, saw living men around it.

Now, to find Hugh. She shielded her eyes and stared across the horde. The skeletons were still crumbling, falling apart in a slow ripple like dominos, but the effect had begun to fade. The survivors wobbled and staggered like drunks, like bees confused by smoke.

There! In the middle of the field of bone, she saw a group of armoured figures. Protected by his lumbering elite, Leth struggled through his soldiers towards the ruins of Saint Allomar's church. Skeletons stumbled around, impeding him. A dozen armour-plated bodies surrounded the necromancer.

Hugh's in there. He must be.

Giulia ran to the edge of the clockwork carriage and jumped. She landed in a crouch, surrounded by white, spindly legs. She stood up, and looked into a sea of skulls.

They wobbled like infants learning to walk. One revenant clattered forward, raising a spear. Giulia darted aside and it made a huge, clumsy swipe and fell to pieces. A second took a step towards her and disintegrated in a cascade of bone. She gritted her teeth and braced herself.

Giulia ran into them as if to smash down a door. Her shoulder crashed into a massive rectangular shield, and it fell aside. Suddenly she was running, stumbling, through rows of the undead, past ribcages and turning skulls and feebly groping hands. One of them grabbed her shoulder; she twisted aside in a rain of ancient finger-bones. A skeleton stepped forward, lifting its sword, and its arm fell apart as it tried to bring it down.

A big revenant stepped into her way. It was some kind of officer, she realised, strong enough to ignore Lannato's poison. Under its plumed helmet was a face the colour of clay. The revenant held an axe in one hand and a wooden rod in the other. It strode forward, swinging the axe.

The officer roared and swiped at her head, but the swing was clumsy and Giulia darted aside. She turned to face it, knife raised, but the revenant ignored her and lumbered past, towards the palace. Giulia glanced back and saw soldiers pushing around the clockwork castle, smashing the skeletons that remained. Perhaps the revenant officer's mind had been damaged by Lannato's green smoke, or perhaps it was too enraged to care. It rushed forward, and the soldiers ran to meet it.

Giulia saw the city gates ahead, and the singed, broken body of Leth's burrowing creature in front of it, like a collapsed tent of hide and bone. There, ahead, was a heap of masonry where it had burst from the earth. She ran forward, knowing that the tunnel would lead her to Hugh. But she saw that it was impassable: the tunnel had collapsed on itself, and was choked with bricks and broken timber. As she slowed, the ground shifted underfoot. Giulia stopped, afraid that the ground might give way. She stood there, at the edge of the ruins, knowing that he had been stolen from her again.

Far behind her, men were realising that they had won. Giulia felt too tired to feel anything. Her vision clouded; she reached up and found that she was crying, more from exhaustion than sadness. *Keep going*, she told herself, but right now, there was nowhere else to go.

Leth had escaped. Giulia pulled her bag down and opened it. She touched the book, and the image of Hugh flickered at the edge of her vision. She took her hand away and he vanished. He was still alive, or as close to alive as he could be. Rescue was still possible. She'd seen all that she needed.

She pushed her hair away from her face and sheathed her knife, so that her allies wouldn't mistake her for an enemy. Then she turned back, towards the prince's men.

Chapter 15

"Cosimo Lannato," Mavlio declared, "you are a genius."

They stood in the square before the palace, surrounded by guards. Soldiers were still scouring the city streets, looking for any revenants that might have escaped Lannato's alchemy. But Mavlio heard cheering, not combat. He closed his eyes for a moment and revelled in it all, buoyed up by the sound of victory.

Palace guards stood nearby, to keep the rejoicing commoners away from their prince. There were still dangers, and the Sciata might make a desperate, last-ditch attempt at an assassination. Besides, Mavlio thought, there was still work to do.

Lannato smiled. "Thank you, my prince."

"No thanks needed. Even by your standards, that was masterful." Mavlio gestured to Vale, who stood nearby. The ambassador had watched the collapse of Leth's army with a calm detachment, like a butcher looking over a beef carcass. He walked over, stroking his beard into a point.

"Prince Mavlio?"

"Look here, Vale. This is the most intelligent man you will ever see. Even if you live a hundred years, you'll never know a man as clever as this."

"Well," Lannato said, "it was quite simple, really. Once I'd figured out the basic principle, it was just a matter of putting it to work on a larger scale—"

"Ah, but would anyone else have done that? One man might think of dropping rocks from the flying machine, or even gunpowder – now there's an idea – and another might have wiped his blade with that potion, but to combine the two – that's genius. I tell you, Sir Francis:

other princes have their wizards, but we have this fellow. I doubt there's been a mind like Lannato's since the days of the ancients."

Mavlio stopped. He looked across the square, and remembered that Leth was one of those ancients. *Old learning against new learning.* The Quaestans had come back to conquer the world, and for the first time in history, they'd faced men more cunning, more advanced than themselves. It was as if an apprentice swordsman had defeated his former master. Perhaps here, Mavlio thought, mankind had finally surpassed the ancients. Humanity had come of age.

A dark figure made its way across the square, weaving between the bright uniforms of the guards and the makeshift armour of the militiamen. *Giulia Degarno*, Mavlio thought. *A woman with a talent for staying alive.*

"It's that woman," Vale said.

"Actually, she was the one who brought me the alchemical recipe," Lannato said. "For the smoke, I mean. If it wasn't for her carrying it here, and for the dryads coming up with it—"

"You do yourself a disservice," Mavlio replied. "History will remember *you*, Cosimo, not some bunch of pixies or a madwoman in a pair of britches."

"Well, I—"

"Prince Mavlio!" Giulia called. Vale pulled a face. "Prince Mavlio!"

She wasn't smiling – did she ever smile? – but Mavlio felt too relieved to care. This was his moment of triumph. He bowed stiffly at the waist. "Madam Degarno. Victory is ours."

"Leth got away. You've got to go after him."

Vale turned on her. "Mind your tone, woman! The prince gives the orders here."

"He'll be hiding in Oppidium, rebuilding his army," Giulia said. "He'll have more soldiers down there, more weapons. This – all this – is just a setback for him."

Mavlio said, "If I was Leth, I'd be running away as far as I could, not hiding in a cave."

Giulia shook her head. "It isn't a cave. It's a city. It's got forges, armouries, barracks, everything you'd need to make an army. And – would you run? Really?"

Mavlio looked across the square. A group of men were cheering. Someone had produced a small barrel of beer, and they were drinking out of whatever they could find. The festivities felt distant, as if he had wandered into a stranger's wedding. "No, I wouldn't." He thought of Leth on the wall, of what the revenant had said about Carmina. "You're right. He has to die. Properly die. I want to see it with my own eyes."

Giulia said, "I'll find Sepello."

"Get him and come straight to the palace." She moved to go, and Mavlio said, "Oh, Giulia? You did a good job. I'm grateful."

"Thank you," she replied, and she walked away.

*

Giulia sat at the edge of the war room on a carved oak bench, the wood smooth and oily from hundreds of polishings. The other leaders – Mavlio, Vale, Goodchilde, Sepello, Lannato and Carmina – sat around the table, like rival giants attacking the model city from different angles. Giulia wondered if they finally felt that she'd earned her place here. They could think what they liked, but they needed her. This was her time.

Mavlio leaned over the model of Astrago. Scraps of dark cloth lay over the fallen parts, along the walls and over the tenements knocked down by the undead. "So," he said, "the city stands. We seem to have won – for now."

Lannato glanced up at him. "Do you think the undead will come back?"

"Oh, Leth won't be back with another army," the prince replied. "At least, I'd be very surprised if he did. I doubt he's got the manpower. Besides, there'd be no point in him keeping reserves. He had to take Astrago to get a foothold on the Peninsula."

Vale stood a little way back from the table, hands clasped behind his back. "But we still have to catch him," he said. "And that means hunting him down."

Mavlio turned and looked across the room. For a moment, Giulia thought the prince was about to address her, and she opened her mouth to speak. "Sepello. Your thoughts on this."

The revenant-hunter stood up slowly. For a young man, he seemed battered and worn-down. "My duty to the Order of Saint Cordelia requires me to destroy the living dead. That means that I have to go after him."

"Me too," Giulia said.

Vale nodded. "So you know where he's gone?"

Sepello said, "I can guess. He'll have gone to ground." He approached the table. "You have to realise how old he is. Time doesn't matter for him the way it does to us. He'll go to ground and wait – maybe ten, twenty years, maybe a hundred – and then he'll try again. Of course, if he does decide to wait it out, then you won't hear from him for a long time – and when he does resurface, it could be a long way from here. But the undead know how to hold a grudge. If he doesn't go after you, Prince, he'll go after your descendants, and he'll be stronger than ever."

He looked straight at Mavlio, and something passed between them that Giulia couldn't quite understand, as if 'descendants' had a secret meaning.

"I see," Mavlio said. "So the tree needs to be dug out by the roots."

"Exactly, my prince. The undead never stop. A man who fights them shouldn't stop either."

"He'll go back to Oppidium," Giulia said. "It's where his equipment is, where he raised his army. Leth is a savant, a sort of natural philosopher. He won't want to leave his laboratory behind." She glanced at Lannato. "That would be throwing all his work away."

Sepello said, "I agree."

Mavlio nodded. "Oppidium it is, then. Cosimo, could we attack it?"

Lannato shook his head. "If Oppidium is underground, it would be nearly impossible to besiege. Were we dealing with men – living ones – we'd simply find the entrances, cut off the food supply and wait, but the undead don't eat. They don't seem to need anything at all. And I doubt we've got the numbers or the equipment to storm a place like that. It must be like Hell down there," he added, half to himself.

"So a conventional attack is out of the question?"

"I think so. And, well, I don't like to say it, but I doubt our men would have the stomach for it."

A heaviness seemed to settle onto the room. *True*, Giulia thought. The people of Astrago might be celebrating now, but an attack on Leth's citadel would be another level of horror. How many of the city's brave defenders would be half-mad before the year was out?

"I could do it," she said. "I could go in there and kill him for you."

They looked at her.

"I've seen what it's like in there. I went in there and I got out alive."

Carmina spoke. "She's right," the princess said. "Giulia knows the way. A small party could slip into this city of theirs, sneak up to Leth and kill him."

"You'd have to get there," Mavlio said.

Quietly, Lannato said, "The flying machine."

The prince looked down at the city. "How many men will it hold?"

"Thirty, at most."

Sepello shifted in his chair. "I'm in."

"You're wounded," Giulia said.

"I'm the expert here. You'll be hunting Leth on his home territory. You need me."

Mavlio nodded. "Fair point. You're both in. We'll need good soldiers, too."

Vale cleared his throat. "I can supply marines," he said. "My own men have suffered a few casualties, but I can put together fifteen or twenty first-class soldiers, used to boarding actions and small-scale raids. They'll be perfect for the task in hand. I will be happy to go with them, to supervise. At your command, of course, Prince."

"Get fifteen men, Vale – volunteers only. There'll be a dozen of my guards, Sepello here, and you and I."

Vale frowned. "You're going as well?"

"Oh yes," Mavlio said. "I want Leth as much as you do. I'm going to look the bastard in the eyes. And then finish him."

"Is that wise?"

Mavlio smiled, deep and thin. It made him look like a snake. "Possibly not, but I'm going to do it anyway. Carmina, Lannato: while we're away, the city is yours. Don't lower the defences, and make sure the people don't get too rowdy. Vale, get your men ready. No need to wait around. Sepello, Madam Degarno: get yourselves shriven, arm up and sleep well. We're going to be busy. I don't know whether you can kill a man that's already dead – but you can make him very unhappy."

Sepello bowed, Giulia curtseyed, and they left the room. The inner circle of House DeFalci remained standing around the model of their city.

They walked down the stairs together. Sepello said nothing. *Soon, Hugh*, Giulia thought. *You could be back here by tomorrow night. So long as none of my new friends decides to kill you.*

At the bottom of the stairs, Sepello turned to her. "Well, goodnight, Giulia. Better get some sleep before we go to Oppidium." He smiled. "I doubt we'll get much rest on the flying machine."

"Goodnight."

Sepello hesitated, and for a weird moment she thought that he might try to kiss her. Then he said, "And thank you for everything. I mean it."

"That's all right."

"*They* may not have noticed, but if you hadn't brought that stuff here from the fey folk, we couldn't have beaten Leth so quickly. Maybe not at all. For all I know, without you the undead might have broken into the rest of the city. Look, Giulia, when we get out of this, there'll be a place for you at the Order of Saint Cordelia, if you'd like. I could recommend you. I'd be proud to work beside you," he added. "God knows you fight hard enough. When I first met you I thought you must be half-crazy, but you're one of the best hunters I've ever met. You'd be a credit to the order."

"Thank you," she said. Her voice caught, surprising her. "That's kind of you." She smiled. "But I think I've

415

seen enough of the undead to last me a lifetime. I just want my friend back – to get Leth back for my friend, I mean." She stopped. She wanted to tell him about Hugh. Sepello would understand. He was a good, kind man, who fought because he wanted to protect people and to do what was right, the way Hugh had done.

No. He can't be trusted. None of them can.

"I'm going to bed," Giulia said.

"If you need anything to help you sleep, I've got a tincture," he replied.

Giulia smiled. "You're like a walking apothecary's shop. Goodnight, Pietro."

They embraced. He squeezed her tightly, and stepped back. "Sleep well."

As she walked away, all the emotion fell away from her like an unfastened cloak. She hadn't told him about Hugh because she was a professional and an expert, just like he was. Sepello would find Hugh, destroy him and sleep soundly, because that was what he did.

No, none of them could be relied upon: not Sepello, not Lannato, none of them. Tomorrow, she would rescue her friend, just as she'd promised to, no matter what anyone else might do. She'd do it the old way: quietly, on her own.

*

The tubby guard near Carmina's door bowed as the prince approached. "Evening, Tomas," Mavlio said.

"Good evening, Prince Mavlio. Are you going to bed, my prince?"

"In a while. I thought I'd see Carmina first. Have they got you standing here all night?"

"I come off in two hours. Then it's back to the wife."

"Good." Mavlio felt a rush of affection towards the man. "When you get off, go down to the kitchens and get yourself a drink, yes?"

"Thank you, Prince. A cup of beer would be good."

Mavlio smiled. He felt generous – not because of the victory over Leth's army, but because selfishness no longer seemed to matter. Life was short; the time for charity was now. "Take a bottle of wine with you, and one for the wife."

"You're very kind, my prince."

"You're a good man, Tomas. I'll see you later." He walked on, to his daughter's door.

Mavlio knocked. He heard the bolts slide back, and Carmina opened it a little way. "Father?"

She opened the door properly and stepped aside so he could enter. She was still dressed. Mavlio closed the door behind her, and bolted it.

"I just thought I'd say hello," he said. "See how you were doing."

"I'm fine, Father."

"Feeling well?"

"As healthy as I get," she replied. She sounded cheerful, but he knew that meant nothing.

"Look, Carmina," he said. "You heard what we said in the map room. Tomorrow we're going to sort Leth out. To finish this. It's unlikely, and I intend to avoid it, but Leth may have tricks waiting for us. If I don't come back quickly, remember what we talked about."

"Yes, Father." She would know what to do if Mavlio was murdered or kidnapped, as did Lannato. Mavlio had drilled them well: hold the palace, close the city, throw known enemies into jail – not that there were any known enemies left in the city now – and formalise Carmina's ascension to the throne as quickly as possible. Then there would be a season of gifts and executions to fix her in place. "Be careful, Father." She hesitated. "I love you."

"I love you too," he said. He stood in the middle of the room, suddenly feeling a long way from everything. "Time for one more lesson," he said.

"I was going to sleep."

"Sleep can wait. One last lesson for the royal princess, I think." He folded his arms. "So, tell me: when should we trust the Pontifex?"

"We never should trust him, Father."

Mavlio drew back in mock surprise. "But he's the head of the Church! What a thing to say! Tell me why not."

"Because he's of House Sciata."

"And what if he wasn't?"

"We can never trust the Pontifex, because the Church seeks power over men's souls." Carmina looked as intense as a novice reciting her vows. "He who controls a man's soul controls his body. And he who controls a man's body controls his deeds. And those deeds can be turned against the prince."

Mavlio smiled. "Very good. Now, say you know that a man in the city has no respect for you. He holds his princess in disrepute. What do you do?"

"Nothing, Father. He's just one man."

"But if he starts to stir up trouble?"

"I kill him."

"Good. Publicly, if needs be, so others don't get the idea to follow him. But remember: what don't we make when we administer justice?"

"Martyrs, Father. Martyrs stay in the churches, not on the streets."

"Excellent. You'll make a great prince. The people will love you — and those that don't will fear you too much to do anything about it." Mavlio paced slowly across the room. "There's a chest in my room, under the bed. Lannato made it; it's got a number on the lock. The number to open it is three-five-two. The papers inside contain information on the main guildsmen and militia captains, should you need them. Make a few examples and the rest will fall in line."

"I know, Father."

What a shitty world, he thought. *Here I am, teaching my daughter to be as much of a bastard as I am, just to save her skin.* A thought struck him. "Carmina, would you consider marrying Lannato?"

She burst out laughing. "Marry? Him?"

"Well, yes. Why not?"

"Well, firstly, he's never shown any interest in a woman for as long as I've known him. And secondly, I'm one of the living dead."

"You're ill, Carmina. He knows how to look after you. And he loves you."

She stopped smiling. "I know. But just not like that. Not… romance."

"It'd be better than most marriages that a princess can have."

"I thought I was staying unmarried so you could – er – keep the other states guessing? Like Queen Gloria does: nobody dares argue with her, because if they do, they'll never get the throne."

Mavlio shook his head. "The other states can piss in the wind. Come here."

She stepped over and he embraced her. *You shouldn't have to be part of this*, Mavlio thought. *The price of survival is to become hard and cruel.* Mavlio held his daughter tight, feeling her body in his arms and the imitation of breath that moved her against him. "You will be a formidable prince," he said.

*

The palace seemed busier than ever. People were coming and going all the time: servants carrying supplies down to the city; soldiers changing guard; runners carrying news from the quarter of Astrago that had been recaptured from the undead. Giulia put on her dress and picked up a large basket full of kindling that stood beside one of the upstairs fireplaces. She pulled a businesslike scowl and hurried downstairs, as if on an important and urgent mission.

She took the back stairs that Lannato had showed her. As she descended into the passageways below the palace, she heard male voices, muffled by stone. The prince's engineers would be back at work, repairing the clockwork castle and readying the defences for the next stage of the campaign. Giulia left her basket at the bottom of the stairs and headed for the workshop where Lannato had tested the dryad serum.

The workshop was empty. To her surprise, the door was open: she had been expecting ingenious locks and traps. That presumably meant that Lannato had only left for a few moments. Giulia entered and went straight to the chest on the far wall. Someone had ransacked it, seemingly for bandages. She found three syringes at the bottom. She picked one up and closed the lid.

On the way back, Giulia stashed the syringe in the basket of kindling and carried it back to her room. She transferred it to her bag, fastened her cloak across her shoulders, and headed downstairs again.

Giulia slipped out of a side door, into the night. She crossed a little garden – the grass was as black as a well

420

in the moonlight – and reached the palace gates. Then she was in the square outside the palace, in Astrago itself. She passed the square, walking quickly, but not fast enough to look as if she had something to hide. In a city of frayed nerves, it was best to give nobody an excuse to attack.

Astrago seemed to be rejoicing, grieving, and standing numb with shock, all at once. Light poured out of a church, and voices were raised in song within. Giulia hesitated, suddenly wanting to go inside. She stopped beside the door and made the Sign of the Sword across her chest.

A handcart came past, pushed and guarded by four men in palace livery. She saw pale sticks inside the cart and glanced down. Bones. They were collecting the bones of Leth's army.

I hope they smash them with a hammer.

As she passed a tavern, a door burst open. Her hand flicked to her knife. Yellow light filled the road, and a man lumbered out. He seemed huge and clownish. "Hey, girl," he said, shoving a big mug of beer at her, "hold this, would you?"

Giulia took it, and the man turned away, opened his britches and pissed loudly against the wall of the pub. Giulia shrugged and took a swig of the man's ale. A minute later, he turned back to her. "You're a good woman," he said, taking the mug back from her. "A good woman. Come inside and have a proper drink."

"Sorry. I've got to see someone."

His face became serious. "You do that. It's been bloody horrible, it has. You do that. Right then!" he declared, and the pub door closed behind him, and Giulia was left in the night again.

Someone was crying further on: not weeping but howling, more from horror than sadness. *This bloody city. Will it ever get back to normal, after this? Will I?*

She pulled her satchel around and took out the book. Hugh appeared beside her. "Funny old night, this," he said.

"We're leaving tomorrow morning," Giulia replied. "To get you back."

"I know. I know what you know, remember? I'm just a memory."

That's all you are. Sadness spread through her like cold. "Hugh, if you die – really die, I mean – I won't be able to see you when I hold this book, will I?"

"No. I'll disappear. Sorry, old girl."

She dropped the book back into her satchel, and he was gone. "Just a memory," she said. "Right, let's get this done."

Up ahead, the road seemed different. It took her a moment to realise why: the houses were lower, broader, held up by panels of shaped stone as well as wood. She was in Smithswell, and these were the homes of dwarrows. Ahead and to the left, she saw the Silver Garden where she'd met Sethis. That felt like half a lifetime ago.

Giulia found the right house and knocked on the door. Nobody answered. She knocked again.

The door opened a little, and a lined, grey face looked out at her. The eyes were wise and wary. The dwarrow nodded and stepped aside. "Come in," he said. "Quickly."

Giulia ducked under the lintel and the dwarrow closed the door behind her. "I need you to get a message to your people; to the dryads, too."

The dwarrow nodded. "I can do that. Much easier now."

"Good. This is really urgent. Tell them that we're going after Leth, to Oppidium. We leave tomorrow morning."

Chapter 16

Giulia woke to the sound of rotors. For a long few seconds, she stared at the ceiling, at the stripes of light slipping through the shuttered window. Then she sat up and rubbed her eyes.

She felt weary and badly rested, as if she'd been drinking. Giulia grimaced and stood up. There was a bowl of water on the table; she dunked her face and looked up, dripping and awake.

Today's the day. Shit.

She opened the shutters and the light flooded in. The racket of the flying machine simmered down a notch, and voices yelled over the sound: engineers, she reckoned, making the final preparations.

They'd better know what they're doing.

Giulia washed, dressed and armed herself. She pushed a knife into her boot and another into the leather bracer under her left sleeve. The big fighting-knife went onto her belt.

She dropped into a fighting-crouch and drove the edge of her hand out at throat-height, sidestepped, kicked low to disable an opponent's knee and stepped through and punched in the same movement. She brought her fists up the way Hugh had taught her. As if waking from a dream, she flexed her fingers and lowered her hands.

I'm not ready for this.

Giulia checked her satchel. All her gear was ready. She reached inside and took out a white cloth bag, its neck tied tight with a piece of black ribbon. Carefully, Giulia opened the ribbon and tipped a little of the contents onto her palm. It looked like finely-cut dried grass, but it glittered as if ground glass had been mixed in with it. "Powerful alchemy", the dwarrows at the clockwork shop had claimed.

It had better be. She picked up the book.

Hugh was standing beside the window, looking out at the battered city. He turned around. "Morning."

His voice put a catch in her throat. "I'm going to get you back today."

He seemed to think this over. "Well, you've got decent weather for it."

She exhaled: slow and deep, to calm herself. "It won't be long now. We'll leave the palace soon."

"Good."

"I've got to admit, Hugh, I'm pretty much shitting myself right now. I'll try everything I can, but I don't know if I can pull this off."

"Oh, I'm sure you'll come up with something," Hugh said. "You know pretty much everything I ever did, all the fighting stuff. And you're clever, too. Crafty, that's the word. Stick one in Leth's back for me, would you? I'd appreciate that."

"I will. I'm going to put the book down now, Hugh."

"Wait." The knight folded his arms and looked out the window; it made him look thin and cold. "I never had a wife, never had children, either. But if I did, if I had a daughter—"

Giulia let go of the book and it dropped back into her satchel. She picked up her crossbow. "Right," she said to the empty room. "Time to go."

Sepello was sitting in the entrance hall, eating a piece of bread. He stood up as she approached. He wore a dull steel breastplate over his coat and a leather collar around his neck. "Giulia."

425

Motes of dust spiralled in the air. It was strange to think of this huge hall being full of guests. "Good morning. You look ready."

"I am." He glanced to the right. "Vale's men will be coming soon."

"I see." For some reason, that made her wary.

"They're praying at the moment. They'll be ready soon."

"I can imagine."

He frowned. "It doesn't make them bad people, Giulia. Some of my best friends are from the New Church. They don't go around smashing icons and beating people for smiling on the sabbath."

"It's not that. It's just… I don't know. I just want things to go smoothly."

"Feeling nervous about this, yes? Me too."

She looked away, made a sudden decision. She strode over – her boots sounded deafening in the hall – and leaned in close. "Listen, Sepello. I've helped you out a lot here. I've brought you information, I've watched your back, I've been a good partner to you. Nobody else gives much of a shit what I do, but I know you do, because you're a decent man."

He smiled. "You're a good person to have—"

"Look, I need something from you. There's going to be a time down there when I want you to look away. I don't want you to break any oaths, or to let anything evil happen – I just want you to look the other way for a moment or two. Just – you remember I told you that Leth killed a friend of mine?"

"Of course. He was a knight."

"He's not dead. He's down there, in Leth's city. And I'm going to get him back."

Sepello reached up and slowly rubbed his forehead, like a sick man. "Oh, Giulia. I *knew* there was something!" He looked around the hall, as if the palace itself was his enemy. "This fucking place. It's like a curse... You mean he's a revenant?"

"He's a hostage. I'll take you to the right place, where you can find Leth. Then, if you give me five, ten minutes, I can slip away and get him back. That potion the dryads gave me can cure him. There'll be no problems – I'll make sure of it. I swear."

Sepello looked up and stared at the roof. Distantly, she heard voices and the tramp of boots: hard, foreign voices.

"Sepello? Are you listening?"

Slowly and carefully, he said, "Are you going to murder anybody?"

"Nobody who's not already dead."

"You realise that if you leave the rest of us, you'll probably die. And if you come back on your own, well, Mavlio won't be taking any chances about you. Nor will Vale."

"I know. I won't be coming back, not with you and the others. Not if it works out."

There were men in the east corridor, their armour criss-crossed with bandoliers.

"I'm getting soft," he said.

"No you're not. You're a good man, that's all."

"You don't know the half of it. This plan of yours – if it goes wrong and you end up as a revenant, I'll finish you myself."

"I realise that. I'd want you to."

Something seemed to wake and harden behind Sepello's eyes. She remembered him on the waterfront at Paraldo, when they had fought the skeletons. "Fine,

427

then," he said. "To hell with it. I *do* owe you. Just say when you want to go."

"Thank you. I know it can't be—"

He flicked his hand up, and she stopped.

A dozen soldiers walked into the hall. Their gear clattered around them: guns and swords, pouches and powder-horns. Most had muskets; several carried multiple pistols. They looked hard and competent.

Vale was at the front of the group, wearing the armour he'd worn the day before. He was talking to a massive man of about forty. The other soldiers looked quick and agile, but this fellow was like a hard old bull.

"And here are our advisers," Vale said, smiling. "Master Sepello is our expert hunter of the undead: he's made a whole career of it. And this, Sergeant, is Mistress Giulia, our scout. Say what you wish, gentlemen, but this is the only person to have entered Leth's domain and returned alive. Apart from me, of course, but she went rather more quietly than I did." He smiled, as if he'd made a joke. None of the soldiers smiled.

Giulia said, "Good morning, Sir Francis."

"Good morning to you. And good hunting."

Footsteps sounded at the rear of the hall. Mavlio walked in, flanked by eight or nine guards. They were equipped like Vale's men, although they wore the palace colours under their armour. Two carried strange handguns that had not just one barrel, but six clustered together, like bundles of metal rods.

For a moment, the soldiers looked like two armed gangs who had come here to fight. Then Mavlio said, "Is everyone ready? Does anyone need time to pray?"

Nobody said anything.

"We're all set then," said the prince. "We'll be going to Oppidium together. Sepello, Giulia, you'll be leading the way. You'll show us the way in. I want you to stay in view at all times. Everyone else will follow. Needless to say, go quietly." He looked from face to face. "Does anyone have any questions?"

Men shook their heads.

Vale spoke. "Prince Mavlio, you don't have to do this. To come with us, I mean."

"Yes I do," the prince replied. "Lannato's got the machine ready for us."

They walked out. The sound of their movement made Giulia think of an army: boots and cloth and the quiet clink of buckles. Giulia glanced at Sepello, motioned him closer.

She nodded at Vale, in his armour. Softly, she asked, "Is this what ambassadors do?"

"Damned if I know," Sepello replied.

They trooped through the hall, down a corridor, and there was sunlight ahead. They walked out onto the back lawn, and suddenly it was open and green.

The flying machine sat on the lawn like a beached ship. A gangplank stuck out, to form a ramp. Men swarmed around the ship, making last-minute checks. The captain, a big bearded fellow, raised his hand to greet them.

Cosimo Lannato jogged out and met the soldiers. He said something to the prince, quick and businesslike, and Mavlio nodded. Lannato turned to the ship. "Captain Comi! Are we ready?"

"We're all set!" the bearded man replied. "Come aboard!"

The Anglians stood aside, and Mavlio's soldiers climbed the gangplank. Vale's sergeant turned to Giulia. "You're next," he said.

She climbed. As she reached the deck, she saw what she'd known would be here: a trapdoor leading into the hold. Fear swelled inside her, fear of being trapped below, locked away with these deadly men with nowhere to hide.

What if they just murder me?

Why would they do that? Of course they won't. They need me.

She reached the trapdoor. To her surprise, the soldier in front of her looked back and said, "Do you need any help, madam?"

He was one of Mavlio's guards, a big man with a round, oddly childlike face. He looked like a giant simpleton. It was a pleasure to hear his accent, gentle and familiar compared to the voices of Vale's marines.

"I'm fine," she replied. "Thanks." Giulia took a last look around, took a final breath of fresh air, and climbed down the steps into the hold.

It was dark and dusty, as if she'd broken into a carpenter's house. The hold reeked of pitch. Benches stood along the walls. At the end of the hold was a door, presumably leading to the workings of the flying machine. Giulia walked in and sat down next to the round-faced man. He was holding one of the six-barrelled muskets. It had to be one of Lannato's inventions. Sepello dropped onto the bench opposite.

At the end of the bench, Mavlio crossed his legs. He was neat and deadly, like a small hawk. As Giulia looked at him, he lifted his head, caught her eye and smiled. She made herself smile back.

Unease simmered in her gut. The Anglians were taking their seats now, bulky and awkward in their armour. They sat with their knees apart, as if their balls hurt.

Vale's sergeant stood beside the ladder. "Now listen!" he shouted. "When I say, you'll go up on deck. I want you off this ship neat and quick. You see this woman, this man?" He pointed to Giulia, then Sepello, with a massive gloved hand. Giulia felt eyes on her, and looked down at her boots. "They are our guides. You will follow them. Do not let them out of your sight! You will go quietly and not attack until I give the word. Now—"

The hull shuddered. Above, the rotor clattered. There was a low rumble, followed by a rattling noise like stones being shaken in a bag. Then something seemed to catch, and the sound was hard and confident: *thum, thum, thum.*

Mavlio said, "We're moving."

The ship jolted upwards. Vale's sergeant stumbled and caught hold of a post. The flying machine shook, as if straining against its load, and steadily, weirdly, it began to rise. Giulia's stomach dropped.

This is it. She closed her eyes. *Blessed Senobina, watch over me. Saint Cordelia, too.*

The hatch opened and light poured in. A crewman scrambled down in a flood of cold air, bundled in a massive coat. He pulled a scarf away from his mouth. "We're nearly there," he called.

Mavlio nodded to his men. They sat up, weapons held close to their bodies.

Nearly there.

Sepello looked at Giulia and nodded.

Vale's sergeant stood up. "All right!" he yelled. "Rise up, whoresons! Time to arm yourselves and meet the day! Get up and look awake!"

Fear was hardening in Giulia's gut, taking shape like fingers curling into a fist. They were closing in on Leth,

431

and Hugh. Soon she'd have to betray these people, to trick them into letting her bring him back.

The sergeant strode down the length of the hull, glaring at each man in turn. "Let's get moving! Get your prayers said and your weapons ready! That goes for you too, dragon lady," he added, glancing at Giulia. His voice was quieter, but there was no sympathy in it.

The machine rocked, and the soldier nearest to Giulia fell against her and muttered, "Fuck". He turned to Giulia and, to her surprise, apologised. Her stomach turned, slowly.

"All right!" the sergeant called. "It's time to do God's work. Are you ready?"

Vale's men yelled "We're ready!"

Giulia thought, *These aren't my friends*. She didn't need to touch the book to hear Hugh saying "Bloody Purists."

Giulia stood up. "I feel sick," she said. "I'm going to throw up. Got to get on deck."

She stumbled down the length of the ship, towards the ladder. Someone tried to grab her, but she twisted aside. The sergeant stepped in front of her. "Sit down."

"Going to be sick." She groaned and puffed out her cheeks, and he drew aside. Giulia reached the ladder and scrambled up.

She climbed onto the deck. The air hit her like a shove to the back of the head. Strands of hair flapped around her face. Wind drummed at her ears.

For a moment her mind raced: the vast, empty sky above her, the deafening thrum of the rotors, the sense that the deck might drop away at any second and she'd fall with it, drop out of the sky to her death – her legs buckled, and she didn't have to pretend that she felt sick anymore.

A sailor saw her. "Hey! Get back inside!"

"Sick," Giulia gasped, and she staggered to the railing and leaned over.

Quickly, she reached into her bag and found the little cloth bag that the dwarrows had given her. She opened the bag and shook its contents into the wind.

A little rain of cut grass fell from her hand. For a moment it looked like nothing, and then the stuff seemed to catch green fire, flickering like candle-flames behind bottle-glass, and it faded out in a shimmer of light.

"Hey," a man called, and she looked around. He was one of the air-crew, short and bearded. "If you want to throw up, go to the stern. I've got to tie off."

The ship was descending. Giulia hurried to the rear of the flying machine, out of the way, but the wind still whipped around her as if it wanted to knock her off. The land stretched out below in green and brown, endless and beautiful and frightening. She'd never thought that the world could be so big, that it could go on so far. The flying machine sank, slowly, and the landscape seemed to rise up below it. Hills stretched upward, the shadows of trees swung like pendulums. Giulia clutched the railing, her stomach churning. They had to be only fifty feet above the ground – thirty now – and the ground looked rough and rocky—

The flying machine hit the ground. The deck jumped under Giulia's boots and she grabbed the railing to stay up. The sailors yelled at each other and hurried to their work, hauling ropes and tying them off. The pitch of the rotors changed, lowered: they were slowing.

Giulia looked across the deck, at the gap in the railings where the gangplank would fit. *I could go now. Just run. Leave these arseholes behind.*

Maybe that was the best bet. But then there was Sepello: Giulia owed him her help. And if she left the others, they'd surely kill her if they met again. She cursed and looked around, at the rocky ground and the grass blown flat by the rotors. *God damn it!*

A man clambered out of the hold, bulky with armour. "Come on!" he bellowed. "Get up on deck!"

It was Vale's sergeant. Another marine scrambled onto the deck, then another. The chance to run had gone.

Giulia stood at the railing and watched them climb out. The group swelled; the men checked their weapons, grim-faced and professional. Mavlio's men climbed out, followed by their prince. Then came Vale and, finally, Sepello.

That was the lot of them. Giulia saw Mavlio standing by the railing, waiting for the gangplank to be fitted in place. He looked quick and thin, like a predatory bird.

The rotors died away. Wind cut across the deck of the flying machine. Two sailors ran over, carrying a long plank between them, and pushed it into the gap in the railings. Giulia took a deep breath and walked over to join them.

"Finished puking?" the sergeant asked.

"I'm ready," she replied.

"Good. You and him, take the lead. And when the fighting starts, get out of the way."

Sepello looked at her and shrugged. He reached into his coat and drew his pistol. The sailors kicked the gangplank out, and it dropped into place.

"After you," Sepello said.

*

Leth trotted up the stairs of the bath-house, pushed open the door and slipped inside. One of the noxi clung to the ceiling of the vestibule; seeing him, it turned and scurried away. Leth felt no urge to rush. He walked into the main hall, sniffed air full of brackish, alchemical water, and nodded, satisfied.

He remembered the time when the air had been full of talk, of laughter and the whooping of children, the sound of splashing. And he remembered a time nearer the present day, when a different sort of screaming had rung around the room, when killers had been busy here, and blood had swirled between the corpses floating in the pool.

It seemed peaceful now. The best sort of peaceful, in fact: dead.

"Leccius!"

He whipped around. Tarrus strode out of the corridor that led to the offices and calidarium, still wearing his armour. "I've been looking for you, you bastard!"

"Is something wrong, Tarrus?"

"Of course it's wrong. Where's Stulcus? Did he make it back?"

"No. He fell in the retreat. It was a soldier's death." Leth knew what Tarrus was about to ask. "As for Crespis, I've no idea. She vanished in the fighting. The fog of war."

"Fog of war? By the gods!" For a moment, it seemed that Tarrus would be overwhelmed by rage. Then he seemed to crumple, to deflate. "So we're all that's left. This fucking bath-house and a few of our men—"

"Our best men."

"A few of them. We can't hold this place. The living will send an army down here and wipe us out. We should be falling back, getting away from here!"

"Wherever to?" Leth smiled, baring his long incisors. "I thought you had more martial pride than that. I'm not done yet, Tarrus. Not by a long way."

Tarrus tensed. "What about me? What about Oppidium?" He glanced down the length of the bath, and Leth wondered whether they shared memories of this place. "You did this, you son of a bitch. You led all of us down here. You ruined this city once, with your fucking magic, and now you won't be finished until every bit of it's destroyed."

Leth put his hands behind his back and rocked on his heels. "Led? You do yourself a disservice. You're not so easily led, and nor were the others. I merely played a tune: it was your decision to get up and dance. Now, our guests will be here soon, and we need to put on a good show for them. Is everything ready?"

"Of course it's ready."

"Thank you. Reliable as ever."

"Oh, I fucking am," Tarrus said. "We all are. I hope the gods find a punishment fit for you," he added, and he turned and strode away.

It pleased Leth to let him go a few paces before calling him back. "Oh, Tarrus?"

The soldier stopped, shuddered, and turned.

"If it wounds your pride so much, I can lend you a sword to fall upon." Leth smiled. "But I wouldn't bother with hemlock. I doubt poison would have much effect these days."

He did not bother watching Tarrus leave: there were more important things to do. Leth paced away, his minions drawing back respectfully to let him pass.

Almost all the skeletons – the lesser undead – were finished now. They were weak things at the best of times, held together by brittle magic. Their real strength was in their ease of construction, and the fear they caused in Leth's enemies. Mavlio had done well not to let his city collapse under their onslaught: the prince had been

436

clever to shut the preachers up before they could cry Armageddon.

Leth passed a side room piled with gymnasium equipment. Here, in the baths, he had mass-produced his forces, turning the living into the living dead.

Given the time, and the raw materials, Leth could make more soldiers. It would be hard to get hold of dragons' teeth in the quantities he needed to raise an army, let alone the bones he had used to make his burrowing creature, but with the right funding it could be done. The noxi took time, and the myrmex were individual works of art, but skeletons could be animated by the regiment. As his work with the Inquisition had taught him, there was no boundary that his skill could not cross, no door it could not open. All the more reason to check on his preparations for Vale and Mavlio. He quickened his stride, heading to the staircase and the chambers below.

*

Giulia ran down the gangplank, her crossbow slung over her shoulder. She saw a big, hard-edged boulder – good cover – and ducked down beside it. Behind her, boots thundered down the gangplank and thumped across the grass. She looked back and saw the men fanning out, their guns held ready to shoot. Whatever else they might be, they knew how to fight.

She nodded to Sepello and ducked out of cover. Side by side, they led the raiding party across the ground. This was open land, exposed and rocky, good only for grazing sheep and goats. Clumps of thick grass jutted up between the stones, their stems shuddering in the wind.

"This way," Giulia said, and picked her way between the big rocks, away from the flying machine. It seemed easy, somehow, much simpler than she'd expected, as if she'd caught Leth's scent. Yes, this was it. She was going the right way, towards Hugh. Towards the end of it all.

Giulia pushed a branch back, held it so that it would not flick towards Sepello's face. Sepello took it from her and held it back for the others. The soldiers followed, footsteps crunching, buckles clinking softly. They felt like a knife at her back, ready to strike.

The ground dipped. She knew more than ever that they were going the right way. "We're nearly there."

Beside her, Sepello was breathing a little heavily. She glanced at him. "How's the arm?" she whispered.

"Not too bad," he replied, looking straight ahead. His face was pale and waxy. "Thanks."

Darkness up ahead. Giulia peered forward, unsure whether it was an opening in the ground or just the shadows meeting between the trees. No, this was it. Her heart and guts moved as she realised that behind a few branches lay the way back into Oppidium.

She stopped. "This is the way in. You'll have to go quietly now."

Giulia ducked down and walked into the dark. The passage smelled of earth and piss. She wondered if the noxi had to urinate. Someone lit a lantern behind her, and the weak light spread out around her body as if she glowed.

The tunnel turned left. She went quickly, the soldiers clattering softly behind her. They thought they were keeping quiet. Giulia hurried down the passage, knowing that without the advantage of true silence, the best thing was to move swiftly.

The tunnel sank deeper underground. She felt the sloping floor under her boots, felt the air becoming moist and clammy as they entered Leth's world. For the first time, she wondered if Oppidium really was below the world of the living, or if descending this path was a sort of ritual that would take them into Leth's realm. The dryads lived in a magical part of the forest, inaccessible to mortal men: perhaps this underground empire was the equivalent for the living dead.

A cold, bluish light came from up ahead. It crept into the passage as if seeping from fungus. *This is right*, she thought.

Sepello said, "Careful…"

Giulia reached the end, halted and raised her hand for the others to stop. She heard them come to a standstill. The tunnel felt incredibly quiet without their muffled bootsteps. "Stay here," she whispered, and she loaded her crossbow. She leaned out and looked left, then right.

Nothing moved in the dim light. Massive chunks of rubble lay ahead of them like thrown dice. The coast seemed to be clear. Giulia took a deep breath and slipped out into the ruins.

The sheer scale of the place was astonishing. She felt minuscule, like a mouse crawling into a ballroom. Veins of ore glittered in the cavern roof. It seemed a mile above her, as distant as the sky.

She had forgotten how monstrous, and how beautiful, Oppidium was. The buildings were larger and whiter than she recalled, the streets broader and without dirt. The cold light gave the edges of the stones a hard, crisp sheen.

Pale domes rose out of the city, bleached skulls in a pile of ribs. Statues gestured at nothing from their pedestals, and raised hands to the cavern roof like drowning men. Giulia wondered what Oppidium had been like in its prime. She felt something like pity as well as loathing for the place, for the undead, and that made it even worse.

A ripple of sharp breaths and muttered curses ran through the men. They stood at the edge of the tunnel, acclimatising themselves. Several made the Sign of the Sword across their bodies.

Giulia felt strangely proud of the effect the city had on the soldiers. They'd be less damn conceited now, and perhaps a little more cautious. *Now do you believe me?* she thought, and she wondered which one of them would be first to try to take the credit for finding this place when they got out.

When she looked back at the city, she felt that something had changed, but she did not know what.

Sepello said, "My God, Giulia. What is this? What happened here?"

A voice quoted scripture behind her. "'And they were cast down, and made to dwell below, and their works were come to nothing'." Giulia recognised the accent: Vale.

Mavlio took a few steps forward. His guards quickly fanned out, and he halted. "What I want to know is how the hell it all got here," he said. "Did they carry all the buildings down here? Did they make it all here, underground?"

"I don't know," Giulia replied. "Maybe the town sank into the ground."

"It doesn't matter," Vale replied. "Let's go."

They walked forward, between two high white shells, past empty windows. Their boots sounded loudly on the cracked stone. The air was still and stale. The cavern smelled of ashes and wet rock.

Giulia passed a statue of some wise man, seated on a throne. His head had either broken or been knocked off,

440

and the shards lay in his lap. An eye stared out from the folds of the statue's robe.

She thought of those stories where a knight rode to some grim castle to rescue a princess. She wished that Sethis was with her now. Or Hugh. She wanted to touch the book, to see his ghost again, but it was too risky. She needed both hands on her weapons.

A massive arch stood up ahead. The buildings on either side had fallen away, giving it the feel of something erected for a ritual, as though it would change them if they passed through it. Giulia swung to the left, and the soldiers parted so that they would not have to go under the arch.

A skeleton lay beside the road, propped against the wall of a house as if sleeping. It wore armour and a crested helmet, and a massive shield stood beside it. She glanced at Sepello: he nodded and raised his gun. They spread out and approached as if creeping up on a sleeping enemy.

Sepello motioned for Giulia to stop. He crept forward, legs bent, and carefully extended his arm. He reached out with his left hand, keeping the pistol aimed at the skeleton's head. Giulia lined the crossbow up with its chest.

If that thing moves…

Sepello reached out and snatched at its helmet. He yanked his arm back, and pulled the helmet and the skull off the corpse's shoulders. The body seemed to sag slightly, as if he'd broken the strings holding it together, and the bones fell slack inside the armour. Sepello stepped back and put the skull on the ground, ten feet away.

Giulia breathed again. One of the soldiers said, "This fucking place makes my skin crawl." Sepello closed his eyes, and for a moment she wondered if he was going to collapse. He opened them again. They moved on, deeper into Oppidium.

The buildings grew larger, the streets narrower as if Oppidium was slowly closing its grip around them. It was absolutely still, but Giulia knew that they were being watched.

The undead had found new uses for their city. An inn had been turned into storage for barrels of some greyish liquid, thick as paint and reeking like swampwater. A row of shops had been knocked through and used to test siege-crossbows. Half a dozen doors were heaped in the far house, each punched with holes the size of a man's fist. A tally had been scratched into a picture of two fighting stallions, white marks on the black flanks of the horses.

Giulia picked her way through a tailor's shop. Mosaics of beautiful women lined the walls, elegant in their sweeping white robes. Each face had been carefully and thoroughly smashed. Sheets of cloth hung from racks like tapestries, marked out with arrows and lines. Something about them seemed familiar. Perhaps they were banners of some kind.

A voice said, "Bastards."

She looked back, and saw Mavlio there. The prince was staring at the drapes, his face set with anger. "They're maps," he said. "Of my city. Sepello, have you ever seen anything like this?"

"Not in my life," Sepello replied. "This level of organisation—"

A soldier stepped into the doorway of the shop. "Prince Mavlio. You ought to come and see this."

They walked out into the road. The soldier led them a little way up the street, where most of the men waited. He pointed down a sidestreet.

A massive white building stood at the end of the road. Torches and lanterns burned around it, making it glow. The orange light looked wrong in this cold, dead place.

"What is that?" Giulia asked.

Quietly, Sepello said, "Some kind of temple."

Vale's voice was low and flat. "Did you see this place, when you were here?"

She shook her head. "No. Did you?"

"No, I didn't . It looks occupied."

Mavlio said, "Let's see what we've got." He looked at Giulia.

She raised the crossbow, pulled the stock against her shoulder, and moved bent-legged down the street. Sepello was at her side. Behind them came the soft clatter of the soldiers.

Her mouth was dry. The air felt cold on her hands and face. She heard Sepello breathing, slow and deep.

The buildings in the street were empty shells, stripped and abandoned. Giulia saw shadows, pillars, windows, doorways and hiding-places. *Soon*, she thought. *He knows we're here.*

They approached the end of the street. Giulia held up her hand, and Sepello stopped beside her. He kept to the side, his pistol raised. Giulia motioned to the soldiers to stay back.

She leaned around the corner.

The building was massive and pale. It stood alone, apart from the houses. There was a small square at the front, with a statue at each corner: gods and goddesses, perhaps. A set of steps led up to huge carved doors. They were closed, flanked by columns. Stone monsters stood either side of the steps. They looked like lions with the faces of women.

Giulia looked around the square, at the windows across the road, at the rooftops and the shadows where an enemy might hide.

Anyone could be there.

"Keep watch," she said to Sepello. She broke from cover, keeping low, and rushed across the square. Giulia reached the nearest statue and ducked down beside it. It protected her from the side, but she was still exposed. She looked across the buildings, half-expecting someone to leap into view. Still nothing.

She beckoned to Sepello. He ran out, coat flapping, across the open ground. Sepello dropped against the statue, his back against the stone. "See anyone?"

"Nobody."

Sepello nodded. "You think he's in there?"

"Maybe. Waiting for us."

"Let's get the others."

Giulia put her hand on his arm. "Wait. You remember what I said to you, back in the palace?"

He looked into her eyes. "Yes."

She let go. "Good."

Sepello leaned out and beckoned. The men ran across, Mavlio and Vale in their midst. They took as much cover as they could, watching the city.

Mavlio pointed to the doors. "We'll go in there."

There was a frieze above the doors. It showed waves, curling around the lintel. A man rose from the waves. His beard was made of more waves, or maybe tentacles.

Vale's captain made a quick hand gesture, as if blessing his men, and four soldiers split from the main group. They climbed the steps in pairs, one pair at either side. As they reached the fifth step, Mavlio tapped Giulia's arm.

"Go up with them."

She nodded and followed.

The soldiers climbed the steps with the same low, scuttling gait: legs bent to run and dodge, weight on the back foot in case the stones gave way. Two of the men had guns, two crossbows. Giulia checked the pillars as she went. They would be an ideal spot for an ambush.

A body lay behind one of the pillars, slumped against the pale stone. It was one of the noxi, and its mask had fallen into its lap. The face behind was awful. One of the men stopped and looked down at it. "Dead," he said.

Giulia stepped over and shot it in the head. "Just to be sure," she said.

She worked the lever under her bow, cranking the string back. She laid a fresh bolt into the groove.

When she looked around, the soldiers were trying to force the door open.

"It's jammed," one of the soldiers said. "There's something behind it." He put both hands on the great handle, braced his legs and pulled.

The door scraped open – six inches, a foot, and Giulia saw a string glittering in the aperture, stretching taut—

"Stop!" Her voice was like a gunshot in the silence. The soldiers looked at her as if she'd cursed them.

"In the doorway," she said, and she scurried up to the doors. "Trap." Giulia dropped down, pulled the stiletto from her sleeve and sliced through the string. "Done."

The soldiers didn't thank her. Maybe she had made them feel like fools. They pulled the doors apart, and Giulia followed them inside.

445

They stood in some sort of ante-chamber, lit by lanterns. Two archways faced them, the left flanked by paintings of women bathing, the right by male athletes. Both led into corridors, twisting out of sight. Someone had scratched all the faces off with a knife. Across the wall, someone had scrawled *'Pulcher' dixit! Calumniae!* A piece of metal pipe lay propped beside the door, mounted on a crossbow-like frame. Nails and glass shards twinkled in the tube.

Giulia took a step forward, but the nearest soldier held his arm out to bar her way. "We wait here."

They waited. Giulia stood with her back to the wall, her impatience building, creeping towards fury. Soldiers entered, quick and careful, until at last Vale strode in, Mavlio by his side.

"*He said 'beautiful',*" Mavlio said. "*Lies.*" It took Giulia a moment to realise that he was translating the graffiti on the wall.

What the hell does that mean?

The prince said, "This isn't a temple. It's a bath-house."

Giulia looked at the pictures, at their obliterated faces, and felt the skin of her back prickle and crawl. *Someone made them promises. He promised them things – beauty, power, long life – and then he turned them into this.*

Softly, Vale said, "Is everybody ready?"

A few men murmured; most nodded. Vale pointed to the archway on the right: the male entrance. Giulia stepped forward and took the lead.

The plaster on the walls had peeled, but the floor seemed to have been swept clean. Sepello followed Giulia, almost by her side. They walked carefully, looking out for wires and loose stones.

The corridor turned, then stopped. They looked out into an enormous room. Blue light danced on the far walls, rippling and pulsing. For a moment, Giulia thought it was lightning. Then she realised that it was reflected from water.

The room was big enough to hold a galleon. Pillars ran down its edges. The centre was taken up by a vast rectangular pool, full of water. Somehow, the pool was lit from below the surface. Reflections rippled and danced on the walls and ceiling. A strange alchemical smell, at once cleansing and unnatural, made Giulia pause. Plants – neither fungus nor coral, but something in between – let out a purple glow in the corners, seeping along the walls. The roof faded into shadow.

"My God," the sergeant said.

Giulia stood at the edge of the room, amazed. The wavering light was hypnotic. Pictures on the walls showed men and women lounging around on chairs, attended by almost-naked slaves. Their flesh was healthy, their bodies strong.

What a place this must have been.

The soldiers moved in and fanned out behind her, checking the pillars. Broken tiles crunched under their boots. Their lanterns broke the dead phosphorescence of the place. The light revealed more murals down the length of the room: chubby bathers and energetic youths, their faces all erased.

"Bloody hell," said one of the marines. "Just look at it all."

But where in God's name was Hugh? Giulia opened her satchel and reached inside.

A voice came from her right: not awed, but disgusted. She looked around, and saw a big soldier

447

crouching by the edge of the pool. "Oh, God," he said. "God almighty. Look."

Giulia walked to the edge and looked down. The water was deep here, and the light hardly reached the bottom. In the depths, corpses drifted. She could not tell where each began and ended: they merged into the same entity. Limbs and hands became fronds of the same underwater plant.

The soldiers stood at the edge of the pool, staring at the dark mass in the water. One of the men swore; another made the Sign of the Sword across his chest.

"They must have turned on each other," Vale said.

"Or Leth didn't need them," Mavlio replied.

Giulia gazed down. She thought of piles of toads, locked together as they mated. There had been a war here, she realised. Leth had unleashed his forces on the town, or else the living had come for him, no longer able to tolerate his evil.

A trickle of dust fell onto the water. Giulia stepped back and the soldiers around her followed. A thin stream of white dust struck the pool, formed grey circles on the surface of the water.

Sepello raised a lantern and the man beside him pulled up his bow. As swift and silent as a striking hawk, a net dropped onto them from above.

"Look out!" Mavlio yelled. Sepello tore at the net in a frenzy. Men shouted. Giulia backed against the wall, crossbow ready. She glanced left and right, looking for attackers. *Where? Where?*

Grey figures scuttled across the ceiling. Guns roared, tongues of fire in the dim light. One of the undead dropped shrieking into the pool. The splash echoed. Vale darted back as if the water would burn him.

Blue light swelled from the end of the hall. A wave of voices spilled out of the far end, whooping and moaning. "Over there!" the sergeant called, and a hand shot out of the water and locked around his ankle.

He hit the floor, his helmet crashed against the stone, and then they dragged him under.

The noxi leaped out of the pool, clearing the surface like frogs. Mavlio pulled a pistol and blew the brains out of one revenant as it scrambled onto land.

A spear sailed out of the dark, almost lazily, and slammed through the chest of one of the marines. Blue reflected light flashed wildly across the ceiling, like captive lightning.

"Shit, shit!" Sepello cried. He tore the net away and raised his pistol. A long-limbed figure bounded into view and he blasted it in the chest. "Fucking die!"

Dead bare feet slapped on the wet tiles; knives and hooks glinted in grey-blue hands. One of Mavlio's guards grappled with one of the beasts, and they staggered like drunken dancers. The revenant's mask ended at the mouth – sharpened teeth snapped and spat. Giulia lined up her bow and shot it in the neck, and the man hurled it screeching into the pool.

A roar from the far end and an armoured bull of a man charged in, face hidden by a massive helmet. It stormed forward, bellowing, and one of Mavlio's soldiers tried to stab it in the side. The thing ploughed a spike into his midriff and tossed him into the water. Half a dozen shots rang off the walls and blasted chips off the broken mosaics. Two bullets hit the giant and it stumbled, groaned.

Giulia's heart plunged in her chest. She thought, *Not Hugh, please not Hugh*, and thin hands the colour of a fish's belly grabbed her and threw her to the ground. She rolled as she went down, saw the water on her left and came up with a knife in her hand. One of the noxi jabbed a trident at her. Giulia darted to the side and drove her knife into its body, between the ribs: it shrieked, blood sputtering from its grinning mask, and Giulia realised that it had been a woman once.

A great keening howl washed down the room and a fresh pack of monsters rushed in, gabbling and shouting, hurling rocks and javelins. Half a dozen men battered the armoured giant to the ground. It flopped down and the helmet came loose. The face below was horrific – but it wasn't Hugh, thank God.

Sepello appeared at Giulia's side. "Fuck!" he yelled. One of the noxi came for him, scrabbling across the tiles. Sepello fired, and the body went sprawling onto the ground. He tossed the gun down and drew his long knife. "For the saint!"

Another colossus lumbered in, shoving the lesser undead aside. It carried a small ballista the way a man would hold a crossbow, and a burning torch jutted from its shoulder-armour. The brute pulled a yard-long javelin out of a quiver and touched it to the flame before dropping it into the bow. The tip of the javelin flickered and spat—

"Down!" Sepello cried, and he threw himself against Giulia. She fell, and the tiles above her exploded. Plaster rained down. Men and undead screamed. Three shots hit the big revenant as it tried to reload its weapon. It stumbled as if buffeted by water. "Kill it!" Sepello cried.

The giant fired its ballista again. The explosion hurled two men into the pool. The air was full of shards and dust.

Giulia worked the ratchet on her crossbow and slapped a bolt into the groove. The monster pulled another spear from its quiver. It held the tip against the coals, until the wad of straw and alchemical oil on the tip was smouldering.

Giulia shot it in the head. The bolt punched into the oversized helmet, through one of the dozen holes, and the creature dropped the burning javelin. Numbly, it began the process again, pulling back the string on its ballista, and the javelin at its feet exploded.

The myrmex stumbled back, howling and moaning. It struck the wall and slid down until it sat on the ground. It lowed like a wounded bull, a loud, sad cry echoing out from beneath the helmet, and fell silent.

The room was clear. Giulia saw that there was nothing left to fight.

Dust hung in the air, settling on the water like scum. The undead lay around the pool: several hung below the surface, limbs held out as if frozen mid-leap. A dozen soldiers lay among them.

The survivors got up slowly, coughing and muttering as if coming to life, and looked around themselves.

"Boys!" a soldier cried. He sounded lost, desperate. "Come on, boys! We've got to keep moving!"

Sepello lay on his side. He groaned and sat up, and Giulia saw that his right half was covered in pale dust. She hauled him upright in a rain of dirt.

They stood together, looking towards the armoured revenant they had just killed. It lay in a heap of metal and boiled leather, barely distinguishable as the shape of a man.

"Are you all right?" she said.

Sepello wiped his mouth on his sleeve. "Just about. You?"

Giulia nodded.

Behind them, the sergeant was shouting his men into order. Mavlio's voice rang out, quieter but more clipped: "Everybody, get your guns reloaded... how many people have we got?"

Giulia reached into her bag and touched the book. Hugh stood beside them. His face was gaunt, his eyes wide and urgent. "You're close," he said. "I can feel it. Down below..."

She let go of the book and looked around the room. The undead had swarmed out of several archways: in each archway, a staircase led downwards. Each looked as good as the others.

"I'm going to go," she said.

Sepello said, "Are you sure? You know that if you come back, Mavlio and Vale will—"

"I know."

He looked her in the eyes. "I'm glad to have met you, Giulia."

"You too. Thanks, Pietro, for everything."

The soldiers were pulling themselves together. Weapons and armour clattered; a man groaned. "Somebody stay back with the wounded," Vale called. "The rest of you get ready. We're not done yet!" The echo made his voice sound hollow and flat.

Sepello looked weary and sick. "You'd better get moving. Good luck."

"You too." She turned and ran, keeping close to the wall. Behind her, someone cried out: "My arm – it's broken!" Something heavy fell into the pool – a corpse, perhaps. Giulia ducked into a doorway and hurried down the steps.

The walls were narrow. It was dry and well-lit.

Murals peeled from the walls as if the building was shedding its skin. She saw frolicking bathers on the edge of some river, trios of reclining ladies attended by slaves. Some of the pictures showed sport, others sex.

Small rooms branched off to either side. Most were dark. Giulia could see couches and empty shelves inside.

She made herself stop. Giulia put her back to the wall and loaded the crossbow. On the wall opposite, three young men were watching a race. One had thrown his head back, frozen in laughter.

Twenty yards on, she reached a crossroads. More peeling walls, more chipped murals. Depending on Sepello and the state of the soldiers, she had about ten minutes' head start on Vale and Mavlio.

She quickened her pace as much as she dared, pacing along instead of creeping, her eyes on the floor eight feet ahead.

At the end of the corridor, a newer picture had been painted onto the wall. The workmanship was less good, but it was in a better state than the other drawings.

It showed a woman swathed in white robes, her breasts and hips exaggerated. Her hair was massive, her eyes huge and edged with black paint. She carried a sort of horn, from which a wad of flowers protruded.

Beside it were capital letters. PULCHERITAS - VIGOR - VITA LONGVS - LECCIVS. An arrow pointed to the right. Giulia had no idea what it meant, but she knew who Leccius was. She turned the corner.

*

Leth waited for his enemies to reach his sanctuary. He wondered who would be first: Mavlio DeFalci, Sir Francis Vale, Pietro Sepello, Giulia Degarno? He was ready for each of them.

One of the noxi waited at the edge of the room, crouching like a goblin in the shadows, its skin ash-grey from stone dust.

Someone screamed. It had come from above – the raiders were not through Leth's last line of defence quite yet, but soon they would find the way downstairs.

Once, this had been a steam-room, where fat nobles had gathered to talk politics and sweat out their ill-humours. The steam was long-gone, and it now served Leth as a library. He felt sad as he pulled his books into the centre of the room. So much work, so much effort to have failed in his bid to take Astrago.

He had not expected such a fierce, rapid response. He had half-expected that Mavlio would never try to chase him down here, or that the prince would just seal the entrances to Oppidium and pray that nothing ever left the dead city again. That was the problem when you made your plans in terms of years and months: you forgot that your enemy might take mere hours to come looking for revenge. He would not make that mistake again.

His survival now depended on what he could offer to his pursuers. He left the drawings and plans pinned up on the wall, so that they would be immediately visible when the intruders burst into the room. They had to see him as something more than just a murderer: a creator, of sorts, a creature who had made something fearsome and great.

At the top of the stairs, something scuffed against the stone. Leth's head twitched towards the noise. He knew that sound: boots, trying to go quietly.

He looked at the noxi. "Someone's trying to sneak down the stairs," he said, in Quaestan. "Kill them."

The revenant padded across the floor, as quiet as water. It unbolted the massive door and disappeared into the dark.

Leth locked the door behind it. He needed to choose his first visitors carefully: some stupid soldier might rush in and attack him before he'd had the chance to speak. All that blood would ruin things. He hauled more of his books out and heaped them where they would be seen. A small table stood by the back wall, and he began to load it with coloured bottles – nothing red, no dead matter, nothing that would remind his visitors of killing. The living were squeamish like that.

A banging had started above, like the beat of a drum in a distant festival. Leth remembered revels and bacchanals, habits that the noxi had kept even after their transformation. He worked faster, his white hands quick and strong.

Hands knocked on the door. Leth opened the peep hole on the door, and saw a grinning mask and crazed eyes behind it. He drew the bolt back and pulled the door open, then stepped aside.

The grey figure behind it was covered in dust, but under the dust were dark clothes. It reached up and pulled the mask away. The face beneath was scarred, but not by undeath.

"It's me," the face said. She drew her knife. "I came back."

*

"No." The revenant stepped back, away from the door. "You – did you kill the prince?"

"He's upstairs," Giulia said. "I want Hugh."

Leth seemed to draw himself up, to harden. He said, "Do you, now? We had a bargain, Giulia. You were

455

bringing me two heads, remember? You went back on it."

Giulia looked straight at him. His eyes were black, like a rat's. The nakedness of his stare unsettled her. It was devoid not just of compassion, but of most forms of curiosity. He could do anything to anyone, she realised, and never even blink.

Carefully, she said, "In ten minutes, maybe less, soldiers are going to come down here. They want to kill you. If you want any chance of getting out of here alive, you'll tell me where Hugh is."

"I'm not alive," Leth replied. "I've not lived properly for fifteen hundred years." he said. "Compared to me, you're a child."

"Where's my friend?"

"You're no fool, though: in fact, you're very intelligent. I respect that. From someone of my experience, being considered a worthy adversary is surely something of a compliment, yes?"

Smiling, he took a step towards her.

"Now then, let's talk business." His pale hand swung out, encompassing the charts, the workbenches, the piles of books and scrolls. "You've got the knife, and I think that makes you the victor here. Perhaps you'd like to take a look at the spoils?"

"Just tell me where Hugh is. Now."

"Look, Giulia: the knowledge of a thousand years, all yours. This is where they came, you know, where it all began. The people of Oppidium lined up to get the treatments I could offer: strength for the men, beauty for the women."

She saw them as if he brought them to life with the sweep of his arm: a row of robed figures, queuing for the death he had been handing out. They had thought that he'd make them better, heal them of their ailments. They must have come in families, the way they would have done to the baths above. Maybe Leth had murdered the doubters, or changed them into revenants by force. Perhaps there had been a point when there had been only one man or woman left truly alive in Oppidium, hunted by the undead, dragged in here to take the medicine...

"You killed them."

"Oh no. I gave them what they wanted. I changed them, that I admit. Remaking the body, as if sculpting it anew. That's what my magic offers, and what the good people of this city hired me to do, of course. And I did it. I still could, if I wanted to. Those scars on your face, for instance: I could alter them, if you'd like..."

She realised that he was not coming any closer. He wasn't trying to creep up on her, to get into range so that he could attack. He was delaying her.

But Mavlio's coming to kill him. Why wait?

Fear spread across her skin like sweat. Leth had something planned, some last card to play. *This is wrong*, she thought, and it hammered in her brain. *Wrong, wrong.*

"Don't try to stall me, you bastard. I want Hugh – now."

"Of course. That's perfectly understandable. I merely think that after all of this, you are surely entitled to some kind of recompense, some peace of mind—"

"*Where's Hugh?*" she yelled. "Tell me where he is!"

"Calm yourself," Leth said. He gestured to his books. "All in good time. All of this—"

"*No.* Now!" Giulia flicked her arm out, and the last three inches of the knife hit Leth's hand. It slit his palm and the tip of his thumb, but there was no blood. Leth whipped his hand back and Giulia dropped into a fighting stance, afraid of his response.

457

"That was unwise," Leth said. His lips slid back, unsheathing his teeth. "Very unwise." He gasped and stumbled. Leth clutched his left hand in his right, as if he meant to tear it from his arm. "Whore! What have you done to me?"

"It's poison," she replied. "The same thing we used on your army back in Astrago. I don't think it'll kill you." She raised the knife. "Not unless I give you some more."

"It *hurts*. I'll remember this, Giulia."

Pain seemed to have shrunk him. She felt six inches taller now. "You'll remember that I gave you a chance," she said. "I could have killed you and I didn't." She took a step closer. "Now, for the last time: where's Hugh?"

"In there." Leth nodded at the arch on the right. "Waiting for you." He drew himself up, tall and serious. He had the bearing of Quaestans that she'd seen in paintings: unflinching, pitiless, grimly honourable. "Go on, take a look. I won't do anything. You have my word."

"You'd better not be lying," she said and, not turning her back to him, she crossed to the archway and looked inside.

A narrow passage led away, lit by a blue, phosphorescent glow, a light without heat. *I'll fix you soon enough*, she thought, as she left Leth behind. But first: Hugh.

A shaky fear swelled in her chest, as if her ribcage held a frightened bird. She saw Hugh's face – smiling, listening, looking contented and vague – and thought, *This is it, the end of the quest.* And then she wondered what horrors might await her: Hugh's head on some monstrous body, some horrible arrangement of limbs—

She turned the corner, sick with apprehension. The room was long, not especially large, and high-roofed. There were benches against the walls. A single figure sat at the far end of the room, made bulky by armour and a massive helmet. The light caught the edges of dented armour plate, threw the cording of ropes into hard relief, made shadows on buckles and straps.

Very quietly, she took a step into the room.

Oh God, Hugh, what have they done?

His hands were bare. They clutched his knees, as bony now as they had been in life. The rest of his skin was hidden by leather, steel and bandages.

Noises filtered in from a long way away. Someone was breaking something: it sounded like a door being smashed down. She realised that she ought to have brought Leth with her, forced him to help bring Hugh back, and she cursed and realised that there was no time for that now.

She stood before him and thought, *Blessed Senobina, watch over me. Easy now…*

Giulia reached out and put a hand either side of the helmet. She lifted it very carefully, as if picking up a bulky vase. The helmet was lighter than she'd expected. It came away quickly, and she turned and put it by her feet. Then looked at the man underneath.

His face was grey, marbled with veins. He smelled like skin that had been bandaged for too long: a sour, vinegary smell.

Hugh's mouth was open, the lower lip damp with spit. Giulia crouched down in front of him and saw his eyes, staring and dead. She raised a hand and waved it slowly before his face.

He blinked – relief shot through her – and, as if learning how to do it for the first time, his eyes followed her hand. Seeing him move was like finding treasure. Part of her wanted to stop now, to try to be satisfied with just this, so she would never risk the anguish of having failed.

"Hugh?"

No response. The face was fixed on hers, as calm and stupid as a cow's.

"Hugh, can you hear me?" She talked through the silence. "I've come to help you. I think I can make you better. The fey folk gave me this stuff…" She rooted in her bag, produced the little bottle. "I'm going to pour this into you. It'll make you better."

Giulia looked from his face to his neck, to the bandages around his throat. Lannato had said something about putting chemicals straight into the vein: it was more effective that way.

There was a crash in the room behind her. They were beating the door of Leth's inner sanctum down. The sound made her urgent. They'd burst in here, avenging crusaders all, and drag her away. They'd think it was witchcraft, and then they'd kill Hugh. *Think!*

She took out the syringe. "I've got to put this into your vein. It might hurt a little." She wondered if he'd even feel pain.

Very carefully, she removed the stopper and readied the bottle. Giulia put the tip of the syringe into the liquid, then pulled the rear of it up – exactly as Lannato had done, so as not to lose any of the magic.

Wood burst and splintered in the hall.

Giulia started: the bottle twitched in her hand and the fluid slopped. She gasped. Nothing had spilled. She closed her eyes.

Just this one thing, please. Do this for me. She took a deep breath. *Here we go.*

"Easy, Hugh. Easy." She pulled the bandages down with her free hand, until she saw the thin dark trace of a vein.

Voices yelled and cried outside. Shit, they'd found Leth. They'd kill him. *No. Forget Leth.* Hugh was the real prize, and his life was the revenge she'd need.

She touched the tip of the syringe to his flesh, took a breath, and pushed it in. Then she drove the plunger home, until there was nothing more to inject. Giulia pulled her hand away and stepped back, in case he lashed out.

Hugh shuddered, twitched. *The tincture must have gone into him. God, what if it's killing him? He's already dead, you bloody fool.*

Would it be worse to leave him as a stupid revenant, or to be responsible for finishing him outright? *God, what if—*

She waited, and for the first time she properly listened to what was going on outside. Male voices were raised, living ones, and she thought she recognised Mavlio, then Vale. But they seemed to be shouting at each other. Had Vale and the prince been beating Leth senseless, she would not have been surprised. Instead, they seemed to be having an argument.

Giulia reached out, picked up the crossbow, and loaded it. Legs bent, sidestepping across the broken tiles, she crept to the doorway.

The corridor was empty. She walked towards the voices, keeping to the shadows.

She could see a sliver of the room beyond. A dozen men stood around, their bows and flintlocks raised ready to shoot.

They were Vale's marines. Giulia tilted her head slightly, and looked out a little more. Leth stood in the centre of the room. Three men pointed pistols at him as a fourth secured the revenant's hands.

461

So what were the other Anglians pointing their guns at? And where were the prince's soldiers?

Mavlio said: "Vale, listen to me. You're making a terrible mistake."

Giulia stepped to the other side of the passage, clean and quick. Now she could see the other side of the room. Mavlio stood flanked by two of his men. They were unarmed.

Mavlio said, "After all he's done—"

Vale stepped into view, dapper in his polished breastplate and black coat. "I'm sorry, Mavlio. But it's better that he comes with us. Believe me, he'll be working for the right people now."

"The right people?" Mavlio moved forward: one of Vale's men shoved a gun against his breastplate.

"Get back," the soldier grunted.

Mavlio ignored him. "Right people, Vale? There are no right people! He tore my city apart, killed my citizens. Can't you understand that?" Mavlio stopped, his face suddenly composed. "You struck a deal, didn't you? You made a deal when he captured you. You'd keep him alive, in return for letting you go. You'd take him back with you."

Vale walked back, out of view. Giulia found her mouth was dry.

"You sly bastard," the prince said, and he laughed. "Is that what you're here for, to find out what he knew? So you could have your own army of skeletons march out for your queen?"

"I'm sorry, Prince Mavlio." Vale raised his voice. "All right, men, get this creature moving."

You bastard. Had Vale gone completely insane? It didn't matter where Leth was, or who he served: all he could do was bring more evil into the world. It would be like hiring the Devil.

Giulia raised the bow and looked down the groove. She leaned to the right, very slightly, and her view through the archway widened. Leth and Vale stood only eight feet apart, framed in the same picture.

She had a clean shot on all of them. She could swing the bow two inches to the right, and line the bolt up with Mavlio's head. Four inches left, and she'd have Vale in her sights. Vale was an enemy of the Peninsula: he'd just admitted as much. Why not shoot a bolt straight through his brain, and end his dreams of exploitation?

Her palms were moist.

There was no contest. Leth the alchemist, the cause of all of this. The bow swung to cover him as if it made the choice on its own. One good pull and all his evil would be gone. There would be no prize for the other two to squabble over any more. Leth had stopped to say something to Mavlio, and as he dipped his head, Giulia closed one eye and squinted down the length of the bolt.

Behind her, something groaned.

For the tiniest part of a second she hesitated, and then she hurried back down the corridor.

Hugh sat hunched over in the bulk of his armour. His big, thin hands gripped his kneecaps, and his face was lowered, as if in prayer.

A slow groan came from between his lips, like wind blowing through empty corridors. He looked down and coughed.

She waited for him to finish. Queasy with apprehension, she said, "Hugh?"

He lifted his head. The knight's eyes seemed terribly sunken, as if mounted on the back of his skull. He raised his right hand and wiped his mouth on the back of his glove.

Hugh stood up.

Giulia drew her sharpest knife, stepped in close and pushed it into the gap between the plates on his shoulder and neck. She sliced out, feeling the blade strike ropes, and sawed down. In two cuts the overlapping metal came loose.

She cut the armour away, piece by piece, and he took shape as if she was sculpting him from stone. Her knife sliced through straps and ropes, and with every section she removed, she saw his old form reappear.

At last he stood before her in his shirt and britches, a sword on his belt, as thin and hard as a dummy in a jousting yard. The room was silent. Perhaps the others had gone by now, back to the flying machine. Maybe she had been left behind, the only living creature in Oppidium.

Hugh did not move.

What now? Giulia thought. *Is this all there is of him?*

She reached into her bag and took hold of the book. The ghostly image of Hugh flickered at the edge of her vision. Then, as if giving the man his soul, she put the book in the knight's hand and closed his fingers around it.

Hugh gasped and staggered aside. She moved forward to help, but he put out his arm and steadied himself against the wall. He took slow, deep breaths, as if afraid that he would shatter.

"Giulia?"

"Yes," she said. "It's me. I'm getting you out of here."

She led him up the stairs, into the maze of corridors. They passed abandoned rooms and peeling murals. Hugh said nothing; Giulia didn't dare speak to him. If she could just get him into the sunlight, out of this city of ghosts...

They passed the huge pool, with its floating corpses. "Careful," she said. Hugh stepped over the body of one of Mavlio's men, as neat and deliberate as a clockwork toy.

The doors to the bath-house were closed. Giulia pushed the door: it swung open easily, silently. She looked onto the big steps as if she'd walked onto a stage.

People stood in the square outside, dozens of them. Leth was beside Vale at the top of the steps, their backs to the door. Vale's marines stood a little way further, their guns ready and aimed. Mavlio and Sepello were to one side, surrounded by the prince's few remaining soldiers.

Beyond them, at the edge of the square, were twenty dryads and half a dozen dwarrows. The fey folk crouched on the lumps of stone and stood in the shadow of the broken pillars, watching, aiming. They carried bows and muskets, and they were all pointed at Vale's men. Giulia recognised three of them, standing at the front: Sethis, Grodrin and Arashina.

The world seemed to have frozen. Giulia glanced from face to face, saw their set expressions, and knew that violence was a moment away. She felt completely exhausted. It was an effort just to stand there.

Hugh drew his sword. Leth turned at the sound, and Hugh stepped forward and ran him through.

The revenant's hands flew up, as if to tear at his own chest. His head flopped back and he shrieked at the cavern roof. The scream escaped and died, and Leth stood frozen in agony, impaled.

He began to fall apart. His cheeks fell in, his lips shrivelled and drew back. Leth's fingers closed up like the legs of dead spiders, and dropped away in a rain of bones. His eyeballs sank back, and the bones pushed through his face, until there was nothing but a skull and papery skin.

Hugh yanked the sword out. Leth collapsed, and burst as he hit the ground. Smoke rose from the remains; skin withered to nothing, bones blackened and crumbled into ash.

Vale stared at Giulia, too enraged to speak. Then he found words. "What've you done?" he cried. "You stupid bitch, what have you done?" He stepped towards her, and the whole front row of the fey folk seemed to tighten, to rise up, to look down their bows and guns.

Vale froze. He was shaking. "You don't know what you've done. You've—"

Giulia's boot flicked out and scattered Leth's ashes. "There's nothing here to argue about," she said. "Let's go."

A long second passed.

Vale nodded to his men. Quietly, they lowered their guns. A second later, the dryads relaxed. Mavlio remained still. His arms were folded, as if he knew that his part was done, but he watched very carefully.

Arashina cupped her hands around her mouth. "Gentlemen, it is time to disperse! Your flying machine awaits you! If you would be so good as to depart…"

"'Time to disperse'," Vale said. His voice was ripe with disgust. "Fine! Back to the boat, men! I'll remember this," he added. "Albion will remember this."

His men began to walk. They moved slowly, reluctantly, as if they had been waiting for a gift that would never now be given.

Prince Mavlio stepped forward. "Madam. I am the prince of Astrago—"

"We know," Arashina replied. "We will come to you, in time."

The prince followed Vale's soldiers, flanked by his own men. Giulia watched them go.

Sepello caught Giulia's eye. He smiled. "Good work," he said. "Bloody good work. I've got to get my pay," he added, and he followed Mavlio out of the square.

Arashina turned to Giulia. "So, you brought your friend back."

"Yes. I don't know—" Giulia felt her voice start to crack, and checked herself. *Not going to cry. Not in front of these people.* "I don't know what state he's in."

A male voice said, "The same as you were when you came to me. Maybe a little worse." Sethis strolled in from the side, looking almost unconcerned. He carried a spare cloak and a bottle. "We'll see."

"You followed us," Giulia said.

Arashina shrugged. "We saw your signal. Some of the elders might not like it, but we knew that it was time to act. Once we are gone, our dwarrow friends will seal the entrance – for good, this time. They know how to shape stone. We'll make sure that nothing ever comes out again."

Sethis offered the bottle; Giulia shook her head. "We're heading back to the forest," he said. "You'd be very welcome. We can look at Hugh properly there."

She nodded. "Thanks. I'd like that."

"Stay as long as you want. Or need."

They walked, and the buildings became smaller and more decrepit. Grand temples became houses, and the houses became rubble and broken walls. The ground rose and rose, and Giulia climbed, Hugh plodding along at her side. At long last there was a tunnel, and light at the end of it: true, pure sunlight. She walked out into trees and sunshine.

Hugh shielded his eyes with his hand. He turned to Giulia. "Where am I? I don't remember. *Who* am I?"

Giulia reached out and slipped her arm into his, the better to lead him into the forest. They could heal there, and rest.

"Don't worry," she said. "I'll tell you."

Chapter 17

The sun rose over Astrago and burned around the towers and the domes. It caught the statue of the prince, and his upraised sword blazed with the dawn light, as it had been designed to do.

Sunshine picked over the rubble in the south-east quarter. Half a dozen soldiers carried water and bread to the churches where the homeless slept. A new shift of workmen walked down from the palace, equipped with hammers and shovels.

Carts made their way through the streets, and soldiers collected up the dead. The citizens who had fallen went first, and they were carried to the grave-sites outside the walls.

The bones of Leth's army were a different matter. Priests blessed teams of men and they gathered the skulls like fruit, smashed the craniums open and threw the fragments into bags. The workers put rocks in with the broken bones and took them to the ferry point four miles east. The ferryman, who had seen some strange cargoes in his time, rowed out half a mile and dropped the sacks into the bay.

"Too many bloody priests," Mavlio said, watching from one of the upper towers of the Quincunx Palace. "People need to remember that it's me who keeps them safe, not a bunch of canting little monks."

Carmina stood beside him. "You should have a festival, Father. A procession, with all the soldiers." She smiled. "I know! You could get some players to come in. They could act out how you defeated the undead. So people will remember how it really was."

"How it really was?"

"Of course. With singers and people doing tricks. It'll help make people happy again. And then they'll remember to be grateful to you."

He smiled at her. "An excellent idea. A bit of festivity would cheer things up a lot. And it would remind people who won this war for them. You know, I think you'll make a splendid prince, when the time comes. Now, come along. We've got work to do."

He headed downstairs, Carmina at his side. He felt deeply proud of his daughter: she might not be cured, but she was safe, and she'd been an inspiration to the commoners. The citizens had started to love her. They would have to learn to fear her, too, but that could come later.

One of Mavlio's operatives waited at the bottom of the stairs. It was Vespasi, a man whose ruthlessness was matched only by his ambition. The young man bowed. "News from Pagalia, my prince. A pigeon came in from across the bay. Princess Leonora is sending soldiers to reinforce the defences."

Mavlio shook his head. "Send her my thanks, but tell her to send masons instead. You might let her know that we defeated our enemies on our own. Oh, and find out whether Leonora's being courted by anyone. Without Lord Vale's patronage, we principalities are going to have to learn to stick together."

Vespasi bowed low. "As you wish, my prince."

Mavlio paced down a long hall, and glanced into the library. It was empty. Lannato would be in his workshop, then.

There was a lot to do. A few looters and ruffians waited in the palace dungeons. He'd haul them out soon, when the shock of the battle was wearing off, and hang them. That would remind the people that their prince was both just and in complete control. He also needed to write to the Pontifex, thanking that old bastard for including Astrago in his prayers, and hinting that the city was stronger than ever – much too strong to cross.

As he reached the east doors, the prince wondered how the fey folk would make contact, as Arashina had promised: they would be useful allies now. Yes, that would work very well indeed: a triumvirate of Astrago, Pagalia and the elder folk, with Mavlio at its apex…

There was one last loose end to tie. He opened the door and stepped into the sunshine.

*

Sepello was checking his horse in the stable courtyard when a slim figure approached. Prince Mavlio rubbed his hands together as if they were cold. Behind him, moving at a gentler pace, came Carmina. She was wearing a broad-brimmed hat, the sort of thing peasants favoured when working in the fields. It made her look strangely like a shepherdess. But then, he thought, she probably burned easily.

"Morning, Sepello," said the prince. "It's a fine day. Good travelling weather, I'd have thought."

"It should be," Sepello replied, "provided it doesn't get much warmer. I've got a long way to go."

"I'm sure you have. All the way to Bergania, yes?"

Sepello slipped his fingers under the horse's girth. It was a little too tight, and he let it out a notch. His left arm had healed well, although the cut was still sore. "Yes. They're expecting me in Darlons."

"Excellent. Well, I just thought I'd thank you before you go. You've done House DeFalci, and the city, a great service. We shall, of course, be making a generous donation to the Order of Saint Cordelia."

471

"Thank you, Prince Mavlio. You've been a very gracious host." He smiled a little. "I don't know if you could call it a pleasure, what we've seen, but I couldn't have chosen better people to fight alongside." He wondered what had happened to Giulia, now that she'd got what she'd wanted.

"I take it you'll be making a report to your order?"

"I shall, Prince Mavlio. Of course, I'll take care to include the right matters."

"I'm sure you will."

"I wondered if I might mention Lannato's use of alchemical vapour against the revenants. Some of my colleagues would find that very interesting."

The prince smiled. "You can mention whatever you like. Within what we agreed, of course."

"Of course."

Mavlio's smile faded a little. "The things we've seen... Well, safe travels. I thought this might help you along the way."

He gestured, and two men emerged from the stables. They wore tough travelling clothes, heavy boots and leather armour. One had his hair cut short, and a thick scar lay along his scalp like a worm. He held out a soft leather bag, tied at the neck. Coins tinkled inside. "Here it is, my lord," he said.

"A little gift," Mavlio added. "Put it on Master Sepello's saddle, please. Share it with your order, if you like," Mavlio said. "My daughter wants to say goodbye."

The scarred man attached the bag to Sepello's gear. Sepello didn't like that: the bag was too prominent for the road. There was no point in giving some two-penny bandit an excuse to try to rob him. He'd stash it out of sight once he had left Astrago.

Carmina took off her hat. "Master Sepello, thank you for everything. You have the thanks of the city." She waited a second. "And my thanks, too." Carmina held out her arm.

Sepello took her cool hand, dipped his head, and kissed the air above it. She might be friendly, but he wasn't going to kiss a revenant.

There was a moment's silence.

"Well," said the prince, "it's time to go, I think. Best make the most of the good weather, eh?" He nodded to the guards. "These two gentlemen will ride with you to the border. We've had trouble with the banditti, and while they're weaker than they were – well, you never know what might happen on the road."

Sepello felt a tiny sense of unease. "That's very kind," he replied. "But really, I'll be fine. I appreciate the gesture, but to be honest, I prefer to ride alone."

"No, no. We can't have that. What kind of a host just throws his guests out the back door? Go with God, Sepello, and with my protection." Mavlio made a small gesture, and the man with the scar walked into the stables.

Carmina fanned herself with her hat. Sepello thought: *The things we've seen.*

"Really, it's not necessary."

"You're a wounded man, Sepello. I insist."

The guards led their horses out and mounted them.

Carmina said, "Thank you for everything, Master Sepello. Goodbye, and Godspeed."

"Goodbye, then," he said. "Both of you." He looked straight at the prince. "I'll see you again, Prince Mavlio. Soon."

Sepello turned and climbed up into the saddle. He grimaced as if it hurt him to do so, and he sat with his

473

bad arm across his chest, as though it was in a sling. He looked weaker than he was.

Flanked by the prince's soldiers, he started on his way. At the gates, he looked back. Mavlio and Carmina were waving goodbye, waiting for him to disappear.

*

A rabbit crept out of the shadows of the forest, onto the long grass at the edge of the pasture. As the branches thinned out, the ground became spattered with sunshine: as the rabbit moved between light and dark, it seemed to blink in and out of existence. It bounced into a pool of light, paused to sniff the air, then lowered its head to the grass.

Giulia watched it down the length of her crossbow. She lined the shot up, put the point of the bolt level with the rabbit's flank.

"Not today," she said, and she lowered the bow.

Giulia stood up and the rabbit bounded into the shadows and disappeared. She wore a tough skirt short enough to show two inches of hunting boot above the ankle. Her shirt was dark green, drawn in with a smart leather belt around the waist.

She took a deep breath and let it out slowly. Sometimes she dreamed that she walked the streets of Leth's dead city. There were days when she swore that she'd never fight or take a life again, any life, that she'd hide in the forest and live off leaves like some kind of deer. And then there were others where she was the warrior who had destroyed the great necromancer, who had brought her friend back from the underworld.

Take it steady, Sethis had told her. *It takes a long time to get better. Just look at Hugh.*

Something red moved beyond the trees, something human. Giulia sidestepped and slipped behind a beech tree. She stared out from the forest, across the rough pasture that led from the woodland's edge to the first of the village fields.

A man walked along the slope, swinging his arms as he strode. He had polished boots and a red coat, a thin sword and no bow.

Giulia stepped out and waited. She had nothing to hide, but it was his decision whether or not he noticed her.

The man saw her and waved. "Good morning," he called, and he started out towards the trees.

"Are you lost?" Giulia asked, when he was close enough to hear.

He stopped six yards away. He had dark hair, neatly parted, a pointed chin and a wide mouth. His eyes shone as if he was amused, but he didn't smile. "I'm looking for my horse," he said. "I was out hunting, and he got startled and threw me. He ran off this way."

"I've not seen a horse around," Giulia said.

"That's a shame. Are you Giulia Degarno, by any chance?"

She stood there, the crossbow in her hands. It would be easy to flick the bow up and shoot him in the gut. "Maybe."

"Well, there's a thing," said the huntsman. "Friends of mine told me you lived round here. They said, 'Seeing as you're out hunting near there, if you see that good lady, be sure to give her a message from us.' And here I am!" He stood there, smiling blankly, waiting for her to ask.

Giulia said, "What do you want?"

"Twenty miles north of here is a village called Sciolana. A river runs through it. When you get there, follow the river east. Three miles on, there's a mercenary camp. The lieutenant at the camp is a young man called Ludwig Kroner. My friends said that you'd know the name."

Giulia said, "Yes, I know him."

"He used to work for you, and for Constantin Leth. He did you a wrong turn, I gather. These days, he works as a freelancer. You're welcome to take his life."

Giulia said, "Why are you telling me this?"

"Think of it as a token of our goodwill. A gift between friends."

"What friends? Who sent you here?"

He opened his hands, as though to apologise. "This whole business with Leth has turned things on their head somewhat, thrown it all into confusion. The fact is, my friends and I are going to take a while before we do anything else. We thought you might want to sit things out. Maybe stay out of the game for a little while."

She tightened her grip on the crossbow, but she didn't raise it. "Are you threatening me?"

"Not at all. Quite the opposite, in fact. We want you to be happy and contented, wanting for nothing. Goodness knows you've earned the right to a rest." He glanced back down the slope of the fields, towards the small houses clustered on the river-bank like animals gathered at a watering-hole. "Well, are you happy and contented? Wanting for nothing?"

"I'm fine," she said.

"You're sure of that? Quite sure? Because if not, measures can be taken to put things right."

"I don't need any 'measures'. I just want to be left alone."

"Excellent. I'm pleased to hear it!" The man looked up at the empty blue sky, shielding his eyes against the sun. "I'd best take my leave, then. I'm glad things are working out well for you. I don't think we'll be seeing each other again, more's the pity. Enjoy your retirement, Giulia." He made the big, thin smile again. "I've got to say, I rather envy you. It's a lovely place, this."

The hunter turned around and started off down the incline. He hooked his thumbs over his belt and hummed.

"Hey!"

He stopped and looked back, still cheerful. "Yes?"

"Did Prince Mavlio send you here?"

He shook his head. "No, he didn't."

"Who did, then?"

"Goodbye, Giulia!" He turned back and kept on walking.

She watched until he disappeared from view.

If not Mavlio, then who? She thought back to the people she'd crossed. Leth was destroyed. Maybe he'd been sent by one of the ex-inquisitors she'd hunted back in Averrio. No, they were all scattered, either dead or in hiding. Maybe it was someone from earlier, one of the criminals she'd worked for and stolen from, many years ago.

A name came back: *Nuntio.* Giulia shivered, and for a moment she wished that she'd shot the huntsman while she'd had the opportunity.

She walked back into the forest, towards her home. Maybe Sethis would have an idea: perhaps Hugh might remember. After all, his memory was beginning to return.

When she had gone a hundred yards, Giulia stopped and looked back. She saw nothing but trees. "Stay out of the game?" she muttered. "Like hell I will."

*

It took two months to reach Albion again. Vale's ship docked at Southaven, and the next morning he rode north, towards the city of Lawton. He had bad news to deliver.

He arrived late at night, and stayed over in an inn. The next morning, he took a boat across the river Lawe. Lawton Castle loomed before him, massive and pale. Light caught on the domed, gilded towers. Vale leaned back in his seat and closed his eyes, listening to the creak and splash of the oars and the sounds of the city beyond.

The red-liveried guards at the gates recognised him. Vale was ushered through, escorted across the lawn and into the keep. The doors closed behind him, and he was in the domain of Queen Gloria.

Vale waited in the ante-room, checking his appearance in a huge mirror. He took a few deep breaths and readied himself.

"Her Majesty will see you now, Sir Francis." Two guards approached. Vale recognised their faces – he had blackmail material on them both.

"Thank you so much," he said, and they led him through the doors.

The room beyond was dark and cool. Massive tapestries hung on the walls: one covered the only window. The tapestry on the right, depicting King Alba and his knights, had come loose at the top right corner. On the table, great masses of candles had melted into each other, forming heaps of wax. The room reeked of ashes, incense and perfume. Smells to blot out something worse.

In the centre was a chair not quite large enough to be a throne. Gloria sat there, her head sagging forward, perhaps asleep.

Vale dropped to one knee. "Your Majesty."

Gloria lifted her head. "Leave."

The guards departed. Vale heard the doors close behind him.

"Come closer, Sir Francis." The queen's voice, alchemically deepened to give her greater credibility as an orator, had long ago settled into a kind of regal drone.

Her wig was dark red and looked heavy enough to snap her neck. Beneath it were bloodshot eyes and pallid skin, an upturned spike of a nose.

"I am glad to see you in one piece, Sir Francis. How was your trip abroad?"

"Difficult, Your Majesty."

"Did you find Leth?"

"I did, Your Majesty."

"And did you capture him?"

"Forgive me, Your Majesty. I tried, but to no avail. The fey folk destroyed him before my men could bring him back."

"But..." the deep voice quavered. "What about his books?"

"Majesty, I learned some things, information I will give to your doctor. But Leth is dead. Destroyed for good. There were complications. I shall of course take measures against Astrago—"

Gloria leaned back in her throne. She reached up and pulled the wig away. It fell to the ground. Without it, her head was a veined, mottled egg in a nest of lace. "So there is no cure?"

"Perhaps Doctor Dorne can make something in his laboratory..."

The queen stared at him. Her white skin was taut like a leather cap. Her teeth were yellow and long. "So I will be like this forever, will I?"

"You will always be our queen, Your Majesty. Greater than any monarch in history. Ruling with strength and wisdom—"

Gloria laughed. It was a low, gurgling sound. "And as pure as the driven snow. Get out of my sight, Vale. Have the guards send for Doctor Dorne. He at least talks some sense."

Vale stood up. "As you wish." He was used to concealing his thoughts, but the idea of Dorne profiting from this infuriated him. Dorne hadn't gone to Astrago. Dorne hadn't been taken prisoner by revenants and nearly murdered in a siege.

"There are other undead, Your Majesty. My men could capture one, and find out how it works—"

The queen raised her hand. "Do as you wish, Sir Francis. Capture all the revenants you want. And take your time. After all, I'll still be here, won't I?"

Her laughter followed him out of the room.

FREE STORIES AND MORE!

I hope you enjoyed this book. For more stories about Giulia and her world, you can join my mailing list, and receive updates on my next books. Furthermore, I'll send you three free stories, exclusive to the mailing list:

"A gift from Pagalia" - Two courtiers plot to assassinate a rival in the Renaissance fantasy setting of *Up To The Throne*.

"Sentimental Value" - Master thief Giulia Degarno is hired to return some compromising letters to their owner, by any means necessary. But the money's too good, and the employer too innocent, for things to go smoothly...

"A Day in the Service" – In an introduction to the world of *The Imposters*, novice spy Richard Cleaver and his android minder, the terribly polite Helen Frampton, deal with botched handovers, corporate assassins and a large number of woolly rhinos. It may be deadly, but it's just another day in the interplanetary Secret Service.

You can get all of this, for free, by signing up at
http://www.tobyfrostauthor.co.uk/

REVIEWS ARE ALWAYS WELCOME!

I'd be very grateful if you left a review of this book on Amazon. Reviews don't have to be long – a sentence or two is fine – and they help my writing career. Honest reviews help bring my writing to the attention of more readers, which in turn helps me to write more novels. So everyone wins!

Thanks!
Toby.

Printed in Great Britain
by Amazon